BLUEBELL HOLLOW

by

Bill Rogers

C A T O N

Published in 2010 by Caton Books

Published by Caton Books

www.catonbooks.com

ISBN: 978-0-9564220-2-6

Cover Design by Dragonfruit
Design & Layout: Commercial Campaigns

Author's Note.
In all of my novels I try to use settings, in and around Manchester and the North West, rich with history and vibrant with a spirit of regeneration. Consequently, all but one of the places mentioned in this story exist. The one exception is the Oasis addiction clinic which - like the plot and the characters - is a work of fiction.

Until recently Bluebell Hollow nestled at the Eastern fringe of Cutacre, once – according to the Guinness Book of Records - the largest coal slag heap in the world. Cutacre is currently a working open cast mine a little over a mile from my home, the subject of several decades of local objections and a fierce community campaign – which is still ongoing - to preserve an area of Green Belt from urban sprawl. Under these circumstances I am particularly indebted to the site manager, Brian Worsley, who kindly gave me an extensive and fascinating tour of the workings.

The earth movers have cleared away the trees beneath which the bluebells flourished, and which have now been replaced – briefly - by a carpet of yellow marsh marigolds. In years to come a business and industrial site will have eradicated the memory of this wild and haunting place, but at least the major portion, landscaped and planted with trees and shrubs will provide a country park with views across the Mersey River, The Manchester Ship Canal, and the Cheshire Plain to the distant Welsh Mountains.

The tiny cemetery on Wharton Lane exists. As far back as 1662 Nonconformists worshipped here under the protection of the Mort family of Wharton Hall. Thereafter Moravians, Congregationalists, and Presbyterians worshipped in a succession of chapels - and finally a church - on this site. The cemetery is still tended by the congregation of the United Reform Church in Little Hulton. It is a rare and magical place, to which the bereaved still come to remember their loved ones, and has always been treated by others with the respect which it deserves. I really hope that it survives the threatened encroachment of warehouses and factory units. If you should chance to come across it, I hope that you'll pause for a moment and reflect on the centuries of faith, protest, and of nonconformity represented here, and active still that helped to bring about the Industrial, Social and Political Revolutions, of which the North West of England can always be proud.

Dedication

This book is dedicated to the Bolton and Salford Cutacre Campaigners, and all those who fought to protect for future generations this site of special biological interest, and our precious dwindling Green Belt land.

And to the memory of David "Alex" Jack
A wonderful husband, father and friend.

1

Caton watched her walk across Albert Square, a touch under five foot seven, a curvaceous size ten, her coat swaying gracefully. As she reached the zebra crossing she spotted him sitting at the table outside Chez Gerard. He waved, and stood up, giving her little choice but to join him. She had a boy in tow. He seemed vaguely familiar.

'Helen, it's great to see you,' Caton said, and meant it.

'You too Tom,' She replied, a little less enthusiastically. She offered her cheek for him to kiss, her chestnut hair brushing his.

'And who is this?' He asked, smiling down at the boy staring quizzically up at him.

'This is Harry,' she said. 'Harry, this is Mr Caton. He's an old friend.'

Caton held out his hand. 'I'm Tom, Pleased to meet you Harry.'

The boy shook it confidently. 'Pleased to meet you Tom.' He smiled; his greeting warm and trusting.

'I'm just about to order a coffee Helen, said Caton. 'Why don't you join me?'

She looked flustered, checked her watch, an excuse forming on her lips. The boy tugged at her sleeve.

'Mum. I'm thirsty.'

Caton pulled out a chair, cranking up the pressure.

The three of them sat down as the waiter approached. She asked for a cappuccino for herself, and a coke for Harry. Tom ordered a double espresso.

'You're looking good Helen.' He said.

Her brown eyes finally met his. 'You're not looking so bad yourself Tom. What's it been, six years? I'm surprised we haven't bumped into each other before now,' said Caton.

'Give or take.' She took a small colouring book and a pack of pencils from her bag, and gave them to the boy. 'Why don't you take them over there Harry,' she said, indicating a neighbouring table. 'You'll have lots more room. Don't worry; I'll make sure you get your coke.' She unbuttoned her coat, taking advantage of the late autumn sunshine. 'I don't get into Manchester as much these days. Not since I moved away.'

'That would explain it,' said Caton. 'Where did you move to?'

'Standish,' she said grudgingly.

'Wigan?' It seemed an unlikely move for Helen, away from the city life style she had so enjoyed. The boy looked up from his colouring pad, grinned from ear to ear, and called across.

'Wigan Warriors! She works for Wigan Warriors!'

She frowned. 'Harry, you shouldn't listen in to people's conversations.'

Head close to the pad, the boy appeared not to have heard.

The waiter brought their drinks.

She sipped her cappuccino, and then wiped a thin line of froth from her upper lip with the back of her hand. Caton registered the absence of rings of any description.

'I didn't have you down as a Rugby League supporter.'

'I wasn't.'

The breeze caught her hair, flicking it across her face. She put down her cup, and tucked the strands behind her ears. It gave her an impish appearance. It was a look that Caton had always found endearing.

'I suppose you could say that I am now,' she said. 'I actually work for the Robin Park Stadium...public relations. It covers the soccer, and the rugby, and everything else to do with the stadium.'

'PR? I bet you're good at that.'

'Look Mum.' The boy held up his pad.

They turned to see. Caton had no idea what it was.

'That's a lovely horse Harry,' said Helen. 'Well done.' The boy beamed, turned the page over, and set off with renewed enthusiasm.

'Your day off?' she asked, lifting her cup to her mouth.

'Not really. My team has just been made homeless while our usual Incident Room is refurbished. We've got to share the one in Leigh. I thought I'd have quiet hour in town while our stuff got loaded onto the wagon. It might be the last chance I'll have for a while.'

'Incident Room. Isn't that CID?' She asked.

He nodded. 'Major Incidents.'

'And you have a team. What does that make you a Detective Inspector?'

'Chief Inspector, actually.'

She smiled approvingly. 'I always knew you had it in you.'

'I just needed to grow up.'

'Me too.' She twisted a strand of hair between her fingers, choosing her next words carefully. 'Are you with anyone?'

'As a matter of fact I am. She's called Kate. She works at the University as a Forensic Psychologist.'

'That must be handy?'

'Sometimes.'

'Is it serious?'

Caton smiled. 'If you call "soon to be married" serious.'

She smiled back. 'Congratulations Tom'.

Caton sensed that she was genuinely pleased, more than that...almost relieved. 'How about you?' he asked.

She shook her head. 'Just Harry and me.'

She picked up her cup and he caught her glancing surreptitiously at her watch. The silence hung heavily between them. Two tables away, the boy put his pencil down, and picked up his drink. As he drank he looked towards them, and smiled.

'How old is Harry?' Caton asked, to get the conversation flowing again.

She wiped her mouth with her serviette, seemingly distracted.

'Harry, how old is he?' Caton repeated, assuming that she hadn't heard.

'Five,' she replied. 'Harry is five.'

At the sound of his name the boy raised his head. 'I'm nearly six,' he shouted.

'You're five.' She repeated sternly.

'Nearly six! You said I could have a bike for my birthday.' He retorted triumphantly, before returning to his latest masterpiece.

Suspicion slithered across the space between them. Caton watched her rummage in her bag. What was it she'd said about their break up? *"Give or take six years."* She had finished the relationship just before their planned week in Rhodes that Whitsun. He did the maths. That made it nearer five and a half. He looked across at the boy. *"I'm nearly six"*. If she had been a couple of months pregnant when she walked away…

She took her purse from her bag, and waved to the waiter hovering by the doorway.

'I'm paying, Helen.' Caton said. When she failed to respond he leaned across the table, and gripped her arm. 'I said…I'm paying.'

She turned, and their eyes locked. Her expression was the confirmation he sought.

'I'm his father.'

'Please keep your voice down Tom. And let go of my arm. You're hurting.'

'You're damn right I'm hurting. How do you expect me to feel?' He let go of her arm, and watched as she rubbed it. In the doorway the waiter picked up the vibes, palmed their bill, and ducked tactfully inside the restaurant. Caton looked over his shoulder. The boy…Harry…his son, was busy scribbling away, head down. Now he knew why the boy had seemed so familiar. In the shoe box at the bottom of the wardrobe where he kept his pathetic store of family memories was a photo his father had taken. A beach somewhere down South. Himself at about the same age, clutching his mother's hand as she bent to brush sand from his hair. Same eyes, same hair, same bright inquisitive expression; same gangly stance. Peas in a pod.

'Why didn't you tell me?'

She looked tired. Like a balloon deflated. She stared down at her empty cup as though she might read the future there. 'Because I couldn't face the complications.'

'Complications?'

'You would have wanted to make an honest woman of me. It's how you are. It's what my parent's would have wanted too. I might well have given in.' She even sounded weary.

'Would that have been so bad?' He asked.

She raised her head and stared at him. 'Come on Tom. Admit it. It wouldn't have lasted.'

He knew that she was right. What they'd had, the sex, the comfortable familiarity, it would never have been enough to carry them through. Even with a child.

'Maybe,' he conceded. 'But it needn't have been like that. I still had rights. I still *have* rights.'

She had no answer to that. She looked down at the cup as she turned it nervously with her fingers.

Caton sneaked a look at his son. 'Is my name on the birth certificate?'

She turned away as she answered. 'No.'

'Why not?'

'I've already told you; I didn't want the complications. I didn't need the maintenance, and you wouldn't have welcomed the call from the Child Support Agency.'

'You don't know that.'

She shrugged.

'What have you told him?'

'That his father was a good man, but we could never

have lived together. That I'd tell him more about you when he was older, if he really wanted to know.'

'At least you didn't tell him I was dead.'

That seemed to get to her. 'You should know me better than that.' She said.

'I thought I did. Didn't you think he was entitled to grow up knowing who his father was, even if we didn't have a life together?'

'Like I said. It's much simpler this way. Less complicated.'

'For you and me, maybe. But what about him?'

She had to think about that. 'For him too I hope.'

Caton shook his head. 'I see young men all the time who grow up fatherless, and end up in and out of prison.'

Now she was angry. She stared at him fiercely, her eyes flashing. Trying desperately to keep her voice down; almost hissing. 'Do you really think I'll let that happen?'

'I don't think it'll be entirely up to you. It's all about what goes on in their heads. Looking up to older boys for their role models – boys who like to take risks, to live on the edge.'

She pushed her cup and saucer away. 'Do you honestly think he'd have had a better chance with a policeman for a father? Shift work. The images of men like you on TV, and the films? The constant threat of violence. You, over protective, wielding heavy handed discipline because you know only too well what the pitfalls are? Him kicking back against it as a teenager?'

'It doesn't have to be like that.' He said, realising that he was repeating himself, like a hollow mantra.

'What kind of detective are you Tom?'

'The kind who detects.' He knew he was behaving like a child, but he couldn't help it.

'I'm not joking Tom. What are you, robbery, vice?'

He took a fraction too long to frame his reply. 'Major Incidents.'

She nodded grimly. 'Like arson, rape, and murder?'

'Sometimes.' He grudgingly admitted.

'And you really think I'd want him to be part of that?'

She was on her feet now. Calling to her son to come.

Caton stood too. He reached across and took her arm. 'Please don't go. I didn't mean to upset you. It was such a hell of a shock. '

She shook her arm free as the boy arrived clutching the book and crayons, oblivious to the storm that had erupted around him. She made him put them on the table, and zipped up his anorak.

'It was really great to meet you Harry.' Caton said, fighting hard to keep his feelings in check; determined not to spoil the first impression his son would have of him. 'I hope I see you again sometime soon.'

The boy smiled.

Tom seized a pencil, wrote on a corner of a serviette, ripped it off, and thrust it into her hand.

'My number,' he said. 'Please call me.'

She placed the pad and pencils in her bag, secured it, and turned to go.

'Goodbye Tom,' she said over her shoulder, as she led the boy away. As they drew level with a black iron wastepaper bin emblazoned with golden bees she raised her hand, and let the piece of paper fall.

'I'll ring you then,' he called after her. 'You can depend on it.'

At the corner of Brasenose Street the boy looked back over his shoulder, and waved. Then they were gone, heading south towards Lincoln Square.

Caton sank into his chair. What the hell was he going to tell Kate? In less than five months they would be married. She'd already made it clear she wanted a family, and that the clock was ticking. And now this. He had no idea how she was going to react. But he did know that one way or another his life would be never be the same again.

Ten miles to the West, where the City of Salford gave way to the Borough of Bolton, Matt Harper used the back of his glove to wipe the condensation from the inside of the windscreen. It left a smear that he knew would show when the sun broke through, and irritate the hell out of him for the rest of the day. He eased into first gear, and moved carefully forward. More accustomed to the wheeled excavator, he was worried that the caterpillar tracks might slip on the frosty surface, and turn them over. Worse still, send them slipping down the steep slope into the gully below. He manoeuvred the telescopic arm to place the teeth of the bucket at the base of the tree, and began to dig.

Less than five years old, the silver birch provided little resistance, its sparse roots torn easily from their precarious foothold in the frozen shale. Matt swivelled the cabin a few degrees to the left, and started on the clump of pussy willow. He had cleared a patch less than three metres square when he was forced to wipe the windscreen again. It was then that he saw it. He had no need to climb down from the cabin to take a closer look. Nor did he intend to. He cut the engine, and with a trembling hand reached for his mobile phone.

2

The van pulled out of the car park at speed, forcing Tom to pull over to the kerb. As it sped, siren wailing, lights flashing, up Derby Street towards Spinning Jenny Way, another van, and two cars, followed close behind.

Caton parked up, entered the station, and made his way towards the major incident room on the first floor. Detective Superintendent James Radford, known popularly, ever since his prostrate problem flared up, as Jimmy - as in *Jimmy Riddle* - met him on the landing.

'Tom,' he said. 'Saw you arrive, thought I'd come and meet you. Welcome to the Wigan Division. You picked a good day to start.'

'Thank you Sir,' said Caton. 'Have my team arrived?'

Radford took him by the arm, and led him back down the stairs. 'They're unpacking. But DI Holmes and couple of the others have been and gone. You'd better get after them. Introductions can wait.'

'Something up?' Caton asked.

Radford nodded solemnly. 'You could say that. Unearthed more like.'

Caton could have aped the others, used his blue light, and switched the siren on, but from what Radford had told him there would be little point. Better to arrive calm, and collected, than surging with adrenalin. At the end of the by-pass he followed the one way system around Atherton, and started the long climb up Newbrook Road. The home team were already investigating two stabbings, Radford had told him, and a serious case of arson; not to mention a tricky domestic murder trial underway. So this one was his. Not his first by a long chalk, nor was it exactly a baptism of fire.

'Be able to take your time on this one. Not so much a cold case, as a new old case,' Radford had said mysteriously. 'Nice one to bed yourself in with by the sounds of it.'

At the traffic lights at Four Lane Ends, he turned right between the Hulton Arms, and the Red Lion, onto the A6. After exactly one mile, at the Watergate roundabout for the M61 motorway, he took the third exit for the entrance to the site.

He stopped the car for a moment to look at the notice board fixed to the fence. It identified the areas of land that were being worked, and in what order. On another board beside it were marked the rights-of-way still open to the public, and those which had been diverted. Today there would be no access to any of them. The dog walkers would have to find somewhere else to complete their morning exercise. Cutacre Reclamation and Surface Mining Site, and all of its environs, were closed for business.

At the barrier across the entrance to the site Caton showed his warrant card to the uniformed officer with the entry log, and was directed down to the cluster of single storey temporary cabins a couple of hundred yards away. He could see the Tactical Aid Unit vans parked up, two marked cars, and several unmarked including Gordon Holmes' silver Mondeo. Three covered container lorries were parked up in a lay by at the side of the road waiting for permission to leave the site. Caton drove past them, around the turning circle, into the car park, and stopped. He took his crime scene bag from the boot, alarmed the car, and took stock.

There were three sets of buildings – all of them portakabins of the more substantial variety - and a half a dozen large steel containers painted green. The nearest building held the reception, and what appeared to be offices. Outside the second building workmen stood in huddles, eating rolls and sandwiches, and drinking from plastic cups. Presumably the canteen.

The third building, much smaller, he gave up on. Behind and beyond it, narrow mounds of earth, twice the height of an average house, and each at least two hundred metres long, stretched out in rows across the farmland. The soil quality appeared to deteriorate from row to row. The first rich brown, the second lighter, the third heavy with clay, and a fourth that seemed to consist entirely of off-white stones and rock. Directly ahead, between the buildings, the road snaked its way south, and out of sight. On the far side, behind the office block, two fresh heaps of earth led the eye away to the west, and a vast spoil heap streaked blue black where the surface showed through white hoarfrost melting in the early morning sunshine.

'That's where we're going Boss. Cutacre.'

Holmes stood in the doorway of the reception block, already suited up in his Tyvek gear. On his feet he wore a pair of boots. He saw Caton look at them. 'You're going to need them too,' he said. He was joined in the doorway by a tall man, six foot three or more, sixteen stone, stronger looking even than Gordon. His weathered face made it difficult for Caton to guess his age. Mid forties perhaps. Together they walked down the three steps towards Caton.

'This is Brian Worden. The Site Manager.' Holmes said. 'And this Brian is Detective Chief Inspector Caton, my new Boss.'

They shook hands.

'This is a bad do Chief Inspector.' Said the site manager. His accent was northern, cultured, the other side of the Pennines. Possibly Sheffield.

'Brian is going to take us up there. Give us a guided tour on the way.' Said Holmes

'My Land Rover's over there.' Worden told them.

'You go ahead. I'll get my boots from the car.' Caton replied.

He opened the boot, and stared at the contents. It was a sad reflection on his work that its primary function was as a store room for all the paraphernalia that a crime scene might entail. Just about the only thing missing was a wet suit. He wondered what Helen would make of it. It would probably scare her to death. Confirm her worst fears. It certainly wouldn't have helped him to win her over. And this, he grimly reminded himself, is the least of what it means to experience my world.

They bounced over the frozen ruts left by the huge earth movers that lined the sides of the road where their operators had left them when the balloon went up.

'Why is the soil graded like that?' Caton asked.

'So we can put it back in the right place, and in the right order.' The site manager told him. 'One fifth of this area will be restored to pasture, three fifths as common land for wild life, and for people to walk on. We have to make sure the top soil from the farmland goes back where it came from, with the right sub soils beneath it. And so on.'

'What about the other fifth?' Asked Holmes from the back of the jeep.

'That's going to become part of an industrial estate, together with what is currently Cutacre Tip.'

'Bloody hell,' said Holmes staring through the window at the mountain of waste. 'Where's it all going to go?'

'Into the holes we made to remove the coal, including the one we'll have created underneath what is currently the tip. We'll also raise the height of some of the common land. Landscape it if you like. Make it more interesting.'

Holmes whistled through his teeth. 'I bet you could move mountains with these.' He said, staring wistfully at the excavators.

Worden grinned. 'I think we could at that.'

'Your trouble Gordon,' Caton said. 'Is that you haven't moved on from playing with your Tonka toys.'

'Come on Boss, admit it,' Holmes retorted. 'Driving one of these is every big boy's dream.'

'Not for Matt Harper, it isn't,' the site manager volunteered, wrestling with the steering wheel as the rear end of the Land Rover threatened to slide away on the icy surface. 'Not today at any rate.'

Beside a steeply angled conveyor belt they passed a mound of shiny black coal that had been washed, sorted, and graded, waiting to be loaded into container trucks. Around the next bend Caton was taken by surprise. Whatever he had been expecting, it was not this. A hole the size of several football stadiums, and three times as deep, had been carved out of the ground. Trackways wide enough to take small excavators, and dumper trucks, snaked their way down into the bottom of the chasm. Beside a narrow seam of coal, some forty metres long, Caton could make out several stationary diggers. From this distance they were the size of the matchbox toys he had collected as a child. It reminded him of the TV images he had seen of South African diamond mines.

'That's a four foot seam.' Worden told them. We've another two of those down there, but any time soon we're going to hit a series of fault lines.'

'What happens then?' Caton asked him.

'One of them, we just go deeper – another fifteen metres. The others are too far down. So we'll just move on to the next area we're going to work, where the seams reappear.' He pointed beyond the workings to a large section of farmland surrounded by a wire fence, and black plastic sheeting. It looked to Caton like the way a crime scene might be marked. They skirted the edge of the abyss, drove past a mound of mudstone, and emerged on open ground.

The steep South Western face of Cutacre tip towered forty metres above them. Thick scrub, and leafless stunted trees, populated the lower flanks.

Above them the earth was steel blue, deeply scarred in places where the surface run off had carved channels at the points of least resistance. The early morning sun glinted on the few remaining patches of ice, and the ochre rusted remains of an ancient truck that had tumbled down the hillside. Caton thought it inexplicably beautiful. Wild, desolate, primitive; almost primordial. A place that man had created, abandoned, and nature had reclaimed for its own. As Worden pointed the Land Rover towards the track that climbed the man made hillside the conversation dried up. When they reached the top another Landrover, a small orange excavator, a huddle of people, and the tell tale ribbon of police tape flapping in the breeze, appeared ahead of them.

'Can we stop here a moment?' said Caton.

He opened the door, jumped down, and walked away towards a high point to his right.

'The Boss likes to soak up the atmosphere first. Get a sense of the place without the people to distract him,' Holmes said as he opened his own door. 'Feel it like the perpetrator must have done. Visualisation,' he added as he climbed down. 'All part of modern policing.' He didn't sound convinced.

To the North, beyond the A6, the ribbon of motorway, and the water tower on Top O' Cow, Caton could see Rivington Pike and the transmission mast on Winter Hill. He turned a hundred and eighty degrees, past the open cast workings, and looked out to the south. Across the Cheshire plain, the unmistakeable ironstone ridge at Frodsham jutted out like the head of a Native American chief watching over the M56 motorway as it snaked towards the ancient and medieval city of Chester. Just visible on the horizon he could make out the snow covered mountains of Snowdonia.

Caton had walked on each of these high places, where people of the Bronze Age, and Iron Age Celts, had built hill forts and the tumuli where they buried their dead. Not buried so much as cremated, he reminded himself. Could there be a connection he wondered? Why else would anyone risk detection by bringing a body up here? Was it too fanciful to imagine that this might be part of some ritual sacrifice? He watched a commuter train, a quarter of a mile away, clatter past on its way to the city of Manchester. A small mound between the boundary of the workings and the railway track caught his eye. He waved the site manager over.

'What's that?' he asked, pointing south. 'Just this side of the track?'

'You mean the spoil heap?' said Worden. 'That came from Wharton Hall Colliery at the turn of the century, before they started dumping here at Cutacre.'

'Why isn't there any vegetation or frost on it?'

'Because deep down it's still burning. You can see it smoking from time to time. As little as a decade or two ago you wouldn't have been able to walk on it without melting the soles of your shoes. Even now, if you were unlucky enough to fall into a void, you'd be roasted to death before anyone could get you out. That's why it's fenced off.'

'So why isn't this one we're standing on burning?'

'It's all about the composition. There's still a lot of coal in that heap down there. In the old days people

24

only wanted large pieces for their open fires. The small stuff wasn't worth what it cost to transport it. It got dumped, in considerable quantities, together with the spoil. The collieries that created Cutacre, on the other hand, were feeding power stations, as well as domestic homes. Power stations aren't that fussy. So there's a much lower ratio of coal to shale and mudstone.'

'But enough to make it worth your while?'

Brian Worden rubbed his chin. 'You've seen the price of fuel,' he said. 'Suddenly it's black gold again. It's still not worth washing the coal out of this one. We're more interested in what lies beneath.'

Me too, reflected Caton as they made their way back to the Jeep.

While their names were being entered in the log, Holmes introduced the new Crime Scene Manager, DS Terry Ryan. Short, round faced, with fierce eyes the colour of the coal around them, she exuded efficiency. As she turned to lead the way along the duckboard marking the common approach path Caton wondered what she'd look like in a business suit instead of her protective Tyvek all-in-one.

The excavator bucket had ripped through the mining waste to a depth of two feet. Suspended in mid air, a skeletal foot hung trapped between two of the bucket's hardened steel teeth. It appeared to have been snapped at the ankle joint; the large toe bent back at an impossible angle. In the trench gouged out by the excavator, the top third of a human skull, the upper section of a rib cage, both knees, and the lower portion of the leg to which the foot belonged protruded from the sticky blue grey soil. The bones were covered by a paper thin coat of shrunken skin. There were wispy strands of hair attached to the skull.

'Bit on the short side.' Holmes ventured.' What do you reckon Boss, female or a teenage boy?'

Caton thought he was probably right. A fraction over five foot. Slightly built. No point in guessing. 'Do we know who the attending pathologist is going to be?' he asked.

'Mr Mullen. But he said in view of our initial description he guessed there wasn't the usual urgency, and if we didn't mind, he'd see if he could bring a colleague along. Might take another hour or so before he gets here.'

'A colleague?'

'Some forensic archaeologist.'

'Not exactly a mummy though, is it?' ventured, the crime scene manager.

'God I hope not,' said Holmes. 'Make nicking the perpetrator bloody difficult. Wouldn't do a lot for our clear up rate.'

'What would you like to do while we wait for the medical examiner, Sir?' asked Duggie Wallace.

'You get your tent up,' said Caton. 'And let the photographer do his work. DI Holmes will have word with the Tactical Aid guys. And I'll try and get the measure of this God forsaken place.'

A few metres away a brown snake, with yellow markings like a collar around its neck, slithered out from beneath the uprooted birch, and disappeared down the greasy slope. As they picked their way across the duckboards, a cold drizzle began to fall.

3

Detective Superintendent Radford was distinctly unimpressed. Caton heard him sigh into the phone. 'I'll pretend that I didn't hear that Tom,' he said. 'Have you the faintest idea what it costs to put the helicopter up? Especially now, with the price of fuel rocketing.'

Caton had read the force budget in preparation for the Selection Board, and knew exactly what it cost. He decided to keep it to himself. 'OK. The fixed wing then; the Defender light aircraft.' He said, pushing his luck.

'Given this is your first day on the team Tom, I'm going to make allowances,' Radford responded. 'But take my word for it. Chester House would not look kindly on our calling on air support for non urgent use. It's not as though you've got the perpetrator hiding out in the bushes is it?'

Caton had heard of Jimmy Radford's famous penchant for sarcasm. He guessed he would just have to get used to it. Try not to rise to the bait. There was no point in antagonising him on day one.

'No Sir,' he said. 'But this is no ordinary crime scene. I have no idea how someone could have got the body up here, what the obstacles are, where the points of access are. The only way I'm going to get my head around this is to see it from the air. In any case, they'll have to provide us with some aerial photos. And...' he added the killer punch. 'It will save a couple of days of overtime for the Tactical Aid Unit.'

He could hear Radford sucking his teeth. The new Chief Constable had been banging on about cutting down on overtime ever since he'd arrived.

'There is a very simple solution Tom,' he said, finding it hard to disguise the triumph in his voice. 'You could always use Google Earth.'

Not such a bad idea Caton reflected. And the likelihood was that the current version would be a year or two out of date; before they started work on the site. Closer to how it would have looked when the body was deposited.

'Actually Sir, that's a good idea,' he said. 'I'll do that when I get back to the office. But...it's not going to solve my immediate problem, how best to secure the site, or the overtime issue. I've got two van loads waiting to be deployed.'

Caton thought the silence captured perfectly the expression *pregnant pause*. Radford's end of the line was pregnant with defeat, and irritation; his own, with expectation.

'All right Tom,' Radford conceded. 'But don't make a habit of it.'

'Thank you Sir.'

'And keep it brief. We've got our Green credentials to consider.'

As far as final ripostes went, it was hardly a winner.

There were four of them in the helicopter; the pilot; Caton, Sergeant Allardyce the air observer, and Worden the Site Manager. India 99 hovered several hundred feet above Cutacre, and fifty metres or so North of the deposition site. Immediately beneath them Caton could see the white tent like structure covering the shallow grave.

'I suggest we hold it here Sir,' said Allardyce. 'You wouldn't want our down draft to scatter all your evidence.'

'No, that's fine,' Caton replied, though he felt sure that with all the mining activity such evidence as there might have been was already well scattered. 'Perhaps you could take her up another couple of hundred? I could do with a birds' eye view of the entire area. And can you send me over a copy of the flight video when we're done? It'll save you coming again.'

'No problem,' the observer replied. The helicopter began to rise. 'You might find it easier to see on the TV,' he said, pointing to the screen positioned in front of him. 'Easier than staring out of the window. Especially through this mizzle.'

Caton nodded. On the screen was a perfect 360 degree view. Cutacre lay, some two miles wide by one mile long, just north of centre in an area, bisected by the train line, The northern perimeter was bounded by the A6 Manchester Road, and just beyond it, the blue grey ribbon of the M61 motorway. To the west, he could see the A579 up which he had travelled, and to the south the road from Tyldesley to Boothstown. He pointed to the eastern boundary.

'What's this road, beside the housing estate?'

The observer had no need to consult the on screen

map. This was an area he had cause to visit regularly, tracking stolen vehicles in and out of Little Hulton, the Heathfield Estate, and, further west, Hag Fold.

'The A5082; Peel Lane, becoming Mort Lane.'

'Mort, as in death; as in Mort D'Arthur?' Caton wondered out loud.

'As in the Mort family who owned both Wharton Hall, and Peel Hall,' chipped in Brian Worden from the seat behind. He leant forward and pointed out a partly wooded area several hundred metres to the east of the spoil tip, and a complex of buildings just beyond Peel Lane. 'Here…and here. '

'How come you know all this Brian?' Caton asked.

The site manager grimaced. 'When you set out to dig up someone's back yard it pays to know all there is to know about it. Where the objections are going to come from, what has to be preserved. The history, ecology… especially the flora and fauna. You'd be surprised how many potential open cast applications suddenly become sites of special scientific interest.'

'Did you get a lot of objections to this one?' Caton asked.

'No more than most. Held it up for over a decade though. Even when we got permission we had to create a new habitat for some endangered species; crested newts among them. We still have to have a resident conservationist watching our every move. Not to mention the Time Team.'

'The Time Team?' Caton half turned in his seat. A team of populist television archaeologists uncovering layers of history buried by the centuries was all he needed on his crime scene.

The Yorkshireman nodded. 'They're planning to televise a dig at Wharton Hall. Already done the provisional survey. They reckon the mediaeval hall was built on earlier foundations – maybe going back to the Iron Age. They're due back in about a month.'

Caton turned back and stared at the screen. That close to the deposition site the press were going to have a field day. He shifted his attention to the scene before him. The great grey coal tip, and the massive hole carved out of the ground, dominated a landscape dotted with a handful of farmhouses and their outlying buildings. White tracks zigzagged along the crest of the tip itself. Close to the site of Wharton Hall, two larger tracks – one in the shape of an athletics track, the other the size and shape of a baseball field – had been stamped out on the ground. Two perfect rectangular sheets of water the size of swimming pools lay just to the south. Orange rivulets tracked their way down deep gullies on the flanks, draining into a narrow wooded valley that ran the length of the east side.

'Tell me what we're looking at here Brian,' Caton said.

Worden hunched forward; close enough to reach out and almost touch the screen. 'Apart from the spoil heap, most of this was farmland criss-crossed by rights of way. Half the farmhouses we demolished before we started.'

'You must have got some protests about that.' Caton guessed.

'Not really. They were all owned by UK Coal – inherited from the Coal Board. The occupants got compensation, or resettlement deals.'

'What are these sheets of water? Were they there before you arrived?'

The observer pressed his key pad, and the camera zoomed in.

'No. We created those ponds to take the drainage from the workings,' the site manager continued. 'Millions of gallons so far. The only problem they cause us is local youths treating them like their own private swimming pools. Bloody silly. The temperature of the water would take your breath away. Before you can do anything about it, you're sinking to the bottom. Anyone dives in to save you, they're a goner too.' He pointed to a lifebelt secured to a wooden stand. 'That's what that's for.'

'How come the water is so clear, when the run off from the tip is orange?' Caton asked him.

'That's because the water in the ponds comes from deeper down, in the shale layer. The run off is from the tip itself. It's caused by iron pyrites oxidation.'

'What about all the trees and shrubs. Was it like this when you arrived?'

'Worden shook his head. 'No, there was a lot more than what you're seeing now. Apart from the cycle tracks, the top of the tip and the approaches were covered with the stuff. This weathered spoil has created what the naturalists call an acid soil habitat; pH as low as 2.5. Mainly pussy willow, silver birch, oak, and alder. Some gorse. Nothing above four foot high. There are not enough nutrients in the soil to sustain anything else. So far we've stripped over a third of it away.'

'Bike tracks. Is that what they are?' Caton glanced out of the window to get a 3D view.

'BMX, and off-roaders,' Allardyce told him. 'The reason I know, is because Salford Division had a big push on them in an attempt to clear them all off before UK Coal moved onto site. We provided air support on a regular basis over a six month period. Pretty effective we were, too. Had to send half a dozen mini motor bikes to the crusher though. Idiots thought they could get away by driving into the estates, along the pavements, up the ginnels, and into their own back yards.'

'That's right,' Brian Worden agreed. 'We still get a handful who insist on trying their luck in the dark. Now they're more or less confined to these tracks on either side of Wharton Lane.' He pointed to the oval shaped track and baseball field. 'Harmless really. Damn sight less of a problem than the lampers.'

'Lampers?' It was an expression Caton had never heard before.

'They come up here early in the morning, before the sun's up, with torches fixed to their air rifles. The rabbits freeze, like they do; bam, bam, they're dead. Regular *Watership Down*. Trouble is, some of them seem to find it difficult to distinguish between the rabbits, and my security staff!'

Caton could see a glimmer of hope in what was beginning to look like a drawn out investigation. 'How long do you reckon it had been going on Sergeant - the bikes and the lamping - before GMP decided to clear it up?'

'God knows. You'd have to ask the locals. But from what I picked up, I'd say a least a decade, probably longer. It's not as though they were really doing any harm. Just about the only playground they'd got.'

'I agree,' said the site manager. 'Even now we try to take a softly, softly approach as far as possible. If we get their backs up, I have a feeling it could be a whole lot worse. Vandalism, sabotage. I'll settle for a little poaching and off-roading any day.'

None of this concerned Caton. It was the revelation that this place had almost certainly been swarming with potential witnesses when the body was buried here that both intrigued and excited him. It told him something about the perpetrator, and opened up possibilities. It gave him a place to start.

'Right Brian,' he said. 'Tell me what access to this site was like before you set up your own perimeter.'

'Presumably you mean for a vehicle capable of carrying a body as well as the driver?'

Caton nodded. 'That's right,' he smiled grimly. 'Though probably not a motorbike and side car.'

Worden had to think about it. 'Well…let's see,' he said. 'From the A6 there was Rosemary Lane, and Back Lane which is where we came in today, but neither of those would have enabled a vehicle to get up onto the top.' He pointed to a spot down by the railway line, seven hundred metres or so to the south of where they hovered. 'There's the track in from Engine Lane, but there's a problem with that. If we could go down there I could show you.'

'Is that what you want to do Sir?' Asked the air observer.

Caton did. The helicopter moved smoothly away. Twenty seconds later they hovered fifty metres above a substantial reinforced stone bridge over the Manchester to Southport railway line. The broad un-metalled track headed north for forty metres, then swung left towards a renovated farmhouse and its outlying buildings. A narrower track headed straight on towards the foot of Cutacre tip.

A four wheel drive could make it up there surely?' Caton reasoned.

Worden shook his head. 'Not really, that's why I wanted to show you.'

The pilot edged the 'copter forward until Caton could see that a ditch nearly three feet deep had been cut across the narrower track. A single plank lay in the bottom. The bikers again, he decided. No way even a jeep could have got across.

'That just leaves two obvious ways in,' Worden told him. 'Off Peel Lane, through the estate on Ashawe Terrace, and then across the football pitches, and a couple fields, onto Wharton Lane.' The Observer traced it on the screen with his finger. Caton could see that it was possible, but it looked a long winded way of doing it. Too much chance of being spotted and a little too complicated in the dark.

'Much simpler to come in off the A6 straight onto Wharton Lane.' The site manager said.

The helicopter turned through 180 degrees, and began to follow the path of a more substantial track through woodland, then out onto the open ground beside the field in which the bikers had created their largest track, past the familiar black polythene clad fencing marking out the site of Wharton Hall. Ahead of them the lane widened, and ran between a high hedge, and a seven foot steel fence marking the boundary of an industrial estate and the local council refuse and recycling dump. At the far end Caton could make out a large white gate across the lane, and beyond it two rows of terraced houses through which the lane emerged onto the road. Sixty metres west of the houses was a pub; beside it, a car park and an area set out with picnic tables.

'That would have been their best way in,' said the site manager following his gaze. 'The bikers. Best way for a four by four too, until the gate went up. Even now, it's just a matter of opening the gate.' He pointed to a path that forked off from the lane just beyond the gate, and wound its way up the less precipitous northern slope of Cutacre. 'Get a land rover or an SUV up there no problem. Just about any urban 4x4 too, providing it's not been raining.'

Caton could see that. It also struck him as an ideal alternative route for his own team to use over the coming days. The car park of the public house would make an ideal location for the mobile incident room, even if someone would have to keep their eye out for inappropriate liquid consumption. Something suddenly caught his eye out of the right hand window.

'What's that?' He said, pointing to a cluster of gravestones huddled below them, on a narrow patch of land approximately fifty metres long by fifteen metres wide. Immediately behind it sprawled a vast grey industrial complex where forty or fifty container lorries were parked up, several at the loading bays.

The helicopter hovered.

'That's Wharton Hall cemetery,' the site manager told him. 'There used to be Presbyterian chapel down there, but it's long gone. Relocated. The cemetery was still in use a couple of years ago though. The grass gets mown. Flowers appear on some of the graves from time to time. But I've never seen who does it.'

'Can you put us down right here?' said Caton.'

'No problem,' said the pilot as he brought the helicopter through ninety degrees, and headed for the centre of the oval track thirty metres away.

From where Caton was sitting there were plenty of problems. Not one of them to do with landing safely.

4

As helicopter lifted off, Caton's phone rang. It was DS Holmes, to say that the Pathologist had arrived. Brian Worden offered to have someone bring over his Land Rover. Caton wanted to walk. To follow the route the perpetrator had likely taken.

They crossed the open ground of rough grass, and the sandy track gouged out by the bikers, then walked North beside the deep valley at the foot of the mountainous slag heap.

'It was in the Guinness Book of Records,' Worden told him.

'What was?'

'Cutacre. The largest spoil heap in Europe; at one time it was thought to be the largest in the world.'

Caton was more interested in the ravine. Sodden brown bracken covered much of the bank this side of the sluggish stream. In the basin, closer to the water, grass and aquatic plants were interspersed with pussy willows. Silver birch had colonised the opposite bank. Some had even taken root on the precipitous slopes; the white bark of their slender trunks stark against the blue grey soil. Sombre sentinels.

'Bluebell Hollow,' said the site manager. 'That's what it was called before the collieries started tipping here. Some of the locals still call it that. We don't get bluebells anymore, but the bottom's a mass of yellow flowers much of the year.'

Caton thought it even more surprising that someone should choose to haul a body to the top of the heap, and dig a grave, than dump it right here in the valley; a far more accessible, and invisible place. A hundred yards further on they swung left, over a makeshift bridge of planks, wide and strong enough to take a small truck, and up the steep broad path the bikers had made their own. The drizzle ceased, and there were glimpses of sun through a layer of grey unremitting cloud that stretched as far as the eye could see. A half a mile ahead of them, along this flat ridge of acid scrub, and spoil, was the spot the perpetrator had chosen. God knows why. Caton had a feeling that that if he could work that out he would be one giant step closer.

'I can confirm that she is dead.'

Mullen crouched over the shallow makeshift grave. He was clearly on form. Caton envisaged being trapped in a pub between the pathologist and DS Jimmy Radford. Sheer torture.

'At least we know it's a woman.' Said DI Holmes, like it was a consolation prize.

'I don't suppose you'd care to hazard a cause of death?' Asked Caton.

The pathologist fixed him with an icy stare. 'Well I could take a wild stab, and surmise that she'd been suffocated. Being buried does that to you. But since there isn't a shred of evidence that she was alive when someone popped her in there, I'd better not. She does appear however, to have suffered a blow of some kind to the back of her skull. Unlikely to have been caused by the excavator. Whether or not it caused her death I can't say. You'll have to wait for the post mortem.'

'And I don't suppose that at this stage you can give us some idea how long she's been in there?'

Mullen smiled thinly. 'You suppose right, Chief Inspector. But Robert here might have a view on that.'

Dr Robert Hulme, senior lecturer in forensic archaeology and investigative science at the University of Central Lancashire, stood up and brushed the soil gently from his gloved hands. 'That depends on how much latitude you're prepared to accept,' He said. 'The problem is that these are not exactly normal conditions – if there ever is such a thing. The high levels of acidity, the above average heat of the soil, even at this relatively shallow depth, the particular nature of the bacteria capable of surviving in this relatively hostile environment, make judgements based on the degree of decomposition very tricky. However, I'd say she was buried here somewhere between four and ten years ago.'

In which case, Caton knew, his best chance of narrowing that down, would be to establish her identity. Someone would surely have reported her missing. 'How easy will it be to identify her?' he asked, staring at the wretched skeleton now fully exposed beneath the protective screen.

'The jaws are undamaged,' said Mullen. 'And the teeth are still in situ. That's going to be our best bet. As for DNA…' He turned to his colleague.

'It should be possible to get something from the hair,' said Hulme. 'Even if the roots have disintegrated.'

Holmes craned forward to examine the skull more carefully. ''I didn't think that was possible. Not from the shaft alone.'

'You need to keep up, Detective Inspector,' Mullen told him. 'A group of Danish scientists showed us how to do that a year or two ago.'

'Using the hairs from woolly mammoths.' Caton added, just in case they were tempted to label him equally ill informed.

'Well what do you know?' said Holmes, unabashed. 'They'll be cloning them next!'

'Yes...make a nice companion for a Neanderthal like you,' said Mullen. 'Whereas you Mr Caton might find this more helpful.' He shifted awkwardly to his left so that Caton could see over his shoulder. The pathologist had one gloved hand under what remained of the corpse's left hand. With the other, he gently brushed at the base of the ring finger, exposing two thin bands; one glinting gold, the other black.

Even in this dull light Caton could see a stone sparkling in the centre of the second band.

It took half an hour to agree the actions. The area to be searched posed a particular dilemma. Given the time that must have elapsed since the body was brought here, the number of people who would have traversed this ground, not to mention the bikers and the excavators – Caton thought the likelihood of retrieving any trace evidence remote. Limiting the search area, however, was not a risk he was prepared to take. Discarded clothing or possessions - the victim's or the perpetrator's - a weapon thrown into the bushes, or down into the ravine; you just never knew what might turn up. Thanks to his helicopter ride he was able to set up the outer perimeter with the minimum number of staff. Nevertheless, there would be a fair few officers and Police Community Support Officers cursing him as they patrolled this dismal setting in the early hours of the morning. Work would cease on the site until further notice. The mobile operations unit was parked up on the car park of the Dun Mare pub. Local officers on the Salford Division were already compiling a list of locals known to have frequented Cutacre over the past ten years. Once that was done, then interviews could begin. Caton suspected this was going to be a long haul. The key would be putting a name to the victim. Those rings would help.

It was five o'clock the following afternoon before the results of the post mortem came in. By then his team had bedded in; DS Radford had been placated; and Caton had discovered that Helen's phone number was ex-directory. Trying to trace her number he had done in his own time, given that the investigation had been restricted to six hours the night before, and a couple of short snack breaks. He had also had a brief conversation with Kate. The time delay didn't help. Just as he was about climb into bed she had been hurrying to her next seminar session in the Conference Hotel in Santa Barbara. It hadn't been the right moment to tell her about Harry, and there was no way that he was going to do it by text. The report on his desk had at least brought some good news.

All of the flesh, including the organs, had gone; prey to bacteria and insects. There was some mummification of the skin and hair. The acid soil had resulted in significant decomposition of the bones which had to be handled delicately. It had still been possible to establish her age. The victim had been in her early forties. Her hair colour at the time of her death was rich auburn; almost certainly dyed from a natural mousey brown shade. Scraps of cloth were adhered to the surface of her skin, and beneath the body, suggesting that she had been at least partially clothed at the time of her entombment. They had been sent off for analysis. Her skull had been fractured by a blow to the back of her head, consistent with striking a blunt object such as a tiled floor. In the opinion of the pathologist it could have happened from a fall, but was more likely to have resulted from a push, or by having been deliberately banged against a hard surface. On its own, it would certainly have been sufficient to cause her death. The absence of blood in the soil around her head pointed to her having died sometime before she was buried. The condition of her teeth suggested someone in good health who had taken care of them. The odontology report had already been circulated to dentists in the region. A DNA analysis was being undertaken by the Forensic Science Service. Both rings, including the badly stained silver engagement ring, were hall marked. The diamond was estimated at approximately 2 carat, and worth upwards of £4,000 at current prices. The time frame in which the victim had died had shrunk to between six and ten years.

Caton sat back in his chair, and rocked gently. Sometime between 1998 and 2002, this woman had disappeared without trace. He already had her height, hair colouring, approximate age, and the rings she was wearing. These alone would narrow the search he had requested of the Missing Persons Unit. Within a day or two he could well have a name. DCS Radford was happy with his progress so far and, given that the victim had died some considerable time ago, there was none of the usual hysteria. Press interest was focusing on the mystery surrounding the identity of the corpse. His phone rang.

'DCI Caton, Greater Manchester Police.'

'This is Emily Hughes,' her voice was young, middle class, educated, and confident. 'I'm a researcher with the Channel 4 Time Team.'

'I thought you might be contacting me,' he said.

'Ah. So you are aware that we are planning to televise a dig at Wharton Hall?'

'Yes Miss Hughes, I am.'

'You see my producer is anxious to know if your investigation is likely to affect our schedule in any way.'

'Well that depends on two things. When you planned to start, and how my investigation develops.'

'We were intending to carry out a further survey next Tuesday and Wednesday and, if that proved fruitful, film the dig proper in March next year.'

'I wouldn't have thought that March is going to be a problem,' said Caton. If he was still at Cutacre by then he reflected, it would be a nightmare scenario. 'But next week will be pushing it. I still expect to have people on site. And the exclusion perimeter currently includes access to Wharton Lane.'

'Perhaps you could keep us informed Mr Caton,' she said, masking her disappointment. 'You have no idea how much of a logistics problem it is setting up a programme like this.'

'Not unlike a murder investigation, I imagine.' He said pointedly.

She chose to ignore it. 'You can reach me on this number,' she said. 'And I should like to give you a mobile number too.'

He made a note.

'I suppose there is one consolation,' she said. 'The body you've discovered. It's going to create quite a frisson around our programme when it does go out.'

'No doubt it will, 'Caton agreed. 'No consolation for the victim though is it, or for her family?'

He didn't wait for her reply.

As Caton entered the incident room Duggie Wallace, the team's senior collator, and crime intelligence analyst, rose excitedly from his chair and waved him over.

'We've got a match already, Boss,' he said. 'She was local. A dental practice in Little Lever rang with a name, and I double checked it with *MissPers*.' He pointed to the screen of his computer.

Caton leant on the desk, and read the missing persons' file up on the screen. Della Farnworth. Fifty years of age when she was reported missing by her husband; February 26th 1998. Nearly ten years and seven months ago. He stared at the photo. Almost certainly taken from her passport, it did her no favours. Not that it mattered now. She looked directly into the camera. Square faced, tight lipped, not daring to smile. Auburn haired, brown eyed. Worry lines on her forehead, crows' feet establishing themselves beside her eyes.   Caton thought he detected an air of resignation about her. Even had he not known how she had ended up, it would still have seemed a deeply depressing photo.

'Print me a copy off, Derek,' he said. 'Then get me Missing Persons on the phone, and put them through to my office.'

By a strange and convenient coincidence, Mary Shepherd, Head of the Missing Persons Team, had been involved in the Della Farnworth case from the outset. As a rookie on the Bolton South Division she had taken the initial details from the husband.

'I always had my doubts about this one,' she said. 'I even dug it out, and had a good look at it when I moved into this post last year.'

'Tell me about it.' Caton said, pulling his pad closer to him.

'The husband left it two days after she'd allegedly walked out, before he decided to report her missing.'

'Did you ask him why?'

'Of course I did. I wasn't that much of a rookie. He said she'd done it before. A couple of times. Always came back within the week.'

'So why didn't he leave it even longer?'

'Because before, he'd always known where she'd gone. To her mother's, or her sister's. But this time she couldn't go to her mum's because she'd passed away, and he said her sister swore blind she'd not seen her for a week. I checked with the sister. She confirmed his story. But the interesting thing was that he left it a day and a half before he rang her.'

'And another twelve hours before he contacted the police.'

'Precisely.'

'Tell me about him.'

'Barry Farnworth. Three years older than his wife. They'd been married for twenty three years. He was a second hand car dealer. She worked on the counter in the local post office, and did his accounts. I say *was* a second hand car dealer because after she was formally declared dead – in March 2005 – it meant that his mortgage was paid off, and after a brief tussle with the insurance company he copped for another £130,000 in life insurance, sold up, and switched to property speculation. Buying, doing up, and renting or selling.'

'Did he now?'

'Got quite a portfolio has our Barry. Here in England, in Spain, Portugal, even Romania.'

'Why did she walk out?'

'According to the husband they'd had a row – a tiff he called it– about her wanting to give the place a complete make over, and put a conservatory on the back. He said they couldn't afford it.'

'Doesn't sound like a reason to walk out for good?'

'That's what I thought.'

'Either of them have anyone waiting in the wings?'

'Funny you should ask that.' He imagined her smiling at the other end of the phone. 'He got married three years ago to a woman he'd allegedly been seeing since 1999.'

'A year *after* his wife went missing.'

Exactly. But we've only got their word for it that they hadn't been at it before she disappeared.'

'What did Della take with her?'

'Her purse containing her bank and credit cards,

46

cash, store cards. Not her passport though, or her driving licence.'

'Did she use the cards at all?'

'No, not one. Hadn't made any withdrawals beforehand either. He reckoned she had no more than thirty quid in cash. Kept her on a tight rein did Barry. Her car was found in a side street near Atherton Station.'

'Doesn't it have a car park?'

'Quite a big one...and I know what you're thinking. Someone trying to avoid the CCTV on the car park. Well for a start they didn't have it then. And secondly, the car park can get pretty full, I checked. Commuters and all those pensioners using their free rail card to go into Manchester.'

Caton was still writing on his pad when she dropped in the *piece de resistance.*

'There was one other thing he claimed she'd taken with her. A month's supply of diazepam. Bought them on the internet. She was using them as a tranquilizer during the day, and as a sleeping pill at night. Her sister said she'd been using them for several months. We found the box in their medicine cabinet with enough for another month still in it.'

'So that's how he managed to get her formally declared dead. I wondered about that.'

'Convenient,' she said. 'Far too convenient I thought at the time.'

Caton pushed the pad away. 'No pressure Mary,' he said. 'But what was your gut feeling at the time?'

There was no hesitation. 'At the time, I thought he was lying. I just couldn't prove it. Not sufficiently to get my boss to take it seriously. If it had been left to me I'd have taken the place apart.'

'And now, ten years on?'

'I think he disappeared her.'

'Are you busy tomorrow morning?' he asked.

'No,' she said. 'Why, is this a date?'

Caton liked her style.

'Only if you're into mortuaries.'

5

They waited in the porch. Mary Shepherd from Missing Persons on the left, Caton ahead masking her from the camera lense in the wall beside the door, and from the door itself. He wanted to see Farnworth's reaction when he first caught sight of her.

The door opened on a chain. Small suspicious eyes, set in a shaven head grotesquely too large for them, peered through the crack. Caton held up his warrant card. 'Detective Chief Inspector Caton,' he said. May we come in?'

He saw the pupils contract. Not so much surprise, more confirmation. He had been expecting them. Farnworth released the chain, opened the door, and stood back to let them in.

'Who's that Barry?' The voice came from somewhere upstairs. A woman's voice; shrill, and unappealing.

He tilted his head towards the sound, and called back. 'No one for you to worry about, darling. You take your time. I'll bring a cup of tea up in a minute.' As Farnworth looked back towards the door, Caton stepped aside to reveal Mary Shepherd.

'Hallo again.' She said, without a trace of emotion.

This time it was not only written on his face, it rippled through the whole of him. He stood there in a pair of white designer jog bottoms, and a gold embroidered black Boss tee shirt, shoulders drooped, belly sagging, dark rings beneath his eyes, his face collapsing into his neck. He was neither shocked, nor surprised, just resigned. This was the moment he had been waiting for ever since the news had hit the stands. Caton knew it for a fact. So did Mary Shepherd. And what's more, Farnworth knew they knew.

Knowing was one thing. Proving it was another. He had invited them in. Pretended unsuccessfully to be surprised that they wanted him to identify a body. Insisted on taking his wife a cup of tea. Accompanied them in the car. Stayed silent throughout the thirty minute ride. Now he stood beside the gurney in the cold grey steel box that was the viewing room. Just him, Mary Shepherd, Caton, and the mortuary technician.

'Are you ready Mr Farnworth?'

There was a slight inclination of his head. Caton nodded, and the technician lifted back the sheet. They watched him as he raised his head, forcing himself to look at the pathetic skeleton that had been his wife.

The first time Caton had been exposed to remains like this it had affected him deeply. Face to face with the ultimate testament to man's insignificance in the world, the universe, eternity, he had felt an overwhelming sense of loss. Now, apart from the identification, it was just a tool. A means to gauge other people's reactions.

Caton had observed scores of reactions, and there was no doubt about it; Barry Farnworth's were extreme. His first was one of reluctance. Caton had seen it several times on the faces of perpetrators. Not the perfectly understandable response of the squeamish, or the grief stricken. This was about facing up to consequences. The second was presaged by the draining of blood from his face, swiftly followed by a yellow flush from his neck upwards. Mary Shepherd, assuming he was about to faint, held out her arms to catch him. The technician, far more experienced than either of them, grabbed him by the arm and steered him over to a steel sink on the adjoining wall, into which he was violently sick.

He was silent again on the ride to the station. Caton decided to interview him under caution. There was no need to arrest him since he had come voluntarily, and nowhere near enough with which to charge him. Best to be on the safe side though. This way anything he said would be admissible. He asked Mary Shepherd to sit in on the interview. Farnworth had waived his right to a lawyer. Probably thought it would boost his claim of innocence. Caton knew different.

'How was I supposed to be able to identify her?' He said, laying his palms upwards on the table in supplication. They were slick with sweat.

'Her?' Said Mary Shepherd, her voice heavy with disapproval. 'I take it you mean Della, your wife?'

'Della,' he croaked, unable to shake the frog in his throat. Caton pushed the glass of water towards him. He picked it up, and drank greedily. His hand shook as he put the glass down, and it rattled on the surface of the table.

'Perhaps these will help,' said Caton pushing a transparent evidence bag across the table towards him. 'I am showing Mr Farnworth two items of jewellery. A golden wedding ring, and a silver and diamond engagement ring.'

As Farnworth stared down at them, beads of sweat broke out on his forehead.

'Do you recognise these as belonging to you first wife, Della?' Said Caton.

Farnworth shrugged his shoulders. 'I don't know,' he said. 'Maybe.'

Perhaps you'd like to take a closer look?' Said Mary Shepherd, pushing them across the table towards him.

He pretended to peer at them.

'Yes, I suppose so. Difficult to tell from the wedding ring, but that diamond look's familiar.'

'So it should Mr Farnworth,' said Caton retrieving the package. You see there is an inscription on the inside of each of them. But you'd know that wouldn't you?' Farnworth raised his head, and their eyes met. 'What did you have inscribed on the rings you gave to Della, Mr Farnworth?'

He tore his eyes away, and looked down at the table. His voice was barely a whisper. They had to make him repeat it for the tape.

'*B&D... Love Eternal*; and *Forever Yours Alone.*' He said.

Caton smiled at Mary Shepherd, and shook his head theatrically. 'The promises we make,' he said. 'Funny how they come back to haunt us.'

Given that Farnworth had waived his right to be represented Caton decided to let him have the break he requested. When they started again he had composed himself; not cocky, but certainly more self-assured.

'You knew it was Della didn't you?' Said Caton. 'As soon as you heard the body had been found.'

'No I didn't.'

'Come on Barry,' said Mary Shepherd, 'It was written all over your face when we knocked on your door.'

'That was different,' he said. 'I wondered if it was her. Of course I did. I've never stopped wondering. Every time a woman's body is found I wonder if it might be her. When I saw you again I put two and two together. I knew then that it must be her.'

'And how do you suppose she found her way there, almost on your doorstep?' Asked Caton.

He spread his hands again. Shrugged his shoulders. The picture of innocence. Like he was back selling cars again. 'I don't know. I assume some man chanced upon her wandering around in her distressed state. Took advantage of her. Then had to dispose of the body.'

'We don't have any evidence to suggest that anyone took advantage of your wife, Mr Farnworth.' Said Mary Shepherd.

Caton placed his hand over hers to stop her saying any more.

'What exactly did you mean by *dispose of the body* Mr Farnworth?' he said.

That shook him. His eyes flicked up to the right, and back again. Then sideways to the right, and back to the centre. Caton could almost see his brain ticking over. He was visually constructing a lie, then constructing the words to go with it. Listening to them in his head. Deciding if they sounded plausible. Standard Neuro Linguistic Programming eye movement directions. Every detective recognised them. Sadly, the courts did not.

'I don't know. I just assumed...with her being found on that slag heap... someone must have killed her, and hid her body up there.'

'Killed her how Mr Farnworth?'

The sweat began to form again. Beads of it at the hair line, on his forehead, at the sideburns. He reached into his pocket, found a handkerchief, and mopped his brow. 'I don't know,' he said. 'I just assumed...'

'So you said.' Caton leaned forward. 'Given that you claim that your wife took all those pills with her when she left, why wasn't your first thought that she might have taken her own life?'

The eyes were on the move again. Ten seconds went by.

'Well Mr Farnworth?'

'I couldn't see her choosing to go up there on her own, could I?' he licked his lips. 'Anyway, if she'd just lay down and died surely someone would have found her before now?'

Caton could tell the moment had passed. He decided to take another tack.

'When we called at the house you didn't seem to be at all surprised?' He said.

Farnworth eased his considerable bulk back into his chair. Caton could tell that he was beginning to relax; sensing that they had nothing more they could throw at him. That it was just a fishing expedition.

'A month after she'd walked out I resigned myself

to her being dead. If she'd been alive, I knew she would have contacted me by then.'

'Did you actually see her walk out?' Caton asked.

'No, I was at the show rooms.'

'So we don't know for a fact that she did walk out?'

Barry Farnworth smiled smugly. 'Well she didn't fly did she?'

They stood at the first floor window, and watched him leave the building. Mrs Farnworth number two was waiting at the kerb in a sleek gold Jaguar. She saw him coming, flung the door wide, jumped out heedless of the traffic, and rushed to meet him. Her fur coat flapped behind her; her shoulder length, blonde, salon straightened hair, a manic slip stream. She flung her arms around him as he struggled to lift her off her feet.

'Mutton dressed as lamb,' observed Mary Shepherd.

'Sixty thousand plus.' Said DS Holmes.

'I think she's got more miles on her clock than that.' Said Caton.

'Not her...the car,' said Holmes rising to the bait. 'XK60. Winter Gold. Flash or what?'

Farnworth put her down, and the two of them linked arms. She hung on for dear life, nestling into his shoulder as they walked to the car.

'I wonder if she knows,' said Shepherd. 'I wonder if she's always known.'

A photographer, a reporter, and a man with a video camera, ran towards them from the direction of the station entrance. Farnworth opened the passenger door to let her in, pushing the reporter aside as he did so. Then he shoved the cameraman in the chest, ran around to the driver's side, clambered in through the open door, and sped off.

'We could always do him for assault,' said Holmes. 'It'll be on the CCTV.'

Caton thanked Mary Shepherd for her help, promised to stay in touch, and made his way back to his room. There was no doubt about it. Farnworth's body language had been all wrong. Come to that, his spoken language had been a giveaway. "*...some man chanced upon her in her distressed state...*" That part was obviously rehearsed. And the bit about having "*...to dispose of the body...*" had sounded more like he was remembering a real event, than one imagined. But since there wasn't a single shred of evidence to link him to her murder, they'd had no option to but let him go. In the meantime Caton had arranged for a search of the house, and Farnworth's former showroom, and set the team tracking down all the vehicles in his possession at the time. According to DS Shepherd, Bolton Division had done that when Della was reported missing, but only half heartedly. If they could find that vehicle, Caton reasoned, it might turn up some traces of blood – even after all this time. Who knows, he may even have kept her purse, or watch; stranger things had happened. If nothing else, it would make him sweat. They would have to get his passport though. Given all the properties he had abroad it wasn't worth taking the risk. There was a knock on the door, and Jimmy Radford walked straight in.

'You've let him go!' He said.

Caton rose from his seat. 'That's right Sir. Why don't you sit down?'

Reluctantly the detective superintendent did just that. He sat bolt upright. Caton wondered if he'd been in the forces, or if his prostate was playing up.

'Did he do it?' Radford asked.

Caton nodded. 'Yes Sir, I believe he did.'

'But you can't prove it?'

He shook his head. 'What I need is a witness, some trace evidence, or an unprovoked confession. Short of that we wouldn't have a prayer on this one.'

The superintendent wriggled uncomfortably on his seat. Not ex forces then. Caton tried hard not smile.

'That's a bugger,' said Radford examining the shine on his toe caps. 'The press were hanging around when you brought him in. Now they've seen him leave. I've been told to make a statement. Release the name of the victim, appeal for witnesses, tell them the husband has been helping us with our enquiries,' he looked up. 'Unless you want to do it?'

It was the last thing Caton wanted to do.

'Well I'd be happy to Sir,' he lied. 'But I've the searches to set up, and I need to check on how we're doing out at the deposition site. But if you could just include a request for witnesses, anyone whose memory has been jogged by the tragic discovery... friends, locals, off roaders. You know the sort of thing.'

Radford grimaced, and wriggled faster. 'Are you sure you don't want to do it? Be good experience.'

Caton shuffled the papers on his desk, giving the impression of urgent tasks to be actioned. I really am pushed Sir,' he said. 'And it's not as though I haven't done it before?'

Radford climbed painfully to his feet. 'Right then. Keep me informed Tom.'

Caton stood up, several pieces of paper clutched in each hand, and watched in amusement as Jimmy Radford hot footed it to the door, en route to the nearest toilet.

Five minutes later he was back, sticking his head around the door. 'Tom. I want you with me. I'll do the bit about her identity, leaving no stone unturned, and so on; you can do the bit about wanting help from the public.' He held up his hand, stifling Caton's objections. 'No discussion on this. Out front, in five minutes.'

He closed the door behind him, leaving Caton to grab himself a quick coffee, and to rehearse his fifteen seconds of fame.

6

It was after midnight when Caton decided to go home, have a shower, and snatch a few hours sleep. He was reluctant to take any time out when there were still so many officers out at Bluebell Hollow. He knew it was daft, because they would be working in shifts, even if they were long ones, but it didn't stop him feeling guilty. In any case, it gave him the opportunity to check his land line.

There were a couple of texts from Kate, to which he responded. Still no message from Helen. But then, he reasoned as he stared into the bathroom mirror, why would there be? Not when she'd thrown his number away. If she relented, she could always look him up in the directory. Had she done, she would already have rung him. This could only mean one thing. She wasn't going to. There was a cracking sound, and sharp pain in the palm of his left hand. He looked down at the shattered remains of the plastic beaker. He dropped them into the pedal bin and examined his hand. There was a tiny drop of blood at the centre of his life line. As he rinsed it under the tap he stared again into the mirror. He saw reflected there the boy who had become a man; and thought about the boy Harry who would grow into one. Come hell or high water, he was going to be there to see it happen.

As the sun came up Caton pulled in to the car park of the Dun Mare and checked in at the mobile incident room. Progress had been slow and painstaking. As he'd suspected, it was proving nigh on impossible to make a connection between the artefacts discovered scattered across the top of the tip, and the gruesome discovery. To make matters worse, much of the litter on the flanks, and down in the valley, had blown in from the council reclamation site on the nearby industrial estate. Morbid curiosity had brought dozens of youths to the mobile incident room – most of them barely out of their nappies when the body of Della Farnworth had been buried. Of the remainder, a few were certain that they would have been up on the rucks, as they liked to call them, at the end of February ten years previously, but as to recalling specific events that might have a bearing on the case, they were a waste of time.

'What about seeing four wheel vehicles up there?' Caton asked the on-site Recorder.

'Plenty of those,' came the reply. 'Custom off roaders, land rovers, trucks, some cars that had been nicked and joy ridden. There are even some burnt out here and there. Where possible, we've got the makes and names of some of the owners, for elimination purposes.' He grimaced. 'But you know what it's like Sir.'

Caton knew exactly what it was like. Few of them would want to dob in a friend, and run the risk of being labelled a grass, even it was to eliminate them. He commandeered one of police force Landrovers to whisk him around the site – rallying the troops – most of whom were coming to the end of a shift and looked like they couldn't wait. Then he had a sausage barm and a cup of coffee at the site office with Brian Worden.

'I don't want to appear difficult Chief Inspector,' said the site manager. 'But we're losing big money here by the hour. I've got my bosses on my back, and sixty percent of the work force hanging around kicking their heels. The last thing I need is for them to get their feet under the table at the Hulton Arms eight hours a day. When I do get them back to work they'll be worse than useless.'

Caton could see his point. As long as the immediate area around the crime scene was secure there was no way he could justify holding up work much longer; especially in the areas they'd already searched.'

'You're right,' he said. 'You'd better show me your maps. See what we agree on.'

Twenty minutes later the excavators were rolling. A covered container lorry full of coal, destined for the Drax power station sixty five miles away in West Yorkshire, pulled out ahead of Caton onto the A6. He followed it to the second roundabout where it took the slip road onto the motorway. Caton kept straight on up Watergate Lane. There were two sets of interviews he had reserved for himself.

'Why did you let the bastard go?' She demanded, stabbing her cigarette like a smoking gun in Caton's direction.

Margaret Stanley, Della's older sister, looked all of her sixty years. Sallow faced, triple chinned, and morbidly obese, she sat chain smoking on the edge of a leather four seater in the lounge of her semidetached, owner occupied, and former council house. Her husband Vernon was in the kitchen where she'd sent him to boil a kettle. Caton took in the new pin brightness of the fireplace, the sparkling windows, polished surfaces, and the freshly shampooed carpet. The contrast between this room, and its occupant, was bizarre.

'Because our investigation is still ongoing,' he said, trying hard to lower the temperature.

'Don't you bloody well patronise me!' She dragged heavily on the cigarette as though drawing on unseen forces, inhaled deeply, and directed a narrow stream of smoke towards the ceiling, where it spread sideways at speed, hugging the surface like a pyroclastic flow. 'You know very well what I mean. You can investigate all you bloody well like; it'll still come down to the same thing in the end. He did it. End of!'

'Now you don't know that for a fact Maggie.' Vernon Stanley appeared in the doorway holding a tray with three china cups and saucers, and a plate of chocolate digestive biscuits. He was a third her size; Bud Abbot to her Lou Costello.

'Nobody asked you,' she said whipping a mat out from under the coffee table with her free hand, and placing it on top. 'And don't be so bloody stupid. Of course he did it.'

Caton could have sworn that her husband flinched.

'I know that Maggie,' he said lowering the tray gently onto the mat. 'But Mr Caton has to be able to prove it. He can't just arrest him willy nilly, now can he?'

Margaret Stanley snorted, took another puff, and directed the smoke in her husband's direction. Caton decided it was time to take control of the situation.

'Your husband's right Mrs Stanley. The best way you can help us to bring your sister's murderer to justice is to put your feelings aside for a moment, and give me some facts to work with,' seeing the cigarette poised to strike he hurried on. 'So, question number one. Why were you so sure that your sister had not just walked out on her husband?'

She took a slurp of tea, and turned to face him, punctuating every point with her cigarette. 'Because, unlike me, our Della wouldn't have had the guts to do it; because even if she'd only thought about it she would have told me so; and because if the silly cow had actually gone ahead and done it, she would have come and stayed here. Good enough?'

It was far from good enough, but Caton believed her. 'How would you describe your sister's behaviour and her emotional state in the days before she disappeared?' He asked.

She stubbed out the cigarette on the china saucer, and pushed it away from her. Caton registered the flicker of disapproval on her husband's face. Mr Tidy and Mrs Lazy Slob; a marriage made in Hell.

'All over the bloody place,' she said folding her arms aggressively across her ample chest. 'That's where she was. Up one minute, down the next. Popping pills like they were smarties. And, before you ask... the answer's no. She was not a junky, and there was no way she was going to overdose on those sodding tranquilizers.'

'She was upset then?'

'Of course she was bleeding well upset. Wouldn't you be?'

Caton counted to five, reigning in his desire to take her on at her own game.

'I don't know,' he said. 'Not till you tell me what was upsetting her.'

She sighed dramatically, and then spelt it out slowly, as though dealing with a simpleton.

'It was him wasn't it? At it again.'

'At what?'

She stared at him, incredulous. 'What the bloody hell do you think he was at? I thought *you* were the detective.'

Caton put his cup and saucer down, and got to his feet. 'Unless you stop messing me around,' he said. 'I'm out of here.'

He could see that had shaken her. Her arms unfolded. She sunk them into the soft leather, threatening to rise in protest. Finding it impossible.

'You can't do that!'

Caton half turned towards the door. 'Try me.'

'He was having it away with someone.'

Caton remained standing. 'You know that for a fact?'

'As good as.'

'She believed he was having an affair. With whom?'

She shrugged dismissively. 'I don't know do I? Someone. It wouldn't have been the first time.'

'How did she know?'

'Going off sex; coming home late; disappearing at odd times; taking his phone into the garden to answer it. Even had his mobile phone password protected.'

'How did he explain it?'

'Problems at work.'

'It's possible.'

She snorted again. 'And pigs'll fly!'

There was more chance of that happening, Caton decided, than Margaret Stanley getting off that sofa unaided.

'So who did she think it was?' He said.

She took a cigarette from the packet on the arm of the sofa, and searched for the lighter under the folds of her right buttock. Vernon Stanley used the opportunity to take a crystal glass ash tray from the mantelpiece and place it surreptitiously on the coffee table. She placed the cigarette between her lips, and held the lighter in suspended animation.

'If she'd known who it was,' she said. 'She could have done something about it couldn't she?'

'Who did *you* think it was?'

'It was that bloody cow he went and married. Must've been, mustn't it?'

'There's no evidence that she was even on the scene at that time.' Caton reminded her.

'If you were screwing around, would you leave evidence lying about?' she asked.

It was the first thing she'd said that made sense. She lit the cigarette, and blew a perfect ring that drifted towards him like a fat full stop.

Philip Carlton had been in the business all of his working life. Approaching sixty, he had seen it all. He passed a hand over the gleaming dome of his bald head, as though expecting to find a sudden sprout of hair.

'I always thought something had happened to her. Foul play I mean. It just never smelt right.'

'That's all it was...a feeling?' Said Caton.

The insurance assessor nodded. 'That's all it was. I put our own investigators onto it, and we even employed a private detective. Watched, him like a hawk. If he was knocking off his future wife before Della disappeared, then he must have been pretty secretive about it. But afterwards the two them would have to have to have exercised unbelievable self-control. It was just under two years after Della disappeared that we first recorded a date between them. They were both in a pub on the edge of the moors.' He consulted the file on his desk. 'Bob's Smithy. They appeared to accidentally sit next to each other at the bar. He offered to buy her a drink. She accepted. That's where it all seemed to start.' He looked up. 'Funny thing is they were both members at the same golf club; had been for three years. If there was chemistry between them, would it really have taken until then to act on it?'

'Perhaps he was still hoping that his wife would turn up. Walk back in?'

The insurance man grinned. 'That's what he wanted us to think, but the way those two went at it after that first meeting I can tell you poor Della can't have made a lasting impression on him. The way it looked to our man, they'd been holding back that long it was like a dam bursting.'

'So why did you pay out?'

Carlton closed the file. 'That was down to your lot.' He said, without a trace of rancour. 'Once you'd satisfied yourself that there'd been no trace of her, passport not used, credit card and savings not touched, no sightings, the courts had no choice but to formally declare her dead. After that we didn't have any option but to pay up.' He stood, signalling the end of the meeting, held out his hand, and smiled.

'Hopefully, now you can help us to get it back.'

DI Holmes was in the incident room when Caton returned just after midday. He had two pieces of news.

'That appeal of yours has turned up trumps Boss,' he said. 'CrimeStoppers got a call from a planning officer with Bolton Council. She thought it might be worth mentioning that our Barry Farnworth had been a consistent – if back seat – campaigner against the revised proposals to begin opencast operations at Cutacre. Regular pain in the arse she said. And what really galled them was that he lived far enough away from the proposed site not to be the slightest bit affected by it.'

'Did he now?' said Caton, sensing that Holmes was holding back the best till last.

'And forensics reckons that the scraps of clothing found with the body are consistent with the clothes that her husband claimed she had been wearing the day she disappeared. Same material, traces of dye the same colour. And that's not all,' he paused for dramatic effect; a tendency that Caton still found irritating. 'They also found traces of blood and engine oil mixed together on some of those scraps beneath the body. Bit of a coincidence don't you think, given that Farnworth owned a garage at the time?'

'How are we doing on the search of his garage and showrooms?' Caton asked.

'Half way there last time I checked.'

'Right, well ask forensics to concentrate on the garage, and the work shop. If that's where she died there's an outside chance they might find something. Whether they do or not, once they've finished, we bring him in again.'

While they were waiting, Caton used the time to clear up some of his paperwork. Then he told the office manager he was nipping down to the canteen. The canteen was quiet; just a couple of police constables and someone from the custody suite getting a drink for a prisoner. He ordered a cup of tea and a sausage barm with plenty of brown sauce, and sat in the corner as far away from the others as possible. He still hadn't convinced himself that pressuring Helen was the right thing to do; only that he didn't have any other option. The waiting was killing him. He took out his mobile phone, selected his address book, and rang Robin Park.

'I'd like to speak with Helen Malone,' he said. 'I understand she's in your PR department.'

'PR and Media actually,' said the woman on reception. 'Who shall I say is calling?'

There was no point in lying. She'd know as soon as she heard his voice. 'Tom Caton,' he said. 'Tell her it's Tom.'

She kept him waiting for less than half a minute, but it felt like forever. Time enough to imagine sitting in the stands with Harry beside him, craning forward eagerly on the edge of his seat. Shouting enthusiastically. Turning to look up into his father's face.

'I'm sorry Mr Caton. But I'm afraid that Helen is out of the office. Can I take a message?'

It was a professional attempt. No tension in her voice, oozing authenticity. Not enough to fool Caton.

'Just tell I her I rang,' he said. 'And that I'll keep trying.'

He left his sausage barm untouched. As he opened the door, and headed up the stairs, one of the uniformed officers walked across, picked up the plate, and grinned at his colleague.

'Waste not, want not.' He heard him say.

7

DI Holmes came across the incident room waving a photograph aloft like a trophy. Which in a way it was. 'We've got a result Boss! You won't believe it.'

'Try me.' Said Caton.

Holmes showed him the photograph. It looked like a greyish black stain on a piece of concrete.

'Forensics thought they'd picked up a trace on the door jamb in the garage with the old ultra violet. So they brought a sniffer dog in with them. And guess what?'

'You're not going to tell me that dark patch is blood; not after all this time?'

Holmes grinned. 'Course I'm not. It's oil. But when Reggie had a go at it...'

'Reggie?'

'The cocker spaniel...his tail went into overdrive. So they cut out a small section of the floor, and took it back to the lab. The Garage owner was spitting feathers...'

'Get on with it Gordon.' said Caton.

'And there was blood soaked into the concrete *under* the layer of oil. A lot of blood'

'Reggie must have a hell of a nose.'

'Apparently he sniffs out blood that's seven years old. Even longer depending on the conditions.'

'One of the mechanics could have had an accident,' Caton suggested. 'Banged his head while working under a car.'

Holmes shook his head vigorously. 'Owner says it was like that when he bought the place from Farnworth. Only it was long since dried, and with the layer of dust on it, it didn't look that bad. Didn't see any point in trying to clean it up. It was only going to get messed up again. Bloody good job he didn't try to steam clean it, eh Boss?'

'I can tell from the grin on your face that you're going to tell me that the blood is hers.' Said Caton.

The grin widened. 'Course it is. One hundred percent hers.'

Caton took another look at the photograph. 'Get him in.'

This time he had a solicitor with him, and he wasn't saying a word. Even when Caton showed him the photograph, and told him the blood matched that of his wife Della. Even when he had been told that a former employee of his had stated that Farnworth was the sole key holder for the show rooms, and the garage. Even when the local nick confirmed that they had a record of the fact on their computer. After half an hour Caton called a halt, leaving him alone to mull it over with his lawyer.

'If he says *"No Comment"* one more time, I swear I'll be over the table and at him.' Said Holmes.

Caton knew how he felt, and that simply saying it was a way to release some of the frustration.

'Are we going to charge him then?' Asked Holmes.

'He's under arrest on suspicion of murdering his

wife. At the moment all the evidence we've got is circumstantial.'

Holmes took a slurp of coffee, and then folded his arms. 'So,' he said. 'They have a row. Della goes off in a huff with the keys to the garage. With the intention of what? Smashing the place up? Nicking a car? Then she falls and bangs her head on the floor. Someone just happens to pass by, sees the door open, goes in and finds her. Decides to bundle her in the boot of whatever he's driving, take her up to Cutacre, bury her, come back and pour oil over the garage floor. Lock up, and smuggle the keys back into the Farnworth's house. The Defence rests!'

'Even so,' said Caton. 'I'd like something more. And why the hell didn't forensics pick it up at the time?'

'Because nobody took it seriously, that's why. You heard what Mary Shepherd said. Couldn't get anyone to listen to her.'

Caton knew he was right. But it still didn't help their case. The best bet was to try and break him. Get a confession. Failing that they would just have to go ahead and charge him. Always assuming the Crown Prosecution Service wasn't going to throw a wobbler. He drained his cup and stood up.

'OK,' he said, checking his watch. 'He's had long enough. Let's do it.'

They had only got as far as corridor leading to the interview suite when the door behind them burst open and a red faced DCS Radford called them back.

'I suggest you suspend the interview, and send him back to his cell,' he said. 'They've found another one!'

As they drove into the car park beside the Dun Mare a familiar figure, accompanied by a photographer, emerged from a silver Toyota Avensis, and started towards them.

'Christ! It's Hymer,' said Holmes. 'How the hell did he get here before us?'

'One of the site workers probably tipped him the wink,' said Caton. 'He'll have seen to it they all had his business card. It's probably pinned up in their canteen.' It was not a difficult assumption to make. Larry Hymer, Chief Crime Reporter with The Evening News had a reputation for scattering his cards like confetti. Caton had barely switched off the engine before the two of them were standing by his door, the lense of the camera poised to capture him leaving the car. The reporter had a voice recorder in his outstretched hand. Caton told Holmes to stay where he was, and opened the window a fraction, forcing Hymer to bend down and speak through the gap.

'Detective Chief Inspector,' he said, with unaccustomed formality that showed how piqued he really was. 'Can we take it that this new discovery is linked with the discovery of Della Farnworth?'

'No Comment.' said Caton.

Hymer pressed on. 'Did Barry Farnworth disclose the whereabouts of this body? Is that how you found it so quickly?'

'No Comment.'

'Barry Farnworth is still in custody though isn't he Chief Inspector?'

'No Comment.'

'Come on Tom,' said Hymer finally showing his frustration. 'You've got to give me something.'

Caton released the window until the reporter was able to lean in. He covered the microphone with his left hand, waved him closer, and whispered into his ear.

'Come on Larry,' he said. 'You know the score. I've only just arrived. I haven't the faintest idea what I'm dealing with. It could be a tailor's dummy up there for all I know. So why don't you grab yourself a swift half, and when I get back you may just get an exclusive.' His finger found the electronic window control, forcing Hymer to make an undignified retreat. 'For what it's worth.' He mouthed as the window clicked shut.

A Police Constable was waiting to open the wooden gate across the bridleway. Ahead of them the lane proceeded between the high steel fence that marked the boundary of the factory, and the hedgerow between them and Cutacre Tip. Part way down, the railings and the hawthorns were festooned with plastic bags and wastepaper that had blown in from the council tip.

'Over there Boss.' Holmes pointed to the right, across the area of rough grass where the hedge ended, and the off-road racing track began. A gap wide enough for a land rover had been cut in the perimeter fence. Beside it stood the site recorder, and a member of the Tactical Aid Unit. Caton parked up, and the two of them climbed out. Parallel lines of tape marked their route along the line of duck boards, and across a makeshift bridge of wooden sleepers. On the far bank of the stream that was once a river they could see the SOCOs in their blue and white Tyvek suits. A tented screen had already been erected around the dump site, no doubt prompted by the single engined bi plane that buzzed over head. Caton guessed it was either a recreational flight from nearby Barton Aerodrome, or more likely one of Hymer's photographers scrambled as soon as he had got word. Either way, it was a distraction he could do without.

'Get on to Chester House,' he said. 'And tell them I want a two mile exclusion zone over this site except for our own Air Support, and commercial flights. Tell them they're creating a hazard.'

As he crossed the boggy ground, and dropped down towards the stream, the plane came perilously close, swooping down above the valley, its wing tips only ten metres or so from the tops of the bare birch trees. He could clearly see the passenger struggling to keep the telephoto lense steady. It occurred to Caton that the perpetrator might be a civilian pilot. That perhaps that was how he had come to choose this site. And then again, maybe he got a kick out of flying over the place where his guilty secrets were buried. It was the kind of perverted pleasure that a serial killer might take. Every visit a vicarious pleasure, and a confirmation of his omnipotence. It was worth checking. He would get the team to match the records of flight plans with this place. He wondered if Farnworth held a pilot's licence. Somehow he couldn't see it.

It was another woman. Caton didn't need to be told, he could see for himself. She was naked. Curled up in a foetal position; her arms hugging her knees close to her chest. Her left ankle appeared to have been shattered, and the heel was missing. Her skin was better preserved than that of Della Farnworth; reddish brown, and leathery. There were blonde hairs on her scalp. She had been buried several feet deeper, and two hundred metres further north than Della, where the steep slopes of Cutacre met the wide banks of Bluebell Hollow. It was just the kind of spot Caton would have chosen had he been sick enough to contemplate such a thing. Accessible but remote. Unlikely to be disturbed by surface mining. Likely to be covered by subsequent land slips as the sides of the slag heap eroded.

'Curiouser, and curiouser!'

He turned to find Mullen the duty pathologist at his elbow, and stepped aside to let him through.

While he waited for Mullen to complete his initial investigation Caton asked Terry Ryan how the body had been discovered.

'To make up for time lost when we had his men all kicking their heels,' she told him. 'Brian Worden set some of the men clearing the scrub on the lower flanks, and along the west bank. Every twenty metres they'd cleared, they drilled a bore hole just to check the sample against their geo maps.' She pointed to a small orange drilling rig standing idle close to the deposition site. 'When they examined the sample from right here there was a sizeable piece of bone in it. After what they found on the top they had the wit to report it. Thanks to the core sample we knew exactly how far down it was. It only took a couple of men an hour to dig down there, and that included sifting every shovel of soil; if you can call it soil.'

'So if it took them that long, how long did it take whoever buried her?' Caton wondered out loud.

'Not as long as you'd think,' she said. 'They reckon there must already have been a depression there where some of the hill had slipped away. The different layers don't match up. Looks like he would only have had to dig down a couple of feet, and then start shovelling from the sides, and from above, until he'd levelled it all off, and then she would have been almost five feet under.'

Caton looked across to the tent from which Mullen was emerging. 'So the missing part of her foot...'

'Is the bits of bone that came up with the sample. Or so it seems.' she said. 'But you'll need Mr Mullen to confirm that.'

Mullen did. He also stated that in his opinion this was a more recent interment than that of Della Farnworth.

'Within the last four years I should think,' he said. 'But don't quote me. Because until Professor James has had a look, and I've completed the post mortem, I'll deny having said it.'

'So how come this body is better preserved?' wondered Caton.

Mullen peeled off his gloves, and placed them in the bag held out by his assistant. 'Different soil composition; greater depth,' he said. 'Something else too. There's no sign of any clothing, and no obvious evidence that she was the victim of a physical assault. I say obvious, because until I've completed a physical examination it's going to be hard to tell.' The hint of a smile teased the edges of his mouth.

'But.' Said Caton.

Mullen didn't disappoint. 'I shall be really

surprised,' he said. 'When I've had a proper look, if it doesn't turn out that she was strangled.'

When Mullen had gone Caton took stock. In truth, his decision to continue to search for further victims following the discovery of the body of Della Farnworth, had been little more than a precaution. Once they had her husband in custody, and the traces of blood in the garage, his hope that it had been a one off had been more or less confirmed. Now that had been blown out of the water. DI Holmes couldn't wait to get back to Leigh, and start in again on Barry Farnworth. Caton was not so sure.

'At the very least we need a connection between Farnworth, and this victim.' he pointed out.

'You never know though,' said Holmes, keen to get on with it. 'The fact that we've found her may just tip him over the edge. There's nothing lost by giving it a try. If he carries on stalling we can charge him with Della's murder, and have another crack at him when we do put a name to this one.'

Caton waited for the thud of the police helicopter to pass overhead, as it shepherded the two seater plane south towards Barton aerodrome.

'Always assuming that the two are connected.' He said.

Holmes frowned in disbelief. 'Come on Boss. What are the odds of this being the work of some other twisted mind?'

Caton scanned the rucks above him, and then the valley in which they stood. 'No worse than winning the Lottery,' he said. 'And someone does that every week.'

8

'Why the hell have you asked for another body search team Tom? Isn't one enough?'

It didn't take a genius to see that Detective Superintendent Radford was unhappy. For a start he wasn't letting Caton get a word in edgeways.

'You haven't even re-interviewed Farnworth yet,' he blustered on. 'If he puts his hands up to both of them you'll have wasted resources, and made us look bloody fools.'

'And what if he admits to more than these two?' Caton managed to get in.

Radford waved it away dismissively. 'If that is the case, he can lead you to them, so you won't need another search team.'

'And how will we know if he's telling the whole truth? He could be giving us a fraction of what's out there.'

Radford gripped the edge of the desk, veins protruding, white knuckles calling attention to the liver spots across the back of his hand. 'Is that what you really think? That he's a serial killer?'

Caton shook his head. 'No Sir, I don't'

'Well then.'

'I don't think the two victims are connected to each other, or to Farnworth.'

Radford's voice went up another notch. 'Think? What's think got to do with it? Where's your evidence? How will you even know till you've put it to him?'

'There are significant inconsistencies between the two...' Caton began. Radford cut him off.

'Then get them ironed out,' he said. 'I do not want to hear about more bodies, or another killer come to that. I am not having another Ipswich here. Not on my patch.'

Caton was tempted to point out that there was bugger all he, or Radford, could do if that was the case. He opted for a slightly less patronising approach. 'The Suffolk Murders were different Sir,' he reasoned, 'Five women killed in less than six weeks. Four of them while the police were still hunting the killer. That's not what we've got here.'

Radford thumped the desk top hard enough to make himself wince. 'We don't know what the hell we do have here Detective Chief Inspector,' he said through gritted teeth. 'So I suggest that you get down to the custody suite and find out!'

It wasn't a problem for Caton. It was exactly what he had been about to do when Radford had so rudely burst into his room.

Farnworth's solicitor made the opening gambit.

'My client would like to make a statement.'

'I have no doubt he would,' Caton told him. 'However, I have something to share with your client first. It may help him to reconsider that statement.'

Farnworth's his piggy eyes narrowed, and beads of sweat appeared at his temples. Something about the manner of the two detectives unnerved him.

'You see Barry,' Caton continued. 'Shortly after we suspended the interview with you this morning we were called back to the Cutacre site, because a body had been discovered. This body had been buried close to the place where we found the body of your wife. There were similarities between this discovery, and the previous one, which led us to suspect that you may be able to help us with our enquiries into this latest discovery.'

The solicitor stared at Farnworth. Farnworth stared at Caton. His face reflected horror, and disbelief. In that moment Caton knew that his worst suspicion had been realised. And Radford's worst nightmare.

Farnworth was fighting to get his breath. His face was flushed crimson, and his hand tugged at his collar. 'It wasn't me,' he spluttered. 'I don't know anything about this I swear.' He turned to his solicitor. Appealing to him with his free hand. 'Tell them. I didn't do this! I didn't kill her! I don't even know who she is.'

'She, Barry?' Caton responded calmly. 'I don't remember saying anything about it being a woman.'

Farnworth looked across at him, his pupils wider now, the sweat running in rivulets. 'I want to make a statement he said.'

His solicitor laid a hand on his arm. 'Mr Farnworth I urge not to say any more until you and I have had a chance to...'

Farnworth tore his arm away. 'I want to make a statement,' he said. Right now! I'll tell you everything.'

'What do you think Boss?' Said Holmes.

Caton looked down at the statement. Farnworth was cooling his heels while they decided whether to charge him, or start again. There was little doubt. He was going to charge him. The only question was with what. Desperate to convince them that he had nothing to do with the second body he had admitted responsibility for Della's death, and for burying her body on the slag heap. Surprise, surprise, he claimed it had been an accident. She came to the showroom to confront him about the affair she suspected he was having. He was in the garage; on the phone to his girl friend. She overheard, went berserk, and came at him fists flying. He tried to push her out of the office into the service area. She fell, smashed her head on the concrete floor, and stopped breathing. There was blood. A lot of blood. He gave her mouth to mouth. Breathing started again but she remained unconscious. She stopped breathing. No pulse. He panicked. Didn't think anybody would believe him. Mopped up the blood with rags then wrapped them with the body in a polythene sheet, and then a tarpaulin. Tied it with a tow rope. He poured some dirty engine oil they had from a service over the place where the blood was. Then he just sat there looking at the body wrapped up like a mummy. Over two hours he reckoned. Finally he got his courage up. Dragged her out to a Land Rover he was selling, got a spade they kept for the flower beds out front of the showroom, and drove up to Cutacre. He drove along the top of the slag heap as far as he could without lights. Then he picked a spot, and started digging. The polythene, tarpaulin, and rags went in a rubbish skip in the council tip next to the site. The barriers were down so he had had to crawl underneath, dragging the tarpaulin behind him. Then he took the Land Rover back to the garage, drove her car out to Atherton Station, and walked it back. Took him the best part of an hour and a half. Then he drove home, downed the best part of a bottle of whisky, and fell into bed. By the time the police were involved he'd already off loaded the Land Rover at a Car Auction in East Manchester. Her personal belongings – purse, bank cards, handbag, and passport – he gathered up the following day, placed in a polythene bag, and buried up on the moors. And that was it. An accident. Followed by a moment of madness when he decided to dispose of her body, and cover it all up. As for the other woman they'd found; nothing to do with him.

'Some moment of madness Boss,' said Holmes, who had been reading over his shoulder. 'Sits around for two hours, and then covers his tracks with all the aplomb of a hit man.'

Caton was impressed. He'd never had Gordon down as a man with *aplomb* in his vocabulary.

'And I liked the way you sucked him in,' Holmes continued. 'With all that talk of similarities? What similarities would those have been?'

Caton ticked them off on his fingers. Let's see,' he said. 'How many do you want? They were both women; both in a grave; both at Cutacre; and they were both dead.'

So, what do you reckon? Murder or manslaughter?' Said Holmes.

'I've no doubt the Crown Prosecution Service will make the final decision but if it was up to me, it has to be murder. And that's what I'm going to charge him with. He's going to plead guilty to manslaughter, so we'll always have that to fall back on.'

'What do you really think though Boss?'

Caton picked up the statement, and headed towards the door. 'He's probably telling the truth, but why didn't he send for an ambulance? The Royal Bolton Hospital is less than a mile away from his garage. They might have been able to save her. As for motivation there's the insurance, and the mistress. It'll all depend on how the jury sees it. If it was down to me, he'd get life.'

Radford put the mug of coffee down on his desk, and looked up expectantly.

'I hope you've got some good news for me Tom?'

'I have Sir,' said Caton. 'I've got good news, and bad news. The good news is that Farnworth has confessed to killing his wife, and I'm about to charge him with murder. The bad news is that it looks like we have another killer.'

True to form, Radford seized on the crumb of hope.

'But you can't be sure?'

'No Sir. I can't. But Farnworth claims he killed his wife in the heat of a domestic argument. It was either manslaughter, or murder in the heat of the moment. In either case, almost certainly unpremeditated. The odds of that happening twice with the same man, and seven years apart, are beyond remote. And I believe him. Secondly, there are significant differences. Della Farnworth was fully clothed. This one was naked. Della Farnworth suffered a blow to her skull. This one – although it's yet to be confirmed – appears to have been strangled.'

Radford picked up a pencil and started playing with it. He was beginning to wriggle on his seat. All that coffee. Caton found it disconcerting. Not least because he was worried that it might set him off laughing.

'Sexually assaulted Tom?'

'We don't know Sir.'

'It could still be him.' Radford tapped his pencil on the desk in time to the gyrations of his lower body.

Caton knew that he had to get out of there. If he did corpse, their relationship would be doomed. Corpsing, he thought. How Freudian is that? 'We'll have a better idea when we know the identity of this latest body, Sir.' He said.

Radford nodded. 'You'd better get on then. I'll let the Chief know. She'll have a view on how we handle the press. Oh, and Tom. Well done on the Farnworth front. Quick result. That's how I like them.'

He was rocking now. A bit like a spitting cobra, Caton decided as he closed the door; only the other end.

His afternoon had flown by. There had been a successful session with Murray from the CPS, and a careful scripting of his piece with the Press Office, followed by a five minute adrenalin fuelled press conference that had gone far better than he'd anticipated. Now he was in Brian Worden's site office at Cutacre with Derek Franklin, the expert guiding the search teams. Spread out on the table in front of them was a detailed plan of the site, the aerial photos taken on day one, and photos previously taken by the Ordnance Survey, and by UK Coal before they began working on the site. By comparing the photos they had been trying to narrow down the search area. The nature of the terrain, composition of the soil, and sheer scale of the encroachment of Worden's men on the landscape had made it the most challenging exercise Franklin had encountered.

'Are you sure that you want me to concentrate on this area?' he asked moving the palm of his hand across the length of Bluebell Hollow.

Caton knew it was a gamble, but he was convinced that Farnworth had been straight with him. This latest body was unconnected, and if there were others, this would be where they would find them. He was as sure as he could be. 'Yes,' he said.

'But you don't know for certain that there are any more?'

'No.'

Franklin stared at the photos, shook his head, and stretched his aching back. Too many hours spent hunched over maps like this; too much craning forward to scan computer screens.

'It's not going to be easy,' he said. 'All this scrub, and trees, not to mention the way all of the diggers have churned up the soil. We would never have had an inkling of your latest one from these photographs.' He pointed to the group of photos showing the place where the naked woman had been found; some in colour, others in black and white. Erosion and land slip had made it impossible to tell that this area had been disturbed by more recent human intervention. 'If we had a photo taken after she was buried, and before half the hillside came down, I wouldn't have had a problem. Your first victim however,' he selected another photo that had been taken by UK Coal shortly before they began work on the site, and slid it across the table with his index finger. 'If I'd seen this when it was taken I could have told you there was something fishy going on down there.'

Caton could see what he meant. Even though the surface colour appeared to be consistent with the soil around it there were two roughly oval shadows. A larger one, perhaps a metre by two metres, and much smaller one near the centre.

'Doesn't matter how carefully you infill a burial, you're going to start off with too much soil, and end up with too little.' Franklin explained. 'Regardless of how far and how quickly the body begins to decompose the soil will start to compress. Over time you're going to end up with a depression approximating the area you've excavated. And then, when the body finally collapses, you're going to have a smaller hollow in the centre. Just like this.'

None of this was new to Caton, but it was the first time he had seen it illustrated so vividly. 'So if there were any more graves up on the top of Cutacre, there's a good chance you might spot them from these photos?' he said.

'It depends on the angle the photos were taken from, and the time of day. But yes, there's a chance. Down here in the valley however, we're going to have to work it out on the ground. Look for changes in the vegetation, bumps and hollows, drill probe holes where there's the faintest suspicion of something. Use the cadaver dogs where we can.'

'Magnetometry?' suggested the head of the Tactical Aid Unit.

'Not unless you suspect the bodies you're looking for have been burned.'

'What about ground penetrating radar?' Caton asked.

The expert shook his head. 'If we were talking concrete, limestone, granite, it might be worth trying, but from what I've been told about this site it's mainly shale, mudstone, clay, coal?'

Brian Worden nodded his agreement.

'In which case,' Franklin continued. 'It's going to bugger up the electrical conductivity. We'd be talking ten centimetres penetration at best. And you've no idea how much it would cost to cover the area you've indicated. Speaking of which, I've got two teams waiting. If you're happy, I'd better get on with it.'

Happy wasn't a word that Caton would have chosen.

9

Caton found it impossible to sleep. It was three in the morning. Knowing that it was because he was sleep deprived only made it worse. What he needed was a solution.

His brain buzzed with overlapping and disconnected thoughts over which he seemed to have no control. One minute he was revisiting the day's events as though he could somehow rework them; the next he was imagining the discovery of another body. He forced himself to refocus. Harry, what the hell was he going to do about Harry? There was no point in waiting to see if Helen would come round to the idea of him sharing her son, disrupting their lives. It was not going to happen. Just one option left then. Look her up on the electoral role. She was bound to be there. Something of a champagne socialist if he remembered rightly. Then he had two choices: write her a letter; or wait for her outside her workplace or her home. Probably the former. He didn't think that stalking her would impress his next promotions board. Nor was the revelation that he had a six year old son likely to impress Kate. He still had that bridge to cross.

He stared at the clock, turned over in despair, and pulled the pillow over his head. A colleague who had served in the forces once told him to imagine that he was in a snowstorm, and think white. He claimed that it worked for him every time. Caton gave it a try. By the time he began to drift off the birds had begun their dawn chorus, and light was filtering through the curtains.

'God you look terrible Boss.'

Caton took the coffee Holmes had proffered him, and found that his hand was shaking. 'What time is Farnworth due in court this morning?' he asked.

'Eleven o'clock. I'll take it if you like?'

Caton blew on the surface, took a sip, and burnt the tip of his tongue. He put it down on top of the drinks dispenser. 'Thanks Gordon,' he said. 'But I'd better go since I was the one that charged him. You get out to Cutacre, and see how the search is going. Before you do that, chase up the post mortem report on the latest victim.'

'No need, Boss. It arrived first thing this morning. Mr Mullen slotted her in late yesterday afternoon. It's on your desk.'

'So?'

Holmes rhymed it off. 'Female, late twenties to early thirties. Natural brunette, dyed blonde. Five foot five, size eight. Can't swear to it, but he's added a note off the record; thinks she may have been quite a heavy drinker. DNA won't be a problem, and her dental profile is going the rounds as I speak. He still reckons she was killed – or at least buried – between three and four years ago, but that's to be confirmed.'

'OK Gordon, you've saved the best till last. 'How did she die?'

Back in his office Caton read it through again. The report was unequivocal. She'd died from manual strangulation. There was classic evidence of damage to the larynx; in particular, the greater horns of the hyoid bone. He double checked the section relating to the victim's hands, rang the mortuary, and asked to speak with Mullen.

The pathologist was cross at being disturbed, and not afraid to let it show.

'This had better be important Detective Chief Inspector,' he snapped. 'I'm in the middle of a particularly interesting dissection.'

'I have your report here. I wanted to thank you for getting it to me so quickly,' Caton said, hoping to pacify him. 'There was one thing I wanted to check with you.'

'Get on with it man.'

'There's no mention of any foreign tissue under her nails. Is that because all the tissue has decomposed?'

'No it is not. If it was, I would have said so. The reason there is none, is that there was none in the first place.'

'So it's unlikely that she tried to stop her attacker by grabbing his or her hands?' Caton persisted.

'God knows,' said Mullen. 'All I know is that there is no evidence that she did. Now can I get back to the dead, and leave you to hound the living?'

'Thank you.' He said as the pathologist cut him off.

It was midday when he arrived back from court. Farnworth's solicitor had tried to get him bail on the strength of his willingness to hold up his hands to manslaughter. The magistrate wasn't having any of it. Not with another body, as yet unidentified. He was remanded in custody until they found a slot at the Crown Court. Despite the fact that they were sharing, the incident room was running like a well oiled machine. His instruction to run a second level analysis of missing persons covering females aged between fifteen and forty five, within a twenty five mile radius of the city centre, was well in hand. They were being listed in four groups – fifteen to twenty, twenties, thirties, and forties. Each group subdivided again into those described as blonde, whether natural or dyed, and non blondes. Given the recency of her demise, and the fact that he was asking for the search to include a year either side of Mullen's estimate, he felt certain she would be in there.

Reports of door to door interviews, and drop-ins to the mobile in the Dun Mare car park, were being put straight onto the computerised system. Two hundredweight of litter, and other artefacts from the two sites, had already been sifted through, and prioritised for forensic examination.

Caton felt a bit like a spare part. He rapidly dispensed with accumulated emails, made a half hearted attempt to clear some of his in-tray, left Holmes to hold the fort, and set out for Bluebell Hollow.

He was just as redundant out there as he had been in the station. There was nothing for him to do except admire the dogged persistence of the search teams, the unremitting boredom for the officers guarding the perimeter, and the monotony of the door to door enquiries. No wonder they call us *The Plod*, he reflected. But at least he had been out in the fresh air. On the way back he stopped at a roadside canteen parked up on Lovers Lane, near the entrance to the Howe Bridge Crematorium. He knew the van would not have been licensed to operate from there, but he was still tired, hungry and thirsty, and didn't fancy another spell in the canteen. He paid for a large coffee in a paper cup, and a sausage barm cake with brown sauce, and took them back to the car. He thought that the caffeine, and the food, would act like a pick me up. The coffee was scalding hot, so he balanced it on the hand brake housing, and set about the barm cake. With that demolished he started to write a text message to Kate on his mobile, realised that it would about five o'clock in the morning in California, and saved it as a draft. The combination of all that carbohydrate and the lack of sleep engulfed him. He switched off his phone and pager, reclined his seat, and closed his eyes. Just a little nap, that's all he needed.

When he awoke, the van had gone. Ten metres ahead of him a hearse was turning right into the broad drive that led to the crematorium. Half a dozen cars followed behind. The word GRAMPS was spelled out in white chrysanthemums along the side of the coffin. Some of the mourners stared across at him as they passed by. Blank stares on pale faces. He thought them accusatory. A paper wrapper smeared with brown sauce lay in his lap. Crumbs were scattered across his trousers, and the floor well. The untouched cup of coffee stood where he had placed it. His shoulders felt tight, and there was a pain at the back of his neck. He restored his seat to its driving position and looked at his watch. His nap had lasted an hour and a half. He flipped down the vanity mirror and stared at himself. 'Tom, you look shit.' He told himself. He crumpled the wrapper, and shoved it in the ash tray. Then he emptied the coffee out of the window, tossed the carton into the passenger foot well, started the engine, and set off. As he turned onto the by pass he tuned into Jazz fm to help him concentrate. Frank Sinatra was singing Bye Bye Blackbird.

Thank God that Helen can't see me right now, he told himself. Some father I'm going to make.

Back at the station, he made the men's room his first port of call. Washed his face, and combed his hair. Half presentable, he stopped by the canteen and grabbed a coffee, then made his way up to the Incident Room. Holmes met him in the corridor. He had Detective Sergeant Joanne Stuart with him.

'Where have you been Boss?' Holmes said. 'We've been trying to get you for the past twenty minutes. They said you weren't up at Cutacre, and I didn't want to set off without you.'

Caton realised that he'd forgotten to switch his phone and pager, back on again. 'Sorry Gordon,' he said, knowing how lame it was going to sound. 'Just got back. I was sprucing myself up in the men's room.'

'Well if you want that coffee, you'll have to bring it with you,' said his DI. 'They've found number three.'

This one was almost a carbon copy of the second. She lay just fifteen metres away, two and a half feet below the surface, curled up in the same foetal position as the second victim. She was naked, and in a more or less identical state of preservation. There were strands of blonde hair on her head. She was significantly taller than either of the previous victims as far as Caton could tell; perhaps as much as five foot nine. He felt a sudden tightness at the base of his chest that had nothing to do with the sausage barm.

'It was a dog that found her,' said Franklin. 'It was one of the bore holes they'd made with a hollow tube. She took one sniff, and went straight into tell mode.'

'Reggie was it?' Asked Holmes.

'Reggie?' Said Franklin who had no idea what he was talking about.

'The dog.'

'I wouldn't know,' said Franklin. 'One of those over there I assume.' He pointed to open ground on the opposite bank of the valley. Three dogs were running free across the off-road race track as their handlers stood chatting.

The dog tired of chasing the others, and reverted to doing what she did best. Nose to the ground, she began to explore the myriad scents, first running zig zags, and then regular figure eights, extending her range until she found one that interested her. This led her towards the lane, where she lost it, and promptly picked up another that drew her into the patch of land that had belonged to the Presbyterian Chapel, and out of sight of her handler.

'That's Bella.' Said her handler. Her bark was unmistakeable. They turned and looked for her. The other two dogs had stopped as well. They stood stock still, heads up, staring in the same direction. 'Bloody hell, don't tell me she's found another.' He said.

'I'd be surprised if she hadn't,' said one of his colleagues. 'That's a bloody graveyard.'

He set off to fetch her back, their laughter ringing in his ears.

'I think you'd better come Sir.' the dog handlers' team leader told him. 'It may be a complete red herring, but it's got to be your call.'

Caton left Holmes and Stuart to wait for the medical examiner to arrive, and set off alone, across the temporary bridge and the open ground, towards the tiny graveyard.

The cemetery was larger than it had seemed when the site manager had pointed it out to him from the helicopter; a rectangle of newly mown grass some fifty metres long by twenty metres wide, partly hidden behind two lines of mature trees. A chain link fence, and a line of ancient headstones wreathed in brambles, plugged the only gap facing west towards Cutacre. Caton estimated there to be well over a hundred graves, many of them marked by headstones. A dozen or so of the most recent were in black or white marble. Small clumps of flowers – real and artificial – adorned a score or more of the graves. It struck him as both peaceful, and incongruous. Peaceful, but for the dog.

Bella was standing in the lee of the trees, on the southern boundary of the cemetery. Her handler commanded her to stop barking, but every once in a while her enthusiasm overcame her. Caton weaved his way between the headstones until he arrived at their side.

'This is it,' said the team leader.

A covering of leaves and twigs had been pushed back to reveal a rectangular patch of overgrown grass that became ragged, and weedy, where it disappeared into the hedge bottom.   It would have signified nothing to Caton had the words of Derek Franklin not been fresh in his head. There was a distinct hollowing of the turf that dipped in the centre.

'But it's a cemetery,' he said. 'We're surrounded by bodies. There must be other unmarked graves?'

'Dead right Sir,' said the team leader. 'But most of them, even if they don't have a cover or a headstone, at least have something marking the perimeter.'

'And the others like this Sir,' said the handler. 'Well they're ancient. All the recent burials are out there in the centre; with the marble headstones, and gold lettering. This one, it's fresh, and likely not in a coffin of any kind. Else Bella wouldn't have marked it like this.'

Caton knew he was right. 'A pauper's burial perhaps...or a suicide?' He knew he was clutching at straws. It was obvious from the way this graveyard was tended that the community would never have allowed one of their own to pass unrecognised. So obvious that nobody bothered to respond.

'A child aborted, and buried in secret?' the handler suggested, trying to be helpful. Not really believing it.

'Even if it was, it would still merit an investigation.' His colleague reminded him.

Caton knew they couldn't just start digging. Not here, in a proper cemetery. There'd be hell to pay if it turned out to be a legitimate burial. He could see the headline. *"Grave Robbers!   Illegal exhumation by Manchester Police.*

'I want this taped off, and guarded, until we've found out who owns this place, and what their records are like.' He said. He turned to the dog handler. 'And tell Bella well done.'

Let's hope she's got it wrong, was what he was really thinking as he walked out of the graveyard, and onto Wharton Lane. He looked across the open ground to the far bank of Bluebell Hollow. The pathologist had arrived to examine body number three. Holmes was leading him across the duck boards and along the common approach path. God, what a mess, he thought. At this rate they might just as well book me a room at the Dun Mare. He shook his head, took a deep breath, and switched on his mobile phone.

10

No one at Salford Council, or at Bolton Town Hall, appeared to be aware of the existence of the graveyard. In the end it was a local police constable who led them to the United Reform Church, less than a mile away, on the Heathfield Estate. The cemetery records were surprisingly comprehensive. There were four hundred and ninety three persons recorded, one hundred and thirty nine gravestones, and one hundred and one different surnames. Every grave had been marked on a plan of the graveyard. They had a copy with them. Caton checked it for the third time.

'So there is definitely no-one buried here?' He said.

The peripatetic minister deferred to the sexton; a local man who had been tending this cemetery most of his adult life.

'Almost certainly not in the past three hundred years; and definitely not in the past forty. In any case,' The sexton pointed out. 'As you can see from the plan, strictly speaking this place is outside the boundaries of our permitted burial ground.'

'So you would have no objection if we were to investigate?'

The minister looked suitably sombre. 'Providing,' he said. 'That if, God forbid, you do discover any poor unfortunate soul, the exhumation is conducted with the same reverence that would be accorded to any person laid to rest in our cemetery; that this Church is represented when you do it; and that you do everything in your power to respect the peace, and sanctity, of this place; including, keeping the press and media away. As you can see, this is an isolated spot some distance from the road, and the estate. It has always been respected by the bikers, and the walkers who come by here, and never subjected to vandalism. I would prefer that it stay that way.'

Caton's question had been a matter of courtesy. There was nothing that anyone could do to prevent him going ahead. Especially now that it turned out that the grave, if such it was, was outside the cemetery proper. But he had no problem in agreeing to what were perfectly reasonable requests. As for how the papers, and the TV, might handle it; that was way beyond his control. Come to that, he doubted there was a lot that God could do about it either.

It was ten o'clock in the evening. A pair of flood lamps cast long, distorted shadows against the sides and roof of the tent. In one corner stood a stack of neatly piled turf; beside it, a mound of sifted soil. Inch by inch they had proceeded; as carefully as though a precious ancient treasure had been concealed here. Just three feet found down the scrape of trowel on bone provided the confirmation Caton had feared. He called a halt.

Heads bowed, they listened respectfully as the Minister stepped forward.

'Heavenly Father,' he began. 'You give us life and hope in this world, and the certainty of resurrection in the next. Take pity on the soul of this, our departed sister, taken cruelly from this world, and denied the reverence of a Christian burial. Help those who now recover these mortal remains, and bear them to another place, to exercise the respect and compassion that she was denied in death. Comfort those who even now grieve for this our sister, when within the coming days our discovery draws to a tragic close their years of alternating hope and fear. Bring this, our sister, safe into your glorious presence. Grant that those here gathered, not deflected by the evil that men do, may continue to grow in faith, hope, and the certain knowledge of your redemption. We ask this, through the Father, the Son, and the Holy Spirit. Amen.'

In the silence that followed, they heard a dog bark in the yard of a farm beyond the rucks; the wind murmuring in the trees overhead; and drops of rain drumming a mournful refrain on the taut canvas roof of the tent.

As the body bag was carefully carried away, Caton reflected that he had witnessed, including those of the past few days, eight exhumations. Two from official graves when foul play had been belatedly suspected, and five others. This was the first where prayers had been said. It was, he decided, no bad thing to be reminded of the sanctity of human life, and for those in his team who believed in a life hereafter to have that respected for a moment before the unseemly scramble to pick over the bones, and hunt down the perpetrator. Had it been a relative of his, he would have wanted nothing less.

'Why down here?' said Holmes. 'Why not along with the others?'

It was good question. Although much more badly decomposed, this bore the essential hallmarks of the previous three. She had been buried naked, on her side, in a foetal position. In the harsh lights of the lamps, once they had brushed the dirt away, even he could tell that the horseshoe shaped hyoid bone had been fractured; snapped like a wishbone.

'You heard Mullen,' he replied. 'This victim was the most recent. The degree of decomposition is down to the much more normal nature of the soil here. If he's right, and she's only been there two years at the most, then the odds are that our perpetrator got a surprise. He'd have come down the lane, blithely expecting to bury her near the others, and discovered that the perimeter fences had been put up. What would you do? Turn round, and have to find somewhere else, or make the best of a bad job? In the event, he chose here.'

'Would have been a stroke of genius if he'd buried all of them here,' said Holmes. 'Chances are they'd never have been found.'

Caton had no doubt that he was right. His dread was that in the intervening years the perpetrator had found another place to dispose of his victims. An even safer location. A place he had been drawn to again, and again. Just as he had to Bluebell Hollow.

The phone was ringing as he entered their apartment in New Islington. He cancelled the alarm and banged his thigh on the sofa as he rushed to grab it before it stopped. It was Kate.

'At last! Are you trying to avoid me?' She said. She sounded more worried than annoyed.

'I'm sorry Kate. It's been manic here.' He said rubbing his leg. 'You've no idea.'

'So enlighten me.'

He told her about the investigation, and could tell by the tone of her voice that she had forgiven him his virtual absence over the past few days.

'God that's terrible,' she said. 'Sounds like I'd be better off over there with you than hearing about American serial killers. Have you contacted my boss yet?'

'Stewart-Baker? Not yet. But I will be doing, now that it's obvious that's what we've got. How about you, how's it going?'

'Mainly boring, occasionally enlightening. My session on Bojangles was well received, and I'm making some useful contacts, so I suppose it's been worth it.'

'I hope so, because I'm really missing you.'

'Not as much as I'm missing you. I can't wait to get back. I've still got loads of arrangements to make for the wedding remember.'

'Might you come back early...break it short?' He said.

'Are you missing me that much? Or are you hoping I'll be able to work with you on this case?'

'Christ no!' He said. 'We agreed that once was enough. I made you a promise and I'm going to stick to it.'

'Keep your shirt on,' she said. 'I believe you. And much as I'd love to hurry back, I've got to see it through. The University paid for me up front, and they won't get any of it back if I cut and run. But I'll see if I can get a flight on the Thursday instead of the

Saturday. It'll mean forgoing the closing celebrations, but I'd rather be with you any day.' She paused. 'You mean the world to me...you know that don't you?'

Physically and emotionally exhausted, he found himself close to tears.

'And you to me.' Was all he could manage.

'Look, you must be knackered,' she said. 'And this call is costing a fortune. Why don't I ring again tomorrow at the same time? Then you can concentrate on your investigation without worrying about when to call me.'

'That would be great,' he said. 'You don't know how much it means just to hear your voice.'

'It better had.'

There was another voice in the background, calling to her. A woman's voice.

'Look, I'd better go and let you get to bed.' She said. 'I love you.'

'I love you too.' He said, as the line went dead.

He replaced the phone, and sat down on the arm of the sofa. His leg still hurt but there was a bigger ache in his heart, and a deep sense of guilt. He still hadn't told her about Harry, and he knew there was no way he was going to be able to until she was back in England, and they were face to face. It was a long time to wait.

The alarm woke him at six. It was the best night's sleep he'd had since they relocated to Leigh. He remembered his GP telling him, back in the early days on the beat when he was still trying to come to terms with shift work, that research had shown that all sleep missed had to be made up sooner or later. Otherwise, she claimed, the immune system would suffer. It was one of the explanations for the poor longevity of the sleep deprived. It was not one of the reasons why Caton had applied to become a detective, but it had proved to be a welcome bonus; until he joined the Force Major Incident Team that was. Now he was beginning to wonder if he would have been better off back on shifts.

By the time he had finished his Weetabix the morning edition was sticking through the letterbox. He took it to the car with him, and tossed it on the front seat. The headline stared back at him; predictable, alliterative, memorable. *'The Salford Strangler Strikes Again!'* Hymer at his best.

The incident room was buzzing.

'The press is having a field day,' said DC Wood. '*Salford Strangler*...why not Bolton? That's where the first woman came from.'

'Because *she* wasn't strangled, and because there's no alliteration with Bolton.' DS Stuart suggested.

'And because Salford is a city...' someone at the back called out. '...the more people they can frighten, the more papers they sell.'

'That's just being cynical.' Joanne Stuart countered.

'But I'm right. Another couple of miles they'd be calling it the Manchester Mauler.'

'I get it,' said Wood. 'If it was a flasher in Wigan, it'd be the Wigan W...'

'That's enough,' Caton told them. 'Forget the media, stick with reality. I want you to concentrate on what Detective Inspector Holmes has to tell us.' Out of the corner of his eye he spotted DCS Radford slipping into the room as Gordon Holmes stepped up to the plate.

'Victim number three...' Holmes began, pointing on the white board to the second of the deposition sites in Bluebell Hollow. '...was in her late thirties or early forties. Her natural hair colour was red, but had been dyed blond several times. The probable cause of death was manual strangulation, just like victim number two. But there is additional damage to bones in the neck that suggests greater force was used than in the two other victims. We are waiting on toxicology reports, but the post mortem found damage to the cartilage of the bone consistent with drug misuse.'

'Snorting Charlie.' Observed DC Wood, as though none of them could put it together without the benefit of his encyclopaedic knowledge.

'If either of the others had been using cocaine, or any drug,' Holmes continued. 'There's a chance forensics will be able to tell us from the samples of their hair. If that is the case, it may provide us with a connection between them.'

'Clutching at straws,' Caton heard DC Wood whisper. For once, he was inclined to agree.

'The Chief Constable wants to know what the hell's going on Tom,' Radford said. 'Come to that I wouldn't mind knowing myself.'

Caton closed the door to his office, and ushered Radford to the leather seat that he knew would put him at a disadvantage; lower down than his own chair, and squeaky. Christ, he thought, what the hell am I doing playing games at a time like this?

'As far as I can tell,' he replied. 'We have two cases here. Della Farnworth's is open and shut. Her husband did it. The other three share the same MO; one that is very different from Della Farnworth.'

'What's to say Farnworth didn't get the taste for it, and go on to develop his own unique style?'

'You don't believe that.'

Radford sighed. 'Of course I don't, but it would have been a hell of a lot easier if he had. So what you are saying is we have a serial killer with at least three victims we know about, and God knows how many more?'

Caton decided it was a rhetorical question.

Radford ran his hand through the widow's peak of his crew cut ash grey hair. Caton felt sorry for him. Less than two years to retirement, and now this. Twenty years ago he might have welcomed it as a challenge; a chance to make a name for himself. Now it was a serious irritation that could easily turn into the biggest disaster of his career. He had only been at Leigh for the past twelve months. Before that he was in Bolton. Technically, these victims had been dumped on his patch, on his watch. As had his new Senior Investigating Officer.

'How long before you have the identity of these women?' He asked.

'Assuming they've all got a Missing Persons file, I'd expect to know within seventy two hours. If not, a dental record match should hopefully turn up by the end of next week.'

'What are you going to do in the meantime?'

Caton had thought of nothing else since he'd got out of bed. 'Apart from keeping the squeeze on forensics, Missing Persons, and the search teams...' he said, determined to show that he was on top of it. '...I think it's time to bring in a Home Office profiler.'

The leather seat squealed in protest as Radford began to squirm. His neck flushed in embarrassment. Caton felt instant remorse that in such a petty manner he had set up for humiliation this man he hardly knew. There was bugger all he could do about it now. Radford's prostate was the least of his problems. The costs of the investigation were spiralling out of control, and here was Caton proposing to pile on even more. Radford heaved himself out of his chair; brushing aside Caton's helping hand.

'If you don't, I've no doubt that the National Policing Improvement Agency will recommend it.' He said.

'We don't have to involve the NPIA,' Caton retorted. 'Not at this stage surely?'

Radford smiled thinly, perceiving a tiny victory. 'Come on Tom, you know the score. Something like this, you don't have any option. You're going to have to contact the Serious Crime Intelligence Section so they can run the MO through their database. See if this bastard's already in the system. In any case, you've already involved them through the Missing Person's Bureau. Don't tell me it didn't occur to you they'd put two and two together, and come up with four?'

Of course he had. But he was hoping to keep them at bay a little longer. Call it professional pride. The last thing he needed was some Crime Support Intelligence Officer, with the rank of Detective Sergeant, giving him the benefit of his privileged position in the national team. Greater Manchester Police had an enviable record in recent times for clearing up murders. There was more than enough expertise in the Force Major Incident Team without having to bring in outsiders. That's what he told himself. But in reality he knew the clock was ticking.

'You're right,' he conceded. 'But in the meantime are you going to give me the go ahead to talk with a profiler?'

Radford headed for the door. He turned wearily, and stared directly into Caton's eyes.

'Go on then,' he said. 'On one condition. You also contact the NPIA, and ask them for a geographical profiler. I'm not having any bright bugger, wise after the event, accusing me of letting you go it alone; of failing to network.'

He had a fair point, Caton conceded. Failing to network was just about the biggest sin you could commit in the modern police force. That...and failing to nail the bastard.

11

'It's not a lot is it?'

Professor Stewart-Baker cleared a space on the desk beside his computer, and pulled up a chair for Caton. He seemed both younger, and older, than Caton had imagined. Older in looks, younger in his sprightly movement, and mannerisms. His hair was a mass of wiry black curls tinged with grey. His high forehead, and broad temples, were etched with creases, yet they gave anything but the impression of worry lines. Those at the corners of his clear blue eyes, and mouth, owed more Caton surmised to smiles than stress. The patterned cardigan he wore over an open necked shirt, once evocative of fusty academics, was right on trend in this year's high street. He was not what Caton had expected at all. The profiler sat down, intertwined the fingers of both hands behind his head, and leaned back, arms akimbo.

'Three naked female bodies, found buried in close proximity.'

Caton thought that more than enough for starters. It must have shown in his expression because Stewart-Baker was quick to clarify.

'Don't misunderstand me,' he said. 'I meant that it is not a great deal from which to build a profile. The more information I have to work with the better. For example, if you had the identities of the victims, and could tell me something about each of them: where they lived, worked; their relationships; life styles; when they went missing, it goes without saying I could be a lot more help. As it is, what I can give you is going to be limited to things I suspect you already know from your own profiling software about deposition sites, and patterns, geographical proximity to the murderer's place of residence, and so forth.'

'There is the psychological dimension.' Caton pointed out.

Stewart-Baker nodded sagely. 'Of course there is. Even in what little you have thus far. There's not much I could usefully say about the perpetrator's antecedent behaviour, although I suppose I could hypothesise potential fantasies and triggers for these murders, but I certainly don't propose to. Equally, since there is no evidence that he has responded in any way to your discovery of these bodies there is nothing to say about his post offending behaviour. As to the typology of his victims, and his chosen method and place of disposal, well it's a place to start.'

He unclasped his hands and folded them in front of him. His brow creased, and Caton realised that far from worry it was the regular process of practised thought that was the culprit.

'Take the strangulation,' he continued, staring disconcertingly at the ceiling; as though seeing there the page of a book he wished to consult. 'This repetitive act, presumably because he derives from it a particular satisfaction, probably sexual, is in itself is a kind of signature. As is the stripping of these bodies, and the placing of them in an identical, almost foetal pose.' He swiveled in his chair, and examined the photographs Caton had brought with him. 'Very interesting that...' he said as much to himself as to his visitor, '...so many possible connotations. Remorse, remembrance, resurrection, return to the womb. Very interesting. He swiveled back to face Caton. 'As is the deposition site. By a slag heap.' He raised his eyebrows. 'Isn't that one of the terms used in common parlance? Interesting don't you think? A slag heap... or, in his own twisted fantasy, has he perhaps turned it into a heap for slags?'

It hit Caton like a punch in the solar plexus. He had no idea why he hadn't thought of it before? Or any of the rest of his team for that matter? They were too close to the trees to see the wood. Which was precisely why he needed someone like Stewart-Baker; someone with enough detachment, and time, to think outside the box?

'You keep saying *he*,' said Caton.

The academic placed his hands behind his head again, crossed his legs at the ankle, and regarded him with faint amusement.

'How long have you been a detective Chief Inspector?'

Caton understood how his students must feel. 'Seven.' He replied.

'And how long with the Major Incident Team?'

'Five.'

'So you tell me. Why do you think I used the male pronoun?'

'Because it has the hallmarks of a male predator. All of the victims were female, in their twenties or thirties, and naked when buried.'

Stewart-Baker's gaze never wavered. 'And?' He prompted.

'And, as far as we can tell, they were all strangled. Two of them manually. The third, either that or garroted. That takes a lot of strength to overcome the victim. The victim almost always has time to struggle...to fight back. To claw at the hands and face.'

Stewart-Baker pursed his lips. 'It could have been a big butch female? That would have come as more of a surprise?'

'Then there's the strength required to get them into and out of a vehicle,' Caton countered. 'Drag or carry them across the stream, and dig a grave up to three feet deep.'

'*Very* big, *very* butch?'

Caton thought he detected the hint of a twinkle in his eyes. 'I don't think so.' He said.

'Then there's the foetal position,' the profiler pointed out. 'Take a feminine streak to think of that.'

The penny suddenly dropped for Caton. This was not merely an academic game. It was a tease. He was being drawn along a path of Stewart-Baker's choosing.

'You think there may be two of them? A man, and a woman, acting together?' He said.

Stewart-Baker shrugged. 'It's possible,' he said. 'There are precedents. Granted, almost all of them involve child victims...but it is possible.'

'Possible, but unlikely?'

'Possible. That's what I deal in you see. Possibilities. Probabilities where I can...but that isn't often.' He uncrossed his feet, and sat up. Game over. 'You, however, are required to deal in certainties. Beyond reasonable doubt, isn't that phrase? So what certainties do you have Chief Inspector?'

There was little else for Caton to share apart from the results of the ongoing forensic search around each of the deposition sites. The immediate vicinity of the graves in Bluebell Hollow had been muddied, in both senses of the word, by the activity, and presence, of the open cast workers; the approaches to all three sites by the scores of off-roaders and walkers who had crossed and re-crossed the open ground; the grave at the edge of cemetery by those who tended the graves, and occasional mourners; and the windborne detritus from the council refuse site continued to produce a mountain of complicating artefacts. In reality, their best bet was the graves themselves. Every inch of soil hade been sifted, sorted, and was being analysed. So far, small fragments of identical heavy duty polythene had been recovered from sites two and three. The assumption was that they had belonged to whatever the bodies had been wrapped, and transported, in. Presumably they had been ripped on pieces of stone as the bodies were rolled into the graves, or the sheeting pulled out from under them where they lay. Soil, pollen and seed had been sent for analysis in the hope of finding elements foreign to the site itself. Apart from the polythene, and the bodies, there was nothing that they could say with certainty had been left by the perpetrator at the crime scene. They were still searching.

'Well, I'll make a start, but please don't expect too much,' the profiler told him. 'When you know who these victims are, and a little more about the circumstances of their disappearance, I should be able to take it a little further. And then, perhaps, the three of us could meet; you, me, and your geographical profiler?' He stood up and crossed to the door. 'I know this isn't the first time that you have personally consulted a profiler Chief Inspector,' he said. 'But let me remind you. What we try to do is based on research, but that doesn't mean that it's gospel. Far from it. Educated guesswork at best. Don't, whatever you do, give it too much credence, and whatever else you do don't come to rely on it. That's all very well for these television series, but in real life it's going to make you sloppy, careless, and myopic. Trust your evidence first, your own instinct second, and my ramblings not at all.' He held out his hand. 'And for the record, let's drop the Sir shall we? My name is Lawrence.'

The first breakthrough came that afternoon. A dental practice in Rochdale had provided a match for victim number two; the first of those discovered at the foot of the rucks. One of the three whom Holmes, in order to distinguish them from Della Farnworth, had christened the Bluebell Girls.

The file from the Missing Person's Bureau was already up on Caton's computer screen. Her name was Shelley Hassell. Born and raised on the outskirts of Rochdale, the daughter of a plumber and a shop assistant, she had been reported missing by her parents on the twenty third of February 2005. She had been three months short of her twenty-eighth birthday.

'She was a real stunner.' Holmes observed.

Caton studied the image on the screen. A head and shoulders shot. It was hard to disagree. Long, straight, blonde hair surrounding a perfectly oval face. Brown eyes, pert lips, a confident smile. Pretty he thought, rather than beautiful. Her tan looked artificial, and she wore a little too much make up for his taste. He thought he detected fragility in her expression. A sense of hesitation, disappointment perhaps, in her eyes. She was trying too hard to project herself for the photographer. And she knew it.

'You can see why they employed her on the perfume counters,' Holmes continued. 'She could have sold me anything.'

Caton didn't doubt it. He read on. She had lived at home until five months before she disappeared. Had then moved into a rented apartment in North Manchester. Her parents had become worried when several days had gone by without contact, got no reply to their phone calls, and let themselves in with a spare key. There was no sign of her. Not then, not since. Until now. Her fellow employees, workmates, and a surprisingly long list of friends and acquaintances, had been interviewed exhaustively. Appeals had gone out on local TV, and radio stations. All to no avail.

'Bloody Hell! Have you seen who we've got here?' Gordon Holmes exclaimed pointing to a name on the screen. 'Only Marcello Barceló!'

Caton didn't need to be told who this was. First choice centre forward for one the leading premiership teams in Europe. Right here in Manchester. His was a household name throughout Europe. Throughout the world come to that.

'What the hell was he doing knocking round with a lass from Rochdale?' Exclaimed Holmes. He saw the expression on Caton's face, and grinned inanely. 'Stupid question.' He said.

Caton leant back in his chair. 'You realise we are going to have to go back over all of these statements?' he said. 'See them all again.'

'Bags I Barceló.' Said Holmes.

'We'll see.' said Caton. Although he'd already made up his mind. There was no way he was going to let Gordon, or any of the other testosterone fuelled, soccer fixated, members of the team loose on a player of Barcelo's status, and reputation. For a start their objectivity would be all to pot. He could just see them ending the interview with a request for autographs, and some inside stories to tell in the canteen, or down the pub. No, he had his own plans for Mr. Barceló. He stood up.

'I need you to prioritise these witness statements Gordon,' he said. 'And pencil names in against follow up interviews. I'm going to break the news to her parents. I'll take DS Stuart with me. I need to see how she works at the sharp end of things.'

He also needed someone who could see through the outward signs of grief, and read what was really going on inside people's heads. Joanne Stuart was good at that.

Fred Hassell sat at the dining table, head in hands. His wife Marge stood behind him, her hands on his shoulder; consoling him. She had proved to be the stronger of the two; on the outside at least. Caton sensed that she had always suspected that her daughter was dead. Shelley had been close to her parents, and had never really fallen out with them. Her meagre bank account had never been raided, or her passport touched. Her father had clung to hope like a drowning man to a piece of flotsam. He needed to believe that she was still alive. His wife had come to dread it. Fearing that if she was, she must have fallen into the wrong hands. Hands that would use her, and abuse her. A fate worse than death. And so she had resigned herself. Almost.

Caton wondered if it was sometimes easier to be a pessimist.

'The second time the officers came to see you,' said Joanne Stuart. 'You mentioned something about a clinic. Could you tell us a little more about that?'

Fred Hassell began to sob quietly. His wife kneaded his shoulders gently. Her voice was calm, detached, and almost expressionless.

'The Oasis Clinic,' she said. 'We paid for Shelley to go there. She had a problem controlling her drinking you see. It started out as binge drinking at weekends...with her friends, and then it suddenly accelerated until she was drinking every day.'

'You said controlling her drinking,' said Joanne Stuart. 'So she hadn't actually become an alcoholic?'

It was a good point, cleverly put, Caton noted. Clarifying the position without assuming anything.

'It's an important distinction I know,' Marge Hassell replied. 'According to the doctors, no, she was not an alcoholic, but she did reach a point where she needed hospitalisation.'

'For detox, or because she had deliberately drunk a life threatening amount?' Asked Caton.

The mother's head turned. She appeared to see him for the first time. Her eyes widened, her hands stilled, and her voice became animated, tremulous.

'Shelley did *not* attempt to take her own life...never had, and never would. Her drinking was a cry for help. That was why we paid for her treatment. Because she needed our help.' She stopped for a moment to recover her composure. 'So yes, it was for detox; followed by an inpatient programme of support, and a further three months of outpatient sessions.'

'When was this?' Caton asked, wondering why it hadn't registered when he'd read the file before setting out.

'Six months to the day before we discovered that she was missing.'

'And was the treatment successful Mrs. Hassell?' DS Stuart asked.

'If you mean did it stop her drinking so much? Yes it did. She still had the odd drink, but she stopped going out at weekends, preferring to come over and see us. She would have a glass of wine with dinner. But that was about all. Her friends and colleagues corroborated all of this at the time. And when we went to her flat there was just an unopened bottle of wine in the fridge.'

DS Stuart looked down at her notes. 'You told the police that Shelley had seemed happy, relaxed, untroubled, the last time that you saw her.'

'That's because she was. She was almost euphoric. That's why Fred and I couldn't understand why she went missing.'

Caton and his DS looked at each other. They had exhausted the questions they came to ask, and a few others beside.

'In that case, we'll take our leave of you.' Caton told her, aware that he missed saying, *leave you in peace*, by a whisker. 'DS Hamer, the Family Liaison Officer, will make sure you're not disturbed. If you think of anything else we ought to know, or that you need to know, please tell her.

'There is just one thing,' she said. 'When will be able to lay her to rest?'

'I'm afraid I can't tell you that right now, but I hope to able to very soon.' Caton told her.

'If you don't mind, you'll have to show yourselves out.' She said, stretching out her arm to soothe the tremors from her sobbing husband's shoulders.

12

'What do you think Detective Sergeant?' he asked as they drove the fourteen miles back to the station.

'I think the mother's telling the truth,' she said. 'Difficult to tell with the father, because he didn't say anything at all. His grief seems genuine enough. Whether there's guilt tied up with it too, that's anybody's guess.'

Caton saw the black BMW SUV, headlights flashing, bearing down on him at an outrageous speed. Although tempted to stay where he was he knew that the idiot might well decide to undertake, and increase the risk to the blissfully ignorant pensioner on his left who had been in two minds about which lane to use for the past two hundred metres. Instead, he pulled across into the third lane, and watched it as it sped into Death Valley.

'Where are the police when you need them?' Joanne Stuart asked wryly.

'He'll get his comeuppance sooner or later...' said Caton. '...if he doesn't take some poor bastard with him first.'

She adjusted her seatbelt where it crossed her chest, and angled her body towards him. 'So what do you think Boss?' she said. 'About the father?'

'I think if there was anything there that might have

prompted her disappearance, his wife would have left him by now.'

'If she knew about it.'

'True. There is one way we might find out though.'

'The clinic?'

She was every bit as bright as he'd guessed; and the rest. 'If her drinking was symptomatic of sexual abuse,' he said. 'There's every chance they would have found out about it. Hitting rock bottom. Then baring the soul. Isn't that what it's all about?'

She grinned impishly. 'I wouldn't know Boss. How about you?'

'Cheeky,' he said, grinning back. 'And no, I wouldn't either. But if this case gets any worse I might just take to drink.' He stopped talking to concentrate on the busy motorway as he signalled left to come off at the Worsley interchange, and make his way up onto the A580. As they passed the Marriot Golf and Country Club he picked up the thread again. 'What impression did you get as to why she let her drinking get out of control?'

Joanne Stuart took her time with that one. 'Well, obviously,' she said. 'A fair few of her friends were lashing it at weekends, but if you ask me, it was a bit of a coincidence it happening at the same time that Marcello Barcelo gave her the big heave ho.'

'That's what I thought,' said Caton. 'And he didn't have a lot to say to the officer who interviewed him first time around did he?'

DS Stuart shook her head in disgust 'Looking at that statement, I'd say someone gave him a pretty easy ride.'

My thoughts entirely Caton decided. Let's see if we can do any better.

Barcelo was more or less everything Caton had expected. Physically fit, although shorter and slimmer than he appeared to be on the pitch and television screen. Handsome, in a sleazy sort of way. Confident to the point of arrogance. Immaculately dressed in a blue Emporio Armani jacket, and open necked white linen shirt, over stone washed Armani jeans, and Marco Tozzi trainers. Not that Caton would have recognised any of them had the footballer not made a point of identifying them.

'And these,' he said, holding up his wrap-around sunglasses that could only have been for anonymity on this overcast October day. 'Are Police, Street Fashion? Funny No? Never see you police wearing them. But then I don't suppose they pay you enough.' He laughed at his own joke. No one else was going to. Not even his agent, or the solicitor provided by the club. The footballer laid the glasses on the table. It saved Caton having to ask. It was always essential to see their eyes. Even if his did keep sliding away to wander unashamedly over Joanne Stuart's body.

'We are clear that my client is here voluntarily?' the solicitor said. 'Though since he has already given the police an exhaustive account of his extremely short relationship with this woman I have to say that I do not really see the point of all this.'

The point is,' Caton said. 'That we now know that Shelley Hassell was murdered.'

'I hope your not suggesting...'

Barcelo put a hand on his arm, cutting him off mid sentence.

'S'alright,' he said. 'Course the man's not saying that I had anything to do with this. For me, it's important to do my bit. Don't want people saying I had something to hide do we?'

'Very public spirited of you Mr Barcelo,' Caton managed without a hint of sarcasm. 'So can you tell us how the two of you first met?'

'At a party.'

'At a party where?'

'In a club in Manchester.'

'What kind of party?'

He raised his eyebrows. 'What you think? An exclusive party. Invitation only.'

'So how did Shelley come to be invited?'

'Same way most of the others got to be.'

'Which was?'

The footballer smiled, as though it was a private joke. 'Talent scouts.'

'I don't follow you,' said Caton.

'Couple of the backroom guys at the club, they know what we like. We got a party coming up; they tour the places and book the talent.'

'Places?'

'Where the talent is. Perfume and make-up counter staff, boutiques, fashion floors. You know. Like Harvey Nicks. Places stacked with Bolly Dollies,' he gave a condescending smile. 'But I guess you don't. Not a lot of time to get out and about in your line of work.'

He was beginning to get under Caton's skin. 'So these talents scouts, he said. 'Are really pimps?'

The agent bristled. The solicitor protested vigorously. 'That's uncalled for Chief Inspector,' he said. 'If you are going to continue like this I must advise my client …' Barcelo brushed it aside.

'If you like. Big difference though. They don't get paid. And the girls don't get paid.'

'Just laid.' Muttered Joanne Stuart.

Barcelo grinned. 'It's up to them. Nobody forces them.'

'In your case, Shirley Hassell was more than a one night stand.' Observed Caton.

The footballer shrugged. 'She was brighter than some. Knew how to respect my moods. I get moods.' He said it in the way that most people would say they got colds. 'Some women, they can't take it. Shelley, she knew when to back off, when to…how you say… humour me?'

'But for all that she only lasted…'Caton consulted his notes. '…three months?'

Barcelo shrugged again. 'What you got to remember, football is a short term thing. Here today, gone tomorrow. All it takes…one bad tackle, and boom! It's over. OK, so right now my world is…how you say? An oyster. Well there's plenty of pearls out there. You can't blame a man for grabbing a few.'

The Spaniard was staring at Joanne Stuart again; undressing her with his eyes, smirking at her obvious discomfort. Yes, I can blame you, Caton was thinking.

'So, Shelley Hassell,' he said. 'Why did the two of you finish?

Barcelo fixed him with his jet black eyes. Daring him to take offence.

'Because she was a slag'' he said.

It took Caton by surprise. Not just the callousness, but also because of the connection Stewart-Baker had made. For a moment it threw him. DS Stuart sensed the hiatus, and jumped in.

125

'Can you explain what you mean by that?' She said.

His gaze was lizard like. 'Maybe it's my English,' he said. 'Maybe you prefer slut, or scrubber? No? Don't' you call women who are promiscuous these names?'

'Are those the only kind of women who are attracted to you?' She responded.

'Don't think because I'm a footballer I'm not intelligent,' he countered. 'I read. I like to learn. Do you know what they say about promiscuous women? Do you?' He leaned forward across the table until their faces were almost touching. 'It is a genetic instinct to seek out men with superior genes with whom to have their babies. Men like me.' She felt betrayed by the flush that spread upwards from her chest, and across her neck. She knew that he was interpreting her anger for something else. She felt Caton's hand on her arm. She eased herself back into her chair, holding Barcelo's gaze, hoping that he saw her contempt.

'Truthfully, I became bored with her,' said the footballer, sitting back. 'There are so many women out there. It's hard when you're famous. You have no idea.' He spread his hands wide, appealing for their sympathy.

'How did she take it?' Caton asked.

'It was embarrassing. She started to drink; more than usual. Started turning up in the places we used to go.'

'What did you do about that?'

'I told the door staff not to let her in. Persuaded one of my friends to start dating her. To keep her away from me.'

DS Stuart slid the file across the desk towards Caton, and indicated a name.   He nodded. Remembering the witness statement.

'And did that work?' He asked.

'Oh yes,' said Barcelo. 'Then he introduced to her to couple of his friends. They *really* took her mind off me.'

And ended up forcing her into a clinic Caton reflected. 'A couple of friends?'

Barcelo folded his hands behind his head, and leant back in his chair. 'Like I said. She was a slag.'

So what does that make you?' asked DS Stuart with barely controlled venom.

His face registered a flicker of surprise, before recovering its customary sneer.   He shrugged his shoulders.

'Unlucky, I guess.'

'He's a slimy, filthy, arrogant, bastard!' Said DS Stuart.

'Hell of a footballer though.' Said Gordon Holmes as he followed her into Caton's office.

She rounded on him, forgetting their difference in rank.   The full force of the pent up emotion she had been forced to curb throughout the interview finding an outlet.

'And I suppose that makes it alright does it? As long he scores on the pitch he can score as much as he likes off it; regardless of their age, or fragility? Grab them, shag them, slag them off! A man's got to do what a man's got to do? Is that it? Well stop the world, I want to get off!'

'Whoa,' said Holmes, swiftly backing off. 'He must really have got to you in there Joanne. Come on I didn't mean it like that.'

'But that's how it is, isn't it?' she persisted. 'You or me, we get done for GBH, drugs, sexual assault, we come out of prison, we're out of a job. Social outcasts. Men like him? It's come back, all is forgiven. Why? Because he can kick a bloody ball around the park on a Saturday afternoon.'

'That's enough.' Said Caton. 'Back off, both of you. Get yourselves out of here, get a drink, and come back when you've cooled down. And while you're at it, mine's a coffee.'

As the door closed behind them he sank into his seat, and stared at the notes he had made. He still wasn't sure about Marcello Barcelo. Apart from his use of the phrase slag there was nothing to suggest he might have had anything to do with her death. One thing he did know. Professional football was not what it used to be. He searched for the phrase they used about the Americans during World War Two. Overpaid, over-sexed, and over here. Only now it was footballers. He found himself hoping that his son Harry had two left feet.

There was a string of urgent messages on his desk, not counting all the emails in his in-box. Radford wanted an update. Hymer had rung three times wanting an off the record conversation. Caton was about to check if there was anything from Helen among his emails when his internal phone rang. It was the Office Manager.

'You've got a call from the Head of Forensics Services Branch, at Bradford Park,' she said. 'They say it's urgent.'

'I can't thank you enough,' he said. 'How did you manage it so quickly?'

He could almost see the wry smile on the face of newly appointed Head of Branch. 'It isn't often a request is immediately followed by a phone call from the Assistant Chief Constable asking for it to be given the highest priority.' She said.

Good for Lillian Lucas, Caton reflected. Jimmy Radford too, assuming he was the one who asked her to do it.

'Even so,' he said. 'Three days. You couldn't have done it much faster.'

'Oh we can,' she replied. 'But don't tell anybody, it'll only hike up the pressure, and we've more than enough of that already. In both these cases a DNA profile had been taken from hairs recovered from the women's hairbrushes shortly after they were reported missing. Given they were already in the system, it was relatively straight forward. Now I suppose you'd like their names? Or do you want to wait until I email them across?'

13

In Caton's experience, there were always things that got left out in the process of creating an official record. Hunches, feelings, evidence weighed, and found wanting. Mary Shepherd had helped to put these files together; she more than anyone else would be able to help him put flesh on the bones. He watched as she spread her papers out on the table top, and made herself comfortable. She looked different from the first time he had seen her, less than a week ago. Perhaps it was the black suit, or the way her hair had been cut shorter, more severe. More probably it was because what had begun with the body of one missing person was now turning into a landslide.

'What can you tell me about them?' he said, sitting down beside her.

She placed her index finger on a photograph, and slid it in front of him. 'This is your victim number two,' she said. 'The one you discovered shortly after Della Farnworth.'

It looked like something from a professional portfolio. A little too good to be true. Maybe even digitally enhanced. Striking for all that. Her head was angled away from her shoulders. It was a strong rectangular face; high cheekbones, green cat like eyes, blonde hair. More confident, far more mature, than

Shelley Hassell, and vaguely familiar. There was a second photograph, full length, modelling an outfit. She was tall, close to six foot according to the post mortem, with a perfect frame to hang clothes on.

'Charlotte Mortimer,' she said. 'Charley, to her friends and family. Thirty two years of age when she went missing. That was sometime between the sixth and eighth of November 2006. Born in Sheffield, mother a shop assistant, father a bookmaker. An only child. She left school at eighteen with 'A' Levels in Art, History, and Drama. Would have gone on to University, but was approached by a top model agency. The work piled in; from catalogues to cat walk. At twenty five she moved to Manchester, to tap the work opportunities in the city, and because proximity to Manchester Airport made her accessible to photo shoots in London, Europe, New York, the Caribbean...wherever. She wasn't quite up there with the likes of Raquel Zimmerman, and Isabeli Fontana.' She noted the look of bemusement on Caton's face. 'Take my word for it, they are where it's at right now,' she said. 'Even so, she was still doing very nicely. Stunning two bed city centre apartment in Regent House, on Whitworth Street. Alfa Romeo Spider in the basement car park. All the trappings.'

Caton remembered now. There had been a lot of publicity when she disappeared. This photo, or one very like it, had been circulated for months, and pinned up in every police station. He was disappointed not to have recognised it; or her name for that matter. 'She was still single wasn't she?' He said.

'Very much so. She had a string of boy friends. None of them partners as such. Too much choice, and too much fun to let any of them tie her down I suppose. There was an Arab from Bahrain who promised her paradise on Earth. She was tempted by all accounts, but he suddenly did a runner.'

'Do you know why?' asked Caton.

She shook her head. 'Not for certain. There was some talk of cocaine, but it could just as easily have been her reputation for changing sexual partners at a rate of knots. If anybody knew, they were not going to tell us; especially not him.'

'Were any of the boy friends suspect at the time?'

'No. As far as we knew we'd got to interview every one of them, but to be honest none of them had what you'd call a real relationship with her. No obsessives among them either.' She looked up at him. 'She used them, they used her; what I'd call a classic definition of casual sex. But in her case it was given a veneer of respectability because of the celebrity world she moved in.'

'What about friends?'

'She had quite a small network really,' Shepherd passed him a list of annotated names. 'Mainly colleagues. She lost touch with her mates on the other side of the Pennines. Except for one.' She consulted her list again. 'Harriet Walker. Went through school together. Best Mates. Charlotte was a bridesmaid at her wedding the year before she dropped off the map.'

He scanned the list seeing nothing that jumped out at him. 'Did any of them report a change in her behaviour before she disappeared?'

'Not one of them. She'd had a couple of longer jobs away in the preceding six months. And she asked her agents to cancel a couple of bookings, and took herself off for six weeks in early summer. Nobody seemed to know where. When she started back at work she was fine by all accounts.'

'Did she have a website, social network, anything like that?'

She passed him another piece of paper. 'That's the website of her model agency. You'll still find a page for her, and links on there. Nothing of her own though. No blog, no Facebook entry. It wasn't her scene apparently.'

'She had money in the bank?'

'Lot's of it. Bonds and shares too. And a couple of villas she bought as an investment, and somewhere to go for a break where nobody would recognise her.'

'Where exactly?'

'Calabria, and a Greek Island.' She checked the file. 'Paros.'

'That's not where she went that summer?'

'No. Definitely not. Interpol checked that out for us when she was reported missing.'

Caton scratched his head. He could see no connection between Charlotte Mortimer and Shirley Hassell; unless it lay hidden somewhere in the list of casual boy friends. 'What conclusion did you draw at the time?' he asked.

Mary Shepherd pushed the file away, and let out a little sigh. 'That she'd come to harm. That someone had abducted, and killed her. Sadly, it seems I was right.'

'How many more are there on your database where you came to the same conclusion?' Caton asked.

'You don't want to know,' she said wearily. 'Believe me, you really don't.' She collected the papers together, and put them back in order into the file. Then she opened the second file, and handed him another 'Speaking of which, this is victim number three.'

At first sight, Verity Parker-Smythe was very different from the other two. She had a square face, blue eyes, and red hair. Older than the others.

'Thirty eight,' Mary Shepherd said without waiting to be asked. 'Her hair is dyed. She's a natural blond.'

'How would you describe that haircut?' Caton asked.

'A pixie bob,' she said without a moment's hesitation. 'It doesn't suit her does it?'

'No,' he said. 'It doesn't. It's too severe. But there's something hypnotic about that combination; blue eyes and red hair.' He felt uncomfortable commenting on this dead woman as though she were still alive. He always did. But having a sense of how the killer might have seen her was a prerequisite for getting inside the murderer's mind.

'She was born Verity Parker, in Stockport, on the eighth of March 1970,' Shepherd informed him. 'Father a math's teacher, mother a school librarian. Had an older brother. He drowned in a quarry aged eleven. She was nine at the time. Him, and two mates, messing around in the summer holidays. Now her parents have to live with this.'

'Parker–Smythe. She was married?' asked Caton.

'September nineteen eighty six. To Peter Smythe, a barrister. He was forty, she was twenty six. He helped set her up as an estate agent on Deansgate.'

Caton looked up. '*The* Peter Smythe...with chambers in Spinningfields?'

'The very one.'

'But isn't he...?'

She nodded, finishing it for him. 'Gay. Or presumably bi-sexual, given the fact that they were married for six years.'

Caton stared at her photograph again. 'I wonder if she knew when she married him?'

'Not according to her blog. It was also one of the reasons that she managed to keep the business after the divorce. Moved out of the house, and bought a very nice apartment right in the middle of Alderley Edge.'

'She kept his name though.' He thought it odd under the circumstances.

'Well, it was also the name of the Agency. *Parker-Smythe Properties*. Very successful it was too, given that she was in at the heart of the property boom. They had been divorced for six years when she went missing. And, whatever the nature of their relationship, she certainly made up for lost time.'

'How do you mean?'

'It was like she'd been let off a lead. Partner after partner. She threw wild parties. Had a reputation for enjoying threesomes. There were even stories that she'd seduce men she was showing around some of the properties. Sale or no sale. Obviously it wasn't going to last.'

'What happened?'

'She ended up having some kind of breakdown, and guess what?'

Caton knew exactly where this was going. He felt a surge of excitement. 'She booked into the same clinic as our first victim, Shelley? She booked into The Oasis?'

Mary Shepherd smiled. 'I thought you'd be interested. She left there three months before she disappeared. And what's more, she started a Blog about it.'

'A blog?'

'Under an assumed name; *Truly...a VIP.*'

'Truly as in Verity...VIP as in Verity Parker,' he said. 'She wasn't that bothered about staying anonymous then?'

'According to her best friend, she was hoping to get an online book deal out of it. Not that she needed the money.'

'Was it really that interesting?' he asked.

'Among other things, she recounts her harrowing slide into sex addiction, and her desperate crawl out of it.'

'I don't suppose her ex-husband would have been too happy about that.' Caton was thinking out loud.

'Probably not, but she was savvy enough to fictionalise the whole thing,' said Shepherd. 'I printed it all out at the time. It's in the file. You can see for yourself.'

'What happened to her business...her money?'

'Her parents managed to persuade a judge to let them set up a Trust for her. They sold the business, and put everything into the Trust. Fair's fair, you've got to hand it to him; Peter Smythe advised them on how to go about it. There was no will, so I assume they'll get it all now. Much good it's going to do them.'

Caton knew what she meant. To outlive both of your children, particularly when they went like that. What difference was the money going to make, except to make them feel even worse?

She closed the second file, and sat back. 'Those are your copies.' She said. 'From my point of view these cases are closed. For you they're only just beginning. If there is anything I can do to help, don't hesitate.'

'Thanks Mary,' he said 'You've been a great help already.' He opened the door for her. 'I just hope this it. That there aren't any more out there in Bluebell Hollow.'

She stopped in the doorway, and looked up at him. It was the first time that he had heard her so despondent. 'To tell you the truth, Tom,' she said. 'If there are, I'd rather we found them. Better to bring them home, and give their loved ones closure, than leave them lost, and unloved, in that god forsaken place.'

The six of them sat huddled around the table; hanging on his every word. 'OK,' said Caton. 'This is how I want to do it. I'm assigning a lead officer for each of the victims. DS Stuart, you take Shirley Hassell. DI Holmes, you take Charlotte Mortimer. DS Hassan you've got Verity-Parker Smythe. Your job is to live and breathe the investigation of your victim. You'll know every detail of the case as it develops. You'll be responsible for liaising with the Receiver, and the Allocator, briefing everyone and anyone who is assigned an action on your case, and especially the briefing and debriefing of anyone who is going to conduct an interview. I want the result of every action entered into the system without delay. You'll also be responsible for briefing the whole team, at the start and finish of every day. Each of you will report to me on a continuous basis. You'll talk to each other, and we'll talk to each other. I never want to hear the phrase *I didn't know, nobody told me.*' Does everybody understand? Concentrate on the following: Last known movements; all contacts; known relationships; secrets confided; state of mind; Detective Constable Langham, you're with DS Stuart.   DC Shaw, you're with DS Hassan. And DC Wood you're with DI Holmes.'

Wood raised his hand. 'What about the Clinic Boss? Two of them are connected to that. And given the Mortimer woman...'

Caton stopped him in his tracks.   *'Charlotte* Mortimer...her name was Charlotte.'

Wood took a deep breath, and gave a good impression of appearing chastened. 'Sorry Boss. Given that Shelley Hassell was an addict, isn't it possible she was in there too?'

Caton nodded. 'Good point. But let's start with the obvious; family, friends, colleagues, and neighbours. I also want the names of bars and nightclubs they might have frequented. Their killer must have met them somewhere. See where that takes us. Then we'll decide who's going to have a look at the clinic.   That's it for now, so let's get going.' As they eased their chairs back, and jockeyed for the door Caton said. 'DI Holmes, a word please.'

'What's the matter Gordon?' he asked when the rest of them had left. 'You look like I asked you to join the traffic wardens.'

Holmes looked sheepish. 'It's just...well...DC Wood,' he said. 'He's about as much use as a sack of potatoes. He knows he's never going to make DS. He's virtually given up.'

'That's why I've given him to you; this is your chance to prove to me you can turn him round. If you can't, then nobody can.'

'Thanks for the vote of confidence Boss,' The DI replied. 'But between you and me, I reckon there's as much chance of that as me climbing Everest without oxygen.'

Caton smiled. 'Tell him that it's his final chance to prove himself. If he doesn't, he could be on his way out this time next year. You can tell him that too.'

In the doorway Holmes stopped, and turned. 'I'm glad I never had a girl Boss,' he said. 'The wife wanted one...women do don't they. Someone to dress up when she's little; who grows up to become her best friend. All those lunches together...shopping trips... grandchildren. These poor women. You know exactly what you're going to see in their parents' faces. All the dreams they had for their little girl ripped into shreds, and thrown in their faces.'

'How's your lad doing Gordon?' Caton asked. 'Robbie isn't it?'

Holmes's face lit up. Surprised that Caton had taken the trouble to remember.

'OK, thanks Boss. His school reports have been really good. Good grades predicted for his GCSE's. He's even planning to go to College next year.'

'Your wife must be pleased.'

'She's really chuffed. Me, I'm just relieved. I remember what I was like at his age.' He closed the door quietly behind him.

Caton sat down at his desk. In ten years time Harry would have just received his GCSE results. Hopefully be in College or the Sixth Form if there was still such a thing. At home, on his computer, he now had Helen's address. His mind was made up. Tonight, after the phone call from Kate. He would write that letter.

14

Under normal circumstances, Caton would have broken the news to each of the parents himself. It was almost a matter of honour. Apart from which, their reactions would be crucial. But these were not normal circumstances. Their daughters had been missing for a long time. There was no doubt about how they had died; only about who was responsible. In any case, he thought it a necessary opportunity for Holmes, Stuart, and Hassan; particularly Hassan. This would be his first. There was nothing like being pushed in at the deep end to see if he could swim. It wasn't the first time the parents had been interviewed. Far from it. He had read all of their statements twice, and doubted if there was anything to be gained by looking them in the eyes. That was what he told himself. The truth was that for once he simply couldn't face it. Instead, he had identified some people he needed to talk to. People who might help clear up a few metaphorical itches he was having trouble scratching. At the very least, it would get him out of the office.

She was a pretty little thing. Elfin faced with curly blonde hair, and wide innocent eyes; only today they were red rimmed with dark blue semi circles that even her professional make up couldn't mask. She'd been chewing her nails Caton noticed. That wouldn't go down too well on the shop floor; not in the beauty care section. The store manager had lent them his office, and some Kleenex. This was after all, the kind of emporium whose clientele expected to be protected from the seamier side of life.

'Take your time Mandy,' he said. 'I've got all day.'

'It isn't fair,' she replied, her big blue eyes searching his face for answers. 'Shelley didn't deserve this. She wasn't like that; she really wasn't.' Tears began to well up, threatening her mascara. Caton pushed the box of tissues across the desk towards her.

'Life isn't fair Mandy,' he said. 'Even a young woman like you knows that.'

He waited for her to dab them dry.

'What was she like?' he prompted.

'She was kind, thoughtful, funny. She was always making us laugh,' she smiled at a remembrance. 'Even at herself. She told this joke once, right? There are these three shoplifters. A brunette, a redhead, and a blonde. The police are chasing them round Tesco. They run into the grocery stores at the back, and hide in some empty sacks. The first policeman pokes the bag with the redhead in it. She goes, "Meow." The officer says "It's only a cat." The second one pokes the bag with the brunette in it. She goes, "Woof Woof." The officer says "This one's a dog." The third policeman kicks the bag with the blonde in it. She manages not to cry out, instead she says in the cutest possible voice, "Potato?"

This time she burst into tears. Caton felt like crying himself. It wasn't the first time he'd heard the joke. He waited until she composed herself.

'So. What was it that changed her?' He said. 'That started her drinking.?'

She looked him straight in the eyes. Her teeth clenched, her eyes blazing; her hands twisting the tissue as though wringing it out. The transformation took him by surprise.

'Those fucking footballers!' she said.

He wondered if she was using it only as an expletive, or also as an adjectival verb. Not that it mattered.

'You'll have to explain I'm afraid.' He said.

You must know about the parties? How they get these blokes to chat up the really attractive girls, and invite them along?'

'I read something about it.' He said.

'Well it happens all the time. Especially at Christmas, and the New Year.'

'Were you ever invited Mandy?'

He thought she was going to cry again, but she managed to fight back the tears. She took a deep breath, and looked down at her hands. Anything, he thought, to avoid his gaze.

'It was shortly before Christmas. The store was buzzing. Sales were going through the roof. We all knew we'd be on a big bonus. These two fit guys came in. I'd seen one of them before in a club in town. They told us about this party. Said there'd be lots of famous footballers there, from several clubs. They needed some more people to give it a bit of atmosphere. Did we want to come? Free buffet...all the champagne we could drink, great DJ. No strings, just a brilliant night out.'

'Weren't you the slightest bit suspicious?' He said, and instantly regretted it. The last thing she needed was a guilt trip. Fortunately, she didn't seem to notice.

142

'Of course we did. Especially Shelley. She said what kind of girls did they take us for? One of them said it was nothing like that. We could even bring our boy friends along if we wanted.'

'So you went?'

A tear formed at the corner of her left eye, and hung there, suspended like dew on the rim of a rose petal. After what seemed an eternity it fell. So intense was that moment Caton half expected to hear the sound of a splash as it landed on the back of her hand.

'Shelley didn't want to, but I persuaded her,' she looked up at him. There was a haunted look in her eyes. 'If it hadn't been for me she would never have gone.'

'There's no point in blaming yourself,' he said. 'No one could have predicted where it might lead. In any case, we don't know that it had anything whatsoever to do with her murder.' And if she didn't get on with it, he reflected, they would never know. 'Tell me what happened.'

'We got there about ten o'clock. It was a private club, with rooms above it. Not that we knew that at the time. There were about twenty or thirty players, and their hangers-on, and nearly a hundred guests; mainly girls. Most of them were really glamorous. Some were gorgeous. They must have been models.'

Now that she was into the story her confidence was growing. Caton decided not to interrupt.

'Waitresses in skimpy French maid costumes were bringing round the canapés, and you helped yourself to pink champagne. There was a DJ on the stage, and quite a few girls already on the floor, dancing. The footballers had obviously been somewhere else first,

143

because they'd already had plenty to drink. Some of them were trawling the room chatting up the girls. Every now and then they'd take one over to a sofa for a snog. I thought it was really sleazy.'

'And Shelley?'

'She thought it was great. She was straight on the dance floor. I felt really self-conscious next to some of those girls. Six foot tall, sex on legs, boobs out there on a platter. The men were all over them; even the few who'd brought a boy friend along. I helped myself to some food from the buffet, and sat on a stool, watching. It was gross. As the night went on, the girls got drunker, and a good few of the men went from chatting to groping. From time to time one of the men would take the girl he was with through a door by the side of the stage, where two bouncers were standing. I thought they were going outside but a girl on the stool next to me said there were rooms upstairs; with beds. I was sickened, because some of those girls were really out of it. One of the bouncers had to help this girl through the door. When it closed behind her they looked at each other, and one of them shook his head. I could tell he was thinking the same as me.'

She stopped talking, as though she'd lost the thread. Caton gently prompted her.

'Where was Shelley all this time?'

She looked up as though surprised by the question. 'Shelley? Oh, yes, she was still on the dance floor. Then about a quarter after midnight the DJ took a break, and the Karaoke started. He was first up.'

'He?'

'Barcelo.' She almost spat out the name. 'Really fancied himself he did. As Enrique Iglesias. Worst of it is, he actually can sing. Shelley was right there at the front. Freaking out. His number one fan. That must have been what caught his eye. When he came off the stage he was all over her, like a rash. Never left her alone.'

'Did he take her upstairs?'

She looked at him sharply, then shook her head. 'No, nothing like that. He's probably too smart to take a risk like that with all those people there. In any case, Shelley would never have gone, not the first time.'

Caton thought she protested too much.

'But she did eventually?' he said.

'I tried to get her to leave with me,' she said, avoiding his question. 'It was just after one o'clock. She told me no. She was having a good time. She'd be alright. Barcelo just gave me a smarmy smile. *"She's with me,"* he said. *"What harm she come to?"* So eventually I got a taxi, and went home. The next day she was like the cat that got the cream. There was no stopping her. It was Marcello this, and Marcello that. Our supervisor had to tell her to get a grip or go home. You couldn't blame her though. A great big bouquet of flowers arrived for her just before lunchtime. Most of the girls – those without bloody great hangovers that is – were really jealous.' She seemed to spot the carafe of water and the glass for the first time, and paused to pour herself a drink.

I'm not surprised thought Caton. If you've just surrendered your virginity, or at the very least your dignity, to no avail, the last thing you need is someone coming up smelling of roses. Mandy put the glass down, and blew her nose on a tissue. She looked around for somewhere to put it, and finding none scrunched it up in her hand with the others.

'According to Shelley, nothing happened that night,' she said. 'But it was only a matter of time. She tried to tell me about the sex they had together, but I couldn't take it. So eventually she stopped telling me. I was between boy friends at the time, and we drifted apart. Then he dumped her, and that's when the drinking started.'

'But she was still seeing other men?' Caton said, remembering what Mary Shepherd had told him. Mandy looked at him with a mixture of sadness and anger in her eyes.

'Oh yes,' she said, the bitterness almost tangible. 'Barcelo saw to that. It's how he tried to wean her off him. Tossing her like a bone to his dogs. Only she was too hurt…too angry to get it. She thought it would make him jealous.'

'And did it?'

She shook her head. 'All it did was make her hate herself for the things she let them do. That's why she drunk like she did. We tried to tell her but she was past listening.'

'So what happened?'

'Thank God, for her parents. They could tell she was falling apart. Somehow they got her to see a GP. He said she needed to go into rehab, but there was a waiting list for patients on the NHS. So they paid for her to go in. God knows how they got the money together. Shelley said something about a loan against the house.'

'How did you find all this out?' Caton wondered.

'She told me didn't she? When she came out, like the old Shelley she was. Funny, lively, but a bit more serious. She was off men. She wasn't drinking either.

Went on fruit cocktails when she was out with us.'

She became quiet for a while, looking down at her feet as though there was something there that might spark off a memory. 'Then I went into work one day...I remember, it was the launch of our Spring range...and she wasn't there. She looked up. Caton could see the tears in her eyes.

'I never saw her again.'

It hadn't been a waste of time. True, he had learnt nothing new, but at least it had brought Shelley Hassell to life; put some flesh on the bones. It also helped to add force to a feeling that been fermenting in his gut, and was close to developing into a hunch. As he pulled into the service area at Hartshead Moor, he wondered if this next interview would take him any further. He took the emergency slip road across to the westbound service area, and parked up.

Harriet Walker was waiting for him in the Primo Coffee Lounge. He spotted her straight away. It wasn't that difficult. She was the only woman the right age, and she was sitting facing the entrance, scanning men's faces as they came in. She had seen him first, and was already on her feet, standing there awkwardly. Conscious of her height he guessed. Best friend aside, he could see why Harriet would have been happy to have Charlotte Mortimer as a bridesmaid. They were a similar height and build, but even with her model looks Charlotte would not have been putting the bride in the shade. Harriet may have been the plainer of the two but she had an inner beauty he thought, that shone through. She flicked her auburn hair aside with one hand, while the other hovered in mid air as she tried to gauge if he intended to shake it.

'Harriet Walker?' he said, thrusting his hand forward to put her out of her misery. 'I'm Detective Chief Inspector Tom Caton.' He reached into his jacket pocket with his left hand, and brought out his warrant card. 'Thank you for coming.'

'Thank you for agreeing to meet me here,' she said. 'I have to be back in Sheffield to pick up my daughter at three thirty. They hate it if you're late.' Her lips crinkled into a frown. '*And* they charge you for an extra hour.'

Preliminaries over, Caton launched straight in.

'I know you haven't long,' he said. 'So I'd like to concentrate on the year in which Charlotte went missing. What do you remember about it?'

'It wasn't a good time for her,' she said. 'To be honest, we had drifted apart a bit. I was recently married, with a baby on the way. So no more wild nights out in Manchester, or Sheffield, just the odd girlie lunch. But we'd talk on the phone. And she was always texting.'

'What did you talk about?'

'The usual things; her work, boyfriends, holidays, the next thing in fashion. Charley was always ahead of the trend…being in the business. Not that I could afford to take advantage of it.' She put down her cup, and smiled. 'Actually, she was really generous. She used to send me some of the clothes she'd been modelling. We're more or less the same build you see. Not that I did them justice…not like her. But it saved me a fortune.'

Caton didn't doubt it, but this wasn't what he was

here for. 'What did she have to say about her boy friends?' he said.

'Her face clouded over. 'It's difficult. I find it hard to talk about. Especially now that she's dead.'

'I understand. But it's precisely because she is dead, and because of how she died, that I need you to be honest with me. For the sake of other girls like Charley.'

There was a suggestion of hurt in her hazel eyes. 'I said it was hard Mr Caton. Not that I wouldn't be honest with you.' She took a sip of coffee before continuing. '*Boy friends*, was something of a euphemism. As far as I know she only ever had one. Abdul Al Jalil. A businessman from Bahrain. She was really taken by him. Swept off her feet I suppose you could say. All of the rest were what she used to call "short stay." Even at school she never went out with a boy more than once or twice.'

'Why do you think that was?'

'She actually told me. Quite early on. It was because she thought that the only reason they went after her was because of her looks, not for herself. They saw her as a kind of trophy. The result was that she built a shell around herself, a kind of carapace, so none of them ever got a chance to find out who she really was.'

Caton already had Harriet down as a bright young woman. Carapace confirmed it. It was the kind of word those fast track graduates came out with. He could see himself tossing it in at a future selection board. Just to see their faces.

'So she ended up treating *them* like trophies instead?' He said.

She shook her head. 'It wasn't like that. I think she needed the companionship, even if it was just for a night. And in her line of work there was no shortage of offers. And she enjoyed the sex, and the risk.'

'There was a suggestion that she was into cocaine,' Caton said. 'Do you know anything about that?'

'It's true I'm afraid. I tried to persuade her to give it up, but she just laughed it off. She said it was a perfectly acceptable social habit. Everybody did it. And anyway, it was better than getting bladdered. *"Drunken sex is like trying to swim in a tank of rice pudding..."* she said, *"...whereas Charlie, on charley, it's un...bloody believable!"* She looked straight at Caton. 'Do you think that had anything to do with her death...the cocaine?'

'I don't know,' he replied. 'Do you?'

She glanced down at her cup. 'I don't know. I do know that it got worse after her Arab gave her the heave ho.'

'Why did he? Did she tell you?'

'Apparently he was serious enough to want to get married. Even went so far as to buy her this amazing platinum and solitaire diamond ring. But his family did some digging and came up with a long list of one night stands, some of whom were more than happy to tell tales in exchange for cash. That was it. He asked for the ring back, and disappeared out of her life.'

'How did she react?'

'Badly. She was on the phone to me all the time that first week. I think she'd seen it as her last chance, and now she'd blown it. I thought she was heading for a breakdown. Then suddenly it all went quiet. She wasn't returning my calls...no texts...nothing. I got quite worried. Nobody at her agency knew were she was. Then, about a month later, she suddenly resurfaced, bright as anything. When I asked where she'd been she just said "Away".

'What did you think she meant by that?'

'At first I thought she must have been to one of her villas. But now I'm not so sure.'

Neither was Caton; but he had a pretty good idea.

When he got back to the office and listened to the reports from his lead officers it was obvious to Caton that nobody had dug up anything earth shattering; nothing that was going to really move the investigation on. But then you never knew which little bit of information squirreled away would provide the missing piece in the jigsaw. There was one development however. Larry Hymer had come up trumps, putting together a great article, using photos of each of the girls. The paper had made it something of a crusade. Appealing to the public to get behind the police, and contact them with any snippets of information no matter how insignificant they might seem. Already the phones were ringing off the walls in the incident room. Just one piece; that was all it would take.

Peter Smythe, the former husband of Verity - victim number three - was another who had been expecting Caton's call.

'I can't see you today though, Detective Chief Inspector,' he said. 'But I could manage first thing tomorrow morning, providing you promise to keep it brief.'

'I'll do my best of course,' Caton told him. 'But it does depend on what you have to tell me.'

'Not a lot I should have thought,' said the barrister. 'How does seven thirty suit? My Chambers?'

It suited very well. It meant that Caton could beat the first major rush hour wave, and have a leisurely breakfast at Carluccio's in Spinningfields. He looked at his watch. It was a quarter to nine. He placed the missing persons file on Verity Parker-Smythe in his briefcase, locked the other two in his filing cabinet, and set off for home.

15

Caton sat up in bed, a double measure of ten year old Talisker single malt on the bedside table, the file in his lap. He rarely took work to bed with him, partly because he'd discovered a long time ago the wisdom of keeping bed and business far apart, and partly because too often he'd fall asleep in the middle of it. He'd convinced himself that a blog sounded less like work, and more like light entertainment. Besides, he'd finished the latest Harlan Coban, and hadn't had time to get another night time read.

He opened the file, and removed the fifteen stapled pages that Mary Shepherd had printed off. He knew beggar all about blogs. It was certainly not something he ever saw himself indulging in. And let's face it, it *was* an indulgence. He doubted that anyone would seriously be interested in the minutiae of his life. But then what did he know? It was all hypothetical anyway because there was no way Chester House would have let him get away with writing a blog. He settled down, and began to read.

It was immediately obvious that this was part journal, part autobiography, part cautionary tale. The further that Caton got into it, the more he could see why she'd thought it might make a good book. He envisaged it flying off the supermarket shelves earmarked for women readers. What's more, it looked like it had quickly attracted a lot of interest. Although Shepherd had only printed out Verity's contribution she had attached a note suggesting he go online, and view the hundreds of comments it had attracted from other bloggers. It didn't take a mastermind to work out that her predator might have come across her this way; may even have left his calling card. But that would have to wait until morning. For now, Caton found her story riveting enough.

She had chosen to call her alter ego Truly Driver; a none too subtle clue to her real identity. Somehow Caton didn't think it would have been enough to dissuade her former husband from pursuing her for libel, but then if what she had written was all true he would have known that his chance of a successful outcome would have been slim. In any case, Peter Smythe had already come out.

Truly was born into what must have appeared from the outside as a perfectly normal middleclass family. Her father was a maths teacher, her mother a librarian. They were devoted parents, if just a little too desperate for their two children to succeed academically. But they were also Jehovah's Witnesses. The result was that Truly and her brother James were forced to lead a life separate from that of other children in the neighbourhood, and at the schools they attended. Looking back she described it as like being in a parallel universe much of the time.

From an early age they were taken three times a week to the Kingdom Hall where their parents helped to organise the meetings. Once a week either she or James was expected to trail from doorstep to doorstep in the wake of their mother and one of her friends, clutching copies of the Watchtower. That had been an education in itself. She had learned the real meaning of a number of words and phrases including, persistence, embarrassment, obstinacy, humility, rejection, verbal abuse, and above all, boredom. Only once had she dared question why their father never accompanied them. Her mother replied that their father served the Kingdom in other ways, and she was never ever to question it again. Truly thought it strange that such an intelligent woman as her mother would always accede to her husband's every wish, and never question his views or decisions. It was only as she approached her teens that she understood the ramifications of a truly patriarchal belief system. Although there was a television in the house it was severely rationed, and as a consequence she and her brother spent much of their time together reading books and doing their homework – including the extra work their father set for them. Then there were the daily interminable readings from the New World Translation of the Scriptures, and the discussions that followed.

It was inevitable that James would be the first to rebel against the stultifying straightjacket that had been thrown around them. It was his practice to wait until his mother had gone out door-stepping, and his father was in his study or out at a parents' evening, and then he would slip out to play with other boys in the neighbourhood. It was on just such a day, in the middle of the summer holidays, that he went out, and never returned.

Their father had gone up to the Kingdom Hall, and their mother was out shopping. Truly was alone in the house when one of the boys burst in through the kitchen door, and burst into tears. She had followed him out, down the lane at the back of the houses, and out across the common land to the woods. She had run ahead of him down the twisting paths and through the ferns, squeezed through the gap in the hedge oblivious to the brambles and hawthorns catching at her dress and tearing at her naked limbs, stumbled on the grassy slope, and tumbled over and over until she landed bruised and battered just feet from the quarries' edge. She pushed herself into a kneeling position, and peered over.

Sixty feet below, beside the bleak grey expanse of water stood two of her brother's friends in white tee shirts and underpants. Even from this distance she could see that they were shivering violently despite the blazing sun. Up the path from the bottom track two men came running. When they reached the boys one of the men removed his top and gave it to the shorter of the boys; the other man followed suit. As they struggled to put on the tops, the boys pointed towards the furthest side of the pond where the quarry came down sheer to the water's edge. The blistered rusting roof of a car was just visible above the surface. Truly could see their mouths moving but was unable to hear what they were saying. Beside her, the boy who had come to the house was sitting clasping his knees to his chest, head down, sobbing uncontrollably. One of the men made as though to enter the water, but the other man pulled him back. They stood there staring at the water. The droop of the shoulders, and their silence, testament to an overwhelming sense of impotence.

Truly had watched as the police arrived, and then the fire brigade, and finally five more men, three of whom donned wet suits, and began to take it in turn to swim out on a line to search the murky depths. The sun beat down from a clear blue sky. A curlew called from somewhere beyond the hill. She felt nothing. Not pain, nor horror, nor dread, nor grief; only emptiness. And the certain knowledge that James had gone. And God did not exist.

Her parents found comfort in their faith. They interpreted her silence and lack of tears as signs of acceptance, courage and forbearance. Nothing could have been further from the truth. With James gone, all their expectations became focused on her. Truly reacted by becoming the perfect daughter; their pride and consolation. It was easier that way. At eighteen years of age she left to go to University. In her first letter home she told them she had renounced her faith. Her father reacted by telling her that he would cease to pay her tuition fees. Truly responded by going out, and getting herself a job; evenings during the week and fulltime at weekends and during the three and a half months of vacation time. Every month a registered letter arrived containing £200 in a mixture of notes. She guessed that it came from her mother, but never formally acknowledged it for fear of the trouble it would cause between them if her father ever found out. She never returned home. By the time she graduated with a 2:1 honours degree in Business Studies she had secured a job in a prestigious property agency, and had saved enough money in the bank to pay the deposit, and the first three months of a lease on a flat.

For the next four and a half years she immersed herself in her work. It was the start of the property boom and the fruition of a decade of redevelopment in the city centre, and along the Whitworth Road and Ashton canal corridor from Castlefield to Piccadilly Village. Properties were selling before they had time to put the details in the window. Truly soon had enough saved to buy her own property. And then along came Piers Black; aka Peter Smythe.

It was a wet and blustery March morning when he burst in from the street, water dripping from his umbrella onto the Italian tiled floor. Truly was the one who relieved him of his coat and hung it up to dry, who placed his umbrella in the stand, and made him a cup of coffee; who found him a new apartment. They hit it off straight away. The fourteen years gap between them was not an impediment. Intelligent and urbane though he was Piers had a certain chubby youthfulness about him. By contrast, Truly was old beyond her years. At the time she would have called herself mature, but looking back she knew it for what it was. Everything about her upbringing had conspired to make her feel and behave like a grown up. Her relative isolation from anyone outside the tightly knit circle of the Kingdom had left her socially inadequate when it came to boys. Even at University the necessity of working from dawn till late into the night precluded boy friends, and she had never learnt the skills that might have stood her in better stead.

All of this suited Piers Black. To all intents and purposes he had a blank canvas with which to work. He swept her off her feet with his charm and cheerfulness. She had never experienced anything remotely like it, and fell hook line and sinker. Six months later they were married in Manchester Cathedral with all the pomp and circumstance of a celebrity wedding. Her mother came; her father did not. Piers took out a lease on a prime office space on Deansgate, and set her up in her own business. And so, for the second time in her life, she found herself in thrall to another patriarch, albeit one more cheerful and outgoing.

So naïve was Truly that it was almost five years into the marriage before she began to guess his little secret. Had he neglected his marital duties she had no doubt that it would never have taken her so long. But he did not. Nor did his perfunctory performance alert her. She had no yard stick against which to judge it. He always seemed delighted to show her off at the parties they attended, and those they hosted at home. His extensive and well connected group of friends and acquaintances proved a boon to her business. Only gradually did it begin to dawn on her that far from being a homogenous group there were two distinct social cohorts in which he moved. And one of these consisted primarily of gay men. Truly was in no way homophobic. In fact she felt distinctly comfortable, even valued, in their company. It was when expressions of empathy from some of them began to feel like sympathy that she started to look around for a reason.

The reason turned out to be a young interior designer called Malcolm; a longstanding friend of Piers who was often at their house. Once she started looking for the evidence it was blindingly obvious that for the past five years it was as though she had had scales across her eyes. When she confronted Piers with her suspicions he admitted it straight away. He told her that he was bi-sexual, and needed the intimacy of both male and female company. That he loved her, and he loved Malcolm. He tried to convince her that the fact that their marriage had been so successful for so long was proof that they could make it work. That there was no need for this to change anything at all. He tried, and failed.

Truly sensed that Malcolm was, and would always be, her husband's real passion. That she had been nothing more than a trophy bride; a convenient means of displaying to the outside world the respectability that he thought that marriage would provide. She realised that he had manipulated and controlled her just as her father had done. She despised him for not having had the courage to come out like the rest of his friends. Above all, she despised herself for having yet again played the perfect role expected of her.

The divorce was swift and uncontested. She kept the shop and the apartment. Not that it was painless. Even before the decree absolute came through she had started drinking during the day.

When it finally arrived,' she wrote. '*It was as though the shackles, not just of the past six years, but of the whole of my life had been removed. If I had learned nothing else in the course of my marriage I had learned how to chat up men. I started by ringing acquaintances and asking out ones who I thought quite fancied me. Most were embarrassed, and cut themselves off from me. A surprising number didn't. Then I started going out to clubs alone, picking up strangers, allowing them to pick me up. Inviting them back to my place...going back to theirs. It was like a drug, fuelled by drinking. I began to throw parties that became increasingly wild. Almost everyone there would mix drink with a cocktail of drugs, until they descended into booze fuelled orgies.*

Even at work I found myself flirting with clients I was showing round some of the top of the range penthouses. On more than one occasion we ended up having sex in the master bedroom. Once, I recall, in the hot tub. The more reckless I became the more I woke up despising myself, and the more I drank to blank it out. Finally I collapsed at work, and was taken to hospital. The doctors said I was suffering from depression and alcoholism. I could have told them that myself. But it was the look on the faces of my staff that finally persuaded me to seek help. And that was how I came to enter the Oasis.

Caton sped read the next three pages in which she depicted her painful yet ultimately healing journey through a process of self examination, and group encounter therapy. He was more interested in the period immediately prior to her disappearance. She described the weeks after her return to work as euphoric. She stopped drinking, had a better understanding of the demons that haunted her, and began to forgive herself, and her parents. The tone of her blog had changed markedly Caton thought. She sounded so liberated, so optimistic, so upbeat. Her final entry was typical.

I am finding it much easier than I expected to do without the demon drink. Ok, so I know it will always have to be one day at a time, but I'm coping with that. It's like I suddenly decided to become a vegan, except that there are so many more alternatives out there. My biggest worry was that my craving for sex, my sexual appetite if you like, would return with a vengeance. After all it's not like I can spend the rest of my life ignoring men is it? The Oasis wasn't so bad - once I started to get my head straight - but for heaven's sake I'm not going to hide myself away in a nunnery am I? Anyway, I've met this guy, and he's really helping me. For the first time in my life I've found a man I really like, really admire, and I know what you're thinking, but no, it's for his sensitivity, his mind, not his body. Not that it might never come to that. It's just that right now that side of it doesn't seem to matter. Intrigued? I hope so. But I can't tell you any more about him because I've promised not to, and I'm not going to queer this one up. Whoops...that looks like a Freudian slip doesn't it! I suppose I must be on the mend if I can laugh about the charade that was my marriage. Anyway, you'll just have to watch this space. Maybe soon. I do hope so.

Caton put the final page down on top of the others, reversed them, and placed them in the file. He had hoped that Verity's blog would help him to find out as much as possible about her as a person, and as a potential victim. It had certainly done that. And while it may not have given him the name he was looking for it had at least provided two possible suspects. Peter Smythe – the callous, suave, and manipulative Piers Black of Verity's blog – and the mystery man whose sensitivity had clearly beguiled her. The threat to her ex-husband's reputation was not in Caton's view a sufficient motive for him to have killed her, or to have had her killed. But if he had learned one thing in his years in the force it was that while just about anyone could become a killer, there was no telling what it would take to turn them into one.

All in all he decided, as he put the file on the floor beside the bed and plumped up the pillows, it had been an interesting day. Not a lot of progress made, but a lot of ground covered. That was half the battle. Then there was the letter to Helen. He would post it on the way in to work. He imagined her picking it up, staring at the vaguely familiar handwriting, checking the postmark, deciding it wasn't a bill. Harry tugging at her sleeve. *"Come on Mummy I'm going to be late!"* Stuffing it in her pocket, locking the door, taking Harry by the hand, setting off down the drive. Later that day, on a coffee break perhaps, she would remember. Retrieve the envelope, and slit it open with her thumbnail. He envisaged two possible scenarios. There is a worried frown on her face that morphs into anger. She curses, tears the letter into little pieces, and drops them one by one into the wastepaper basket. Or alternatively, she looks surprised. She begins to smile as she reaches the bottom of the page, and turns over. She folds the letter, places it back in the envelope, and reaches for the telephone.

The only prayers Caton could remember these days, apart from the Our Father, and the 23rd Psalm which seemed to be an obligatory part of the all too many funerals his work had lately forced him to attend, were those his mother had taught him to say last thing at night. None of them seemed to be appropriate. For the first time in years he was forced to come up with his own. 'Dear God,' he said out loud. 'Help.' He switched off the light, and lay with his head on the pillow, trying to think white; waiting for sleep to engulf him.

16

Peter Smythe was running late. Either that, or the barrister had deliberately kept him waiting to emphasise the voluntary nature of the meeting or, more likely, to keep it brief. It had only been a five minute walk for Caton from his apartment overlooking the quayside on Castlefield, so it didn't really faze him; quite the reverse. It had given him time to rehearse his questions.

'Mr Smythe will see you now.'

The office manager was a matronly woman in her late fifties, wearing a tweed suit, and brogues. Caton wondered how she had handled the revelation of their senior partner's sexual preference. She had probably known all along.

'Ah, Detective Inspector.'

Smythe was seated behind his desk. He made no attempt to get up. Power play.

'Sorry to have to keep you waiting,' he waved almost dismissively at the chair on the other side directly facing him. 'Do take a seat. Haven't long I'm afraid.'

Although in the past Caton had seen him in and around the courts, he had never been involved in a case where Peter Smythe had acted for the Defence or the Prosecution. This was the first time in nearly three years that he had been this close to him. He was shocked by the way in which plump had become fleshy; by how his face had lost its definition, and his body too. He was now a cross between Orson Welles, and Alfred Hitchcock. Caton thought it appropriate given that he exuded much of the arrogance of Citizen Kane and, if Verity's blog was to be believed, the predatory manipulation that characterised so many of Hitchcock's male leads.

'This shouldn't take long,' Caton told him. 'And I can always come back.'

'Let's hope that doesn't become necessary,' the barrister replied. 'My time is money, and as I am sure you are aware, I don't come cheap.'

Caton smiled innocently. 'In which case, we both have good reasons to want to get to the truth as quickly as possible.'

Smythe raised his hands theatrically. 'As Pontius Pilate is reputed to have asked of Christ – *What is truth?*'

'Is this your way of saying that you wash your hands of your ex-wife's death Mr Smythe?' said Caton.

Smythe's face remained expressionless but there was a sudden tension to his body that told Caton he was rattled. If nothing else it had put him on the back foot and stopped this from becoming the cosy chat Smythe might have hoped for.

'That was uncalled for Detective Chief Inspector,' he responded. 'You know very well what I meant. I was certainly not casting myself as Caesar's Friend, nor can I believe that you see yourself as Jesus Christ. Or perhaps you do?'

Caton ignored the jibe. 'So you don't think your marriage, or the divorce, had anything to do with it?'

The barrister began to fold his arms then suddenly, as though he had become aware of how defensive that would look, placed his hands on the desk instead.

'Yes I regret the marriage. Yes I did deceive her from the outset. But contrary to what you may think I never set out to use Verity. So I was both sorry, and somewhat chastened, when she demanded a divorce. But that hardly constitutes responsibility for her death does it?'

'Was the divorce amicable?'

He gave a wry smile. 'I would hardly describe it as that. But it was swift, and I made sure that it was generous as far as Verity was concerned. I felt I owed her that at the very least.'

'Did you remain friends?'

'No, nor did we become enemies.'

'Did you have any contact with one another.'

'No, but I have to admit that I did hear from shared friends and acquaintances how she was getting on. Or should I say, carrying on? I have to say that the way her life changed after our divorce upset me. Guilt I suppose.'

'Why guilt?

'Come Mr Caton, you can't be that naïve. Her entire personality changed, as did her behaviour. We both know that what she saw as my betrayal of her was the trigger that set her off on that trail of self-destruction.'

'*She saw* as your betrayal? Are you suggesting that it wasn't?'

The barrister leant forward, taking the weight of his upper body on the palms of his hands. 'Now you are trying my patience Detective Chief Inspector. I understood this to be a search for the truth, not an exercise in polemics; which, as I'm sure you are aware, is my field of expertise, not yours. Yes I betrayed her. But that was not my intention. Surprising though it may seem, I did love Verity. And we were as happy... I venture to say happier than, the average husband and wife. I never intended her to discover my little secret. Had she not, I have no doubt our life together would have continued harmoniously, and she would still be alive today.'

He paused for a moment to catch his breath. Caton could see he was on a roll, and resisted the temptation to point out that this was one of the worst defenses, the worst examples of casuistry, he had ever heard. Smythe hooked a finger under his collar, trying in vain to loosen it.

'I was deeply saddened...' he said. '...when I learned that she had died, and more so because of the manner of her death. Yes I felt some responsibility for it. Had I never married her perhaps she would have gone on as before. She might now be a very wealthy single businesswoman with her own agency; North West Businesswoman of the Year. Who knows?'

He looked into the detective's eyes. It was surprising, Caton reflected, how often people did that; hoping to find some kind of absolution there.

'But I was not the bastard who did what ever he did to her,' Smythe's voice caught in his throat, and for a moment Caton though he might be choking. He recovered enough to complete the sentence. 'And then dumped her like a piece of a garbage.'

He reached across the desk, and poured himself a glass of water from the crystal decanter. This wasn't a piece of court theatrics Caton decided. He really had loved her in his own twisted way.

'What did you feel when you heard that she'd disappeared?' He asked.

'I heard intimations of it from several of our mutual friends who had become concerned about her. Then your colleagues came to see me. I was concerned. Very concerned.'

He took another sip of water. Not playing for time Caton decided. His mouth was dry, and there was a wet slick on his face and damp patches in his armpits.

'When the police told me that none of her cards had been used, or her accounts accessed, I feared for the worst. You'll have read the transcripts of the interviews. You'll know that I co-operated fully. That I was exonerated.'

Caton shook his head, expressing surprise and disappointment. 'Nobody was exonerated, Mr Smythe. They never are in the case of a missing person. Not until we know exactly how and when they disappeared. And as for murder...well.' He let it hang there.

The barrister responded by looking at his watch. Caton didn't want to have to come back to these Chambers to interview him again. Apart from anything else he doubted he could achieve the same dynamics again. Smythe would be better prepared a second time. 'Just one more question Mr Smythe,' he said. 'Did you know about your ex-wife's blog?'

It was Smythe's turn to be disappointed. He raised his eyebrows. 'Come, come, Detective Chief Inspector, you know from the transcripts that I did. Yes I was first made aware of it by one of my legal executives who knows about these things. Was I upset by it? Yes, I suppose I was. On the other hand I knew she had to get it out of her system somehow, and I suppose I thought I deserved it. Was I minded to sue? That would have depended on how far she went with it. Most of what she'd written about was true I'm ashamed to admit, and there are plenty of people out there who would have backed her up. Could it have damaged my reputation? Hardly. The divorce forced me to come out, and frankly it was the best thing that could have happened. Malcolm and I are now open partners, and may well decide to go through a civil ceremony. Not get married you note. Call me old fashioned but I still think that's a term that should remain exclusive to heterosexual partnerships. Would I have killed her to shut her up? Absolutely not! And let's face it Detective Chief Inspector. If her death was linked to that of any of those other poor souls you've dug out of Bluebell Hollow what's the likelihood that I would have known them too, let alone had a reason for killing them? Unless of course you think I might be a serial killer? Now that *would* make a good story.'

He looked at his watch again, and levered himself up by pressing his podgy hands against the desk. 'I'm due in court in half an hour. You know where to reach me. And Mr Caton, I do hope you catch the bastard who killed her. Having read that blog I know this much. I never really knew her. I certainly didn't deserve her; and she didn't deserve that.'

He walked around the desk, over to the door, and placed his hand on the brass knob.

'Do you know what the Greek word for Truth is Detective Chief Inspector? It is *alethia*. It means, *that*

169

which is revealed. In other words, you get what you see. And more often than not that's as good as it gets. I hope you get to see enough to nail the bastard who killed her.' He opened the door, and stood back.

'Good day Mr Caton.'

17

Caton had half an hour to get back to his car, and drive the one and a half miles against the incoming rush hour traffic to the Didsbury Campus of the Metropolitan University. Lean and lanky Henry Sobel of the National Policing Improvement Agency, whom he knew from several previous investigations, was already there in the office of the Home Office profiler.

'I was just telling Dr Stewart-Baker that I hadn't realised that the Henry Fielding Centre had closed.' Sobel said, as Caton took off his coat and hung it on the back of the door.

'It was complicated,' the forensic psychologist told him. 'Not least by the kind of work you and your colleagues have been doing. But nevertheless, here I am. Different university, different office, different department, same field, ploughing the same old furrow.' He waited for Caton to take his seat, and said. 'I hope you have a little more for us to go on?'

Caton took a slim file from his document case, and handed it to him. 'See for yourself,' he said. 'I've already emailed a copy of this to Mr Sobel. I hope you got it Henry?'

Sobel held up a small sheaf of papers. 'I got it. I've just been explaining to the professor that I've fed the data you sent me into our analytical models and I've brought the results along. Normally, we would want to see the offender profile first but since you don't seem to have any firm suspects yet, in this instance, and with all due respect to Doctor Stewart-Baker, I'm not sure that the profile will change the results all that much, other than to confirm them.'

Stewart-Baker shook his head. 'No offence taken,' he said. 'And please, forget the Professor and Doctor malarky, just call me Lawrence. And to speed things up a little why don't you run through the factors common to your victims Tom, then Harry can share his results, and then I'll try to give you a starter for ten on a likely psychological profile for your perpetrator.'

Caton began to take his copy from the case, and then thought better of it. He knew them by heart. 'Three women, ages twenty eight, thirty two, and thirty eight. They lived within ten miles of each other. All of them had been buried in the immediate vicinity of a massive tip consisting of waste from three former coal mines. All of them were naked, and had been strangled. They were also lying in what appeared to be a foetal, or recovery position. It was impossible to determine whether or not any of them had been sexually assaulted. All three were attractive women. All three had natural blonde hair; although the hair of one of the victims was dyed red at the time of her disappearance. All three were only children; one of them de facto following the death of her brother when she was only thirteen.'

Stewart-Baker interrupted him. 'Why have you included the fact that they were only children?' he asked.

'Because I thought it might have some bearing on their personalities...their behaviours?'

'I know what you're thinking,' the profiler replied. 'That they are more likely to have been spoiled for example?'

Caton noticed that the academic was staring again at the same imaginary spot on the ceiling.

'But,' he continued. 'Research evidence tells us that it doesn't follow, although only children do need to work harder to win friends. Certainly they are more likely to have been close to their parents, and outwardly to be more mature than children with siblings. They are generally dependable, high achieving, and make good leaders; leaders however who tend to be both demanding and unforgiving. They may well possess good self-control, and yet conversely tend to be quite needy. Lone children in a family generally have better self-esteem and are higher achievers. But like all generalisations the exceptions to the rule are many, and far more interesting.'

He tore his eyes away from the ceiling, and looked at Caton. 'I'm sorry,' he said. 'I shouldn't have interrupted. Please, carry on.'

This time Caton did consult his notes to check where he was up to. 'All three were single. One of them was divorced. Their occupations were sales assistant, model, and property agent respectively. All three of them had addictive personalities. Alcohol and sex in all three cases, drugs in the case of numbers two and three. The youngest and the eldest both attended the same private clinic – The Oasis in Cheshire - for a course of rehabilitation. The two youngest frequented some of the same bars and restaurants, although not, as far as we know, together.'

'Ethnicity?' Prompted Stewart-Baker.

'Caucasian. White British to be precise.'

'Religious persuasion?'

'One a lapsed Catholic; one christened C of E; but never practising; one a former Jehovah's Witness.'

'And none of them had a prior conviction of any kind.' Henry Sobel added, effectively completing Caton's summary.

'Very interesting,' said the academic. He turned to the man from the National Policing Improvement Agency.

'So, what does your analysis have to tell us Harry?'

Sobel spread his papers out the desk in front of him. 'Right,' he said. 'You're both aware that what we try to do is to pin down the most likely location for what we call the offender's anchor point. The place where he feels most comfortable...anchored if you like. That's most often his or her place of residence, but it could just as easily be his workplace, or somewhere connected with his social life. We do that by looking at the locations of connected offences, the neighbourhood where they happened, and, if we've got it, the profile of the offender compiled by the Home Office profiler. In this instance I've had to work with their last known location before they were reported missing; and the deposition site.'

Caton had learned his Murder Investigation Manual by heart for the Selection Board. He was aware of the shortcomings of all of these analyses, but he also knew that they were right nine times out of ten for the easy to solve cases. It was the other ten percent that bothered him.

'We started off...' Sobel continued. '...by charting a ten mile zone within which we would expect to find the anchor point using our only consistent point of contact with the perpetrator – the dump site. The question we can't answer is whether that is proximal to his home, or his place of work. And of course it's complicated by the fact you've got seven different interconnecting motorways that he could use to get in and out of this area. Much as Peter Sutcliffe the Yorkshire Ripper did. His thirteen victims fell within a quadrant with a radius of thirty eight miles covering Leeds, Bradford, Manchester, and Halifax.'

Caton had studied that case inside out. Mainly to learn from the mistakes made. If the detectives working that case had had Sobel's Geographical Statistical Analyses available to them the odds are they would never have been taken in by the hoax tapes that led them to focus on the North East. And that would almost certainly have saved the lives of the last three victims.

'I did the same,' Sobel continued. 'In relation to each of the victims' home addresses and their work places. This is the result.'

He handed them each a printed map of Greater Manchester on which two almost identical circles of ten mile radius, with focal points close to the city centre itself, overlapped with a third circle centred around Cutacre and Bluebell Hollow. The area thus covered formed a larger circle with its outer edge beginning in Darwen in the North, passing through Middleton and Ramsbottom, Hollingwood and Rochdale in the East, Poynton, Sale, and Warrington in the South, before swinging up through Wigan and Chorley in the West, and back to Darwen.

'What's that, about a hundred and fifty square miles?' Guessed Caton.

'A hundred and eighty seven,' Sobel told him. 'What's more to the point, we're talking two and a half million people. But it's not as bad you think. We know that our victims were between twenty eight and thirty eight years of age. Our database tells us that thirty five percent of murderers of victims in that age range are themselves between thirty and thirty nine years of age. Twenty three percent are between twenty five and twenty nine, and only fourteen percent are forty years and over. If we make the assumption that we're looking for a male offender, or offenders, then your potential offender range is going to include between 312,000 and 156,000, males. Enter a few more variables – such as prior convictions of a sexual or violent nature, possession of a driving licence, and so on, and depending on what Profess...' he caught himself. '...Lawrence, has to say, you could be looking at as few as 40,000 or so.' He sat back. Letting them digest it. Pleased with himself.

Caton was computing the number of man hours it would take to work through that lot. Not that it couldn't be done, only that it he'd need a hell of a lot more to go on before he started down that route.

'My turn,' Stewart–Baker declared. 'But before I start, how about I get us all a coffee....unless that is, you prefer tea?'

'Same person! Too much in common not to be.'

Stewart-Baker put his mug down on the floor perilously close to his feet, and rocked back in his chair. 'For a start, you're looking for a male. Someone physically strong, intelligent, resourceful, and sexually motivated. That may not be the primary motivation, but it will be a strong motivation nonetheless. A man who is controlling – not that that's unusual – and who is outwardly attractive and charming, especially to women. How else would he manage to abduct three attractive young women? I also think it likely that he will have an addictive personality. I took the trouble to go out and see the deposition site for myself Tom. I think he chose that very carefully. The Cutacre site, and Bluebell Hollow in particular, has some kind of symbolic meaning for him. It wasn't a random choice. I think he had prior knowledge of it. Either worked or lived locally. My guess, and it's nothing more than that, within a three mile radius of the tip. Possibly a little further, given that it is visible for some distance away from the south.

'Not recently, surely?' said Caton. 'Or he would have been aware that they'd got the go ahead to start open cast mining.'

The psychologist nodded his approval. 'Good point. The bad news is that he's almost certain to have continued to kill after February 2007 when the last of your victims was killed. There were ten months between his first and second victims, three months between his second and third. He will have continued to kill, and quite possibly at increasingly frequent intervals. Like any drug, he will be trying to recreate, more importantly to re-experience, the feelings of that first high. But it will become increasingly hard for him to do that. That would explain the additional injuries to victim three.

'Given that when he turned up there with victim number three the open cast was already underway,' said Caton. 'Won't he have chosen a new deposition site?

'Yes.'

'In the same area?'

'Possibly, assuming that he still lives locally, but he may have looked further afield in order to find a similar opportunity to conceal.

'Is he looking to get caught – consciously or subconsciously?'

'Probably not, because he initially chose an isolated site – albeit that it was popular with the off road bikers – and he buried the bodies deep, and away from the well trod paths. The third victim, he had to dispose of in a hurry, and extemporise. And he has made no attempt to contact you in the way that some serial killers do; to taunt you or, to flaunt his invulnerability.'

'What age would you put him at?'

Stewart-Baker steepled his fingers. "I would place him somewhere between thirty and forty five. Fifty at the outside. Mature enough to appeal to victims two and four, young enough to appeal to victim three.'

'Married or single?'

He shook his head. 'Impossible to say. A recent study showed that a woman's libido plummets almost as soon as she feels she has secured a long term partner. Within four years of securing a long term partner less than fifty percent of thirty year olds reported wanting regular sex. Whereas although a man reaches the peak of his virility at 18 years of age, the desire for sex in men hardly flags at all over the first forty years of a marriage. Throw a personality disorder with an addictive compulsion into that mix, and anything can happen. Look at Sutcliffe.'

He stared up at the ceiling again.

'To summarise – you're looking for a sexual predator who has become a serial killer. He is likely to have engaged in early abnormal sexual behaviours such as spying on women, stealing their underwear, flashing, escalating over time to possibly involve stalking, sexual assault, and rape; although that doesn't mean that he was ever caught. There is one element in his modus operandi however that intrigues me.'

'The way in which he displays the bodies?' said Caton.

'Exactly right Tom. There are a number of possibilities. It may relate to something in his past. He may be copying something he's seen before – in a photograph or a painting. It may be also be an indication of remorse, which would suggest that whilst he acknowledges that what he is doing is wrong that moral awareness is not going to be enough to stop him doing it again. Let's face it, at some time in our lives, we all repeat acts of which we are momentarily ashamed. I know I have.'

'Not on this scale.' Said Sobel wryly.

'This is precisely what makes him unusual. Anyway, whatever the reason, it does indicate someone with at least a vestige of emotional intelligence, however bizarre that may seem. Don't forget he doesn't seem to have expected their bodies to have been found. He's arranging them like that for himself, or for the victims.'

'You're saying he's capable of showing compassion?' said Caton.

Stewart-Baker nodded sagely. 'If you like, but only because he needs to...can't help himself. But not mercy, clearly.'

Caton checked his list of questions. 'Is there anything we can do to bring him out in the open?'

The profiler had to think about that one. He stared back up at the ceiling. 'Given how long he's been operating he may begin to feel the need for recognition...the need to trumpet it. But so far as we know he has shown no sign of reaching that stage where the frequency of his attacks fails to satisfy his needs. The stage where some serial killers begin to reach a crisis...to unravel...to come apart. To take risks that will inevitably lead to their arrest.'

'Like the Suffolk Murderer.' Said Caton.

'Exactly.' But there are others who don't, and are only caught by accident; like the Yorkshire Ripper, and Jeffrey Dahmer. But just as many are never caught. Like Jack the Ripper, or the Zodiac Killer in North Carolina back in the 1960's. And there will be others who never even figure on anyone's radar.'

'Like this one, had they not decided to start the open cast on Cutacre.'

'Precisely.'

'Now that his crimes are out in the open...Caton began.'

'Some of his crimes.' The professor interjected.

'...some of his crimes are out in the open, how will that affect him?'

'It's impossible to say. He may be tempted to play to the gallery. He may decide to stop for a while...to see how far you get with your investigation... then start again when the trail has gone cold. Or he may feel so sure of himself, as most serial killers do, that he'll just carry quietly on, more cautiously than before.'

It was the scenario Caton had feared most.

'Oh, and one more thing,' said Stewart-Baker.

'When you do find him, given that the bodies had been stripped, but not mutilated, you can expect to find that he has hoarded trophies of one kind or another. Clothing, jewellery, photographs, tapes, video tapes.'

'To enable him to relive the experiences without the risk.'

'Just so. Ordinarily I would say his over weaning self confidence would lead him to keep them in the home somewhere. But given the care with which he has sought to hide these bodies I think it more likely you may be looking for somewhere less prone to accidental discovery.'

'Like a safety deposit box?'

'I don't think so. Not enough opportunity to pore over them whenever the mood takes him. A lock up perhaps.'

'Or a Self-storage unit?'

'Now that would be perfect.' Stewart-Baker stretched out his feet, and sent the mug flying. 'Sod it!' He said.

A pool of coffee began to soak into a carpet already so badly stained that it was evident to Caton this was a regular occurrence. The profiler took a white handkerchief from his pocket, and used it as a mop, wringing it out into the mug several times before dropping it into the beaker which he then placed back on his desk.

'Where were we?' he said. 'I know…trophies. I'm surprised Tom, that you haven't asked me about the connection between the victims, other than their age, sex, and the colour of their hair.'

'I was just about to.' Said Caton.

181

'There is always something you know. Something that makes them vulnerable. Like their profession – prostitution for example, or something which means they work alone – like an estate agent. Or, as in this case, their addictions. They also seem to have one single point of connection; the clinic.'

'But we don't have any evidence that Charlotte was ever in the Oasis,' Caton pointed out.

'I'm prepared to wager that she was,' Stewart-Baker replied. 'Check it out. She had an addictive personality just like the others. It's too much of a co-incidence. I'll be very surprised if that wasn't where he met them.'

Caton walked back to his car, deep in thought. So preoccupied was he that he almost collided with a group of students as he turned the corner of the Education Research Centre. He had barely recovered when his cell phone rang. It was Larry Hymer.

'Hello Tom,' he said. 'I've got a story going out in the late edition. Thought I'd better give you a heads up so it doesn't come as a surprise. You might even want to give me a quote, though I doubt it.'

The hairs on the back of Caton's neck went up. Go on.' He said.

'It's about the connection between the victims, and The Oasis.'

'Christ Larry. How the hell did you find out about that?'

'…using my journalistic skills Tom, it's what I do.'

It was the pause before he replied that gave it away. 'It was a leak wasn't it?' Caton said. 'Someone inside GMP.'

'No comment Tom.'

'You just did. Why the hell didn't you tell me first?'

'I just have.'

'You know what I mean. Before you wrote it up.'

'And run the risk of Chester House leaning on my editor; maybe some kind of injunction not to publish.'

'We haven't even decided how we are going to pursue that line of enquiry.'

'Well it sounds like you'd better get on with it.'

'I can't believe you're doing this. Just because I wouldn't let you get close up to the crime scene'

'Don't talk daft Tom. This is a headliner in anybody's book, you know that. What was I supposed to do? Wait till one of the tabloids gets hold of it and steals our thunder?'

Caton knew he was right, and cursed himself for not making the Oasis a priority sooner.

'You could be blowing one of our leads out of the water here.' He said.

'Sorry about that Tom,' the reporter replied. 'But how was I to know if you didn't tell me?'

18

'I'm not sure we're ready Boss.'

Caton was in no mood for humouring anyone. Not even DI Holmes. 'What was it you didn't understand?' He said. 'The story is going out this evening. By tomorrow morning there will be reporters crawling all over that place. Paparazzi camped at the gates. That's not going to win us any friends with the staff or clients is it? So we don't have any option. What do we know about the Clinic?'

Holmes opened the sub folder marked *The Oasis*, and clicked on the link to the web site. Caton pulled up a chair, took control of the mouse, and scrolled down as he read through it. Part of the UK Holistic Care Clinics Group, the Oasis, on the outskirts of Northwich, specialised in the treatment of a range of addictions for both private and NHS patients. Four areas of service were common to both men and women: detoxification, forensic addiction treatment relating to alcohol and substance misuse, treatment for sex addiction and gambling addiction, co-dependency, rehabilitation, and the treatment of personality disorders. For men there were programmes for arsonists, sex offenders, and internet addiction. For women, programmes were offered for sufferers of anorexia, bulimia nervosa, self-harm, and shopping addiction. A sister clinic nearby provided secure accommodation and treatment for patients suitable for medium security detention under Section 12 of the Mental Heath Act 1983, and residential programmes for women who have killed.

'What's co-dependency when it's home?' asked Holmes.

I'm not sure,' Caton admitted. 'Why don't you look it up?'

He was surprised by the number of links that came up. The first was mercifully succinct.

Co-dependency, he read, *is an unhealthy reliance on relationships. It is often termed "relationship addiction". A learned behaviour, it most often results from exposure to abusive, controlling and dependent relationships. As with all addictions, low self-esteem lies at the core. Co-dependents may also seek to overcome these feelings by engaging in substance abuse, workaholism, indiscriminate sexual activity, or gambling.*

Caton immediately thought of Verity Parker. Maybe her outwardly confident hardworking exterior had hidden massive insecurity. It would not have been surprising given the bizarre nature of her upbringing. It would also have explained her ill fated marriage to the older man, and her rapid slide into addiction, and high risk sex.

'They offer in-patient, out patient and day care, Boss,' said Holmes who had already switched back to the Oasis home page. 'Must be making an absolute mint. And all on the back of other people's misery. Still I suppose if it helps them to recover it helps to cut our work down.'

'Not with these three it hasn't,' said Caton taking his jacket from the back of the chair. 'Not by a country mile.'

The tree lined tarmac drive opened up beyond imposing wrought iron gates and a high brick wall that encircled the property. Beech, elm and specimen conifers dotted the sweeping manicured lawns. Caton thought he recognised a Cedar of Lebanon, and a Californian Redwood

'Bloody hell Boss,' Holmes exclaimed as he swung the car onto the gravel lined apron. 'Would you look at this!'

The house looked more like a castle than a clinic, with crenulated ivy clad towers, stone mullioned windows , and a Gothic arched doorway. A clock and a bell tower adorned a more recent extension, itself at least two hundred years old. Over the doorway, on a white stone plaque, were the letters JCR, and a coat of arms. Two bay trees and a pair of sculpted box, in stone planters, completed the effect. It looked to Caton more like a five star hotel than a clinic; no doubt with prices to match.

The entrance led directly into a hall in the centre of which was a coffee table covered with magazines and newspapers, and surrounded by a variety of sofas and armchairs. On either side, a double staircase led up to a galleried landing. Caton spotted a porter carrying a large suitcase and small overnight bag up the left hand flight. When he reached the landing he paused for a moment to catch his breath, and stared down at them. He nodded curtly then stooped to pick up the bags and set off through a doorway on the left.

'I'd say he knew who we were,' said Holmes. 'Someone must have briefed him. I can't see him greeting paying guests like that.'

There was a sign marked Reception over the door on their immediate right. Inside the room was a standard hotel reception desk with a pair of computer screens. On the counter was a vase full of white lilies and chrysanthemums, and a brass bell push. On the wall behind the desk was a set of wooden pigeon holes containing room keys, and the odd piece of mail. On the walls were a series of framed photographs of woodland and lakes through the seasons. Caton pressed the bell, and stepped over to take a closer look at a moody photograph of a winter scene. The late evening sun, out of a grey cloud laden sky, threw leafless and partially fallen trees into sharp relief against the silver surface of a bleak expanse of water. He thought it an incongruous introduction to a place supposedly dedicated to healing.

'Shemmy Moss, in the Delamere forest.'

Caton turned to face the owner of the voice; an attractive woman in her mid to late forties. Black hair, brown eyes the colour of caramel, smart black suit, white blouse, and a red scarf. Her smile was polite, cool, contained. 'I know what you're thinking; it looks a little too miserable for a place like this.' She waved her arm around in a half circle taking in the other photos. 'But if you see it in context with the other three, it's actually part of a natural cycle in which spring and summer inexorably follow autumn and winter. It was our Director's idea. A way of reminding our clients that however bleak things might seem, a new beginning lies just around the corner.'

Caton was tempted to point out that it all depended on where you started; it was equally true that Autumn and Winter inexorably follow Spring and Summer; hardly an encouragement to manic depressives or struggling rehabilitees.

'You must be Chief Inspector Caton,' she said, lowering her voice so like a conspirator that Caton glanced over his shoulder on the reasonable but erroneous assumption that someone else must have entered the room. She held out her hand. 'Mr Weir is expecting you. I'm Sally Roper, Head of Policy and Marketing.' Her hand was cold.

'*Detective* Chief Inspector,' Caton corrected her. 'And this is Detective Inspector Holmes.'

She shook hands with Holmes. 'If you would please follow me?' She led them through the door behind the Reception, down a wood panelled corridor, past several doors, to one at the end of the corridor on which a gold embossed sign proclaimed *Jason Weir, Director*. She knocked lightly once, opened it, and stepped aside to let them enter. She stepped into the room, closed the door behind them, and stood with her back to the door as though guarding it.

'Jason,' she said. 'Detective Chief Inspector Caton, and Detective Inspector Holmes.'

The clinic's director, his back towards them, stood looking out of the single large bay window that dominated the room. Over his shoulder Caton could see a stone walled terrace with gravel paths and flower beds, and lawns that sloped down to a large lake. Weir turned slowly to face them, reinforcing Caton's impression that that this had been a pose intended to impress. If so, it had failed. It didn't help that the Director was short and stout, about five feet four and thirteen stone, which Caton found surprising for someone in his mid forties. Weir walked across the heavy duty velvet Wilton carpet to shake hands with the detectives, before inviting them to sit down in a pair of chairs that faced his desk.

'I would like you stay please, Sally,' he said as settled himself behind his desk on a chair that must have been ratcheted up to its maximum height. 'If Mr Caton has no objection.'

'None at all.' Caton told him.'

'Good, because I have also arranged for one of my consultant psychiatrists to join us.' Weir responded. 'There may be ethical and clinical issues that arise from our discussion here today, and I feel that Dr Vickers will be best placed to advise me.'

One of *my* consultant psychiatrists, not *our* consultant psychiatrists, Caton noted; and the decision already made without the courtesy of finding out how that might sit with us. Not that it mattered, all of the staff would have to be seen. Better sooner than later.

'Thank you for agreeing to see us at such short notice Mr Weir.' He said.

'And thank *you* for the heads up with regard to the newspaper article.' The director replied. 'It has given me time to tighten up our security. The main gates will remain locked to all but my staff, and our guests will be asked to come and go through a rear entrance via the woods, and a neighbouring property, that I am confident will remain hidden from the press.'

'You'll be lucky.' Gordon muttered just low enough for Caton to hear him.

'To be honest I was surprised that you hadn't asked to come and see me sooner.' Weir continued.

'Why is that?' Caton said feigning ignorance.

Weir frowned. 'Because as soon as it became evident that three of the young women whose bodies you have found had been patients here at the Oasis surely it was inevitable that you would want to ask some questions?'

Caton picked up on it straight away; Charlotte Mortimer *had* been a patient at the Oasis. That made it a full house. Too much of a coincidence. 'And when exactly did you make that connection,' he asked. 'That all three of them were treated here?'

'Well I can't say exactly when.' Weir began. From her position by the doorway Sally Roper came to his rescue.

'Four days ago, when you released Shirley Hassell's name, a number of us recognised it straight away. And then two days ago, when you released the other two names, one of our therapists came to tell me he had heard it on the news, and I told Jason.'

'And you recognised those names so quickly because...?' Caton asked.

'Because they were all patients who had suddenly ceased to follow their continuing care plan as outpatients, and with whom we were unable to make contact.' She replied.

'We make a special note of patients who seem to just drop off our radar.' Weir said, eager to demonstrate that he was on top of things.

'Why is that Mr Weir?' said Gordon Holmes.

'For a number of reasons,' replied Roper. 'For research purposes mainly; both clinical and commercial.'

Caton finally lost his patience with their ping pong dialogue. Apart from anything else he needed to be able to see her body language, to pick up the non verbal cues. 'I wonder if Ms Roper could come and join us?' he said. 'It's very difficult carrying on a conversation with someone who is standing behind you.'

'Of course,' said Weir, without conviction. 'Sally, why don't you pull up a chair over here?' He gestured to his immediate right.

She took one of the antique carver chairs from the bay window, and placed it beside him. She looked neither contrite nor the faintest bit embarrassed; if anything her cool demeanour had headed south towards the chiller. That's more like it Caton decided; us against them.

'What I don't understand,' he said. 'Is why, having made the connection, you decided not to contact the police straight away? I take it you saw, heard, or read, of our appeal for information? It wasn't as though we, or the media, were keeping it low profile.'

To their credit, this time they did look embarrassed. Jason Weir actually squirmed in his chair reminding Caton for a second of Detective Superintendent Radford. It was Sally Roper who replied.

'There were a number of things we had to consider first.'

'Such as?'

'Ethical issues...and the implications for the privacy of our current patients.'

'Nothing to do then with the reputation of the clinic once the press found out?' Caton asked.

'I resent that Mr Caton...' Weir started to bluster. Caton cut him short.

'Three young women, all patients of yours, are found murdered and buried in the same location, and your first thought is not for them, their families and friends, or the safety of your current patients, but for privacy and *other ethical issues*.' Said Caton. 'I don't think you're in a position to resent any questions we might put to you, do you Mr Weir?'

A pink flush appeared above the scarf around Roper's neck, and began to spread to her cheeks. Caton couldn't tell if it was embarrassment or anger. Not that it mattered.

'So let me explain what my agenda is,' he continued. 'Then we can all save ourselves a lot of time. Firstly, I need you to tell us about the clinic. What you do here, the kind of patients you treat, the staff you employ. Then you can tell us everything you know about the three victims. And finally, I'll let you know who we wish speak to, other than yourselves.'

For a moment it looked as though Jason Weir was going to object, but whatever he was proposing to say was interrupted by a firm knock on the door. A knock that was clearly not a request for permission to enter since the door immediately swung open, and someone walked in.

'Sheila, thank you for coming.'

The relief in the Director's voice, and on his face, was such that Caton instinctively turned to see who it was. She made an imposing entrance. The oldest person in the room – in her late fifties Caton estimated – she carried herself with assurance and gravitas. It helped that she was also the tallest by far; at least five eleven and a half. She wore a smart brown tailored suit, with the jacket buttoned to the neck, and the skirt three quarter length over high heeled shoes that made no concession to her height. Her immaculately feathered hair bounced on her shoulders as she walked. As she drew level with Caton her hazel eyes stared down at him through purple framed designer glasses that seemed to intensify an already piercing gaze. She held out an immaculately manicured hand just high enough to force him to rise from his seat. 'I am Doctor Sheila Vickers ' she said in a voice as cool and fresh as menthol. 'You must be Detective Chief Inspector Caton.

19

It was obvious that Weir was relieved to see her. More than that, he was eager to defer to her.

'Mr Caton would like some background on the clinic Doctor Vickers,' he said. 'You've been here longer than any of us. Perhaps you could tell him about it?'

Weir had not used her first name, as he had with Sally Roper, Caton noted. Not much doubt about the pecking order then.

'I am aware of the range of conditions you treat here,' he said. 'So could you could just tell me about the clinic, who works here, and how it works?'

She looked intently at Caton; trying to get the measure of him. 'We don't treat conditions here, Mr Caton,' she said. 'We diagnose conditions, and treat patients. That's what a psychiatric practice is all about.'

He could see that she didn't intend it as a rebuke, merely a statement of fact.

'We are relatively new, fifteen years old, and small compared with some of our neighbouring clinics, and others within the Group. We were set up to focus on a narrower specialist range of addictions due to the growth of demand for these services in the region. We have twenty five beds for inpatient treatment, almost exclusively for forensic addiction services. We also have a five bed unit for our eating disorder service for which we provide specialist outpatient, inpatient and day patient treatment. We have fifty full and part-time staff, of which twelve are full-time clinical staff, fifteen are part-time counsellors and therapists, and twenty three are support staff.'

Caton checked that Holmes was getting all this down, and then said. 'Could you break that down for us please Doctor?'

She looked across to the Director who immediately opened a desk drawer and removed a leather bound folder. He flicked it open, and started to read. 'On the clinical side there are our two consultant psychiatrists, five nurses –two of whom are nurse practitioners - five care assistants, fifteen therapists and counsellors working in three teams of five, and one social care worker. Five people work in catering, two porters, five cleaners, one on IT, and three on buildings and grounds maintenance. We have a health studio manager, two full time and two part time health therapy professionals, two in sales and marketing, and six in management, finance and administration.' He stared at the list for a moment and then looked up.

God, he's revelling in his little empire, Caton thought, when what he should be doing is asking himself which one of them might be a killer. Doctor Vickers was already launching into the second part of her virtual tour.

'The process is as follows,' she said. 'Following an approach, either directly or through a family member, employer, union, GP, or NHS Trust, we offer a free, unconditional, no obligation initial assessment of the potential patient within forty eight hours. The purpose of that assessment is to determine the nature and extent of the patient's condition, and suitability and relevance of our programmes in relation to that patient, and that condition.'

'Do you conduct that assessment yourself?' Caton asked.

She shook her head. 'No. That is always carried out by one of our highly experienced therapists. Where there is a physical condition, or detoxification is required, the patient will also be assessed by one of our nurse practitioners.'

Caton found it surprising that no doctor was involved.

'Once the patient has signed up,' she continued. 'Our multi-disciplinary team use the assessment to put together an individual treatment plan. I am always involved at that stage.'

'So each of the three victims would have had a different treatment plan?'

'No, not substantially different. Our addiction treatment programme is more or less standard, based on a proven twelve step therapeutic model.'

'So in what way can it be described as individual?'

'Every patient is different; medically, psychologically, and in their life style. Whilst the therapeutic model is standard we are able to be flexible about the way in which it is delivered. Some will require immediate de-toxification of between one and two weeks, others will not. Some will be admitted to an inpatient regime of anything up to six weeks. For the majority it will be one month or, more accurately, twenty eight days. In less severe cases we are able to offer day patient and outpatient treatment, but only following an initial, if brief, in-patient stay.'

'For those with alcohol and cocaine dependency what form would the treatment take?'

'For alcohol detoxification we generally use chlordazepoxide, a form of benzodiazepine, followed by a drug commonly known as Campral to reduce the cravings. There are no comparable drugs to treat cocaine addiction...' From out of nowhere Jason Weir interrupted her.

'But we are currently trialling a revolutionary vaccine developed in the United States,' he announced proudly. 'That blocks the drug from reaching the brain, and therefore prevents it delivering the high that the addict craves.'

'Thank you Jason.' she said, with a withering look that caused him to shrink into his chair. She turned back to Caton. 'It is not common knowledge that we are using this drug Mr Caton, and I must stress that Mr Weir has mentioned it in confidence. In any case, it was not available when these three women were here at The Oasis, so it can have no possible bearing on their deaths.'

'In that case,' he assured her. 'Your secret is safe with us. So how would they have been treated?'

'Well, initially we would have tried a number of medications used to treat alcohol dependent patients to get them over the early stages, but in the main it would have come down to the same programmes we use with all of our other addicts; abstinence, and cognitive behavioural therapy, or CBT as it is often known. In any case, only one of the three victims had a cocaine dependency if I remember rightly?'

'You do remember rightly,' Caton told her, knowing full well that she would have done her homework as soon as they'd heard about their former patients. 'How tough would these regimes have been?'

'Making the decision to commit to the programme is often the toughest part, since they will normally be at rock bottom when they arrive. If not, the withdrawal of access to their substance or behaviour of choice, followed by the initial process of self-examination, will take them there. After that, the only way is up. Our facilities are excellent Mr Caton. Every patient has a hotel standard en-suite room with the accessories and appliances you would expect; except an external telephone line. Room service is available, although we prefer and encourage our patients to use the dining room. The less they think of themselves as abnormal, or as victims, the better. You may have noticed that we pride ourselves as operating a Holistic Care Clinic. That is because we ascribe to the philosophy expounded by the Roman poet Juvenal.'

Mens sana in corpore sano,' said Holmes looking up from his notebook. 'A healthy mind in a healthy body.'

Caton found it impossible to hide his surprise.

'It was our school motto.' Holmes explained with a cheeky smile.

'Very good Detective Inspector,' she said. 'Close enough.' She tilted her head slightly and began to recite.

'It is to be prayed that the mind be sound in a sound body. Ask for a brave soul that lacks the fear of death, that places the length of life last among nature's blessings, that is able to bear whatever kind of sufferings, does not know

anger, lusts for nothing, and believes the hardships and savage labours of Hercules better than the satisfactions, feasts, and feather bed of an Eastern king. I will reveal what you are able to give yourself. For certain, the one footpath of a tranquil life lies through virtue.'

She smiled modestly. 'Not such a feat as you might think; we have a framed copy on the wall in every room. It is a perfect companion for our Twelve Point Plan. Hence, we have a gym, health studio, spa, and swimming pool. Some of the holistic therapies that take place in there include swimming, water aerobics, aerobics, dance classes, Pilates, Alexander technique, yoga, full body massage, reiki and head massage. Elsewhere in the building we hold individual and group therapy classes that focus on CBT, and art group therapy classes. In the grounds we offer horticultural therapy. Your victims would have had access to all of these. Once their chemical addictions had been treated these other therapies – especially the CBT – would have been used to work on their sex addiction, and underlying insecurities.'

'Not my victims,' Caton reminded her. 'Our victims...society's victims. When the community at large disassociates itself from victims of violence that's when our work becomes nigh on impossible.'

'That's very profound Mr Caton.' She said without a trace of sarcasm.

Caton turned his attention to the Director. 'Now I need to know as much as possible about the victims,' he said. 'Who treated them, fellow patients and staff who may have come in contact with them.'

Weir looked to his consultant psychiatrist in the vain hope that she might answer for him. Her face remained impassive.

'It's not that simple,' he said. This is a medical establishment. There are ethical issues and issues of confidentiality.'

'Let's start with the easy part,' Caton replied. 'These three women are dead. There's not much chance of them claiming a breach of data protection is there? As for your staff, none of them are in a privileged patient relationship with you are they? At least I hope not.'

'As a matter of fact, quite a few of them are,' said Sheila Vickers. 'All but one of our therapists and counsellors is a former and recovering addict of one form or another. Who better to guide a patient through the process? Empathy, not sympathy, is the key you see.'

'But I take it none of them is currently involved with you as a patient?'

'Not in the strict sense of the word, no.'

'So having a list of their names, and the opportunity to speak with them, would not constitute a breach of any kind?'

'No.'

'But as for our other patients…' Weir began.

'*Ex*-patients, 'Caton reminded him. 'Unless you have a remarkably high failure rate?'

Weir sat forward in his chair, attempted to pull himself up to his full height, and took a deep breath. 'You can have the victims records, and I can tell you who treated and supported them from among the staff, but I cannot give you a list of other patients who may have come in contact with them We promise, and they expect, total confidentiality and anonymity. It would destroy our reputation if we were to break that trust.'

'And where do you think your reputation will be,' retorted Caton. 'When it emerges that three former patients of yours were murdered, and you failed to co-operate with the police? If there is a link to this clinic the sooner we find it the better for your reputation. If there isn't, the sooner that's made clear the better. In any case it's academic, because without your co-operation I shall simply apply for a search warrant to cover your patient records for the relevant three years.

Caton could see that Weir was beginning to sweat. He looked again to Sheila Vickers who remained stony faced. Caton decided to help him out.

'We'll be sensitive Mr Weir,' he said. 'I promise to keep their names completely confidential. We'll agree to meet with them outside of their work, or home, if necessary. You can explain, and even act as a mediator if that would help.'

'I certainly won't have the time to do that,' Weir protested.

'But each of our outpatient clients has a sponsor...' Sheila Vickers said calmly. '...who could certainly fulfil that function.'

Her intervention was the shove that Weir had been waiting for. 'All right,' he said. 'If that is Dr Vickers' advice.'

'And I shall need the names of those people who sponsored each of the victims.' Caton said.

'They have all been police checked, Detective Chief Inspector.' Weir replied.

'A check by the Criminal Records Bureau is a precaution,' Caton said firmly. 'Not a guarantee. I need all of them...today.'

Sally Roper was despatched to arrange for the details to be compiled, although Caton suspected that had already been done. It took no time at all to discover that Weir had had no direct involvement within any of the victims, although he vaguely remembered having seen Verity Parker Smythe several times when she came in as an out patient. He was relieved when Caton let him go, leaving Dr Vickers alone with the two detectives.

'If I understood you rightly,' Caton began. 'You would have been involved in tailoring the programmes for these three women, and for providing on-going advice to the therapists.

'That is correct.'

How exactly did you do that if you hadn't actually met any of them?'

'I would have read their assessment reports, their life stories, and journals, and would have been given feedback from the group and individual therapy sessions they attended.'

'In addition to your work here you have your own private practice?'

'Yes.'

'And do you see any of the Oasis patients privately?'

She raised her eyebrows, affronted by the suggestion. 'No, that would be a conflict of interest. And unethical. I have referred clients to The Oasis, and I have on several occasions agreed to take on a former patient from The Oasis when they have exhausted the resources of the programme, but never for addiction related conditions…always for separate mental health problems.'

'Were any of the three victims ever private patients of yours?'

'No. Had they been I would have told you.'

'Might your colleague,' he checked his notes. 'Dr Kumar, have been consulted in relation to any of these women?'

'No.'

'You seem very sure.'

'I am, for two reasons. Firstly, Anish is exclusively responsible for our eating disorders unit, and secondly, he has only been with us for eighteen months.'

'What about his predecessor?'

'There was no predecessor. He helped to set up the unit. Prior to that I was the only consultant psychologist on the staff.'

'Don't your patients feel cheated when they discover that their fees don't buy them direct access to a consultant?'

'Not at all. We make it clear that is the case from our marketing material.'

That wasn't Caton's recollection, but he let it go unchallenged.

'Potential clients are also reminded of our procedures,' she continued. 'Before they sign any paperwork, and in any case they have the benefit of my experience and expertise through our highly effective multi-disciplinary team all of whom I train, advise, and supervise.'

She brushed invisible specks from the front of her skirt where it fell across her knees, and prepared to stand. 'Now, if there is nothing else I really have to go.'

Caton stayed her with his hand. 'There is, as a matter of fact. Since you were involved in the assessment of all three of the victims perhaps you could tell me if there was anything they had in common which might have led to them being singled out by whoever it was that killed them?'

'You're asking me to remember the details of three patients stretching over three years, from among one and a half thousand patients. I would need to have their case files with me.' She slid back her sleeve and looked at her wrist watch. Caton could tell that she was using it to avoid having to look at him.

'I find it difficult to believe,' he said. 'That you haven't accessed them since we released their names, either out of curiosity or to prepare for a meeting such as this?'

She looked up slowly, and he could see that she had done exactly that. To his surprise she as good as admitted it.

'There is a big difference,' she said. 'Between refreshing one's memory and having the notes in front of one.'

'Why don't you just do your best, and then we can both get on?'

She placed her elbows on the arms of the chair, crossed her fingers to provide a rest for her chin, and stared at an imaginary spot on the floor. What was it about psychiatrists, Caton wondered, that meant they couldn't manage to remember anything without the aid of the floor or the ceiling?

'Like everyone else in this profession I have at least an academic knowledge of the characteristics of supposedly serial killers, but I am not trained in offender profiling, so I think I should leave that to your own experts. I do however, have some experience with stalkers, and those whom they stalk. Am I right in assuming, whether or not they were stalked before they were killed, that you believe them to have been selected purposefully rather than at random?'

'We think it likely.'

She nodded. 'In which case, they will have been observed in much the way that a stalker tracks his victims. Depending on whom you choose to believe between one in six and, one in twelve women, and a quarter as many men, will be subject to stalking in one form or another during their lifetime. The internet has made it even more likely to be the case. It follows that most victims of stalking are as normal and ordinary – not that I believe there is any such thing - as you and me. In the overwhelming majority of cases the stalker will be an ex-partner who has been rejected. As I'm sure you're aware, over ninety per cent of women murder victims were stalked, and killed, by an ex-partner; the remainder, by persons who are delusional and, most often, schizophrenic. Sadly, the practice among young women today of indulging in short term relationships, and one night stands, can only increase the numbers, if not the percentages.' She looked up at that point. 'There is no such thing as a no-strings relationship Detective Chief Inspector. Someone is always holding the strings, and that person may prove reluctant to let go.'

Was there any evidence in their life stories, or their journals, that any of these women had been, or were being, stalked?' Caton asked.

She shook her head, her hair swaying hypnotically. 'No, which in view of what I've just said must sound remarkable. In reality, it's not. All three of these young women had such low self esteem, and need for affection at almost any cost, that they would not in my view have attracted the attentions of an ex-partner. Put simply, I believe that once their addictions got the better of them they would have been too high maintenance to be worth the effort. However, that vulnerability might have been what attracted them to their killer. Someone with a need to control who would despise their weakness, and perceive that weakness as legitimising his desire to humiliate them. Even to kill them. And don't get me wrong. I don't buy into theories of gender based victimhood. What I'm describing could – and does – happen to men too.'

She stopped talking, which gave Caton time to think about it.

'But according to friends and family,' he said. 'At the time of their disappearance all three of them appeared to have put their addictions behind them, and exhibited a positive frame of mind.'

'In which case, their killer might have thought he was losing them, or alternatively, he might just have got them exactly where he wanted them.'

'Either way, Caton said. 'The implication of what you're telling me is that unless their killer had been a former partner of all three, he is likely to have become aware of them in some other way, when they were at their most vulnerable, and killed them when they were beginning to recover?'

She folded her arms, and let his question sit there; unanswered.

He answered it for her. 'Which means that he met them here, or through a connection with the Oasis.'

Her sleeve had slipped back exposing her wrist watch. She looked purposefully at it, unfolded her arms, and began to rise. 'Possibly, but not necessarily. And I do hope not.'

She stood there for a moment staring at him, her gaze unwavering. Her eyes were devoid of emotion. It was as though she was trying to see inside his head. To probe his mind. And yet it felt neither personal nor intrusive; more a professional inquisition. Much as the one he had been carrying out.

'Now I really do have to go,' she said. 'I have a patient waiting.'

20

'It's going to be a hell of a list,' said Holmes after she'd left. 'Fifty staff, and God knows how many sponsors, not to mention former patients.'

'Well be that as it may, we can't afford to miss out any of them,' Caton told him. 'I'll be surprised if it tops the hundred mark. We'll just have to set up five teams of two. You and I can start with those that had contact with all three of the victims. No reason why we can't begin right now, with any of the staff who happen to be here. I'll set about prioritising the list with Roper. You get a copy over to Derek Waldon so he can check them on the PNC to see if they've got any form.'

'Weir reckons they've all been CRB checked.' Holmes reminded him.

'But he'll only have acted on ones that might preclude them from working with children and vulnerable people,' Caton pointed out. 'I want to know everything about them; everything.'

'This is all of them?' Caton said.

Sally Roper nodded. 'That's right. I double checked them to make sure.'

There were fewer names than he had expected. Most of the therapists and counsellors also doubled up as sponsors, each of whom had a cluster of mentees. None of the patients had been an in-patient with, or attended group sessions with, more than one of the three victims; nevertheless, Caton was going to have every one of them interviewed. Taking staff turnover into account there were only thirty four staff that had been at The Oasis at the same time as all three victims. Of those, one nurse practitioner, one nurse, two care assistants, two therapists, and two counsellors had had the most contact.

'I'll want to see these first,' he said. 'In that order if possible.'

'I'll try,' she said. But I can't guarantee what order you'll see them in. We have half day sessions of therapy booked in - morning, afternoon and evening - and we can't let our current patients down.'

'You don't need to,' Caton told her. 'Just do the best you can. DI Holmes and I will stay here till we've seen everyone who's on duty, and come back again at seven in the morning. The rest of my team will be here by nine am.'

'I can arrange for you to have dinner tonight, and breakfast tomorrow, in the dining room if that would help?' She said.

Either someone had had a word, Caton decided, or the ice maiden was really thawing. 'I'll get back to you on that,' he said. 'But if we do eat here I insist on paying.'

She started to leave.

'And there's one more thing you can do for me, Caton told her. 'I'm sorry, but I should have thought of this earlier. I'll need the names of all of the female patients you've treated for addictions over the past five years.'

She froze in the doorway. 'You can't be serious? Whatever for?'

'Don't worry,' he said. 'I don't need to question them, or bother them in any way. But I do need to check their names against the Missing Persons Register.'

The enormity of what he was suggesting hit her. The blood drained from her face, and for a moment he thought she might keel over. 'You don't think... surely...that there are more?'

Caton couldn't believe that it hadn't already occurred to her, or to her boss. 'I don't know,' he said. 'But I think we should find out, don't you?'

An hour later they sat in a seminar room that had been set aside for them to use, drinking mugs of coffee, and preparing for the interviews. On the lap top in front of them was the list of names that Derek Waldon had just emailed through. It listed members of staff with convictions. There were twelve in all. Unsurprisingly, seven, including the Director himself, had one or more convictions for speeding offences. One of the therapists had been done for drink driving six years previously. One of the porters had a previous for affray at a football match. One of the kitchen staff had been prosecuted for non payment of the television licence. Two of the counsellors, one of whom was also a therapist, had convictions for possession of cannabis, and amphetamines, respectively. As Holmes pointed out that was hardly surprising given they'd been addicts. Both of them had received conditional discharges, the condition being that they went into rehab.

'Obviously worked Boss,' said Holmes. 'Not only did they dry out, they copped a new job as well.'

Caton was disappointed. 'There's nothing that fits the pattern is there?' He said. 'No priors for low level sex offences. Either our perp is a late developer or he's been extremely careful.'

'If he's a late developer, he sure as hell is making up for lost time.' Holmes observed grimly. There was a knock at the door, and Sally Roper entered. She was holding a sheet of paper.

'Here are the names and times for the one's you're seeing this evening,' she said. 'I'll let you have the others before you leave. I've arranged for them to wait next door in the staff room.'

'You'd better let them know these times are arbitrary,' Caton told her. 'We could get through them faster or slower depending on what comes up. I don't want them thinking they can wander off, and drift back in at the last moment. The sooner we get it done the better.'

'I'll do that,' she said. 'Oh, and on the back of that sheet you'll find the names of the people that acted as sponsors for the three victims.'

Caton turned the sheet over. 'They're all female.' he observed. 'Is that by chance or by design?'

She frowned, not, Caton decided, because it was bad question, only that she needed to think about her reply.

'By chance. They could just as easily have been men. I suppose it was because of the nature of their addictions...'

'You mean because they were also sex addicts?' Said Holmes.

'Yes, because there was a sexual element to their addictions they may have requested, or their therapist or counsellor may have advised, a female sponsor; but it doesn't always follow.'

'I'd like you to add them to the list of people DI Holmes and I are seeing tomorrow,' Caton told her. 'Can you do that?'

'Of course Detective Chief Inspector.' She smiled brightly. 'And may I get you both some more coffee before I send in the first one?'

'No thanks, Miss Roper' said Caton. 'We're fine.'

'I think she fancies you Boss,' said Holmes when the door had closed behind her.

'I hope not,' said Caton. 'I've got enough on my plate right now.' He wasn't only thinking about the investigation either. Helen had not got back to him. He was beginning to wonder if she ever would.

'I don't know about you Boss, but I'm exhausted.'

Caton checked his watch. It had taken three and a half hours to see everyone on the list. He was bushed, and only relieved that he had not been the one making the notes. Beside him Gordon Holmes shook his wrist to relieve the cramp that had set in.

'I can see myself suing for industrial injury… repetitive strain,' he complained. 'Better still, early retirement on grounds of ill health.'

'Be careful what you wish for.' Caton told him. He ran his finger down the list of names. The two nurses, both female, seemed to be beyond reproach. The same for the two care assistants. Likewise the two counsellor's, both of whom had been through the mill of alcohol and sex addiction themselves, a combination that Caton was only now beginning to realise was more common than one might have suspected. The two therapists had had the most intensive contact with the three victims, and hence had come in for the greatest scrutiny. His finger lighted on one of the names. Gordon Holmes saw it resting there.

'Frank Croft. Now he's a weird one.' He said.

'What makes you say that?' asked Caton, knowing full well what his DI meant, but needing to hear it anyway.

'Well, for a start what's a man doing working with an all female group? Secondly, he's forty five years of age, and single. I'm surprised he's not still living with his mother.'

'He's not though is he?'

Holmes grinned. 'She probably chucked him out. I know I would've. And he packed in a perfectly good job with the CIS that brought him home ninety thou' a year, plus all the perks, and probably a massive pension, just to play mind games with a load of losers.'

'Cognitive Behavioural Therapy,' Caton reminded him. 'Which is a highly reputable technique and a damn sight more effective long term than pumping them full of anti depressants. Come to think of it, you could do with a few sessions yourself. And another thing, strictly speaking addicts *are* losers in more ways than one, but I don't think it helps to talk about them like that….especially not here. If it didn't start out as an illness, it certainly is by the time they end up here.'

Holmes shrugged his shoulders. 'OK, but I still say we put Croft under the microscope.'

Caton couldn't disagree with that, although he had a hunch it would draw a blank.

'What about the next one....Carmen Miranda?' Said Holmes.

Caton moved his finger down. Carmen *Sanders*. What about her?'

'Well she's out of the picture obviously.'

'Why obviously?'

'Because she's a self-confessed lessie. Why else?'

'Come on Gordon,' said Caton, surprised that his DI was still exhibiting homophobic tendencies despite his excellent working relationship with DS Stuart. 'She happens to be a lesbian. It's not a life style choice, nor is it a crime. It's what she is. Confession doesn't come into it.'

'OK. But it still rules her out.'

'It doesn't follow. She might have a pathological hatred of attractive, heterosexual, sex obsessed women. She may have a partner who is jealous of her association with these women.'

DI Holmes rolled his eyes. 'You don't believe that.'

'No I don't,' Caton admitted. 'But I can't rule it out, and neither should you.' He ran his finger swiftly down the remainder of the names. The art therapist and the three complementary therapists who worked in the spa and the gym; lightweight, every one of them. All female, all married with children, and nothing remotely suspicious about any of them. Not that they wouldn't be fully checked out. All in all though, no obvious suspects. There was a knock, and Sally Roper hesitantly entered.

'I'm sorry to disturb you,' she said. 'But there's a phone call for you at Reception. A DI Shepherd. Something about sending a fax?'

Gordon's face was a picture. It wasn't pretty.

'You know you wanted to know if any of the women who've dropped off the Oasis's radar are on the Miss Pers register,' he said. 'Well there are.'

It was worse than Caton had feared. There were three names on the sheet of A4. The first, Eileen Godfrey, disappeared in October 2007, seven months after Verity Parker-Smythe; the second, Laura Cuxham just over six months later in April of this year; the most recent, Noor Shada bint Umar – also known as Nadia Umar - 4 months after that, on August 12th, only two months ago. The intervals had shortened at a dramatic rate. It was the familiar pattern Stewart-Baker had outlined. The perpetrator was finding it harder to achieve sexual gratification by replaying his previous actions, and was becoming increasingly needy, arrogant, and reckless. Caton knew it would eventually be his undoing. But if they didn't get to him quickly more women would die, and at an ever increasing rate.

'I've already asked for copies of their files Boss,' said Holmes. 'It's not good is it?'

'No Gordon,' Caton replied. 'It's a bloody disaster. And you know what really worries me?'

Holmes shook his head.

'We're assuming that he only selects his victims from The Oasis. What if he's got other sources? Other clinics? Other places altogether? Thanks to Larry Hymer he'll know by now that we've made the connection with the Oasis. What if he turns off that tap, and turns on another one?'

Gordon Holmes nodded his understanding. 'You want me to run the Mis Pers list past all the other clinics in the area?' Said Holmes.

Caton nodded. 'You do that Gordon. Only you'd better make it the entire region. And let's pray to God I'm wrong.'

21

'Not bad are they?' said Holmes waving his second sausage barm. 'Bloody sight better than the one's in the canteen down the nick.'

'Watch it Gordon, you're spraying it everywhere,' Caton replied testily, wiping a splatter of brown sauce from the sheet of paper on which were typed the names for the morning's interviews.

'I can't decide if it's the sausage, or the barm cake,' Holmes persisted. 'Probably both.'

'The coffee's pretty good too,' Caton conceded. 'Only at this rate we're in danger of drowning in it.'

'I told you she fancied you.' Holmes grinned, and took another bite.

'And I told you to let it drop.'

'Mind you,' Holmes's words were barely intelligible. Caton quickly moved the list out of range of a spray of breadcrumbs. 'That Dr Vickers...now she's more your type...and what a challenge!'

In more ways than one, Caton reflected. The thought of having everything he said, and did, come under the scrutiny of those eyes, that mind, was enough to make you frigid. He finished his coffee, wiped the table top with his serviette, stacked the plates and mugs, and took them over to the trolley. He brought back a carafe of water, and three clean glasses.

'Just like the Selection Board,' DI Holmes observed. He looked at his watch. 'Five minutes before the first one's due. I'm going for a jimmy riddle if that's alright with you?' He got up and headed for the door, chuckling at yet another of his amazing witticisms.

'One of these days Detective Superintendent Radford is going to hear you saying that,' Caton called after him. 'And then your life won't be worth living.'

As soon as the door was closed he switched on his mobile and made a call. It had come to him at four o'clock in the morning, in that wakeful hour between deep sleep and slumber when most of his good ideas tended to surface. Mark Swettenham, former DI and colleague of Caton's, had got early retirement on ill health grounds back in the Spring. It was alcohol that did for him. Strictly speaking, it was his inability to cope with some of the more gruesome and heart breaking aspects of the job, coupled with his wife walking out, that had pushed him over the edge. GMP had been more than fair. Not least, by paying for him to be treated at The Oasis. Caton had thought hard and long about contacting him, but on balance he knew it was the right thing to do. He was just about to give up when Swettenham answered.

'Hello?'

'Mark, it's Tom here, Tom Caton.'

'Hi Tom. Good to hear from you.'

He sounded OK. Reasonably chipper. Sober at any rate.

'How are you keeping?'

'I'm alright thanks Tom. One day at a time, you know how it is.'

Caton didn't, not really, but he knew what he

meant. 'Did you get that job you were going after last time we spoke?' he asked.

Swettenham laughed. 'That depends on where you're ringing from, and whether there's anyone with you.'

Caton laughed with him. If the pensions people found out he was working they'd be onto him like a pack of hounds. 'In which case I assume the answer's in the affirmative,' he said. 'But I don't want to know.'

'You didn't ring up to ask after my health did you Tom?' Now he really sounded sober. Still too good a detective to fool that easily.

'No Mark, I didn't. But I am pleased to hear you're doing OK.'

'I know you are,' he said. 'And don't think I'm not grateful. You're one of the few who does still keep in touch. It means a lot.'

'You were a bloody good detective Mark, and a really nice bloke,' Caton told him. 'You've still got the respect of all your colleagues...it's just that the work piles up, and sometimes you don't have the time to see over the top...'

'It's alright Tom,' he said. 'I've been there, remember?' There was a brief pause. 'It's about the Bluebell Hollow murders isn't it? You want to ask me about the Oasis.'

'If you're not happy with this,' Caton told him. 'I'll understand. I thought hard and long before ringing you, but I know we're missing something here, and I don't know what. If you...' Swettenham cut him off.

'It's alright Tom,' he said. 'Really it is. Just tell me what it is you want to know.'

'In a nutshell, all three of our victims disappeared shortly after having been treated in the Oasis. More or less the same length of time after they left. So far we've found no other connection between them. And you know as well as I do it can't just be a coincidence.'

'I agree. What were they being treated for?'

'Two of them for alcohol addiction, one for alcohol and cocaine. All three of them for sex addiction.'

'Blimey, and I thought I had it rough! Which came first, the booze and drugs, or the sex?'

'Varied I think, but on balance it looks like the sex was an accelerating factor. Does it matter?'

'Might do. Cause and effect. Drinking to perform, or drinking to forget. I suppose after a while it would be impossible to tell which was the head and which the tail.' There was pause while he had a think. 'I'm guessing they would have been supported on an abstinence regime around the 12 steps programme once they were out, but if it was the sex addiction that was the trigger they would need support to keep their modified behaviour patterns going. Who are you looking at?'

Caton told him who had been interviewed, who was left. 'The way things are going though,' he said. 'I've got this nagging feeling that while the Oasis is the link, the perpetrator is on the outside looking in. In which case I have no idea where we go next.'

'What about their sponsors?' Swettenham asked.

'We're seeing them this morning. But I don't think it's likely. They're all women. No form.'

'It doesn't follow Tom. They might have sociopathic boy friends. Might be a witches' coven. Stranger things have happened.'

'But at the moment there doesn't appear to be any connection between them.' Caton told him. 'They were in the Oasis at different times. They live and work apart. Not known to associate with each other according to the staff here.' He heard Swettenham sucking his lips at the other end of the line. It made him smile. It was habit Mark had when he was thinking through a tough problem.

'I see your point,' Swettenham responded. 'There is one possibility…some of the clients, when they've used up their free outpatient allocation, turn to private counsellors or therapists. I didn't, partly because I couldn't afford to, but mainly because I didn't think I needed to. Got to throw the crutch away sooner or later.'

Caton could see another lead opening up, and an even bigger call on resources. It was always swings and roundabouts. 'How do they know who to turn to? Where do they get their recommendations from?' he asked.

'Like most things. Word of mouth referrals. Mainly from other patients or staff.'

'Did anyone offer you any recommendations?'

'Not me personally,' he said. 'But some of the others in my group told me it goes on. The staff are not supposed to, but they do. I wouldn't be surprised if it's a nice little earner for some of them.'

'Could you do me a big favour and ask around Mark? See if you can come up with any names?'

He had to think about it. 'I could try my sponsor, and a couple of the group I see from time to time.'

'That would be brilliant.'

'No problem. And good luck with this, it sounds like you're going to need it. I can almost feel Chester House breathing down your neck.'

'You don't know the half of it,' Caton told him. 'You're well out of it.'

'Too true,' he said, although Caton sensed he didn't really mean it. 'I'll be in touch.'

As Caton put his mobile back in his pocket, the door opened and Gordon Holmes walked in.

'There's two of them sat in the staff room right now, comparing notes,' he said as he pulled out his chair. 'That's hardly what we want is it Boss?'

'No it's not,' Caton agreed. 'So instead of sitting down why don't you go and fetch the first one in?'

As he watched his DI retrace his steps Caton chided himself for letting him get under his skin. It wasn't as though he didn't do his job well; it was more that he seemed able to rise effortlessly above the cloud of heartbreak and tragedy that surrounded brutal and coldly calculated deaths like these, when others like Frank Swettenham were brought to their knees by it. Caton's own sleep patterns had been badly disrupted since the second body was found. Maybe he, reflected, I'm envious of Gordon Holmes. And then he remembered that there might well be other bodies out there, and more to come. On second thoughts he decided, better to be haunted by it; if nothing else it concentrated the mind.

It was half past ten when the last of the sponsors left the room.

'Well I don't know about you Boss,' Holmes said, stretching his arms behind his back, and shaking his hand loose. 'But I don't see any of those having anything to do with it.'

Caton was inclined to agree. There was not a sign of anxiety or nervousness among any of them. They had been straight, honest and forthright in their responses, he was sure of that. If they felt any guilt it was that they hadn't managed to prevent it happening to their client. Not that Caton could think of anything they could have done that would have made a difference; not now that it had been explained to him. The point was that the initiative came from the recovering addict. They rang when they needed advice, support, or reassurance. It was not the job of the sponsor to intrude, to check, or even to monitor their recovery. They were there if needed. Simple as that. And all in their free time. No money changing hands. Just an empathetic shoulder when needed. Even in the middle of the night. According to each of them the last contact they had had with their respective clients had been upbeat, positive, even happy. That was the one thing that struck Caton. It was too much of a coincidence.

'One thing I have learnt though,' said Holmes breaking into his thoughts.

'What's that Gordon?'

'Well, if those three are anything to go by, sex addicts come in all shapes and sizes.'

Whatever goodwill Caton had managed to generate towards his colleague evaporated in an instant. He was about to reprimand him when his cell phone rang. It was Detective Superintendent Radford. Spitting feathers again.

'Caton? Is that you?'

No Tom this time.

'Yes Sir?'

'I've had Chester House on the phone. They've been fielding complaints from just about every private hospital and clinic in the North West. They want to know what the hell's going on, and so do I!'

'*Just about* every private hospital and clinic,' Caton replied calmly. 'That can't be right Sir. I asked for every one of them to be contacted.'

'Don't play silly buggers with me Tom,' Radford stormed. 'I haven't got time for it. What's it all about?'

Caton imagined him jiggling around on his seat, and couldn't resist a smile. He explained as quickly as he could, with due regard to his superior officer's medical condition.

'Christ,' said Radford. 'You don't really think he's been at it all over the region surely?' There was desperation in his voice.

'I don't know Sir, but I can't risk it. We need those names.'

'Right, well I can see their point of view,' Caton's boss replied. 'And if they want to stonewall us it could take weeks to get it sorted. So here's what we do. Instead of them sending the names to us, why don't we get Shepherd to send her list of names to them, and let them check them against their own records? That way they don't have to divulge anything to us unless there's a good reason to do so.'

Caton could have kicked himself for not thinking of it first. Radford had just gone up in his estimation. 'I don't see why not Sir,' he said. 'That's a great idea.'

'Good.' Radford already sounded mollified. 'And the minute you've finished there, I want you to bring me up to date. ACC Crime is getting anxious. If we don't get some movement on this I can see them bringing in reinforcements. There's already talk of Suffolk Constabulary sharing their experience from the 2006 murders in Ipswich.'

'I don't have any objection to learning what we can from them but it's hardly the same Sir, is it?' Caton said, well aware that he was being unnecessarily defensive. 'They were all sex workers after all.'

'Sex workers, sex addicts, what's the difference?' Radford demanded.

Caton wanted to tell him that the answer was obvious, but held back. The last thing he needed now was to alienate his boss. 'Let's discuss it when I come in,' he said. Now if you don't mind Sir, we've a few more interviews to complete, then I can come straight back to Leigh and give you everything we've got.'

Radford made a sound that Caton could best have described as a hurrumph. 'Better get on then,' he said. 'I'll be waiting.'

'*Everything we've got*, Boss?' said Gordon Holmes as Caton put his mobile away. 'What is that exactly?'

Caton was wondering much the same himself. Bugger all if truth be told. 'Who's next?' he asked, running his forefinger down the list. He felt his mobile vibrate and took it out again. There was one text message. From Helen.

I got yor lettr. Dont txt me back. And dont ring me. I need 2 think about it. Will let U know. Helen.

Well at least, he told himself, that's a start.

'Not Jimmy Riddle again?' said Holmes. 'He's a persistent beggar isn't he?'

'*Detective Superintendent* Riddle to you Gordon,' Caton replied. 'Now, like I said, who's next?'

The door opened, and in he came. Fred Hatch, the porter. Early forties. Medium build. Short cropped hair. Tattoos on the backs of his hands, and peering over the top of his collar. He licked his lips, but not nervously, his tongue grotesquely pink against the yellow of his teeth. He sat opposite them picking at what was left of his fingernails, stained to match his molars. Whatever addictions he might have conquered, smoking wasn't one of them. This had to be the football hooligan. Caton didn't need to check, but he did anyway.

'Something we should get out of the way first Mr Hatch,' he said. 'Have you ever been convicted of a criminal offence?'

His pupils narrowed, almost to pin points. 'You know I have or you wouldn't be asking.' His voice was husky. Probably damaged by the drink Caton concluded, or the fags, or decades of chanting on the terraces. Probably all three.

'Affray wasn't it?' Gordon Holmes said. 'Why don't you tell us all about it?'

'It was years ago,' he said, his lizard eyes sliding across to take in the detective. 'It's got no relevance to this.'

'Humour us.' Holmes told him.

He addressed himself to Caton. 'Ninety nine,' he said. 'Man City versus Bolton. There was a group of us surrounded by their fans down by the station. Your lot were off swanning around somewhere leaving us to get battered. Probably on purpose.'

'So you took it into your own hands, and decided to kick the shite out of a dozen lads half your age.' Said Holmes.

'You know how it is Mr Caton,' he said, continuing to ignore the DI. 'Guilty by association, that's the beauty of affray isn't it? You don't actually have to touch anyone, just put the fear of God into them.'

'And is that what you did?' Holmes persisted.

'What I did Mr Caton, was stand in the middle of our group advising our rival fans to piss off before they got a seeing to. Anyway, that's history. I'm officially a reformed character. Ask anybody here.'

'And unofficially?' Said Holmes pointedly.

Hatch stared directly into Caton's eyes, and smiled insolently. 'Do you put him in a kennel in the yard, Mr Caton, when you go to bed at night?'

'It may or may not be relevant to this investigation Mr Hatch,' Caton said. 'But you have shared *some*thing significant with us, haven't you?'

His eyes narrowed again, and his eyebrows suddenly seemed to touch.

'What's that?'

'Reformed or otherwise, you've still got an attitude problem.' Caton read his reaction as relief rather annoyance or surprise. That in itself was interesting. It told Caton that Hatch had something to hide.

The porter leaned forward. Far enough for Caton to smell stale tobacco and junk food flatulence on his breath.

'That's only because I'm being asked stupid questions by your sidekick here,' he said. 'The answers to which you already know. Why don't you ask me about those women, like you've been asking everyone else? Then you'll discover I can be as civil as the next man.' He looked pointedly at DI Holmes. 'And a damn sight more civil than some I could mention.'

'Alright,' said Caton. 'Let's get on with it. You know what we're doing here, whose deaths we're investigating. Just to refresh your memory, here are copies of photographs from the patient records. Just tell us what contact you had with each of them, and you can get back to your work.'

The porter looked down at the photos for a full half minute. Holmes was about to nudge him along until Caton stayed him with his hand.

'Take your time Mr Hatch,' he said.

Another twenty seconds went by, the porter pointed to the photo of Shelley Hassell. 'I didn't have much to do with this one at all,' he said. 'Just carried her bags in when she arrived, and took them down to the reception when she left. These other two, they had a harder time with the detox. Stayed in their rooms a lot more to start with. I took meals up to their rooms a few times, and I showed them how to find their way round the building; to the health studio and the spa, and where the GT rooms were, that sort of thing.'

'GT rooms?'

'Where they hold the group therapy meetings.'

'Did you get to talk to them at all?'

He shook his head. 'Not really…passed the time of day, the weather, that sort of thing. Patients value their privacy here. We're not supposed to intrude.'

'Of course, you'd know all about that having been a patient here?'

The eyes locked onto his; blank, unmoving. They had a similar quality to those of Dr Vickers, Caton thought, but without the intelligence.

'That's right,' he said. 'I came here to beat the demon drink; that and anger management. And as you can see, it worked.'

'You must have got to know the staff and the routines really well, what with having been a patient, and now working here.' Caton observed.

'I suppose.'

'You probably get to hear about what works for different people when they've left...you know, which sponsors are really good, private counsellors and therapists, that sort of thing?'

He shrugged. 'Not really. When they've gone, they've gone.'

'But some of them come back surely?'

'That's right, then they go again.'

'So if someone wanted to know of a particularly good expert outside the Oasis would you be able to help them? Maybe put them in touch?'

His eyes never wavered. 'I'm a porter,' he said. 'What would I know? You want to ask the medical staff. I would.'

'Well that was a waste of time.' Said Holmes

'I'm not so sure,' Caton told him.

'What do you mean Boss?'

'Towards the end, when I was asking him those questions about recommendations to people outside the clinic, did you see his eyes?'

'Well I know he was staring at you, but I couldn't tell much else...I was making notes half the time.'

'He wasn't just staring, he was blanking me. No eye movement, no blinking, no muscle contractions, nothing; dead eyes. You tell me Gordon, when do people do that to us?'

The DI nodded. 'When they're lying.'

'Or when they've got something to hide.' Said Caton.

There was a knock on the door, and Sally Roper

came in.

'Sorry to disturb you again,' she said. 'But your next one, Max Vine our Health and Fitness Manager, he's got patients using the pool at the moment and our Health and Safety Regulations mean he has to physically be there. Could you come over and interview him in his office? At least then he can watch them on his monitors?

22

They sat in the chairs reserved for patients needing to discuss their workout programmes. There was a desk with a computer screen and keyboard, pin boards on three of the walls, and a number of charts showing exercises and parts of the anatomy stacked up beside the door. One wall, made entirely of safety glass, looked out onto a fitness room full of aerobic machines and weight training equipment. A bank of CCTV monitors close to the ceiling covered the health studio reception area, a small gymnasium, and the twenty metre swimming pool. Caton could just make out a couple of swimmers doing lengths, and someone in the poolside Jacuzzi. Max Vine was outside, speaking to the Marketing Manager.

'Max is about right,' whispered Holmes. 'Maximum weights, maximum sit ups.'

'Abdominals,' Caton told him. 'They're called abdominals.'

'Whatever they call them, he does them,' said the DI. 'He's either training for the World's Strongest Man, or Mr Gay Universe. I know which one my money's on.'

'I've told you before,' Caton replied. 'You keep your homophobia to yourself; especially when you're on duty.'

Before Holmes could respond the door opened, and Vine walked in. Five foot ten tall, blue eyes, blond hair cut short and spiked, wearing a pair of loose track bottoms and a tight sweat shirt that emphasised the firmest muscle definition Caton had ever seen; he looked like a cross between David Beckham and Superman. Caton thought him a strange choice for a place like this. God knows what his effect on the sex addicts must be.

Vine's voice came as a surprise. For all that he still radiated confidence and strength, it was surprisingly gentle and high pitched.

'I'm sorry you were dragged all the way over here,' he said. 'I hope Miss Roper explained?'

'It's not a problem,' said Caton. 'As long as you're confident you can talk to us, and watch the monitors at the same time?'

Vine sat down in his swivel chair. It sunk several inches as the springs took the strain. 'They're right behind you,' he said. 'I have to do it all the time. You soon get used to it.'

Caton took the three photographs from the file Roper had given him, and laid them out on the desk

'Did any of these women use your facilities; the spa, the gym, fitness room or the pool?'

Vine looked carefully at the photographs although it was obvious that he had had plenty of time to think about it as soon as the details had been published in the papers.

'These two, Shirley and Charley, used the gym and the pool. This one, Verity, only used the pool I think. All of them would have used the spa and beauty centre I would have thought but you'd have to check with the staff.

First name terms, Caton noted. 'How did they strike you Mr Vine?' He said.

'Shirley was the youngest. A bit more fragile than the others I'd say. Less used to physical exercise too, though she'd come on quite well by the time she left. Charley, now she was the best of the lot. As a model she'd been used to exercising and it all came back pretty easily. Good swimmer too.' His finger lingered on the final photograph. 'Verity, now she struggled. She was the eldest of the three, but it wasn't just that. She was never really in to it. No previous experience you see...nothing to lock on to. And her mind was elsewhere most of the time.'

'Did any of them come on to you?' Caton asked.

Vine raised his eyebrows theatrically. 'Sadly, and surprisingly Detective Chief Inspector, no. Actually they rarely do. Most of them are too knackered, physically and emotionally when they arrive here, and my exercise programmes don't allow much time or opportunity for hanky panky. In any case, there's no way I would encourage it.'

Holmes raised his head from his pad. 'More than your job's worth?'

Something on one of the monitors caught Vine's attention and he watched it for a moment or two before replying. 'Partly that, but mainly because all of these patients are damaged in some way. Even if I did fancy them, and they happened to fancy me, I reckon high maintenance would be an understatement.'

It was good answer Caton thought. It was the one he would have given.

'One last question,' he said. 'Do you ever recommend

to the patients professionals they might turn to for continuing support once they've left the Oasis?

'All the time,' he said.

Caton resisted the temptation to catch Holmes's eye, but his peripheral vision told him that his DI had stopped writing, and was closely watching the health studio manager.

'And can you remember if you recommended anyone to any of these three women?' said Caton.

Vine looked down at the photos. 'Remind me, where did these three live?'

Caton told him, and watched as he opened his right hand desk drawer and took out a black plastic wallet like the ones used for credit cards. It was full of business cards. Vine flipped the sections over, stopping several times to remove a card. He placed one on each of the photographs, and sat back. 'There you go.' He said.

Caton and Holmes leaned forward in unison. Two of the cards were for health studios, the third, for a private trainer who claimed also to be a chiropractor. Caton flipped them over. On the reverse of the two for the health studios a name had been scrawled. None of the names were the same.

'Whether they're in here for the full twenty eight days,' Vine explained. 'Or as in-patients, it's never enough to keep them going after they've left. You know what it's like, people sign up straight after Christmas and they've stopped going by Easter. What they need is a personal trainer to keep them motivated. It's what I do in here,' he tapped the business cards with his forefinger. 'And it's what they do out there.' He gathered up the three cards, and pushed them across the table. 'You keep can these if you like.'

Caton put them in the file together with photographs. 'Do you offer this service to all of the patients?' he asked.

'Only the ones who come in here, and even then only to the ones who tell me that they want to keep up the exercise regime.'

'Are you on a percentage for recommending clients,' Holmes said before Caton could stop him. 'Or a retainer?'

Vine looked at the DI with a mixture of surprise and disappointment. 'Neither,' he said. 'It could lead to my being dismissed, so I'd hardly do it this openly would I?'

'How do you decide who to recommend?' Caton asked.

'That's easy. I only recommend people and places I know. I've got my own reputation to think about. Some of them are places where I've worked, some are friends or people I trained with. But really I'm doing it for the patients. That's why I choose places convenient to where they live.'

'Do other members of staff offer a service like this?' Caton said.

'To be honest, I'm not sure,' Vine replied. 'It wouldn't surprise me, but I really don't know.'

Caton placed the file in his document case, and stood up. 'Well thank you Mr Vine,' he said. 'You've been most helpful. If you think of anything that's relevant please give me a call.' He took a card from his breast pocket and handed it to the Health and Fitness Manager. 'Here, you can put it with your others.'

'What do you think?' asked Caton as they made their way back to the main building.

'Mr Adonis? Too good looking to have to resort to what our perpetrator's been up to I would have thought.' Said Holmes.

'I don't understand how women would find that kind of thing attractive.' Caton observed.

'You're just jealous Boss.'

'No I'm not,' he said a little too forcibly. 'I'd say he was addicted to the body beautiful. That's hardly a good example for patients with eating disorders is it? And there was one other thing. Did you notice what he said when I asked if he knew of anybody else flashing business cards around?'

'That he wasn't sure?'

'Check your notes Gordon. What he actually said was *"To be honest,* I'm not sure." And what's the first thing they taught us about people who say *to be honest*?

'That they're probably lying?'

'Precisely,' said Caton. 'That makes two that we know about. I wonder how many more have been giving us the run around. Come on, we'd better see how the others have been getting on.'

By early evening they were back in the major incident room in Leigh. Caton, Holmes, DS Stuart, DS Aashif Hassan newly transferred in from uniform, and Detective Constables Gerry Langham, Dave Wood, and Jackie Shaw; his core team.

All of the staff at the Oasis had been interviewed. On the face of it, there were still no obvious suspects, and no new leads, only the suspicion that there might be a link with someone on the outside. What they did have, was another stack of people to check up on.

'What makes it worse is there's no physical evidence that might link anyone to the perpetrator.' Said Holmes.

'Unless the perpetrator kept trophies.' Jackie Shaw pointed out.

'Trouble is we've got to find him first.' Said DS Hassan.

'I know it's relatively early in the investigation,' Caton told them,' but I don't like groping around in the dark like this. Not when there's a good chance he's not only still at it, but killing with increasing regularity. I think we should do something proactive.'

'Something to draw him out Sir?' asked Shaw.

'It's something DI Holmes suggested when we were driving back this afternoon.' Caton replied. He could instantly see from the look on their faces that they already knew. Holmes must already have floated the idea. That was one of the DI's failings; the inability to curb his enthusiasm, to pick the right moment. 'I think we should set up a covert operation. Put someone in undercover.' Caton told them.

'As a member of staff or as a patient?' Wood asked.

No Boss, no Sir, Caton noted. 'As a patient,' he said. 'Someone the perpetrator might see as a potential victim.'

Wood whistled. 'That's *really* high risk isn't it? D'you think Chester House is going to go for that?'

'We won't know till we ask them will we?' said Holmes hinting that he should just shut up, and listen. It didn't work.

'If it's going to be a potential victim,' said Wood,

with a smirk on his face. 'It has to be some one suffering from a sexual addiction surely? Any volunteers?'

Nobody laughed. He saw the expression on Caton's face and immediately backed down. 'I'm sorry Sir,' he said. 'Inappropriate.'

'Bloody right it's inappropriate!' Caton stormed. 'We've got three young women abducted, and killed, that we know about. Likely others we don't, and even more at risk. Anybody thinks that's grounds for a good laugh has got another think coming. Sort yourself out DC Wood, or get out of this room, and off this investigation.'

You could have cut the atmosphere with a knife.

'The essence of what DC Wood said was correct,' he told them. 'Even if the spirit in which he said it wasn't. What I'm proposing here is that someone put themselves into the mindset and role of a person with a sexual addiction, and play that out under the closest scrutiny of people who treat such patients every day. And what's more, they've got to do that knowing that our perpetrator could be homing in on them.'

'None of the victims were actually attacked inside the clinic though were they Sir?' Said DS Hassan.

'No they weren't,' said Caton. 'That's the only reason I'm willing to consider it. The real risk will be when they come out. That's when we'll be watching whoever it is twenty four hours a day.'

'In which case I'd like to volunteer Sir,' said Hassan.

They stared at him in a stunned silence. Partly, Caton knew, because he was an outsider – until he'd been here a while and proved himself – but mainly because he was Muslim. They were all thinking the same thing. How could a Muslim possibly be taken seriously as a sex addict? He could see Holmes's mind working overtime, trying to decide the safest way to put it. Only there wasn't going to be a safe way. Not without sparking off accusations of racism; and rightly so. So he got in first.

'Three problems with that Aashif,' he said, conscious that their eyes were on him. 'Firstly, you're still on probation as a detective, secondly, you've not been trained in undercover work, and more importantly, it has to be a woman. Always assuming we've got this right, you might be able to discover who on the staff is making recommendations, but not necessarily ones to our predator.'

'I am Boss.' Their attention switched to DS Joanne Stuart. 'A woman that is; and I've not only been trained in covert work but I went undercover half a dozen times when I was with vice.'

Wood sniggered, and Langham was having difficulty keeping a smirk off his face.

'My private life is my private life,' she said looking directly at them. 'Just because I'm gay it doesn't mean I've never experienced straight sex. And even if I haven't I'm sure I could fake it as well as all the women you've ever known…assuming there have been any.'

That earned a round of applause from the others, and looks that could kill from the detective constables.

'All right, calm down.' Caton told them. He waited until order was restored. 'OK Joanne,' he said. 'Convince me. You can start by telling us how you think you're going to persuade the clinic that you're a real patient.'

239

'PGAD,' she said. 'Persistent genital arousal disorder.'

'That's a disorder? Give me some of that!' said Wood.

'You should be so lucky!' said Langham digging him in the ribs.'

'You clowns have no idea have you?' She said. 'It's no laughing matter I assure you.'

'How do you know about it Joanne?' Caton asked.

'I read about it in a woman's magazine.'

'You haven't met Dr Vickers, their consultant psychiatrist,' Caton told her. 'Fooling her on the back of an article in a women's magazine isn't going to cut it.'

'I'm sure one of the force medical examiners could brief me enough to get by.' She said optimistically.

'There's no guarantee the force medical examiners will know enough about it themselves.' He said.

'Anyway, she's never going come up against the intriguing Dr Vickers is she? Said Holmes. 'She only gets to see a therapist and counsellor. Mind you,' he added. 'Vickers is that cold blooded she could do with taking a leaf out of a nymphomaniac's book.'

'It has nothing to do with nymphomania.' Said Stuart, who seemed to Caton to be well on the way to getting inside her part. Then she checked herself. 'Well actually, I suppose it has, but not like you think. What you call nymphomania is actually disinhibited sexuality, and there's a lot of evidence that that's to do with damage to, or small seizures or strokes, in the frontal temporal lobe of the brain. It accounts for some of the flashers and rapists we get, although I never knew it till now.'

Neither did I, Caton was thinking, and it helped explain some of those bizarre cases he'd investigated involving sex offenders living otherwise perfectly normal lives, whose behaviour seemed to have changed for no apparent reason.

'If that's the case what would be the point of going somewhere like the Oasis,' Holmes pointed out. 'Wouldn't you be better off with a brain surgeon?'

'You don't get it do you?' She said. 'What I'm talking about is physical engorgement when there's no external stimulus for it. Unwanted orgasms at inconvenient times. A bit like you getting a hard on in front of the Selection Board Gordon, or just when you're about to have a pee.'

'Happens all the time,' he said, in a vain attempt to divert their laughter.

'Why can't you just go on a bender or take an overdose?' Wood suggested.

'Because the connection between the victims is sexual addiction, you pillock.' She replied.

'That's enough,' said Caton. 'This is a serious proposition.' He waited for them to settle, and then turned to Joanne. 'DS Stuart, what do you see as the relevance of this condition to the programmes provided by the Oasis? What kind of treatment would it involve?'

'There are some drugs that help some patients – I would have to pretend that I'd tried all those. After that, it's a bit like treating OCD; obsessive compulsive disorder. Cognitive behavioural therapy and bio-feedback are both used here in the UK. Strictly speaking, it's more of a condition than an addiction. And it's one that leads women to feel real shame, and isolation, and loneliness. Not to mention buggering up their personal and family relationships. I could also pretend that it led me into on-line porn addiction as a way of trying to get some relief. I did a spell on that in vice.'

'You really have been looking into this haven't you?' he said.

She blushed. 'As soon as I heard you were talking about the possibility of someone going undercover, I remembered that article, and went on the internet. Half an hour on the web is all it took. And just in case you're wondering…yes I have discussed the possibility with my partner. She's thinks I should do it.'

Caton steepled his fingers, and thought about it. The room fell silent. He looked around the table.

'Does anyone have a better suggestion?'

On the way to his car he switched on his mobile. There was one missed call, from Helen. She'd left a message.

Ring me.

He returned the call on hands free. She answered after the third ring. Either she had been waiting for it, or happened to be near the phone.

'Hello? This is Helen Malone.'

A bad idea that, Caton thought, giving out her name. He would have to wait for the right time to tell her though. Not now, definitely not now.

'Helen, it's Tom. You asked me to ring you.'

Hearing her take a deep breath, as though steeling herself, he feared the worst.

'A fortnight on Saturday is Harry's birthday,' she said. 'Wigan Athletic are playing at home. It's a three o'clock kick off. If you want to, you can take him for something to eat after the game.'

Caton's heart began to thump in his chest. Of course he wanted to. But he hadn't been prepared for this, and the words wouldn't come.

'Tom?'

They came in a rush. He knew he sounded pathetic, too eager, too grateful, not the least bit cool. 'Of course I would...I'd love to...I mean...thank you Helen, it can't have been...you know...easy for you.'

'It wasn't,' she said. 'So don't screw it up.'

'I won't, I swear.'

'You'd better not. You can pick him up from the house. I've no doubt you've already found out where it is. Then you can bring him back here. I shall be going out with a friend, but I'll be back before you. Waiting for you. You'd better not be late.'

'I won't.'

'Good, because if you do louse this up it will definitely be the last time. Oh, and Tom...I haven't told him yet about you being his father. I don't want you to either. Not until I'm sure it's going to work out.'

'But...' he began.

'No buts. It's not up for discussion. You can take it or leave it Tom.'

He had never experienced this side of her; so hard, so certain. Perhaps that's what being a single mother did for you. Or maybe it was what they meant by maternal instinct.

'I'll take it,' he said.

'Twelve o'clock a week on Saturday,' she said. 'Goodbye Tom.'

'Goodbye Helen, and thank you,' he said. He had no idea if she had heard him, but the click as the receiver was replaced suggested that she had.

He sat back in his chair. Don't get too excited, he told himself. What was it Sheila Vickers had said? *There is no such thing as a no-strings relationship. Someone is always holding the strings.* There wasn't much doubt about who was holding them here. Not that he minded. Not if it meant he was going to get to know his son.

23

They were waiting for him on the fourth floor. Detective Superintendent James Radford, Commander Lillian Lucas, Assistant Chief Constable Crime, and someone he had never seen before. The three of them had their backs to the window. His seat was facing them. Classic inquisition mode.

'Take a seat Tom,' Lillian Lucas said. 'And thank you for coming at such short notice, and so quickly. I trust you didn't go through any lights on red?'

She said it with a smile, but Caton knew her reputation for safety first. At least she'd chosen to dispense with the formalities. He hoped it was a good sign.

'Perish the thought Ma'am.' He said.

'This is Harry Spencer from the Crown Prosecution Service,' she said. 'I don't believe you two have met?'

'We haven't had that pleasure have we Detective Chief Inspector?' Spencer held out his hand for Caton to shake. A firm grip, and enquiring expression, told Caton all he needed to know; he was nobody's fool.

'Mr Saxon may pop in at some stage,' Lillian Lucas informed him. 'He's keen to hear where we're up to with this investigation as I'm sure you'll appreciate. He would like to hear it from the horse's mouth as it were.'

The Chief Constable popping in was all Caton needed right now. He wasn't too keen on the metaphor either. They shot horses didn't they?

'I look forward to that,' he said, as enthusiastically as he could manage.

She raised her eyebrows just enough to let him know he wasn't fooling anybody, and picked up her briefing notes.

'Right, time is precious, let's get straight to it shall we? Detective Superintendent Radford has brought us up to date with the progress of this investigation, and we have a copy of your proposal. It's probably best if I let you know at the outset that we all feel very uncomfortable about what it is you intend to do. If you want to change our minds you're going to have convince the three of us of four things: firstly, that this is the only means of making swift progress in identifying the perpetrator; secondly, that it has a reasonable chance of success; thirdly, that it isn't going to result in the case being thrown out before it even reaches court; and finally, that you can guarantee that you will be able to protect your undercover officer. 'She glanced at the clock on the end wall. 'You have five minutes. Your time starts now.'

Caton managed it in less than four. Fail to prepare and you prepare to fail, had been drummed into him by his father. In any case, five minutes of one person's voice, even one as sonorous as his own, was more than most people could take. He waited to see who was going to start. He wasn't surprised when Spencer from the Crown Prosecution Service stepped up to the plate.

'You claim Detective Chief Inspector,' he began, 'that the only purpose of this covert operation is intelligence gathering.'

'That's right.'

'You are aware that evidence gathered by this means may well be ruled inadmissible by a judge... that it must therefore be about identifying leads that may result in evidence gathering through other, admissible means, such as questioning, and searching under, and within, PACE guidelines.'

'I am,' said Caton, resisting the temptation to point out that every rookie detective had that drummed into them, and that he, Tom Caton, was very far from a rookie, having been involved one way or another with more than a dozen covert operations, including having been undercover twice himself.

'There is no question in your mind that the actions of your officer might later be construed as those of an agent provocateur?' Spencer persisted.

Probably a barrister who's found a comfortable niche in the CPS, Caton decided. Not as well paid as working in Chambers, but a sight less stressful. He didn't have a lot of truck for them. *Championing justice*, was a neat little strap line, but too often in his experience it meant throwing out cases because they demanded too much effort, or might cost too much, regardless of the merits of the case, or the victim's right to justice.'

'None at all.' He said.

Spencer raised his hand to the ceiling as though invoking the Holy Spirit. 'Come on,' he said. 'She's going to pose as a sex addict, in the hope of ensnaring a serial killer. What's that if not entrapment?'

'I think you'll find that I've just explained that she will be endeavouring to gather information which may then enable my team to identify and arrest the perpetrator,' Caton reminded him. 'There is no question of her seeking to meet with him at all, let alone entrap him. It *is* entrapment you are talking about isn't it Mr Spencer?'

'It may not be her intention,' the lawyer countered. 'But what if in the process of gathering the information you need he becomes aware of her, and embarks on making her his next victim?'

It was a fair question. One to which Caton had given a lot of thought. 'First off, if he does it won't be because she persuaded him to. Secondly, if we have enough evidence at that point, we'll arrest him.'

'And if you don't?'

'Then we'll let it run, with every safeguard in place. As soon as we know for sure that it is him, I'll pull her out.'

Spencer turned to the others. 'This is exactly what I was afraid of,' he said. Have you any idea what the pay out was in the Rachel Nickell case?'

Caton answered for them. 'Seven hundred thousand pounds.' he said.

The ACC Crime looked impressed. Parker was taken aback that he knew, but quickly recovered.

'Exactly,' he said. 'A Home Office compensation award. From the public purse. There's no way we can risk that happening again.'

'I agree Ma'am,' Caton replied deliberately addressing himself to the ACC. 'Nor a wrongful conviction, or an acquittal on appeal. There is no way I would sanction my officer coming on to a suspect, feigning a romantic interest, pretending to be turned on by these murders. You've got my word on that.'

Harry Spencer was about to respond but Lillian Lucas raised her hand to claim the floor. 'You mentioned safeguards Detective Chief Inspector,' she said. 'What exactly did you have in mind?'

'Round the clock surveillance on my officer from the moment she comes out of the clinic. If a suspect does emerge, then we put twenty four seven surveillance on him. If it is deemed appropriate to allow him to make contact she will be equipped with covert audio equipment.'

'Listen and record, or two-way?' She asked.

'That would depend on the circumstances,' Caton replied. 'Ideally it will be listen and record. Not two-way. I wouldn't want to risk a perpetrator picking up on her facial cues when she's trying to listen to us as well as him.'

She nodded her understanding.

'At all times she'll have the means to defend herself – a taser, a rape alarm, and a pepper spray. I'll make sure we're in a position to respond if we hear anything untoward. The tapes will be open to scrutiny by the CPS, and if they have the slightest concern that she's getting into murky waters they can tell us so.' He looked at each of them in turn. 'All this pre-supposes that contact is made between her, and the perpetrator. I don't intend for that happen.'

'Maybe not. But if does, I expect you to come back here and justify her meeting with him, in advance of that happening.' Said the Commander Lucas.

'Of course Ma'am,' said Caton. 'I'd welcome that.'

'No you wouldn't,' she replied. 'But you'll do it anyway.'

He was happy to be rebuked, because it looked like he'd won her over; and Radford too, even if he hadn't said a word. Not so the man from the CPS.

'Do you intend to let the Director of the Clinic in on it?' Spencer said, desperately trying another approach.

'Absolutely not,' Caton told him. 'We can't risk anybody outside the team knowing.'

'When he does find out he's going to go berserk,' Spencer persisted. 'As will their lawyers.'

'He'll only find out if we actually identify the perpetrator. In which case if they do complain they're going to look mean spirited – more so if we've established a connection between these women's deaths, and the Oasis. If I were them I'd keep my head down. The less publicity the better.'

Lucas and Radford nodded sagely. For a moment Caton thought that must have sealed it, but Spencer had one last stab.

'The Oasis. How much is it going to cost exactly?'

Reluctantly, Caton told them.

Jimmy Radford came to life. 'You are joking!' He said. And that's not including the cost of the surveillance teams, and all that overtime.'

Spencer was trying not to look smug, and failing. Lillian Lucas looked pensive.

'What's the minimum we can get away with?' she asked.

'That depends on the initial assessment, and the programme the clinic comes up with.' He told her.

She shook her head. 'Well I can tell you now, I'm not authorising an open ended spend on this one. She can tell them she has limited resources. Enough for a one week maximum as an in-patient, and then she's out. If she hasn't got what you need by then she's never going to.'

Caton disagreed, but he could see it was the best he was going to get.

'Very good Ma'am,' he said. 'One week it is.'

She studied him closely. 'Don't count your chickens DCI Caton,' she said. 'I didn't say you can go ahead. I need to discuss it with DCS Radford and Mr Spencer first. Why don't you take a seat outside, and I'll call you back in shortly.'

It was like waiting outside the High Master's office at MGS. Something Caton had only experienced a handful of times but had never forgotten. He could hear their muffled voices; Spencer's louder than the other two; more strident. He had the impression that the odds were two to one in his favour.

The door opened, and Lillian Lucas invited him in herself. He thought it typical of her self-effacing style of leadership.

'Well Tom,' she said when they were both seated. 'Somehow you've managed to convince us.'

Judging from the scowl on Spencer's face, Caton thought the '*us*' a little too inclusive.

'The conditions I outlined stand,' she continued. 'And there is one new one. The Head of the Dedicated Surveillance and Intelligence Team has to be in on this. You'll be using some of his people anyway, for the audio and suspect surveillance, and I don't suppose he'll be all that happy that you've got one of your own going undercover, even if she has had covert experience.'

'Nothing less than I intended Ma'am.' He assured her.

She nodded her head. 'Good. Because your decision to check with all of the other clinics in the region has put the cat among the pigeons. I know you cleared it with DCS Radford, and I don't doubt your motives, but it's really got the gutter press going.'

Pigeons. Caton liked that. Rats with wings.

'Then you'll be pleased,' he said. 'To learn that we have all the responses in, and every one of them has come back negative. There were five missing persons, but four of those were male.'

'And the fifth?'

'A fifty two year old schizophrenic, who had been sectioned, treated, and released into Care in the Community.'

'Typical,' muttered Radford. 'Careless in the Community more like.'

'Well the sooner we let the press know, the better,' Said the ACC. 'That should slow down their feeding frenzy.'

'It's just as well they haven't found out about the other three ex Oasis patients who are still missing.' Caton said.

'And it better stay that way.' Her voice was steely. 'As for this covert operation, it had better be worth it.'

'It will ma'am,' Caton said, crossing his fingers under the table. 'I'm sure of it.'

It had taken three days to set it up, including a coaching session from one of the psychiatrists the force used on a regular basis, a briefing by Craig about what to expect, a visit to the hairdressers to dye her hair blonde, testing the equipment, and setting up the operational plan for when she came out. It was their final meeting before she left to pack her suitcase.

'You do realise you won't be able to have face to face contact with any of us from the moment you go in, until we wind the operation up?' said Caton.

She grinned, to reassure herself as much as himself he guessed. 'I'll be alright Boss,' she said. 'I have done this before remember.'

'Even so, I don't want you taking any risks in there.'

Her grin widened. 'I know one thing I will be taking.

'What's that?

'My cossie. Have you seen the pictures of the health spa? And all those treatments?'

'You go easy on the extras,' he told her. 'Don't forget who's paying for this.'

'Ah but it's all included,' she said. 'Be a shame not to take advantage of it. When I come out you won't recognise me.'

'I'll look forward to it.'

She pretended to be crestfallen.

'What did I say?' He asked.

'Typical man, It's what you didn't say.'

'Which is?'

'That I look just fine as I am.

'Well you do. Blonde suits you.'

'Too late Boss,' she said as she headed for the door. 'You've blown it. Now I'm really going to town. Manicure, pedicure, body wrap, full body massage, the lot,' she smiled and waved theatrically. 'See you when I see you'

He could tell that it was mainly bravado. They were all like that before going undercover. The downside was he was now twice as nervous about what she was doing, and already questioning his decision to let her do it.

24

'Haven't I picked you up before?'

From the moment she told him the address, and saw the expression on his face, Joanne had known this was coming. For the past ten minutes he had been studying her in the rear view mirror, trying to place her.

'I don't think so.' She said.

'No...I'm sure I have. Don't tell me. Where was it...Granada TV Studios?'

'No.'

'The BBC then, just off Oxford Road?'

'No.'

'I know...Old Trafford, VIP entrance.'

'Look,' she said, as politely and firmly as possible. 'I have never been your fare before. All I want to do is get there as quickly and as peacefully as possible. Alright?'

He looked in the mirror again, oozing false sympathy. 'I understand,' he said. 'If I was you I'd feel just the same.'

'I doubt it.' She muttered under her breath.

Fifteen minutes later the taxi dropped her by the impressive front entrance. He opened the boot, and took out her bag. She seized it, gave him the fare without adding a tip, and started to wheel it towards the doors.

'Good luck.' He called after her, not meaning a word of it. 'You're goin' to need it.'

You're so right, she thought, but not or the reason you think. She was met in the entrance hall by a bright and efficient looking woman in her mid thirties. Her name badge said Tania, but Joanne had no chance of pronouncing her second name correctly.

'Miss Wilson. Welcome to the Oasis,' she said in excellent English with a distinct East European accent. 'Please leave your bag there, and come through to reception. Don't worry, it will be perfectly safe.'

Tania led Joanne to the reception desk, and handed her a form.

'I wonder if you would be so good as to complete our registration form? I realise you have already done this on line, but it's important that our patients verify the details for us. I'm sure you understand?'

Joanne did. The last thing they needed was to have checked out their patients in advance and then find some undercover journalist or celebrity stalker was pulling a fast one. She wrote down the name she was using – Jane Wilson - her supposed date of birth, and the address of the safe apartment set up in Piccadilly Village by Special Ops.

'I'm afraid I'll need to take an imprint of your credit card,' Tania told her. I'm sure you understand?'

'Of course,' said Joanne handing it over. After all, she reasoned, who'd trust people who can't even trust themselves not to do a runner? The card was processed and handed back. Tania smiled her most engaging smile.

'Now I don't know if it was explained to you when you confirmed your registration, but I'm afraid I will have to ask you to let me have your mobile phone for safe keeping. You will get it back when you leave, I promise.'

Joanne handed over the pay-as-you-go cell phone she had been given for just this purpose. Her own was still in the shoulder bag she had with her. Not that she planned to use it during her stay, just in case the rooms were bugged, or her conversations were overheard. It was just a precaution, in case she needed to quickly get information to the outside.

Tania placed the phone in one of the pigeon holes behind her, handed Joanne a key card, and pressed the brass bell push. 'Your room is on the second floor. Mr Hatch will show you the way, and bring your bag.'

As if by magic a man appeared at her shoulder. Early forties, medium build, short cropped hair, tattoos. Joanne recognised the description Caton had given her. This would be Fred Hatch the porter.

'Room 203, Fred.' Tania told him. 'Miss Wilson's bag is in the hall.'

Joanne caught a whiff of stale smoke as he brushed past. 'This way Miss.' He said.

At close to four thousand pounds sterling, for six nights, the room was smaller than Joanne had anticipated, but it had a queen bed, an ensuite shower room, a desk and chair, fitted wardrobes, colour television, hair dryer, kettle and beverage tray, mineral water, and a bowl of fresh fruit.

Hatch placed her case on the trestle provided for that purpose, and crossed to the small bay window. 'Good room this,' he said. 'Nice views across the terrace, and down to the lake. You can open the windows, but only so far.' He demonstrated by lifting one of them a couple of inches until it reached the stopper. 'I'll leave you to guess why that is.' He gave her wink, crossed to the door, and turned to give his final spiel. 'Lunch is from twelve in the dining room. There's a room service menu on your desk. The phone is internal only; the list of numbers is in your bedside drawer. There's no alarm clock but you can set an alarm using your TV remote, or ring reception for a morning call. No morning papers, but you'll find some in the entrance hall, and the lounge. Your programme for today is also on the desk. If you need anything else, just ring reception.'

Before Joanne could thank him he had turned on his heels and slipped out, closing the door quietly behind him. Either tips were not encouraged, she decided, or he didn't need them. At these prices he'd have been lucky anyway. She walked over to the window and took in the view. Ancient rose beds sat among a gravelled terrace bordered by a carved stone balustrade. A broad flight of stone steps led down to a lawn that swept gently downhill for eighty metres or so to a large lake, the furthest bank of which climbed to meet dense deciduous woodland where only the yellow leaves of the larch still clung stubbornly to their branches. On the lake she could make out a pair of swans, and some Canada geese. She thought it a good setting for a weekend break, not that there was much chance of this turning out like that. She unpacked her case, and picked up the programme. There was a knock on the door. She opened it. A tall woman in her forties, with curly red hair tucked up beneath a nurse's cap, and wearing a crisp blue uniform, stood there radiating cheerful efficiency.

'Miss Wilson? May I call you Jane?' She asked. 'I'm Nurse O'Malley. I'm your number one.' She saw the confusion on her face and pointed to the sheet of paper Joanne was holding. 'On your programme there. I take it you've not had a chance to read it yet?'

Joanne laughed nervously. 'No, I was just about to. Please come in.'

O'Malley breezed past her, and put her medical bag down on the bed. 'Well there's nothing to worry about at all. Standard procedure, that's all. And aren't you the lucky one? You're not going through detox so there's none of that nasty stuff to worry about. But I will need to ask you a few questions, and check your blood pressure.' She patted the bed. 'Now you sit down here, and we'll have it over with in no time at all.'

Joanne sat down beside her.

'Now then,' the nurse practitioner said. 'Are you on any medication?'

Yes,' said Joanne. 'I've some prescription drugs.'

'Right then, can I see them?'

Joanne opened her bedside drawer, took out the two packets she had brought with her, and gave them to O'Malley who studied them closely, and noted the details on a clipboard.

'I'll have to keep these I'm afraid,' she said. 'House rules. Either Nurse Bhati or me will bring the dose prescribed each evening. When do you normally take them?'

'Before I go to bed,' Joanne told her. 'About ten o'clock or so. Do you really have to take them?'

'Oh I'm afraid so,' O'Malley told her. She lowered her voice conspiratorially. 'We've had some unfortunate experiences in the past here, and at other clinics and hospitals in the Group; very few, but enough to make us cautious.'

Since the pills were completely harmless it didn't really matter to Joanne one way or the other, but her worry was if they analysed them they would find that out. Even if they did, the theory was that they'd assume that her doctor had given her placebos, which might just indicate that the doctor thought she might be faking her condition. But then wouldn't that have been a justification for her being in the Oasis in itself? She hoped so.

The nurse practitioner placed the packets in her bag, wrapped the blood pressure cuff around Joanne's arm, held her stethoscope to her chest, and pumped away. As she let the air out, and the cuff deflated, O'Malley stared intently at the dial. Joanne suddenly realised that it was making her nervous.

'Well your heart sounds great, and your systolic is perfect for someone of your age,' said the nurse as she unwrapped the cuff. 'But your diastolic is a bit on the high side. Not that that's unusual on your first day in here. Why wouldn't you be a little anxious?' She put the equipment back in her bag and picked up her clipboard. 'Is there anything else we should know about?'

'Such as?' Joanne asked.

'Dietary requirements, allergies, phobias, panic attacks, mobility problems, that sort of thing?'

Joanne wondered if she should make something up, and decided against it.

'No, nothing at all,' she said.

'Of course not...a fine young thing like you.' said O'Malley putting her clip board and biro into the bag.

There was only a decade between them and Joanne was a little surprised but more than happy to accept the flattery.

O'Malley stood up. 'I understand that you're only with us for the week Jane. So it's going to be a bit more intense, and a bit more individually structured than might normally be the case. You do know that don't you?'

'Yes they made that clear when I booked my place.'

'Good. So have you had a chance to start your Life Story then?'

Joanne nodded. 'I need a couple of hours to finish it I guess.'

O'Malley beamed a smile. 'That's great, because you're due to see Diana, your senior therapist, for your initial assessment at three o'clock this afternoon. You've time for a quick tour, a spot of lunch, then it's nose to the grindstone. Is there anything you want to ask me?'

Joanne shook her head. 'No I don't think so.'

'Right, I'm off then,' she said. 'Nurse Bhati will bring your pills this evening, and I'll see you tomorrow night.' She paused in the doorway. 'Good luck.' Then closed the door behind her.

Joanne was getting tired of being wished good luck. But so far, so good. The meeting with the therapist would be her biggest test to date, she knew. Possibly the biggest test of all. A lot would be riding on her life story. She went to the desk, and opened the notebook in which the first four pages were already filled with her handwriting. They had insisted that she write it longhand. She assumed that had something to do with them analysing her handwriting, but she didn't really know. Maybe they were worried that if she brought her laptop with her she'd be tempted to use to it to access pornography. She sat down, and began to read.

It felt weird, because on the advice of both Craig and the force psychiatrist she'd kept as close to the truth about her own life as possible – just changing her name and blowing up into major crises the small things that had affected her as a child. That way she would have less difficulty in sticking to her story. So she had included things like being an only child, being bullied at school, and having teenage arguments with her parents about who she associated with, smoking, drinking under age; all of which had happened. She had described her first fumbling sexual encounters, and the sense of guilt that went with them. True again, except for the reasons behind the guilt.

The reality was that she had never really enjoyed her sexual relationships with men – such as they'd been – because they had never felt right. And even after she'd realised why, and had come out , she had only ever enjoyed sex as part of a meaningful relationship rather than as end in itself. Not that she was going to tell them that.

The recent stuff she had largely drawn from other women's stories in a PGAD support group on the internet, and some of the medical papers she had come across through the various search engines. There was a critical incident she'd invented about how she had been knocked off her bike by a taxi while cycling to work down Deansgate four years previously. That had become the trigger for her addictive problems. She recounted how she had suddenly lost the urge to smoke, and had then started suffering from persistent genital arousal. If that wasn't distressing and embarrassing enough, so the story went, she then got hooked on online porn. It had started as an attempt to try and get some relief, and satisfaction, because the worst part was that what others might have expected to be the upside of these inconvenient urges rarely happened. She repeated a description one of the women on the self help website had given; that it was like having a full bladder, and not being able to pee. Then when you finally do it turns out to be painful. That was as far as she had got. She looked at her watch, picked up her biro, and started writing.

Joanne closed the notebook. Jane Wilson's life story was finished. She checked the time. It was ten past two in the afternoon. She had become so engrossed she'd missed lunch. Not that it mattered because she was so nervous she didn't really feel hungry. She decided to go for a walk instead. Have a quick look around the Oasis, a breath of fresh air, and then come back and have a cup of coffee before facing up to her biggest test of all; fooling the senior therapist. She consoled herself with the fact that at least it wasn't going to be that consultant psychiatrist Gordon Holmes had been banging on about. Now that really would have been something to worry about.

25

'Miss Wilson. Do come in.'

Diana Lewis, the senior therapist, was just as Joanne had expected. In her early fifties, shoulder length brown hair, slightly unkempt; more natural than neat. Confident and self assured, with some of the guarded empathy Joanne associated with the many child protection social workers she had met along the way. She had smiling brown eyes behind which her analysis of her patient had already begun. The room on the other hand was softly furnished, not the clinical space one associated with medical matters. No desk, only four comfortable chairs arranged around a coffee table, on which lay a small voice recorder connected to a tiny microphone, three glasses, a jug of water, and a packet of tissues. There were several undemanding abstract prints on the walls, in muted colours, and high windows that let in plenty of natural light, yet provided total privacy. Everything designed to reassure. Almost everything.

'I am Diana,' she said offering her hand. 'And this is Dr Sheila Vickers, one of our Consultant Psychiatrists.'

The doctor remained seated, and settled for inclining her head a fraction in greeting. Her smile was less expansive than that of her colleague, and her eyes much harder; more penetrating.

Shit, thought Joanne. Now I'm in trouble.

'Dr Vickers would not normally sit in on the initial assessment,' the therapist was explaining. 'But it's part of our own appraisal process, so really it's me she's assessing, not you. And coincidentally, she found your case particularly interesting.'

I bet she did, Joanne decided as she nervously sat down. And I'm a case now am I? I don't like the sound of that.

'I can see you're a little nervous,' Diana Lewis said. 'But there's nothing to worry about. I do need your permission though to switch this audio recorder on. That will allow me to concentrate one hundred percent on what you're saying. There's nothing worse I find than trying to talk to somebody who is busy scribbling away.' She waited for a reply, and when it was obvious that one was not forthcoming said. 'Jane, Is that all right?'

'Oh, sorry,' said Joanne. 'I was miles away.' More accurately, her mind had gone blank in the face of Sheila Vickers intense scrutiny.

'The audio tape,' the therapist pointed at it. 'May I switch it on?'

'Yes, of course. I'm sorry, I thought you were telling me, I didn't realise you were asking my permission.'

Diana Lewis waved it away. 'Don't worry Jane. Like I said, you are bound to be nervous at first. It will pass, believe me. Oh, and there's a word I want you to try to avoid in here; *sorry*. I am not here to judge anything you have done, or might say. OK?'

'I'll try.'

'Good.' She switched on the tape, checked the level indicator, and pushed the microphone a little closer to Joanne's side of the table. 'Now let me first explain what this meeting is all about. I am going to listen to your story without interrupting. Then I shall ask some questions, just to clarify things in my mind and yours. Then you can me tell what it is you are hoping for; your goals if you like. And then I will give you some idea of the range of building blocks that might make up your programme over the next five days. Then you can take a well earned rest in the refectory, or the lounge, even go over to the health centre and have a swim or a sauna, while Dr Vickers and I put together your programme, and decide who else we would like to work with you. How does that sound?'

'That's great.' Joanne said

The therapist smiled encouragingly. 'Good, in which case why don't you start at the beginning. You can consult your Life Story as much as you like, even read from it if that helps. And there's no rush. Just take your time.' She poured a glass of water, and placed it close to Joanne. She eased her chair back a little, stretched out her legs, and relaxed like a child preparing for story time.

Joanne took a sip of water. Opened her notebook, and began.

'Well done,' said Diana Lewis. 'That wasn't so bad was it?'

Joanne felt completely drained. The pressure of remembering and retelling the story with as little reference to her notebook as possible had been exhausting. Not only that, but she had begun to get inside her assumed persona so well that to her surprise it had stirred her emotions, at one point enough to bring her close to tears. Furthermore, she suspected, it had started to surface things in her own life that she had managed to bury away in the furthest recesses of her mind for years.

'It was hard, but not as hard as I expected.' She said, taking a drink of water. As she did so the doctor leaned forward, and whispered something to the therapist, who then reached out and placed her hand on the notebook.

'Dr Vickers would like to have a look,' she said. 'If that's OK?'

Joanne was unable to stop a small involuntary gasp that caused her to choke.

'Of course,' she spluttered as she tried to get her breath.

'Here,' said the therapist, passing her a tissue with one hand, and palming the notebook with the other.

They waited until she had recovered.

'OK Jane. I'd like to check a few things,' Lewis said. 'You said that your consultant managed, through the drugs you are taking now, to dampen down the physical symptoms of your condition enough to make them bearable?'

'That's right.'

'But your online porn addiction remains?

Joanne nodded. Best to say as little as possible.

'So, what was it exactly that led you to decide to come here, to an addiction clinic?'

This was a part she had rehearsed so often that she was worried it might sound too pat. 'Between the PGAD and the addiction,' she said. 'I found it impossible to concentrate at work, to the point where I recently received a final written warning. My weekends and evenings are taken over by it. Like I said, I started losing sleep, and now there are some nights I don't get any at all. I don't go out anymore, except to work, and even then only because I need the money. I used to go horse riding, but I can't do that anymore, and I wouldn't dream of riding a bike.' She grimaced. 'I used to use the Metrolink but now even those vibrations set me off.' She looked down at her hands. 'It might sound funny but it's horrible.'

'I don't find it funny at all,' said the therapist. 'I can't imagine what is must be like, but it must be very distressing. In so many ways what you are describing is a very disabling condition; as is your addiction.' She paused for a moment to take stock. 'What about boy friends?'

Joanne shook her head. 'It's out of the question. Meaningful relationships with men went out the window two years ago. To start with, the problem was that as soon as they started kissing or touching me it would start me off, and that was anything but sexy. It was more of a cruel distraction than anything else. Not to mention that most of them immediately began to get the wrong idea. Not I that blamed them. Then when I got into the internet porn I found that no boy friend could live up to the virtual reality. Now I feel I'm a sort of stuck somewhere in the middle, with neither real life nor porn providing any kind of satisfaction. Quite the reverse.'

'You've been without internet access for seven hours now. How has that made you feel?'

'Actually,' Joanne told her. 'It's longer than that.

Because I knew I was coming in here I made a real effort not to go anywhere near it, starting yesterday morning.'

'And?'

'It's made me nervous, jumpy, and frustrated during the day. And I couldn't sleep last night. I kept getting hot sweats, unwanted arousals, and vivid images floating round in my head.'

Just when it all seemed to be going well Sheila Vickers came to life.

'Do you mind if I ask a few questions Diana?' she said.

'Of course not Doctor,' the therapist replied, a little too readily for Joanne's liking.

Vickers waited until she had gained uneasy eye contact from Joanne, and then said in an off hand manner that was a little too carefully crafted. 'It would have been nice to have your medical notes, Jane, or at least a letter from your consultant.'

'She's off in the States I understand,' Joanne replied using the statement they had prepared. 'Some kind of symposium I think.'

It felt to Joanne as though the psychiatrist's eyes were boring into hers.

'I see from your Life Story that your GP tried sedatives?' she continued. 'What effect did they have?'

Joanne pretended to think about it, worried her answers might have started to seem too glib. The problem was remembering to force her eyes to move to the left indicating auditory remembering, rather than to the right which would indicate that she was probably constructing a lie. Both Special Ops and the force psychiatrist had warned her that to let her natural instinctive eye movements take over would almost certainly result in discovery in front of specialists like this. That's why it had been so important to memorise her back story and all manner of responses to the kinds of questions they might ask. Then at least, they had argued, she would be remembering them rather than constructing them.

'They did make a difference to the arousals,' she said. 'But only when she put me on big doses, and then I could hardly function at anything. I just wanted to sleep all the time. So she took me off them. That's when she sent me to the consultant, and he tried this new medication. He said it would never be a cure, only a help.'

'Did he suggest anything else?'

'He did say a programme of cognitive behavioural therapy might help both the PGADS, and my addiction. He said I could go on the NHS list and wait six months for a place on the programme, or I could go private. Well I couldn't wait that long, so that's why when my employers began to lose their patience with me I contacted the Oasis.'

'That's one of the things that intrigues me,' said Vickers. 'That your employers have not offered to meet at least some of our fee.'

One of the things; Joanne wondered what the hell the others might be. 'I couldn't tell them about my problems,' she said. 'It's too embarrassing.'

'Mmm, I can see that.' Said the psychiatrist unconvincingly. 'Has anyone suggested ECT to you?

Joanne's heart began beat faster. 'ECT?' she said, hoping she had misheard.

'Electro Convulsive Therapy.' Said Vickers.

It was one thing to role play her way through some confrontational groups and skill based sessions, but the thought of being strapped down, and letting this woman zap her brain with electric shocks filled Joanne with dread.

'He thought that would do more damage than good.' She said just a little too quickly.

The doctor studied her for a moment or two, then nodded to her colleague, and sat back.

'OK Jane, you've been brilliant,' said the therapist. 'And you'll be relieved to know that we're nearly there.' A high pitched tone from the little black box warned her that she needed to change the tape. That done she said. 'So, what are your goals? What is it you want to achieve?'

Joanne already had that off pat. She worried that it was going to sound like a load of platitudes that they must have heard thousands of times before. On the other hand she thought that might work for me; make it seem more plausible. Perhaps it did, because it didn't elicit any response from Vickers, and the therapist smiled encouragingly throughout.

'Tell me Jane,' she said, changing tack. 'Do you believe in a higher authority?'

'Like a God d'you mean?'

'Like a God, or a Life Force perhaps. A higher moral authority at least?'

'This was better Joanne decided. At least I can tell the truth. 'Not really. I'm afraid that my view of God has been heavily influenced by those who claim to follow him.'

'What does that mean exactly?'

'That I'm more a John Lennon *Imagine* sort of person. Religion and war seem to go hand in hand. I think we have to be our own salvation.'

'That doesn't seem to have worked too well for you so far.'

'I suppose not.'

'Well I'm not sure that you've actually reached rock bottom, nor that the twelve point plan approach is going to work for you...' She looked across at Sheila Vickers who nodded her agreement. '...not in the space of a week at any rate.'

'So are you saying that I'm wasting your time and mine coming here?' Asked Joanne, worried that they might be turfing her out before she'd had a chance to achieve what she'd come here to do.

The therapist shook her head. 'Oh no, far from it Jane. We are far more flexible than that. Given that your addiction is not substance based – although I do realise that there are chemicals released from your brain when and if you do achieve orgasm, or at the very least some relief from your condition - and given that you are clearly going to have problems with aspects of our twelve step plan, in your case I'm thinking about a seven step plan.'

'What would that involve?' Asked Joanne, genuinely interested to know, and willing to try anything as an alternative to the ice maiden's *shocking* proposal. Diana Vickers began to tick it off on her carefully manicured fingertips.

'Step one; will help you take a good hard look at what your addiction is doing to you. Step two will help you to begin to understand why and how you have allowed this addiction to take control. Step three will set out clearly what breaking this addiction and recovering from it will mean for you. During step four you would begin to learn some of the skills and actions that will help you to begin the process of changing your behaviours, not just with regard to your addiction but to your PGAD as well. Step five will enable you to understand what you need to do, and put in place, to keep you free of this addiction in the long term. Then we introduce a reality check. Step six will introduce you to some of the facts about relapse, how to spot the warning signs, and how to deal with temptations, and those times when you may actually falter and lapse. And finally, step seven will help you to develop and leave here with short, medium, and long term programmes of action, and support. How does that sound?'

'That sounds great.' Said Joanne, hoping that she didn't come across as too enthusiastic, and wondering what the hell she'd let herself in for. 'But a bit scary.'

A word of caution,' said Dr Vickers leaning forward. 'Five days, however intensive, and it most certainly will be, is nowhere near long enough to guarantee that you will overcome your addiction, and learn to minimise, and live in harmony with, your condition. You will need to seek, and continue to use, support outside this clinic.'

'I realise that,' said Joanne. 'And I'm prepared to do whatever it takes, within my means, to get myself back on track.'

'And stay there.' The psychiatrist said pointedly.

'And stay there.' Joanne agreed, secretly wishing they would just skip the seven point plan and give her the names she'd come for.

Fat chance of that.

26

Joanne lay on top of the bed trying to relax. Her head ached with the strain of what had felt like an hour and half of interrogation. Even the exploratory tour of the buildings and the grounds had failed to shift it. She was also physically and emotionally drained. In the end she gave up, and decided to run a bath. While the bath filled she drew the curtains, and stripped off in the bedroom. Her clothes were damp from the sweat that had trickled down her armpits and inner thighs as she had laboured under the intense scrutiny of Vickers and Lewis. It suddenly occurred to her that if the rest of the week was going to be like this she wouldn't have enough clothes. That would mean having to rinse them off each night, and hang them over the towel rails to dry. God, she thought, it's like being back in the police hostel when I was training. She scooped up her underclothes and put them in the laundry bag she'd brought with her. Then she picked up the room service menu. Having neglected lunch she was starving. She dialled the number at the bottom of the menu, and ordered dinner. A veritable feast. To hell with it she told herself. You've earned it. Then she went into the bathroom, checked the temperature of the water, adjusted it, emptied a full sachet of bath salts and another of bath and shower gel into the bath, and climbed in. Then she lay back, and let the water wash all of the tension away.

Caton looked at the clock on the wall of the incident room. Had it only been that long? It had made sense to instruct her not to use her mobile unless there was a problem, but already he was regretting it. He looked around the room at the neat piles of paper whose data was being entered into the computer system by members of his team. Somewhere in that lot he knew would be a vital piece of information that would eventually help him to track the killer down. The trouble was that until some of the other pieces of the jigsaw began to emerge there was no way of recognising it for what it was. In the meantime all they could do was to keep collecting until they found a piece with a face on it. Hopefully that's what Joanne might be able to deliver. He found himself looking at the clock again. This, he told himself, is going to be the longest week of my life.

For Joanne it turned out to be one of the shortest. Doctor Vickers had been right about the intensive nature of the experience, and Joanne had no trouble sleeping. Each night she crawled into bed exhausted. She wondered if it was like this for all of the patients, or because they were trying to cram four weeks therapy into one.

Day two of her stay, and the first of her programme, began with an introduction to a supposed self-help group. Destruction group was how she would later describe it. At the beginning she suspected that this particular group had been put together with the sole purpose of breaking her down. Quite soon, however, it became obvious that they had been together for some time, and had been briefed to do a job on her.

There were eleven of them sat in a circle, with an empty chair for her. Diana Lewis sat outside the circle observing in silence. Five of them were fighting alcohol addiction, three of them drugs. One was addicted to gambling, one to love, and, to her dismay, the one sitting immediately opposite her introduced himself as a porn addict. They stared at her intently, like a group of medical students watching a dissection. She had never felt so exposed. Her brain told her to get out of there. Her feet were rooted to the spot.

She was invited to tell her story. In the main they listened in silence, but every now and then somebody would mutter something like *bullshit*; *pull the other one*; *load of bollocks*; and, *who the hell does she think she's kidding?* If it was meant to destabilise her it worked. What started off as a blush turned into a hot flush that spread from her chest up to her neck, and across her face. That prompted a cold sweat, and her words began to falter. She prayed that they didn't realise that these reactions were because she was lying.

When her story was told they began to question her. Belittling her replies. Making ever growing accusations.

'You're a fucking hypochondriac aren't you? Aren't you?'
'Admit it girl. You're a filthy whore!'
'You're excuses are pathetic, just like you!'
'You're no more serious about becoming addiction free than going to the moon!'

She waited for the intervention from the therapist that never came. When she had finally burst into tears, they were genuine.

In her mind Joanne was age thirteen, and in her high school playground, surrounded by a jeering circle of girls; some of them her supposed best friends. Her crime was twofold; to have been one of the brightest in her class; and for her single mother not to have been able to afford to send her on the class trip. This single piece of mob bullying had not been the worst of it. It was being sent to Coventry for the rest of the term that had led her to plead to be moved to another school. And now she realised that she had spent the rest of her life believing that she had been a coward to run away from them. Not to have faced them down.

She was still sobbing when the first arm encircled her, quickly followed by another, and another, until she was the centre of the biggest, warmest group hug that she had ever experienced.

'I have a secret to tell you Jane,' Diana Lewis had told her when they were all seated. 'Everybody else here is in the final week of their programme with us. They have reached the stage where they feel ready to go and face their demons armed with the self knowledge, the skills, and the tools they have developed in their time here. Today is an opportunity for them to show how far they have come by helping you to start off on that same journey. Believe me, you could not be in better hands. And now, we are going to have a break. Ten minutes everyone.'

In the session up to lunch the group shared with her their own experiences, focusing on the reasons why they had allowed their addictions to take hold. Then, through what she thought was incredibly skilled and sensitive questioning; they helped her to do the same. In some ways she had found this even more challenging than the first part because it meant she had to work so hard to remember her back story in detail, and extrapolate from that. After lunch they explained what starting to break free from their addictions had meant for each of them, and invited her to describe how doing so herself would change her life. By the end of the day she was so deep into her role that she had almost forgotten her real purpose here. She was also surprised to discover that she felt real warmth towards some of the group. Some…but not all.

On the third and fourth days, from nine in the morning until seven in the evening, she attended a mixture of one to one and group sessions that focused on cognitive behavioural therapy techniques. So intense were these that she was advised to break them up with visits to the health studio, and walks around the grounds. Twice she used the swimming pool, Jacuzzi, sauna and steam rooms. On one occasion she had a spell on the aerobic machines deliberately so that she could seek advice from Max Vine the health studio manager. She found him knowledgeable, professional, and friendly. But nothing more.

On the fifth day the morning and afternoon were spent on alternative techniques and practising those she had already learnt. The evening session involved a group session to which former and recovering sex addicts - one was now a therapist and most of the others were sponsors - shared their experiences of their painful journey down the road to recovery. A journey, she was constantly reminded, that would never end. At the end of the session, one of the group was introduced to her as the person who would sponsor her after she left the Oasis.

Marcia Coyne was a brunette, in her late forties. On both counts, probably lucky to have fallen outside of the predator's target group Joanne reflected. She had a pretty face, but sad eyes, and a very serious manner.

'It's not going to be easy,' she told Joanne. 'But if you've come this far, you can make it. I'll be there for you night and day, at the end of the telephone,' she smiled briefly. 'Preferably before midnight, but if you're really desperate don't hesitate. You can email me too. Less chance of being overheard. If things get really bad I can meet up with you, either here at the Oasis or somewhere inconspicuous; a coffee bar, a pub, whatever. The point is you are not alone.'

'What about your partner?' Joanne replied. 'It must be a nightmare for...'

Marcia Coyne smiled again. 'Her,' she said helping Joanne out of her dilemma. 'It was hard at first, but a damn sight less than before I came into the Oasis. My partner's just glad to have got me back. The real me, not the sex obsessed lunatic I became. In any case, I still contact my own sponsor from time to time; I call it charging the batteries.'

Blimey, Joanne was thinking, so much for my Gaydar. But then if I hadn't got her down as lesbian there's a chance she hasn't seen through me either. 'There is one thing,' she said, 'When I leave here, if I need more professional support where am I going to find it?'

Her sponsor looked surprised. 'Why here,' she said. 'That's where I got it from. You do know you have a certain number of free outpatient sessions included in your package?'

'Yes. But I've paid for a week's programme so there's a limit to how many sessions I can access.'

Marcia Coyne pulled a face. 'I'm not sure that's entirely true. But even if it is, after you've used them up unless you're prepared to rely on the NHS you're still going to have to pay for specialist support. I can't help you there; you'd have to ask around. If I were you I wouldn't worry about that now. The odds are you won't need it. Tell yourself you need a crutch and you'll never believe you can walk without one.' She tapped her forehead. 'It's all about positive thinking; you must have learnt that much in here.'

Day six went past in a blur. It was all about planning. There was a quick recap of everything she had learned, then a session of visioning how she wanted her life to be, and then the putting of the building blocks into place. By the end of the afternoon it felt as though every 'i' had been dotted and every 't' crossed; all eventualities planned for.

'Only life isn't like that,' the senior therapist told her. 'As sure as I'm standing here, something will happen out of the blue, when you least expect it, and like an earthquake, avalanche, or tsunami, it will threaten to sweep all of this away. And at that moment you will stand or fall on the strength of your resolve. And if you think for a moment that you are going to fall, you've got to…?'

'Ring my sponsor. Ring Marcia.'

Lewis smiled. 'Exactly. And she'll listen. And

between your telling, her listening, and the questions that she asks, you will remember why you came to the Oasis, what you learned here, and why you are not going to fall.'

'And if I do?'

'Then at least between the two of you you'll know how to get back up again.'

Joanne zipped up her bag, and looked around the room. So intense had been the experience, heightened further by the stress of staying in role, that it seemed like she had been here two nights, not six. It also felt as though she had run two consecutive marathons; one with her body, one with her mind. And what did she have to show for it? A better understanding of what it was to be an addict, greater self awareness, and some insight into her own fragilities, and where they had come from. The most important thing she had discovered was that to some extent her work had become an addiction through which she was diverting herself from having to face up to the way her childhood and adolescent years had been affected by her uncertain sexuality, and the way it sometimes played itself out in her relationship with her partner Abbie. Funny that, she reflected. Here I am in The Oasis, thinking about Abbie. It was something she now meant to address. To put the past to rest, and sort out her work life balance that the Boss was always droning on about. Some of the CBT techniques would come in handy after all.

But as for the investigation, she had learned absolutely nothing. Nobody had made the slightest approach, or made any recommendation. Several people – her sponsor and Diana Lewis in particular – had made a point of not being able or willing to do such a thing. She suspected that in the case of Lewis it was because the Oasis was first and foremost a business, so why would she want to support the competition?

She heaved the suitcase from the bed, and wheeled it over to the door. The taxi would be here shortly; there was no point in keeping it waiting with the meter running, even if it was Chester House picking up the tab. As she reached for the handle, there was a knock on the door. She opened it, and found Fred Hatch the porter standing there.

'I've come to take your bag Miss.' He said.

'I didn't ring reception for anyone,' she replied.

'I know Miss,' he said. 'But when you ask them to get you a taxi they automatically arrange for one of us to collect the cases shortly before it's due to arrive. All part of the service.'

'I'm sorry,' Joanne said. 'But I'm afraid I don't have any change to give you a tip.'

'It's not necessary,' the porter grinned, showing his atrocious teeth. 'In fact it's actively discouraged. You needn't worry, I'm very well remunerated.'

'I'm sure you are.' Joanne was minded to tell him she could manage all the same, but it seemed unnecessarily churlish, he was after all only doing his job. She pulled the case level with her, and angled the hand towards him. 'Thank you.' She said.

To her surprise, he didn't take it. Instead he appeared to be feeling in his trouser pocket. For a moment she suspected the worst until his hand emerged holding two business cards.

'Maybe I could give *you* a tip?' he said holding them out towards her.

'What's that?' she asked with what she hoped was the right combination of curiosity and suspicion.

'These are the contact details of a couple of people who I know have been extremely helpful to people like you once they left here. It can be very hard out there on your own. And these two are highly regarded. Very professional.'

Joanne took the cards and read them. The first was a woman: Madeline Hunt UKCP Registered. DipCP. DipCT. European Certificate for Psychotherapy.

The second was also a psychotherapist: Simon Stone. Psychotherapist. CPEAB Certified, DipCP, DipCT. Dip.CAH. Specialising in Cognitive Behavioural Therapy, Narrative Therapy, and Hypno-Psychotherapy.

'He's particularly good I'm told,' said Hatch pointing to the uppermost card. 'Mr Stone.'

'I'm not sure I'd want to see a man.' Said Joanne feigning hesitance.

'Can't speak from personal experience obviously,' said the porter as he took the handle of her case. 'But he's very popular with the women by all accounts. Put it this way…I've never known any of them to complain.'

27

The taxi dropped her off outside the entrance to the apartments in Piccadilly Village. Mercifully, the driver had remained silent throughout the journey. Presumably, Joanne guessed, his discretion was one of the reasons that the Oasis used him. Unfortunately, his discretion was not matched by his powers of observation because had it been he would have noticed the silver Nissan Micra that had tailed them all the way from the clinic, and had just pulled in to the kerb eighty metres behind them.

Before she could get her key out of her pocket the door of the apartment opened from the inside. It was Tom Caton; in navy blue overalls with some kind of company logo on the lapel.

'Welcome back,' he said, grinning all over his face.

'Bloody hell, Boss,' she said, relief flooding her veins. 'You frightened me half to death.'

He stepped back into the hallway to let her inside. 'You'd better stop saying *Boss* or you're going blow your cover before you've started.'

She closed the door behind her. 'Before I've started? You must be joking. You've no idea what I went through in there.'

'So tell me about it.' He led the way into the lounge diner where a member of the surveillance team, dressed in identical overalls, was sitting by the breakfast bar. 'As far as the rest of the world is concerned Clarke and I are electrical contractors doing some maintenance for the landlord,' Caton explained. 'Clarke has brought your covert audio equipment. You don't need to wear it all the time, only if and when you know you're going to make contact with a suspect. He needs to fit you up, test it, and make sure you know how to use it.'

'I've done this before you know.' She reminded him.

'With respect ma'am, that was three years ago,' Clarke said getting off his stool. 'Things have moved on. I'll show you.'

Clarke had left some time ago. Joanne had told Caton everything about her stay in the Oasis. Now they sat on the sofa nursing mugs of coffee.

'So apart from the porter no one came up with any names?' He said.

'Nope.'

'What about the manager of the health studio, what's his name?'

'Vine, Max Vine.'

'That's the one. Gordon had him down as a distinct possibility.'

'Sorry to disappoint you. I gave him every opportunity.'

'How so?'

'I told him I'd quite like to start training regularly but I wasn't sure where best to go.'

'What did he say to that?'

'That there were plenty of places around. His

advice was to get a free trial, including a session from a personal trainer, and find one that suited me before I signed up to anything.'

'Good advice,' Caton looked her up and down. 'Why don't you give it a try?'

'You cheeky beggar,' she spluttered. 'I bet I'm a damn sight fitter than you are.'

'In you dreams.'

'Tell me about tomorrow,' Caton said.

'What about it?'

'Humour me,' he said. 'Take me through what you're going to be doing.'

She drained her mug, and put it down on the floor. 'I start work at the bank. Bright and early. Got to make a good impression. My back story is that I've just been transferred from another Branch. My addictions were beginning to affect my work. Human Resources gave me a written warning. That's why I went into the Oasis. This is their way of giving me a fresh start. And guess what? I'm going to be as good as gold.'

'And who knows that you're undercover?'

'Only the Head of HR, and the Centre Manager.

'Not even the person you're working for?'

'Nope.'

'So what have the rest of the staff been told?'

'Nothing. Just that I requested a transfer.'

'What if they ask where you've transferred from? They might be tempted to do some digging.'

'I'll tell them I'd rather not say. I had a problem with one of the senior staff. A man. They can think what they like so long as they can't check up on me.'

'You're sure you'll be able to cope with the work?'

She nodded. 'It shouldn't be problem. It's just as well I worked at the Co-op Bank before I joined GMP, and that they've only got me doing clerical stuff here, but I won't be surprised if I come in for the odd bollocking or two from my manager.'

'Just so long as he doesn't rumble you.' Caton said.

'*She*, won't,' said Joanne, pointedly. 'So what do you think about the names he gave me?' she asked changing the subject.

'The man is favourite obviously, but we can't rule the woman out, she could be a go between. We'll check them both out.'

'You'll let me know what you dig up?' she said.

'As soon as. Not before tomorrow evening though, unless something really important turns up.' He studied her intently, with his serious face on. 'You're clear about the rules aren't you Joanne? You ring me, not vice versa. Every day before you leave here, and every evening when you get back, and again before you retire.'

'I know that.'

'And keep your eyes peeled. If you get any sense that you're being followed, or watched, get your phone out. Don't hesitate.'

'But I will be won't I?' she said innocently.

'What?'

'Be being watched. By the surveillance team.'

'You know what I meant,' he said. 'Seriously, don't take any chances.'

'I didn't know you cared,'

'I wouldn't be much of a Boss if I didn't would I?' he said. He stood up, and picked up his tool bag from beside the sofa.

'You don't think anyone *is* watching me do you; not already?' She said as they walked towards the door.

'I doubt it very much,' he said. 'But look at it this way, if they are, it means we're a step closer. That's what you're doing this for isn't it?'

It was a sobering thought. For them both.

'This is interesting Boss,' said Holmes. 'The woman, Madeline Hunt, she's a psychotherapist all right. In her sixties. But get this. The phone number on the card DS Stuart was given is discontinued, and according to the United Kingdom Association of Psychotherapists her registration has lapsed, and they reckon she retired from practice two years ago.'

Caton sat down on the edge of the desk. 'That porter, Hatch, must be aware of that,' he said. 'There's no way over the course of two years someone didn't let him know. In which case, maybe he's being clever. He can't be seen to be offering only one option, and a man at that. This way, Joanne tries the woman, can't contact her, so she gives the man a go. Clever.'

'So let's pull him in. The porter.' Said Holmes

'Not yet,' said Caton. 'If he's being paid, his loyalty might be to the perpetrator whether he knows about him or not. And if he's not being paid then that would be even more worrying.' He picked up the other business card. 'If this Simon Stone is involved we can't risk Hatch tipping him off. See what you can dig up on him first.' His mobile rang.

'DCI Caton,' he said. 'What? Are you sure? No don't do that. Get onto uniform at Bootle Street, and get them to pull him in on suspicion. I'll be there as soon as possible.' He rang off, and punched in another number.

'What is it Boss?' Asked Holmes.

Caton shook his head, silencing him, and spoke into his phone. 'Joanne?' he said. 'Listen. There's no need to panic, but make sure you've got your door secured. Don't open it to anyone until I get there. What? We don't know. It may be a burglar, or a prowler, a domestic, someone completely unconnected with this case. It's being dealt with. Just stay there.'

'Surveillance have spotted someone?' Holmes guessed.

Caton nodded. 'A man's been watching the apartments for about half an hour. Seemed to take a particular interest in DS Stuart's lounge window. Lights on, curtains not drawn. He's just gone in through the main doors carrying a small rucksack. They wanted to take him, but I want uniform to do it, just in case. Whoever it is we don't want him to know we're watching the place. You drive into Bootle Street; I'm going over to the safe house. '

'What if he breaks in before uniform arrive?' Said Holmes.

'DS Stuart isn't going to let him in.' Caton replied as he made for the door. 'And anyway, she can look after herself. We don't call it a safe house for nothing.'

So why am I so worried, he asked himself as he started to run down the corridor.

Joanne peered through the peephole lense in the front door. It would have been much easier if they had installed a camera but none of the other apartments had them, and they'd told her they thought it would have been a giveaway to any one who happened to see the inside of the flat. So far so good. The hallway was empty. Someone rounded the corner from the stairway. It was a man; about five foot five tall she estimated, in a black anorak, carrying a small rucksack in his left hand. He looked vaguely familiar, but the distortion of the fish eye made it impossible to be sure. The man advanced until he was standing in the middle of the hallway. He looked from door to door, trying to work out which was the one he was looking for. His mind made up, he approached her door and rang the bell. Even though she'd been expecting it, the sound made her jump. He tried a second time, and when he failed to get a response his hand moved to the letterbox. Joanne stepped quickly sideways, and pressed herself against the wall.

'Jane, are you there? He shouted. 'It's Gerry, from…you know. Gerry. 'I've brought you something.'

Now she recognised him. Gerry was the name he had used in the group session. The supposedly recovering porn addict who had sat immediately opposite her. From the beginning she had taken against him. He was too much of a stereotype. She could imagine him in a dirty raincoat, sitting in a peep show booth in some sleazy sex dive, or in a lap dancing club. How the hell had he got her address? She held her breath and waited. He called out once again, then stood up, and pressed the bell twice more. She heard him curse, and then move away from the door. She risked another peer through the peep hole and could see him pacing up and down the tiny hallway. He advanced towards the door again, this time with a greater sense of determination. Just when she thought he was going to put his shoulder to it he stopped mid stride, and turned. Over his shoulder she saw first one, and then a second, uniformed officer round the corner and head straight for him.

'You've got it wrong!' she heard him say as they took him by the arm and began to lead him towards the stairwell. 'I know her. She's a friend. Ask her…'

Only when they'd gone did Joanne realise that that she had been holding her breath, and that her heart was pounding ten to the dozen. God, I'm getting too old for this she told herself.

Twenty minutes later the door bell rang again; it was Caton.

'Are you OK?' he asked even before he'd got through the door.

'I'm fine,' she said. 'You needn't have come you know. I take it you realise you're breaking your own rules?'

'Rules are for breaking,' he said, closing the door behind him. 'Anyway, surveillance say it's all clear, and there's no chance of your prowler having seen me because he'll be snuggled up in an interview room right now with DI Holmes and DS Hassan.'

'What's in there?' she asked pointing to the carrier bag.

He opened it up, and revealed a bottle of vodka, and a couple of cans of coke.

She laughed. 'I've only just come out of rehab, and I'm supposed to be on duty 24/7.' It didn't stop her heading for the kitchen to get a couple of glass tumblers.

'I thought you might need to steady your nerves.'

He said, crossing to the window, standing in the shadows, and looking out into the street. Then he found the curtain pull, and drew them.

'Don't you think you might be giving the lads from surveillance the wrong idea?' she asked, as she unscrewed the top of the vodka bottle.

'They were the ones who suggested it.' He told her. 'They reckon you're just asking for it. *Lit up like a shop window in the Amsterdam Red Light District* to be precise. 'I think they've got a point,' he said. 'You're supposed to be undercover, not on display.'

She made to fill the other tumbler. He put his hand over hers.

'Not for me,' he said. 'I'm driving.'

'Let me at least make you a coffee.'

'OK,' he said. 'So long as it's a quick one.'

She was fixing his coffee when his mobile went off. By the time she brought it over he had finished the conversation.

'That was DI Holmes,' he told her. 'Your prowler claims he was at the Oasis with you. Gerry Whitehead ring any bells?'

She handed him his mug. 'Gerry from the recovery group. I recognised him. God, he gave me the creeps the first time I saw him. He claimed he was a recovering porn addict.'

'Maybe he's been fooling himself,' Caton said. 'The tale he told Gordon was that he was coming in for an optional half day session when he saw you get into your taxi. On a whim, he decided to follow you. He said he thought a bond had developed between you.'

'Bloody hell!' She said. 'I can't imagine anything worse, except maybe MRSA.'

'He says he sat outside for ages trying to pluck up the courage to come inside; he just wanted a chance to get to know you. He says he was going to offer to be your sponsor.'

'Talk about the blind leading the blind.' She knocked back her vodka and coke, and poured another one.

'I don't think you say can that these days Joanne.' He teased.

'Well, you know what I mean. Does he fit the profile?'

'He's got a history, drunk and disorderly, and he's been done a couple of times for soliciting. In 2007 he got a twelve month driving licence ban for repeated soliciting of prostitutes in Whalley Range.'

'That makes him a possible surely?'

Caton shook his head. 'He's a merchant seaman by trade. When two of our girls went missing on each occasion he claims he was halfway round the world. Holmes's checking it out as we speak, but he's pretty sure he'll be in the clear.'

'Has this blown our cover?' she asked, genuinely concerned that all her hard work might have been for nothing.

'Holmes says not. The story they gave him is that there's been a spate of burglaries, and when a resident spotted him hanging around they rung the police. He's actually invited us to search his place just so he can clear himself.'

'So we're still on course?'

Caton put his mug down, and stood up. 'I don't see why not. I'd better go. You need your beauty sleep, and I've got checks to run on Hatch and Stone first thing in the morning.'

She got up from the sofa, and started to walk towards the hallway. 'And we wouldn't want those two out there to get the wrong idea would we?'

'I'll stick my head through their window so they'll know I haven't been drinking,' he replied, his hand on the door knob.

'In which case,' she said coyly. 'I won't kiss you goodnight, in case they get a whiff of perfume.'

He laughed, shook his head, opened the door, and walked towards the stairway. At the corner he turned and saw that she was already inside. As he started down the stairs He wondered why he had bothered to worry about her. Tough as old boots was DS Stuart.

28

It was almost midday. By now Joanne would have completed her first morning at the Bank. Caton wondered how she was getting on. He got up from his desk and went through to the incident room. Holmes was busy writing on one of the white boards.

'Where are we up to Gordon?' Caton asked.

Holmes finished writing, stepped back to view his handiwork, and pointed to the scary photograph staring back at them. 'Our friend Hatch. Nothing since the affray back in '99. Still associates with some of the low life known to us, mainly petty criminals, counterfeit traders, ticket touts, receiving and selling stolen goods, you know the kind of thing. Kept himself clean though. There's a rumour he belongs to the BNP, but his name's not on the list that was leaked on the internet last week.'

British National Party? That figures. Not illegal though is it?'

'Not unless you're a policeman.' Holmes pointed out.

Caton thought he caught a worrying edge to the DI's voice. 'Even then it's not illegal, just prohibited.' He said, watching for a reaction. Holmes shrugged, and carried on with his report.

'I can tell you he's a heavy gambler though,' he

said. 'He's into the bookies for over £900 pounds. That's a hell of a lot on his wages.'

'Is that what he was in the Oasis for?'

'No. That was drink and anger management remember. Looks like he's swapped one addiction for another.'

Caton weighed up the options. 'OK,' he said. I think we need to speak to him again, without tipping him off. You can do that; take Hassan with you.'

Holmes looked uneasy. 'But he's already been interviewed Boss. All the staff have. If we pick on him he's going to put two and two together and come up with DS Stuart.'

Caton knew he was right. 'So you tell him it's just a follow up we're doing with all of the staff. You'd better line up a few more of them to see while you're there to make it look right. In the meantime I'm going to find out where Derek Waldon is up to with Dr Simon Stone. Let's hope at least one of these two turns up trumps.'

It was quarter to seven in the evening when Holmes got back to the station. He looked like a wrung out dishcloth.

'I thought I'd give the M56 and M60 a miss, and came back up the M6,' he said. 'We got caught in a jam on the other side of the Thelwall Viaduct for an hour and a quarter, and then the air con' got stuck on twenty four degrees centigrade.'

Caton sat him down in his office, and brought him a beaker of ice cold water from the cooler.'

'How did you get on?' he asked.

Holmes drained the plastic beaker in one, crumpled it up in his fist, and tossed it into the wastepaper basket in the corner. 'I softened him up with a few openers, and then I asked him if he knew of any other practitioners outside the hospital who clients might have gone to for further treatment. He cottoned on straight away that I knew about his little sideline. I could see it in his eyes. So I told him he didn't need to worry, I wouldn't tell his boss, that it wasn't as though he was doing anything illegal.'

'Smart move.' Caton acknowledged.

'We were in his room. He reached into his drawer and pulled out a stack of cards; twenty in all. Everything from aromatherapy to psychobabble. Seems he was approached by a couple of people to start with, and then he decided to go proactive. Says he went through the Yellow Pages, and then rang them in turn, offering to promote their services.'

'Quite the entrepreneur,' Caton observed. 'Next thing he'll be on Dragon's Den. How does he know who to recommend to whom?'

Holmes smiled. 'One of the nurses got careless. Stuck her password to the side of her keyboard. He uses it to access patient files. He was terrified I'd tell the Director. I told him a white lie; that would depend on whether he was straight with me.'

'What does he get out of it?'

'Most of them pay him commission – a tenner for every referral. A couple pay him in kind,' He grinned. 'I got the impression that included the tantric sex, and the Swedish massage.

'What about the two people he recommended to DS Stuart?'

Holmes wiped a thin line of perspiration from his brow, and sat up. 'That's the interesting part. The woman paid him commission. He told me straight he hadn't heard from her in years.'

'So why was he still giving out her cards?'

'Exactly. Needless to say I wasn't going to let him know we knew. That would really have blown DS Stuart's cover.

'What about Stone?'

'He's one of the ones he claims pays him a retainer. A flat fifty quid a month regardless of whether he gets any referrals that month.'

Caton thought about it. 'So Hatch never gets to know who followed it up, and who didn't?'

'Exactly.'

'Interesting. Well done Gordon.'

'It wasn't just me Boss,' said the DI. 'Hassan had a hand in it too. He's shaping up alright.'

Just his saying that pleased Caton more than Holmes would ever know. 'Glad to hear it,' he said. 'Now how about I tell you what Derek turned up on Dr Simon Stone?'

Holmes downed his second beaker of water, and tossed it at the bin. This time he missed. 'So much for the power of rehydration,' he chuckled.

'Just make sure you pick it up before you leave,' Caton told him. 'Now, where was I?'

'Cognitive Behavioural Therapy, Narrative Therapy, Hypno-Psychotherapy CPEAB Certified Dip.CP. Dip CT. Dip. CAH.' Holmes told him showing off his amazing short term memory. 'What are all those Dips?'

Caton consulted his notes. 'Diploma in Counselling and Psychotherapy; Diploma in

Counselling Therapy; Diploma in Clinical and Advanced Hypnotherapy.'

'Holmes whistled. 'Hypnotherapy. How interesting is that?'

'Nowhere near as interesting as this,' Caton told him. 'Stone is 40 yrs old. When he was just 17 he was one of two football apprentices lodging in a house in Daubhill, in Bolton. Their landlady was found strangled.'

'Bloody hell!' Holmes sat bolt upright. 'You're joking?'

'Her clothing had been disturbed; buttons on the blouse torn, the dress rumpled. No sign of sexual assault. No semen. Both boys were interviewed.'

'Don't tell me,' said Holmes. 'They had alibis?'

Caton nodded. 'Seems they were both in town on a pub crawl celebrating the fact that some of them had been retained, and commiserating with the lads who hadn't. Stone was one of the ones who hadn't. The other lads all swore that Stone was there with them. They remembered having a laugh because he'd too much to drink, and spilt a pint of beer all down his trousers.'

'Was there anyone else in the frame?'

'Suspicion fell on the husband. There had been previous domestics. His alibi was that he was at work; he was a night security driver. His logs and milometer seemed to back this up, but he could still have slipped back and done it.'

'What about forensic evidence?'

Caton shook his head. 'None that would stand up in court. Don't forget this was twenty four years ago. Six years before DNA was first used in criminal proceedings. The lads' fingerprints were all over the place, but then they would have to have been wouldn't they? There was no obvious motive. Case remains unsolved.'

'Have the cold case team got to this one yet?' Holmes asked.

'Yes, but like I said, there was no semen on the body. Nor were there any swabs taken back then that might have yielded DNA. There is one thing though.' Caton said, adding a hint of mystery.

'What's that?'

He swivelled the large folder he had in front of him so that it faced his DI. Holmes could see it was a Murder Book. It was open at a photograph of the victim.

'Bloody Hell.' He said for the second time in as many minutes.

The body lay on its side, with one leg straight, and one curled up. One arm was straight down beside the body, the other across the body at right angles.

'That's the classic recovery position,' Holmes said.

'Caton nodded. 'That's what I thought. The sort of thing you might be taught as part of a football apprenticeship do you think?'

Too damn right!' Holmes exclaimed. 'And not so very different from how we found those girls in Bluebell Hollow.'

It felt to Caton like a bad case of déjà vu. Harry Spencer from the CPS was in his element.

'You can't possibly let DS Stuart pose as a prospective patient of this man.' he said. 'If he is the perpetrator it will be far too dangerous,' Caton was about to interrupt but Spencer thrust his left hand out aggressively to stop him. 'If he isn't, you lay the police open to being sued by Stone, and ridiculed in the press. And more to the point, it would be folly from a legal perspective. I've told you before there is no way you can risk entrapment. Even if you can show him to have been responsible your case would never get to court, and a guilty man would be laughing in your faces.'

DCS Radford could see that Caton was bristling to respond, and stepped in as adroitly as a Middle East peacemaker. 'We should at least check out his alibi for these murders Tom,' he said. 'Check his patient records. Search his place for trophies.'

Caton shook his head. 'With respect Sir,' he said.' The grounds are pretty thin.' He addressed himself to the man from the CPS. 'Would *you* say we had enough for a search warrant?'

'Probably not,' Spencer replied. 'It's barely even circumstantial. You have no evidence that he ever met, let alone treated any of the victims. You can't even show that he knew any of them. You can't place him anywhere near them when you think they went missing. You have no DNA evidence, fingerprints, or other forensic evidence that you could try to match to him. As for the murder of his landlady, the investigating team had not a shred of evidence to support his involvement in that. They didn't even caution him.'

It was the reply Caton had been hoping for. 'So, no search warrant,' he said. 'Even if we were able to get one, if it is him, and he's as clever as we think, he's likely to claim he can't remember where he was after all this time. Remember he's self employed. No clocking in and out. What's more, the case files suggest that all of the victims went missing sometime in the evening, and most often at weekends. He could claim he was watching TV, at the pictures, whatever. We could never disprove that. If they were his patients he'll have likely destroyed any records, and he's hardly likely to have stored any trophies he might have collected where we could find them.

'Where might he keep them?'

'A lock up. Or a self-storage unit. '

'Or a cold storage unit perhaps?' Said Derek Saxon.

They all looked at him. It was the first thing the Chief Constable had said since the discussion began. It also suggested he had not bothered to remind himself of the facts.

'The perpetrator buries the bodies Sir,' Caton reminded him as respectfully as possible. 'There's nothing to suggest that he kept them in a freezer first. Nor were any body parts taken. But I would like a warrant to get the names of everyone renting a self-storage unit within twenty miles of the city centre. Then we can cross match them against all of the names we come up with during the enquiry.'

Harry Spencer snorted derisively. 'Can you imagine the uproar that would cause? These places guarantee confidentiality. Without that they're going to lose half of their customers. You wouldn't expect a bank to disclose the names of all of their safety deposit holders – always assuming they gave their real names - nor a judge to issue a warrant to force them to do so. Especially not on the basis of anything more than a hunch.'

Caton could tell that he was wasting his time pursuing it. But Lucas's response had at least given him ammunition for his main objective.

'Even assuming we did get a warrant just to search his house,' he said. 'Which you say is unlikely; all we'd have done is alert him to the fact that he's a prime suspect.'

It took another half an hour to wear them down. As before, Commander Lillian Lucas and Jimmy Radford came to his rescue, and provided just enough pressure to convince the Chief Constable. The decision was made to proceed, with caution. The rules were still the same but Derek Saxon spelt them out again. More, Caton sensed, for Harry Spencer's sake that anything else.

'DS Stuart,' he said with as much gravitas as he could muster. 'Cannot…must not…be seen to act at any point as an agent provocateur. That would be inadmissible, not to mention far too great a risk to herself. Nor can she ask questions about the murders that you might have wanted to ask under caution. That would also be inadmissible under PACE section 78.' He paused to check that Caton was in agreement. A simple nod of the head sufficed. 'She's to go in with a wire for two reasons only,' he ticked them off on his fingers. 'Firstly, for her own safety. Secondly, to enable you to decide if there are sufficient grounds for you to proceed to gather evidence by other means; a warrant for example. During the period that she is working undercover both of them are to be kept under 24hr observation. And you pull her out at the first hint that he may have designs on her. Do you understand?'

Caton nodded his head gravely. 'Absolutely Sir,' he said.

'And one last thing. I want you to link up with the Operation Talon Team, and the Force's sexual crimes unit.'

'It's already been done Sir.' Lillian Lucas assured him.

'In that case, he said. 'There's only one more thing to say.' He stared directly at Tom Caton. It was a hard cold stare full of threat, and devoid of warmth, or empathy, or anything that could have been described as caring. 'Be careful.' He said.

Caton closed the door behind him, with a sigh of relief. It was exactly what he'd wanted. So why did that phrase *be careful what it is you wish for*, keep spinning round in his head?

He dug his phone out from his pocket and flipped it open as he started down the corridor. The number answered just as the lift door opened.

29

'He agreed to see you when?'

'Tomorrow evening,' Joanne Stuart told him. 'Five o'clock. He said he had a cancelled appointment.'

'Did you believe him?' Caton asked.

'I couldn't tell,' she said. 'But I do know one thing. He recognised my name.'

'So Hatch must have told him he'd given you his card.'

'Either that, or he'd already singled me out somehow, and Hatch had been told to make sure I got his details.'

There was silence while they thought about the implications. For one thing it would make it even more likely that Stone was their man. Secondly, it would mean that he had some kind of plan. They already knew that Hatch had access to her details. Perhaps Stone had already checked up on her. Not there was much for him to discover beyond her age, occupation, the address of the safe house, and whatever was on her patient file.

'There is one consolation,' she said. 'It was quite a while after each of the victims left the Oasis that they actually disappeared. Months in most cases.'

Caton wasn't convinced. 'Except that the gap shortened with each successive victim,' he pointed out. 'And if, as seems likely, there have been more victims since…' He left it in hanging the air.

'Then I'll just have to be that much more careful.' She said confidently.

'These should help,' said Clarke pointing to the devices on the coffee table. 'Now we know for certain you're going to have contact, and under what conditions, you can give me back the other one, and take your pick from one of these.'

She had the choice of a button, a biro or a brooch. Each of them attached by thin black wire to a small rectangular transmitter the size of a mobile phone. She picked them up, and examined them in turn.

'They give us a range of one and a half kilometres line of sight.' Clarke told her. 'Good building penetration. Battery lasts four days. Built-in GPS tracking just in case. You can stick the transmitter unit anywhere you like on your person, so long as the wires are hidden. Our advice is to wear it in the small of your back, with a loose fitting blouse, and a jacket over the top. I'd go for the button if I were you. Less chance of exposing the wire.'

'Just so long as he doesn't ask me to strip.' Joanne joked.

Caton didn't see the funny side.

'Why not a miniaturised wireless video camera?' He asked.

Clarke shook his head. 'Nowhere near as reliable, bulkier, and unnecessary,' he said. 'As I understand it, you want to decide if he's your man, not find out what he looks like. And since you won't be using it in court, what's the point?'

'It would be quite useful, I'd have thought, for you

to be able to see if he's about to strangle me.' She said calmly.

'All you have to do is yell, and we'll be there,' said the man from Special Opp's. 'Just don't drink anything while you're there, then he can't drug you first.'

'Thanks a bunch,' she said grimacing. 'I don't think I've felt this good since I did that parachute jump for the Police Benevolent Fund.'

'You don't have to do this.' Caton told her. 'We can find another away.' A part of him hoped she would back out now while she still could.

'Just try and stop me.' She said, handing Clarke the button.

The atmosphere in the van was electric. It wasn't the first time for Caton, or Holmes for that matter, but it was the first time he had felt this personally connected to the covert asset to whom they were listening. *Asset*, meaning positive advantage, skill, benefit. Joanne Stuart was certainly all of those and more. Here she was at the sharp end, and all he could do was impotently sit, and listen. It would take a minimum of fifty seconds from leaving the van to bursting into the room where she sat. He had worked it out as soon as they'd arrived and parked up. He had been through it in his head a dozen times trying to shorten the time. It still came out the same. And how long did it take to strangle someone? No wonder they were hanging on every word.

'So why have you come to see me Jane?'
    'Someone at the Oasis recommended you.'

'I'm sorry. I meant, how is it you think I can help you?'

Joanne looked down at her hands, and squeezed her fingers into tiny fists.

'I have this disorder.'

'Go on.'

'Its called Persistent Sexual Arousal Disorder.'

He nodded. 'PSAD, or PSAS as they call it in the States. You're not the first person I've seen with the condition, but I'm interested in why you've chosen to come to a male therapist?'

'Because when I was in the Oasis, although I found it easy to relate to the women there, the psychiatrist, the therapist, and the counsellor, the men in the recovery group were somehow more... understanding.'

'Understanding? Do you mean soft? Sympathetic?'

She shook her head. 'No, not that. I'm not looking for that. They were less, I don't know, judgemental.'

'He frowned. 'Judgemental. I'm surprised that any of the staff there should come across as judgemental.'

'I don't think any of them meant to be,' she said hurriedly. 'It's just a feeling I got.'

'Why do you think that might be?' he asked.

'I don't know. Perhaps I expected them to empathise more with my addiction. Maybe the men understood it better because...when I think about...' she looked down towards her hands clasped tightly in her lap. 'The way I was behaving...the things I was doing...it's more what you'd expect of a man isn't it?'

Simon Stone did not reply. When she looked up his eyes locked with hers. She felt herself under the closest scrutiny she had experienced since going under cover. She was surprised to discover that she found it unthreatening; natural even. He was simply making up his mind. It was a neutral, professional assessment. After what seemed an age he smiled. She found herself smiling back. Like the mirroring technique they'd taught in the group sessions. Only this time it was automatic; unthinking.

'Fair enough,' he said. I'm prepared to give it a try if you are. Why don't you start by telling me how it affects you?'

More than anything else this was the part that Joanne had been dreading. It had been one thing sharing these intricate and personal details with complete strangers but now she had the Boss and DI Holmes listening too. It didn't matter that the whole thing was a fabrication, a pack of lies. Somehow the fact that it was coming out her mouth, and they were listening to it, made it seem dirty, and made her feel uncomfortable. If nothing else, she told herself, the fact that I feel like this might just make it more believable for Stone.

'It comes on without warning,' she said. 'Completely unrelated to sexual situations, or thoughts. Just driving in the car; even the vibrator on my mobile phone can set it off. It's so intense – the feeling – I can hardly concentrate on anything else.'

'Does achieving an orgasm – self-induced or with another person – bring you relief?' He asked.

'Sometimes it does – more often than not it doesn't. The trouble is that's resulted in my having...my developing ...fantasies that led me into risky situations which left me feeling increasingly frightened. That's why I turned to porn on the internet. Then I found I couldn't stop.

He nodded sagely. 'I understand.'

'I'm not a nymphomaniac.' She said.

He smiled supportively. 'No, you're not. Your addiction is really a pattern of behaviour you have developed in order to help you cope with a condition which is beyond your control. In any case, the medical profession no longer recognises nymphomania as a condition.'

'It doesn't?'

He shook his head. 'No. We refer to hypersexuality – a very strong sex drive if you like. In itself that's not a problem. Some might even regard it as a blessing. It only becomes a problem if it causes you distress, or makes it impossible for you to function in a normal social context. That might equally be the case for someone with a low sex drive.'

'I see.' She said.

'Have you consulted your GP about this?'

'Yes.'

'What did he do about it?'

'She said it was unusual for someone of my age to have it. That it was usually women who had gone through the change, the menopause, and pretty rare even then. That it was pity I wasn't a man.'

'What do you think she meant by that?'

'She said that it was easier to treat men with the condition…something to do with hormones?'

He nodded. 'Antiandrogens.'

'Anyway,' she continued. 'She put me on antidepressants, but they were even worse for my concentration. They made me sick, and left me tired and confused. So then she prescribed an anaesthetizing gel. That didn't really work. In fact applying it made it worse.'

He nodded. 'So what did she do then?'

'I got the impression she'd given up on me. She said I'd just have to learn to live with it.'

'But you haven't been able to?'

'No. Although the Oasis has helped.'

There was a long silence.

In the van, Caton and Holmes looked at each other, and then at Clarke. 'It's still sending,' he assured them. He pressed the volume button several times, and suddenly they could hear her breathing. Twice more, and they could hear the rhythmic beating of her heart.

'She sounds pretty calm to me.' Said Holmes.

A damned sight calmer than me Caton was thinking. Suddenly the psychiatrist's voice seemed to fill the van.

'Shit!' exclaimed Clarke quickly returning the volume to normal.

'Since you don't actually experience any pain,' Stone was saying. 'The issue is really two fold. How you deal with the impact on your levels of concentration, and how you deal with your understandable feelings of frustration. Is that how you see it?'

She nodded eagerly. 'Yes.'

'In which case cognitive reframing of the arousal as a healthy response, could make a big difference. Do you follow?'

'I'm not sure.' She said.

'Basically, at the moment, you regard the arousal as unwelcome, as abnormal, and possibly even as something to be ashamed of. Am I right?'

'Yes.'

'Therefore you worry about it. It makes you anxious; desperate to make it go away.'

'She nodded.'

'So desperate, that you find yourself doing things of which you are even more ashamed, and which are putting you at risk.'

She nodded again, this time head down as though experiencing that shame.

'Now we know that there is no surgical cure for this,' he continued. 'And that the drugs have had only a limited effect. All that remains is for you to learn to control your reactions to what is currently an unwelcome sensation, and make it seem either welcome, or completely normal and therefore bearable. Many people manage to cope with real pain, or with annoying distractions such as tinnitus, in just this way.'

'I see,' said Joanne.

'I don't know what advice you were given in The Oasis,' he said. 'You can share your recovery plan with me at the end of this session, but I think that it's important that you don't cut yourself off from sexual feelings, or regard sexual urges as anything other than normal. I'd like to help you to learn to separate out your response to a physical condition – which according to our telephone conversation yesterday is improving – and your need for, and control over, sexual activity.' He made sure that they had eye contact before continuing. 'Sex is not your enemy Jane. It may be that depression, fear of intimacy, negative childhood experiences, or issues of self esteem, are; but sex is not.'

'I think I understand.' She said.

He smiled, and moved so that he was leaning forward, perched on the edge of his chair. 'There are three ways in which I can help you to do that,' he said. 'Cognitive therapy, which you experienced to an extent in the Oasis, substitution, and hypnosis.'

'No way hypnosis.' Said Caton out loud. He needn't have worried; Joanne Stuart was way ahead of him.

'No, not hypnosis.' She could tell that Stone was surprised by the strength of her objection. His expression had changed. He was staring at her intently, with a hint of suspicion.

'Why not?' He said softly.

'Because I couldn't bear the thought of not being in control...of being dependent on someone else,'

'That's only true if you perceive it that way.'

'What other way is there to perceive it?' She asked.

Holmes shook his head despairingly. 'She's getting too smart Boss. He's going to suss her out. I told you we shouldn't have let her do this.'

Caton knew that he was right. She was beginning to forget that she was supposed to be depressed, weak, and pliable. 'Give her a chance,' he said. 'We don't know that she's blown it yet. Maybe we should have insisted on her having a camera in there. At least then we'd have some idea of how he was reacting.

'Shush,' said Clarke. 'He's started talking again.'

'Let's say you wanted to give up smoking,' Stone said. *You* want to give up, remember...it's not the hypnotist who is making you do it; he is simply planting your own conscious desires deep in your subconscious, The surgeon, who guides a shunt into your artery, or a mitro valve into your heart, is doing it for *you*, at *your* request, not for his own gratification.'

Joanne softened her voice, bowed her head in a manner that she hoped he would interpret as submissive, and said. 'I understand, but even so...I still don't think I would be comfortable with being hypnotised.'

'There is an alternative.' he said.

She looked up. 'There is?'

'Self-hypnosis. It would complement cognitive therapy, and substitution. And you'd be completely in control. Nothing to object to there, surely?' He scooted his chair across to his desk, pressed the keys on his computer keyboard, and scanned the screen. 'I could fit you in for a session the same time tomorrow.' He swivelled in his chair, and smiled at her. 'What do you say?'

'I can just about manage that she said, if I leave work dead on time, before the worst of the rush hour.'

'Good,' he said. 'There is just one thing Jane,' he folded his arms and studied her closely. 'It goes without saying that everything that passes between us in these sessions is completely confidential. I am in the fortunate position of having as many – if not more – patients than I can manage. I have to admit that I only fitted you in because your case intrigues me. I don't need to advertise, since all of my patients come to me through recommendations. So my only condition for continuing to work with you is that you give me your word that you won't tell anyone that I have been treating you until our work here is completed. Then, hopefully, you will want to tell everyone how successful it has been, and I will be in a position to take on new patients.'

'Of course,' said Joanne, hoping that there were no external symptoms of the sudden surge of adrenalin that this first real sign that Stone might be the predator had caused. 'I haven't told anyone, and I won't be doing. It's not the kind of thing you can share with people. The only time I tried – apart from in the Oasis - it turned out disastrously.'

'What happened?' He asked.

'I'd had too much to drink, and I blurted it out. Half my supposed friends thought it was hilarious, the other half started to disown me.'

'In which case, we can proceed,' he said standing up. 'Till five o'clock tomorrow then.'

'I'll look forward to it.' Said Joanne.

'Don't push it Joanne.' Caton muttered.
DI Holmes punched the air with his fist. 'We've got the bastard,' he said. 'We've bloody well got him. '
Not yet we haven't,' said Caton. 'But we will."

30

DS Stuart waited till she got back to the apartment before ringing him.

'What do you think?' Caton asked.

'What did *you* think?' She replied.

'By the sound of it you did a great job,' he told her

'I found him surprisingly normal,' she said. 'Charming in a much understated, professional sort of way.'

'Don't tell me you're falling for him?'

'Don't be daft. But I can see why someone who fancies men might. Especially someone who's been damaged by men in the way the victims were.'

'Do you think he bought your story?'

'Did you?' she wanted to know.

'Hook line and sinker.'

'So did he I think. It helped that I'd been through it so many times at the Oasis. So much so I've almost started believing it myself.'

'DI Holmes and I nearly had a heart attack when Stone suggested hypnotising you.' Caton told her.

She laughed. '*You* nearly had one, how do you think I felt?'

'Are you sure you should go ahead with this self hypnosis session,' he asked. 'There's no guarantee he might not actually try to hypnotise you.'

'No worries,' she said, sounding like an Australian. 'What both he and you don't know is that I've done it before.'

'When?'

'When I was taking my driving test. I failed the first time because I was a bag of nerves. My instructor suggested self hypnosis. My GP did it for people with asthma, and stress related diseases. She gave me three sessions. Worked like a charm.'

'Good for her,' he said.

'Well it worked,' her tone became serious. 'There was only one point today where I got really anxious.' She said.

'At the end?' He guessed.

She nodded even though he couldn't see her. 'When he said I couldn't tell anyone. Then I knew it was him. That here I was having this bizarre conversation with the bastard who killed all those women.'

'That's what Gordon thought.' Said Caton.

'And you don't?' She responded sharply.

'I'm not saying that, what I'm saying is that I still don't know.' He heard the quick intake of breath, and sensed her eyebrows shooting up. 'I trust your instincts,' he added hurriedly. 'But let's face it, what he actually said sounded perfectly reasonable. If we weren't investigating these deaths we'd have accepted what he said at face value.'

'You weren't there.' She said coolly.

'I know,' he replied, but then neither was the jury.' There was silence at the other end of the line. 'If you're absolutely sure Joanne,' he said. 'I'll pull you out now, and we can get a search warrant, and take it from there.'

'No,' she said. 'Being sure is one thing. Having enough to move on is another. If I've learnt one thing as a detective it's that. Things are just beginning to warm up. I want to stay.'

'If you're sure?'

'I am.'

'OK,' he said, secretly relieved that she had made the decision without having to be pushed. 'Ring me tomorrow. And take care.'

'You bet I will,' she said.

It was ten in the evening when Caton's land line rang. He was hoping it was Kate. It was Larry Hymer the crime reporter from the Manchester Evening News.

'Have you any idea what time it is?' Caton asked him.

'I'm sorry,' said Hymer. 'But you wouldn't have thanked me for running this story without giving you the opportunity to comment.'

Caton's heart sunk. 'Go on.'

'In a nut shell, is it true you've had someone undercover at the Oasis clinic?'

Caton struggled to disguise his anger. 'For Christ sake Larry,' he said 'If we had done that you know as well as I do that the slightest hint in the press would put an officer's life in danger. Not to mention jeopardise the entire investigation.'

'So I can take that as a yes?'

'No, you can't!'

'OK. So I'll take it as a no. In which case I can still run it as a rumour, and accompany it with your denial.'

'What the hell would be the point of that?'

'It sells newspapers.'

Caton knew that he had been painted into a corner. Whatever he said now Hymer would publish, and put Joanne in jeopardy…unless.

'Are you taping this Larry?' he asked.

'Tom, how could you?' He sounded as though his honour had been irretrievably impugned.

'Hymer, are you listening to me. I can't believe you would be this irresponsible.' Said Caton.

There was a pause. When Hymer spoke his tone was suddenly all warmth and reason. 'Well obviously I wouldn't, Jack. That's why I'm telling you. But since I have told you, and we're not going to publish the story, I'm assuming you're going to give me an exclusive when you nail the bastard?'

'Come on Larry,' Caton said realising that he had allowed himself to be suckered. 'You know your editor would never risk undermining an undercover operation.'

'Maybe not, but I know some editors who would.'

'Are you threatening me Larry?'

'No, just pointing out that since I'm not going to publish, my source could easily take the story somewhere a lot less fussy.'

'Caton knew he was right. This wasn't about the story. He never was going to publish it. It was all about the source. Rather than trying to compromise him, and the operation, Hymer was actually doing him a favour. Caton wasn't going to apologise but the man deserved a favour in return. 'You know there's a limit to what I can promise Larry,' he said. 'A case like this, all the press and media communications have to be approved by Chester House. You'll just have to take my word for it that I'll do what I can to give you the heads up. I'll make sure you get your photographer to where he needs to be, and that your researcher's a step ahead of the rest of the field.'

'Fair enough,' said the reporter. 'You know that I can't just give you a name Tom.'

'You can tell me if the leak's from Chester House, or the CPS.'

'I would if I could, but I can't'

'Why not?'

'Because Tom,' he said. 'I think he's one of yours. He gave me his mobile number. I told him that I'll get back to him by ten o'clock in the morning,' he paused theatrically. 'When would be a good time for me to ring him do you think?'

Holmes and Caton stood in the corridor, looking through the window in the door. The incident room was crammed.

'Why the whole team Boss?' Said Holmes. 'There's only six of us know about this.

'Because I don't believe a secret like this can be contained that easily in a team our size.'

'And your sure Hymer is telling you the truth?'

'Hymer may be cunning,' said Caton. 'But he's always been straight with me.'

Holmes pushed the door open. 'That's like saying you can always trust a snake, just because you keep it in your pocket.'

The atmosphere in the room was charged with anticipation. It was a reasonable assumption that with the whole team there something big was in the offing. As soon as it became clear that this was just a bog standard rallying of the troops, an attempt to inject a bit more urgency and enthusiasm, Caton had seen the shoulders sag, and the eyes glaze over. He was hoping that one pair of eyes at least would have a look that marked them out. Anticipation perhaps, fear of discovery, guilt even. Some hope. He checked the clock on the back wall for the final time. At the back of the room he saw a sudden movement. Someone had turned his back, and was slipping quietly through the open door to the adjoining office. Must have the phone on vibrate, Caton decided, since there had been no tell tale tone. No matter, Gordon Holmes was only a couple of seconds behind, closing the door gently as he went.

'What the hell made you do it you pillock?' Shouted Holmes. 'That's you finished. You do know that don't you? You can kiss your pension goodbye for a start. You could even go down for this.'

'That's enough.' Said Caton. It wasn't as though DC Wood needed telling. He sat there head bowed, his world collapsed around him. He had a wife and two children. No job, no pension, no references. He wasn't going to go to prison though. Chester House wouldn't want the publicity. Especially with the investigation still ongoing. Had it not been for what it might have meant for Joanne Stuart, and the operation, Caton might even have felt sorry for him.

'Why did you do it?' he asked.

Wood replied without looking up. 'Five years ago the wife wanted to move...a bigger house, detached, just like her sister. We took on a mortgage we could barely afford. We were already in arrears when the credit crunch hit. The mortgage rates gone up, petrol, gas, electricity. The building society's threatening repossession. I thought this would see us through till things look up again.'

Caton thought he sounded pathetic; in the true sense of the word. No trace of his customary bravado; just a sad defeated whine. He hadn't even bothered to deny it. Not that there was much point with the mobile on the table in front of them. He hadn't even asked for his Police Federation representative. Not that he was going to get much joy there, not with him having put a fellow officer at risk.

'And what about DS Stuart.' He said. 'What the hell did you think was going to happen to her?'

'That you'd pull her out straight away,' he said, the first trace of appeal appearing in his voice.

'And to hell with the fact that it would have blown the operation and undermined the investigation?' Said Holmes.

'I didn't think.' He said, putting his head in his hands.

'Famous last words.' Muttered Holmes.

'Have you told anyone else?' Caton asked.

He shook his head. 'No.' He looked up. 'What happens now?'

'Now we go and try to sort out the mess you left behind,' Caton told him. 'And you get a visit from the Professional Standards team. Take my advice. Don't try to bullshit them. Just tell them the truth, and face the music.'

'*Exit* music,' said Holmes wryly as they headed down the corridor. 'What are you going to do about DS Stuart?'

'Tell her what's happened,' said Caton, and let her decide. If Wood's telling us the truth, and Hymer hasn't spoken to anyone, then it's been contained. If not, she's out of there. It's got to be her call.'

It had been easy to say, much harder to stick to. In the event he found himself pushing her to call it a day. He soon discovered how much he had underestimated her.

'You must be joking,' she said. 'After everything I've put into, this d'you think I'm going to chuck it all away because of some scrote like Wood? Forget it!'

'At least be even more careful.' Caton told her.

'I don't think I could be any more careful than I am being,' she said. 'If Stone suspects, I'll know. There'll be a change in his manner…something. Trust me I'll know.'

'Let's hope you do,' Caton said. 'And then you've got to promise me, you'll get out of there any which way you can.'

31

They followed Stone into the Great Northern car park, out onto Watson Street, across the square, and onto Deansgate. They watched as he entered Starbucks, picked up one of the complimentary newspapers, and ordered an Americano. He settled in a window seat. One of the watchers entered the café, ordered a drink, and sat close to the doors. The other one waited under the covered way close to the Christian Book Shop. He took out his mobile phone and rang the number.

'He's watching her Boss....' said Gordon Holmes, almost before he was through the door. 'Stone, he's watching DS Stuart.'

Caton leapt to his feet, and started to pull his jacket from the back of his chair.

'It's alright,' said Holmes. 'He's not going anywhere without them knowing.'

Caton realised that he was over reacting; not least because it would have taken at least twenty minutes to get into the city centre, and park up. He sank back down into his chair. 'Go on.' He said.

Holmes flopped down into one of the chairs beside the table. 'The surveillance team followed him from his house, into the city. He parked up on the Great Northern. Now he's sitting in the Starbucks' window, pretending to read a newspaper. What he's really doing is watching the entrance to the RBS building where DS Stuart is working.'

'He's checking that she really works there.'

'Or what time she gets off.' said Holmes.

'How did he know where to go?'

'She told him. You heard her telling him when we were in the van.'

'Only that she worked at the RBS regional office in Spinningfields. They've got at least three different buildings within a hundred metres of each other. She didn't tell him which one.'

'You're right Boss. Maybe he doesn't know that there's more than one. This building is the most visible. Maybe he just got lucky.'

'Serial killers don't get lucky,' Caton told him. 'They plan meticulously. That's why they get to be serial killers. Because they don't get caught.'

'The Yorkshire Ripper got lucky twice,' Holmes pointed out. 'Once because the investigating team didn't have their database sorted, and the second time because of that idiot who sent the faked tapes with the Geordie accent.'

'Lucky or not, I don't see him picking her up in broad daylight,' said Caton. 'Not right outside her place of work; she's bound to be suspicious.'

'Do you think DS Stuart should show herself?' Holmes wondered. 'If she goes out of the staff entrance, and he never gets to see her, he might doubt that she works there at all.'

'Good point,' Caton conceded. 'But we don't want to make it look as though she knows he's there. I'll send her a text, and suggest she waits half an hour, and if he's still there she can make an excuse to pop out for five minutes. She can nip down to House of Fraser, or over the road to the chemists. So long as she goes back in carrying a purchase of some kind.'

The watcher by the door took a call on his mobile phone, finished his coffee, and left. Thirty seconds later the second watcher entered the café, ordered a coffee, and took it to a different table four away from the one where the target was sitting. This watcher had started on his second newspaper when he saw Stone lower his paper, shift his position in the chair, and then raise it again. There was something about his body language. The confirmation came when the psychotherapist lowered his newspaper again, half turned in his seat, and was clearly observing someone walking north on the opposite side of Deansgate. Five minutes later the identical sequence happened, this time in reverse. As Stone lowered his newspaper for the final time the watcher was able to see her disappearing through the imposing doors of the building opposite. Two minutes later Stone got, up and left. Watcher One picked him up as he passed by the arcade, and followed as he retraced his steps to the Great Northern car park.

'It looks like he's swallowed it Boss,' said Gordon Holmes. 'They reckon he's heading back to his place.'

'To ready himself for his five o'clock session with DS Stuart no doubt,' said Caton. 'Funny how someone who is supposed to have a diary overflowing with appointments can find the time to sit in a coffee bar all afternoon. Now I wonder why that is?' He took his jacket from the back of his chair and stood up. 'If we're going to get settled in before they start, we'd better get a move on.'

'How do you feel Jane?'

Caton glanced at his watch. They had been at it for over half an hour now. He could have told him exactly how he felt stuck in this van; hot, sweaty, and impatient. Joanne Stuart's voice came through so quietly that the three of them found themselves craning forward to hear.

'I feel completely relaxed; as though I'm almost floating.'

'Good,' said the psychotherapist. 'Now remember, you are completely in control. You are conscious of everything that's going on, and you are in control of it. Yes?'

'Yes.'

'Good. Keep breathing like that, slowly, deeply, steadily. Let your tongue sink to the bottom of your mouth…there should be no strain, no tension, in your face…your neck…anywhere in your body.'

In the silence that followed they could hear her softly breathing. Caton was conscious that his own breathing had quickened. Several minutes passed. The tension in the van mounted. When Stone finally broke the silence it came as a relief.

'I am going to show you an image Jane,' 'Of the kind that you described to me in your first session. No, don't sit up; I'll bring it to you. When I tell you, I want you to open your eyes and look at it. Do you understand?'

'Yes.'

'Before you open your eyes, Jane, I want you to make sure that you've cleared your mind completely. Don't try to imagine what the image is going to be. Don't think about anything at all apart from your own breathing. Concentrate on that. That's good. When you open your eyes, and see the image, I want you to observe it without thought. Try to suppress any thoughts that might come into your mind. Instead I want you to concentrate on what you're feeling. On your breathing, on the beating of your heart. I want you to concentrate on keeping them slow and rhythmic. If any of your muscles begin to tense, I want you to deliberately relax them. Remember, this is your body. You are in control. If you feel any sensations that threaten physical arousal I want you to close your eyes, and focus on a point in the centre of your forehead. Do you understand Jane?'

Caton strained to hear her reply. There was none.

'She must have nodded,' said Holmes without conviction.

'Open your eyes Jane.'

There was silence in the van as they listened to sound of her breathing. After what seemed an age, but can have been no more than twenty seconds or so, her breathing became louder and more rapid, almost as though she was panting..'

'She's some actress, I'll give her that,' said Holmes admiringly. 'If she is acting.'

'Of course she's acting,' said Caton sharply.'

'How'd you know Boss?'

'Because if she wasn't, we'd be able to hear her heart racing,'

'Close your eyes Jane,' they heard Stone say. 'That's it. Now focus on that spot and slow your breathing down.'

Almost a minute passed before they heard him speak again.

'Well done. Now I am going to show you another image. When I tell you, I want you to open your eyes, and do the same again. This time see if you can manage to control those sensations a little longer. Because you *can* Jane. You just have to concentrate. Ready? Open your eyes.'

And so it continued. Three times more, each time the intervals between her opening her eyes and closing them lengthening until the final time her eyes remained open, and Stone took the image away.

'Well done Jane,' he said. 'You've done it. You managed to desensitise yourself to that particular image. And to control those unwanted sensations. How do you feel?'

'Exhausted but exhilarated, 'she said.

'Good. Because I want you to try one more thing. It may be premature, but I think you may be ready for it. Do I have your permission to touch you?'

'No!' said Caton, loud enough to startle both Holmes and Clarke.

'If I just place my hands on either side of your forehead, on your temples, would that be alright?'

'Yes,' said Joanne.

Caton reached behind him and checked the position of the door handles. Fifty seconds, he told himself. Fifty seconds. Nowhere near long enough.

'I think we should trust her instincts Boss,' said Holmes picking up on it straight away. 'After all, she's there, we're not.'

'Alright,' said Caton checking himself. 'But if we go, we go out shouting at the top of our voices, and I want the horn on this van sounding over and over again. Is that clear?' He could tell from the look on their faces that they thought he was over reacting. He didn't give a damn what they thought; only about the safety of his officer. Only about Joanne.

'Close your eyes.'

They could hear her breathing again, and her quickening heartbeat.

'Now I am going to slide them down onto your shoulders. Keep concentrating on that spot on your forehead, and on your breathing.

To Caton it sounded as though her heart beat had filled the van, and was merging with his own. His hand was on the door handle.

'Slowly Jane. Breathe slowly.'

There was something about the tone of his voice…there was a tremor in it. The door was open. Caton was moving.

'Hang on Boss.' He felt an arm clutching his shoulder, pulling him back. 'It's alright Boss, Listen.'

'Well done Jane,' Simon Stone was saying. 'That's it for today. When you sit up, do it slowly. We don't want you fainting, do we?'

While DI Holmes drove Caton took the opportunity to check his phone messages. One was from Kate telling him how much she missed him, and that she couldn't wait until next week. There was another, from Helen, reminding him that he had promised to take Harry to the football the following afternoon. God, he thought, is it Friday already?

32

Caton waited until he was on his own in his office before ringing Helen back.

'I'm sorry I didn't get back to you straight away,' he said. 'I don't want you to think I'd forgotten. It's just that we're right in the middle of something.'

'So long as you're not still in the middle of it tomorrow afternoon,' she told him. 'Because if you let him down Tom, I'm not going to give you a second chance.'

'I won't.'

'Just make sure you don't.'

'I told you, I'll be there.' He said, wondering how many times he would have to say it.

'Good.'

'It's Wigan Athletic then?'

'That's right.'

'I thought he was a Wigan Warriors fan?'

'You're obviously not a rugby league fan,' she said. 'Or you'd know that their season finished back in September.'

'You're right, I'm not.'

'Well now you're working in the Wigan area,' she said, 'I suggest you brush up on your knowledge, because otherwise your street cred' is going to suffer.'

'Harry can help me.' He told her.

'That I don't doubt,' she said. 'You can pick him up at half past one. Don't be late.'

Only then did it dawn on Caton what he was taking on. Helen was right. He couldn't play fast and loose with this boy's affection; even if he was his son. No, *because* he was his son. It was too important to mess up. If he couldn't hack this, he told himself, if he didn't think he could keep juggling his work and his personal life to make room for his son, he shouldn't even start. Harry seemed happy as he was. Helen looked like she was doing a perfectly good job. Why be a selfish sod? Why not leave him be? The answer was obvious. With the exception of his Aunt, Harry was the only family he'd got. He wished that Kate was here right now. She would know what best to do. And he would be able to gauge how it was likely to affect their own relationship. He told himself it wouldn't do any harm to keep the appointment. He would speak to Kate next week; as soon as she got back to the apartment. Then they could decide together. Now was not the time to make a rushed decision. He'd keep his options open, and concentrate on Simon Stone; and keeping DS Stuart safe.

It was gone eight in the evening by the time Caton had cleared his in tray, and his emails. He went through to the incident room to find DI Holmes hunched over his computer screen, hugging a beaker of coffee.

'You still here Boss? I thought you'd be long gone.'

'I stayed on because I won't be coming in tomorrow,' Caton told him. 'I don't think you should either. We've worked every weekend since this investigation began. I don't think one day's going to make much difference. DS Stuart's not due to see Stone until next Tuesday, and he is still under surveillance.'

'You're right,' said Holmes. 'But I'd only be kicking my heels. Marge is over in Hull with the kids; staying with her mother. So if it's alright with you I'm coming in.'

'Well if you do, and anything comes up, you'd better contact Detective Superintendent Radford. I'm going to be incommunicado. Unless it's really serious.'

Holmes leaned back in his chair, and raised his eyebrows. He had a stupid grin on his face. 'Going somewhere special?'

'No Gordon, just to watch Wigan take on West Brom.'

'Wigan?' Holmes was incredulous. 'I thought you were a City fan?'

'I am, when I get the chance,' said Caton already halfway out of the door. 'But my nephew supports the Latics and the Warriors. Good night Gordon.'

Holmes was left scratching his head; literally and metaphorically. He could have sworn that the Boss was an only child.

'We park here Tom. This one here!'

Caton signalled right, pulled up before the red and white barrier pole, and wound down the window.

The security guard leaned in to check the pass that Helen had given him. He smiled at the boy on the booster seat. 'Hello Harry,' he said cheerfully. 'Wot d'you reckon…we going to win today?'

'Easy peasy Phil,' the boy replied gleefully. 'We're going to wallop them!'

'Bay 17 on the right sir,' said Phil. 'Enjoy the game.'

'Can we go to the Megastore now Tom?' Harry asked as Caton locked and alarmed the car. 'You promised.'

'Of course Harry,' he said. 'You show me the way.'

His son grasped his hand, and led him past the wide frontage of the reception area. In the glass panels above the doorways a mass of menacing grey clouds were reflected like a vast skyscape. Harry led him down the path that led to the adjacent retail park.

'What would you like for your birthday Harry?' Caton asked. 'How about a home strip?'

'No thank you,' he replied. 'I've' got one of those. I want an away strip.' As an afterthought, he squeezed Caton's hand and added. 'Please.'

Joanne Stuart strolled down to Carluccio's on Hardman Square, the heart of the new financial district in Spinngfields. She rewarded herself for her morning's work with a large glass of Pino Grigio Puiallino, and a plate of the Antipasto Massimo. While she waited for them to arrive she tried to spot the watchers from the surveillance team. Having been one herself she expected it to be easy. There were a number of possibilities. A man standing in the doorway of the Grant Thornton building, another hovering outside the HSBC headquarters, another sat on a bollard watching the passers by, and her favourite, sitting at an outside table beneath an electric heater, reading the Manchester Evening News. By the time her food arrived only the last of them remained, and he was in the process of standing up to greet a female companion. Arm in arm they sauntered off towards Deansgate. Wherever the watchers were they were very, very good. She comforted herself with the knowledge that if she couldn't spot them then Stone, who didn't even know he was being watched, wouldn't have a cat in hell's chance. She sipped the luscious melon and pear flavoured wine, and turned her attention to the colourful plate of Napoli and Milano salami, roast ham, fresh green beans and mint salad, caponata, sun-dried tomatoes, roasted peppers filled with pesto and olives, and the lightest, tastiest, slice of focaccia she had ever had. And all on expenses. It's a hard life, she reflected, but someone's got to do it.

'Are you sure you want this Harry?' Caton stared at the fluorescent yellow shirt trimmed with black, and the black shorts. He couldn't decide if the shirt was yellow or lime green.

'Yes please Tom. I want that one.' Said Harry.

'That's the mini kit away strip. It's £29.99,' said the assistant. 'But there's twenty percent off the training range.'

'Does that include the away strip?' Caton asked.

'No'

'But he wants the away strip.'

'That's full price.'

'If you'd asked for a Mercedes top of the range would you go and buy a Fiat Punto just because it was twenty percent off?' Said Caton, becoming increasingly exasperated.

The assistant thought about it, then shook his head. 'No,' he said. 'But I might go for a curried chicken pastie, instead of a meat pie.'

They left the Megastore, and headed back towards the stadium. Harry trailed the bag containing his birthday present along the ground, and when Caton tried to relieve him of it they ended up in a tug of war. Caton won, but Harry decided to sulk, and wouldn't hold his hand.

'Kids…who'd have them Tom?'

Startled, Caton looked up. A big, burly, uniformed chief inspector stood grinning at him. Beside him stood a sergeant Caton didn't know. The chief inspector was Harvey Bateson from Bolton Division. Presumably drafted in for the match.

'Tell me about it.' Said Caton.

'I didn't know you had a lad.' Said Bateson.

'I don't,' Caton replied, the lie sticking in his throat. 'Harry's the son of a friend of mine.'

'It's my birthday.' Harry declared

'Good for you. What did you get then?'

'Uncle Tom bought me an away strip.' He said.

'Uncle Tom?' Said Bateson raising his eyebrows.

'It's just an expression,' said Caton. 'You know how it is. Come on Harry.' He grabbed the boy's hand, and started to walk away.

'I know how it is,' Bateson called after them. 'Enjoy the match.'

That's all I need, Caton reflected. When he was promoted, the article in *Brief*, the GMP news magazine, had described him as single. Knowing Bateson, this would be all over the Bolton, Wigan and Manchester Division by Christmas, if not before. He tightened his grip on Harry's tiny hand. Bugger it he muttered to himself, they can think what they like.

'Bugger what Tom?' Harry chirped up.

'Rugger,' said Caton. 'Rugger, as in Rugby football.' He could tell that the boy wasn't buying it.

Joanne paid her bill, and walked out into the cold November air. The sky was overcast and threatening rain. Maybe even sleet. She turned up the collar of her coat, and started off in the direction of the Rylands Library. Here comes the real reward she told herself. A major shopping spree. Whatever else the credit crunch had done it had got the high street prices tumbling. It was just a shame she couldn't put this on expenses too.

Behind her, Watcher Three stepped out from the Giraffe Restaurant doorway. Up ahead, Watcher Four was already on Deansgate, moving slowly, listening to his colleague's situation report in his earpiece; ready to change direction as required. Bo Peep was nicely boxed in. Bring it on, he was thinking. The sooner the better, I'm freezing my balls off out here.

Caton rubbed his hands together. It was warmer up here just behind the Directors' box, but it was still very cold. Helen had kitted Harry out with gloves, a scarf, and a bob hat. He looked as warm as toast, but his cheeks were pink, and his nose had a permanent drip. Caton was surprised at how knowledgeable his son was about the Latics, and even more astounded that he had managed to concentrate on the game for so long. Not least because the visitors had just scored the first goal of the match within two minutes of the start of the second half. Ishmael Miller had pounced on a mistake by Titus Bramble, and put the ball beyond reach of a despairing Chris Kirkland in goal. And still his son was following the game intently, providing his own commentary to the amusement of those in the row in front. My hands and feet may be cold thought Caton, but I'm warming to this little person perched on his chair beside me.

'I have visual on The Shepherd. I repeat... I have visual on The Shepherd.'

'Understood,' replied Watcher One. 'You stay with Bo Peep; We'll stay with The Shepherd.'

The two surveillance teams had been aware long before Joanne had left the RBS building that Stone was waiting to catch sight of her. His every move had been recorded. At the very least they had a stalker on their hands. Control had been alerted, and DI Holmes and DCS Radford were following every move back at the station. They had agreed that there was no point in bringing up the communications van because DS Stuart was not wired up. But it was sitting in the yard behind Bootle Street nick in case they needed it.

'Shall I contact DCI Caton?' Asked Gordon Holmes.

Radford shook his head. 'No need DI Holmes. Stone is probably doing what he did the other day; watching her, getting to know her routines. I don't think there's any need to disturb Mr Caton, not unless Stone actually makes contact with her. Then you can let him know.'

Holmes's instinct told him that Boss would want to know, but Jimmy Radford didn't take kindly to being contradicted. Anyway, she was in the city centre in broad daylight, with four officers boxing the two of them in. What could possibly go wrong?

'*GOAL…!*'

Caton leapt to his feet to steady his son. Harry was jumping up and down, punching the air. Caton hoisted him up so he could see the celebrations on the pitch, and the replay on the big screen. Paul Robinson had made a careless back pass which the Senegalese striker Henri Camara had seized upon, before striking the ball acrobatically past the hapless Scott Carson. The scores were level. Twenty nine minutes to go, plus added time. Game on.

Joanne bought a pair of boots in Shoon, spent half an hour in Marks and Spencer where she bought some fashion jewellery, ten minutes in Selfridges, and thirty five in Harvey Nichols, in neither of which she bought anything. Now she was in the Triangle, looking for a dress in Jigsaw.

'He must have nerves of steel following her round that lot,' said Radford. His leg was going up and down like a piston. 'I get bored stupid after ten minutes shopping with the wife.'

'He's taking a hell of a risk,' Holmes said. 'God knows how many cameras he's been picked up on. I'll be surprised if the city centre monitoring team haven't already marked him down as suspicious. All we need is for a uniformed officer to stop and question him. That could blow the whole operation.'

'Don't worry about it,' said Radford. 'One of the surveillance team will move in and forestall them if it looks like that's going to happen. Anyway, I'm going to get a drink. Do you want one?'

'No thanks Sir,' said Holmes, trying hard to concentrate on the chatter between the watchers. 'You look like you need one more than me.'

'GOAL...!'

Twenty three thousand people were on their feet, cheering. Harry was up on his chair. Caton was trying to persuade him to get down, worried that even if he didn't fall off, the seat might break. Three minutes to go, the Latics goal under intense pressure that brought a string of fantastic saves from Kirkland and, just when it looked like a certain draw, Emmerson Boyce had latched onto a Jason Koumas corner at the back post, and headed what looked like a certain winner. Harry flung his arms around Caton's neck, and his little legs around his waist, and hugged him tight. Caton hadn't felt like this in a long time.

It felt good. Really, really good.

33

Caton suggested Rigoletto's, the stadium's own Italian restaurant, for their post match meal. Harry was having none of it. It was his birthday after all. They ended up in Burger King on the retail park.

'The chicken burger looks nice,' said Caton.

'I'll have the Aberdeen Angus mini burgers please,' said Harry.

'How about a Five Alive to drink?' said Caton. 'Five kinds of juicy fruit in a neat little bag, with a straw?'

Harry looked disgusted. 'I'll have a Coke please. And a double chocolate fudge cake ice cream.'

Caton gave up trying to persuade him down the healthy eating route, added a Sweet Chilli Royale Chicken on a sesame bun to the order for himself, and found them a table.

'Did you enjoy the game Harry?' Caton asked.

'It was mint.' The boy replied through a mouth full of burger.

Caton couldn't believe that he was hearing 1950's slang from a six year old. God I'm out of touch, he thought.

'What are you smiling at Tom?' asked Harry.

'I was just thinking about that last goal.' Caton replied. 'What a killer.'

Joanne Stuart had one last call to make. She always bought a book token from Waterstones for her brother at Christmas. It was never too early to do her Christmas shopping; in this job you never knew what might turn up if you left it till the last moment. In any case, it was pouring down with rain and it was an excuse to get into the dry; maybe have a coffee in the café on the second floor. As she joined the queue to pay she noticed Simon Stone standing at the end of the counter trying out the eBook Reader on display. It was the last thing she had been expecting. Like Caton she never believed in coincidences. She took a deep breath, and walked over.

'Dr Stone,' she said. 'Fancy meeting you here.'

'Jane, what a pleasant surprise.' He said convincingly.

'Are you thinking of buying one of those?' She asked.

He shrugged. 'I don't know. I must admit I am into gadgets, especially techno ones, but to be honest I don't think you can beat getting your hands on the real thing, do you?'

There was playful smile on his lips. Something about the way he said it sent a chill through her

'I know what you mean,' she said, smiling back at him. *And I really do you bastard*, is what she was thinking.

Stone returned the screen to the menu page, and stepped away to give her his full attention. 'Look, he said. 'I know we don't have a session booked until next week, but I think it would be really good to have a chat outside of my practice rooms. I was thinking of have an early dinner here in town. Why don't you join me? My treat?'

'I don't know,' Joanne said hesitantly. 'Is that a normal part of a doctor client relationship?' She felt confident that both of them were being watched, and in that respect it would be safe to accept his offer, but she desperately needed to get back home and put her wire on first.

'But this isn't like seeing your GP is it?' he said. 'What you and I do is talk. Does it really matter where we talk? And when it's pouring down outside where better than somewhere warm and cosy, over a glass of wine and a good meal? I know a great gastro pub, just a stone's throw a way.'

'The Bridge?' she guessed.

'Close. Sam's Chop House.'

'I know it,' she said. On Chapel Walks. Stone flags on the floor, assorted wooden tables, and hearty British food.'

He smiled. 'Exactly. So you'll come? We don't have to talk shop, just chat.'

'I would,' she said. 'But I've still got some shopping to do, and then I need to go home, and get changed.'

'Well if you let me know when you've finished shopping you can give me a call, and I'll come and pick you up, and take you home. I can wait while you get changed.'

There was no way Joanne wanted him to know where she lived. Nor did she want to blow what looked like a solid gold opportunity to find out more about him. Maybe even to put an end to all this. 'There's no need, really,' she told him. 'If you can give me an hour, as soon as I'm ready I'll call you, and you can pick me up at the entrance to Piccadilly Station, where the cars pull in.'

'He studied her for a moment, and then smiled. 'Brilliant,' he said. He took a leaflet from the box beside the eBook Reader, and wrote his mobile number on it. 'Here you are. I'll get a coffee upstairs and have a browse through the books. When you call it'll take me ten minutes to get to my car, and drive over to Piccadilly. Are you sure you don't want me to pick you up at your place?'

'I'm sure,' she said.

It was the last thing she wanted.

Stone made a call on his mobile phone, then he climbed to the third floor, selected a book from the crime section, took it to the café, where he bought a double expresso, sat down, and began to read. Watcher One ordered a macchiato, selected a newspaper from the rack, and chose a seat around the corner, from which he could see the back of The Shepherd's head, and both exits from the café area.

'We've got to tell DCI Caton,' said Holmes.

'But we don't know what's going on,' said Superintendent Radford not unreasonably. 'Alright, so he's made contact. But if she's walked off, and he hasn't followed her, what's the panic? I say you wait until she contacts us.' He shrugged half heartedly. 'You're the acting SIO. It's up to you. But don't be surprised if DCI Caton tells you you're wasting his time.'

The way Caton had been behaving lately Holmes doubted it. Fortunately he didn't have long to wait. Joanne rang to bring them up to date.

'Where are you now?' asked Holmes.

'I'm just approaching the apartment,' she told him. 'It'll take me about twenty minutes to have a shower, change, and set things up. Have you told the Boss what's happening?'

'Not yet, I was waiting till I'd heard from you.'

'Good,' she said. 'Because I don't think you should bother him just because I'm having a meal with the man.'

'Are you sure?' said Holmes. 'The football match will be over by now, and it's only his nephew.'

'Take my word for it.' She assured him. 'Let him be. The place where we're eating is going to be heaving with you know who. If he puts so much as foot wrong they'll be on to him.'

'If you're sure?'

'I'm sure.'

'OK,' he said. 'The van will be outside in ten minutes. I'm driving over to take up residence with Clarke. Give me a ring when you're ready to go.'

By the time he got back to Helen's place Caton had learned that his son could count in fives and tens up to fifty, tell the time on his watch, say the days of the week, the month, and the year, knew most of the parts of the body and what the five senses were, knew his address and phone number, knew the story of The Very Hungry Caterpillar by heart, could sing five songs all the way through, and knew seven rude words. Caton had no idea if that meant he was a genius, normal, or a slow learner. It felt like he was a genius, but then he would be wouldn't he, with his genes. He let Harry out of the car, made sure he had the bag containing his birthday present, and rang the door bell. Nobody came. He checked his watch. It was half past six. Helen had said she'd be home by five. He tried the side gate but it was locked.

'Have you got a key Harry?' He asked.

The boy shook his head. 'No I haven't. Can we go in please, I'm cold.'

'Does mummy keep a spare one anywhere?' he asked, lifting the pot of winter pansies beside the door to look underneath.

His son shook his head. 'I don't know,' he said stamping his feet. 'I'm cold.'

Caton tried Helen's mobile number again, and got the same recorded message. He left another message asking where she was, and telling her they were locked out, and would she ring him straight away.

'Is there another house we can go to while we wait Harry, until your mummy gets home?' He asked.

'There. We can stay there.' The boy pointed to the neighbouring detached house. There was early 1990s Rover car in the drive, and a For Sale sign lying on the lawn.

'Do you know who lives there Harry?'

'Mrs Jones,' said the boy. 'She's nice.'

Caton took him by the hand. 'Come on then.' he said.

'Can I help you?' He was in his mid sixties. Grey haired, tired looking, thin.

'Harry is it?' He said smiling down at the boy.

'Is Mrs Jones in?' said Caton. 'Only Harry's mother isn't home yet, and we're locked out. I'd wait in the car but it would mean keeping the engine running.'

'And I'm cold!' said Harry.

'I'm sorry, she isn't, said the man. 'But you're welcome to come in and wait.' He stepped aside, and let them in.

'I'm ready to go.' Said Joanne. 'I'm going to ring him now. I'll ring you again when I get back.'

'OK,' said Holmes. 'Take care.'

Joanne switched off, and prepared to make the call to Stone. I wish people wouldn't keep telling me to take care, she reflected, it only makes it worse.

'The Shepherd is on the move.' Reported Watcher One.

Ten minutes elapsed, and then they heard his voice again; loud and clear. 'The Shepherd is in place.' He said.

As soon as Joanne was back at the safe house, and the van was parked up outside, Watcher's Three and Four were sent on to Sam's Chop House. One to book a table in the restaurant, the other to have a drink at the adjoining bar that would already be heaving with shoppers on their way home, and revellers warming up for the night. There was no point, the Head of Special Op's had reasoned, in having the four of them trying to tail DS Stuart and Simon Stone when the two of them were travelling together. It only made it that much more likely they would be spotted. Holmes agreed.

'What about the van?' he said. If we stay where we are, and follow DS Stuart the three hundred yards to the station, we're going to stand out like a sore thumb.'

'You're right,' said Radford from the relative comfort of the incident room. 'Why don't you drive down, and park on the opposite side of the road to the forecourt exit. Then when your man drives out you can follow behind Watcher One, park up on Chapel Walks, and keep tabs on the conversation between DS Stuart and her target?'

'Good idea,' said Holmes, rolling his eyes in the direction of DC Clarke.

'God, I hope no one's monitoring this channel,' muttered Clarke. 'You can tell he's never done any covert work.'

'I don't really want to get that far ahead of her.' Said Holmes. 'Why don't we drive a couple of hundred yards down to the bottom of Chapeltown Street and then, when we can see her in the rear view mirror, we can drive the last couple of hundred yards to the station.'

'Sounds good to me.' Said Clarke.

The rain had lessened to a miserable drizzle. Joanne raised the collar on her coat, and started down the steps. As she reached the gates she felt a massive jolt in the middle of her back, and her legs collapsed from under her. She lay on the ground, helpless, her limbs jerking uncontrollably like a rag doll on speed. She was vaguely aware of her hands being bound behind her. She tried to scream, but nothing came out. Something hard and cold was forced between her teeth, and secured roughly behind the back of her head. Some kind of mask was placed over her eyes. She felt herself lifted bodily, and carried through the gates. She was bundled into the passenger floor well of a waiting vehicle, and heard the door slammed shut behind her.

'We've lost signal,' said Clarke suddenly. He started twiddling dials, and pressing the keys on his control board.

'Which signal?' said Holmes instantly alert.

'Both of them; audio and GPS.'

'How's that possible?' asked Holmes.

'I don't know, unless she's switched them off'

Holmes moved to the back of the van, and stared out through the rear windows. 'I can't see her,' he said. You'd better turn round.'

The driver had to wait for a black VW Toureg to cruise past. As he made the turn, Holmes called up Watcher One. 'Where is The Shepherd? He asked.

'The Shepherd is standing by the main entrance, looking at his watch,' came the reply. 'What do you want me to do?'

'Keep watching,' said Holmes. 'If he moves, or does anything…anything at all, I want to know.'

They were outside the open gates to the apartment complex. Holmes leapt out and searched the courtyard, then he entered the building and unlocked the door to the apartment. It took thirty seconds to establish that DS Stuart had gone. Holmes dashed out to the van and began to follow the protocols. Despite being surrounded by all that high technology equipment he had never felt as helpless in his entire life.

34

The tremor in her legs had gone. She felt weak and nauseous. There was a ringing in her ears. Her head was jammed up against the passenger foot rest, and her knees squeezed up towards her chest. Every time she tried to change position the plastic cable ties bit into her wrists. There were now ties around her ankles too. A solid nylon bar clamped between her teeth was attached to brass rings either side of her mouth, and a leather strap that fastened behind her head. Her mouth was dry, and she found it impossible to swallow. There was something hard resting against her thigh. She cursed herself for her stupidity.

'Stop struggling or I'll have to do it again.'

It was a man's voice. Slightly high pitched. It was a voice she had heard before somewhere, but couldn't place. She only knew that it wasn't Stone's.

'Cattle prods have been known to kill a human being,' he said. 'They're nowhere near as safe as those tazers the police use, but I'm afraid it's all I've got.'

He shifted it so that the delivery end was jammed between her legs, and the handle rested between the handbrake and the gear stick.

'I suggest you sit back and enjoy the ride.' He said. His laugh was cold and pitiless.

Caton kept trying to reach Helen. Eventually, he gave up. Almost immediately his phone rang. It was Gordon Holmes.

'I'm sorry Sir,' he said. 'I've been trying to get you but your phone's been engaged.'

'Is there a problem?' said Caton. He could already tell there was, from the tone of his voice and that fact that he'd called him Sir.

'I'm sorry Sir,' said the DI. 'But it's all falling apart. DS Stuart…she's disappeared.'

A cold hand clutched Caton's heart. His grip on the phone threatened to crush it. 'What do you mean, she's disappeared?'

Holmes told him.

'Who's in charge?' Caton asked.

'I'm acting as Bronze Commander on the ground. Mr Radford as Silver Command out of the MIR, and Commander Lucas is heading in to Chester House to take over Gold Command and muster whatever extra resources we might need.

'Where are you now?'

'I'm in the Comm's van, we're quartering the area in the hope of picking up a signal.'

You're not going to, Caton was tempted to say, but what was the point; Holmes would already know that, but what else could he do. 'Where's Stone now?' he asked.

'He hung around waiting for DS Stuart to arrive, used his mobile a couple of times, and then drove home. The lights are on, the TV's flickering in the lounge, and there's some music playing in one of the other rooms. His BMW's in the drive with the tracker still on it, and that signal is working. The Watchers have got a visual on the car and the house; they're parked one at each end of the street.' He paused, summoning up the courage to say it. 'Looks like it isn't Stone, Boss. '

Caton didn't even want to think about that possibility. 'What about DS Stuart's tracker?' He said.

'God knows,' said Holmes. 'Her unit still isn't sending. We know it was working when she left the apartment.' He lowered his voice to a whisper. 'Radford's twitching like a blue arsed fly Boss, and he doesn't seem to have a clue what to do. I think he's hoping Commander Lucas will do it for him. I can't just sit here driving round in circles. There must be something we can do?'

TV flickering, music on in another room. Caton didn't buy it. 'Send them in there Gordon, and pull Stone in. Shake his tree till the leaves fall. You said he'd made a phone call. Find out who he was calling. You've got to either rule him in or out. You don't have any alternative.'

'Radford isn't going to like it,' said Holmes.

'Just do it!'

Caton paced anxiously up and down in the hallway, his mind a blur. None of it made any sense. And it was his fault. He should have been there. Had he been, he would have insisted that they had a visual on her from the moment that she stepped outside the apartment. But you weren't there, he told himself again. You should have been there.

'He's not there!' said Holmes. 'The bastard's gone. Television's on full blast, all the light's are on, his car's still there in the drive, but he's gone.'

'How the bloody hell did they let that happen?'

'There's a lane at the back. He's got a gate in his fence leads straight onto it. According to his neighbour he occasionally has some kind of 4x4 he parks on the lane from time to time.'

'I thought he only had one car?'

'According to the DVLC.'

'Shit.'

'So it must be registered to someone else. We don't even know the make, only that it's black.'

'He can't have got far,' said Caton. 'Get out an all cars alert.'

'I've already done that,' said Holmes. 'And Commander Lucas has arrived at Chester House. She's going to get the traffic police watching all the arterial routes, and the main motorways.

'Right,' said Caton. 'Get the locals to pick up Hatch, and get Superintendent Radford to send some of our team down to work on him; I can't believe he doesn't know something.'

'What if it isn't either of them Boss? What if we were wrong, and Stone isn't the perp?'

'Christ Gordon, I don't even want to think about it. Just do it. And get back to me as soon as you've got anything. I'm coming in.'

Caton looked at his watch. It was twenty five minutes since Joanne had gone missing. Whoever had taken her would almost certainly be beyond any cordon that they threw up now. And they didn't even know what they were looking for. It was a complete and total mess. His mess. He walked back into the living room. Harry was curled up on the sofa wearing his football kit over his clothes, and watching the television. Mr Jones was in the other chair reading the television listings. Caton made a decision. When he explained it all, Helen would understand.

'I've got a problem,' said Caton. 'I've got to go. Can I leave Harry with you until his mum turns up? She can't possibly be much longer.'

Mr Jones lowered the magazine. 'Don't worry about it,' he said. I'll keep an eye on him. We'll be alright won't we Harry?'

The boy nodded, his gaze fixed on the action on the television screen. His thumb had gravitated to his mouth.

It must be nice to be six, thought Caton, to live in the moment, with nothing to worry about.

'Goodbye then Harry,' he said, ruffling his hair. 'I'll see you soon.'

'Goodbye.' said his son.

As Caton reached the door he heard his son call after him.

'Thanks Tom,' he said. 'It was mint.'

Caton sat in his car, keys in the ignition, eyes closed, trying to concentrate. Where the hell was he supposed to go? Into Manchester where Joanne had last been? To the major incident room in Leigh? To Chester House? More to the point, where would the perpetrator be heading for? And who *was* the perpetrator? There were only two possibilities; either Stone was not their man, and there was someone else not even on their radar, or else he had an accomplice. If it was the former, then it was a hell of a coincidence that Stone should have also disappeared, and surreptitiously at that. Caton didn't believe in coincidences.

It wouldn't be Cutacre or Bluebell Hollow. Not with all the activity going on there now, and the night patrols. Maybe somewhere near the Oasis, assuming that was still the connection. Wherever it was, it would be an area the perpetrator knew well. He screwed his eyes up tighter. What the hell was there near the Oasis? Suddenly he recalled the prints in the Reception area at the Oasis, and Joanne's voice on the tape.

'That's a nice a photo. Where is it?'

And Stone had replied.

'Shemmy Moss, in the Delamere Forest. Have you never been there?'

'No.'

'You should. It's one of my favourite places. It's beautiful. Haunting and peaceful at the same time'.

He slammed the steering wheel with his fist. Then he rang Holmes on his Bluetooth.

'Gordon, I think I know where he's headed,' he said. 'Delamere Forest. It's only a couple of miles from the Oasis.'

'I know it Boss,' said Holmes. 'I've been there loads of times. It's bloody massive. It'll be like looking for a needle in a haystack.'

'Tell them to start with Shemmy Moss,' said Caton. 'I'm on my way.'

He started the engine, punched the name into his sat nav, placed his magnetic flashing light on the roof, and set off towards the M6 roundabout at Orrell Post.

He was over the Thelwall Viaduct and preparing to join the inside lane for the M56 South when his phone went. It was Holmes again.

'You're not going to like this,' he said ominously. 'Hatch. He's dead.'

'Christ!' Caton exclaimed. 'How?

'He fell down the stairs at his flat. Broke his neck.'

'Or he was pushed.'

'A neighbour found him. Cheshire CID were already on the scene when DCs Langham and Shaw got there. They agree with you. Said he must have literally flown through the air to have landed where he did. D'you think it means the perpetrator's sussed out DS Stuart is police?'

'God, I hope not,' said Caton. 'It'll only make him all that more careful.'

'Maybe he's just been spooked by all of the attention we've given the Oasis,' said Holmes. 'Maybe he's just covering his tracks.'

'Maybe,' said Caton. In his heart of hearts he doubted it. Whoever he was, he either knew or suspected. Either way it was him, Caton, who had let her put herself in danger. Who had wanted her to hang on in there. And when she needed him, where had he been?'

'I'll be with you in less than fifteen minutes,' he said. 'Get the whole of the Team to converge on the Forest. I'll get Gold Command to send the Tactical Aid Armed Response Team down there. And see if you can get hold of the Forest Rangers. It's our only hope.'

The driver dipped the lights on the Taurus, turned off the road, and drove slowly down the narrow track deep into the forest. It bumped along for several minutes. Each time it hit a rut Joanne's head banged against the side panel, and the passenger foot rest dug into her back. The only sounds she could hear were the swishing of the windscreen wipers, and the steady hum of the engine.

The car came to sudden halt, throwing her forward into the confined space beneath the glove compartment. The engine stopped, and she heard the driver's door open, and then the passenger door. Two hands grabbed her beneath the shoulders, and dragged her roughly from the car. She lay sprawled, face down, against the dank and stinking leaf mould on the forest floor. She felt the cable ties around her ankles being cut, and then she was hauled to her feet. Whoever this man was he was strong. He grabbed her by the hair, and pushed the cattle prod into the small of her back. The mask had slipped at an angle, and he it pulled off so that for the first time she could see him. He was head and shoulders taller than her, and muscular with it. His hair was short and blond with spikes, once gelled, that now dripped water from the drizzling rain. He wore a black fitted waterproof jacket and matching trousers over lightweight walking boots. She recognised him instantly. Max Vine the heath studio manager, from the Oasis. With frightening clarity, she realised that they had got it wrong. And that Tom would be frantically pursuing Stone. Chasing shadows. But at least there was the GPS. At least there was that.

'Let's go,' he said.

He pushed her ahead of him. The only light came from the sidelights on the Taurus, and the moon shining dimly through a double filter of clouds, and the leafless branches of the trees. She stumbled several times. Each time it felt as though her hair was being torn from her scalp as Vine hoisted her back onto her feet.

They reached a small clearing where rotten trees had been removed. There was a silver birch close to its centre. He directed her towards it, and turned her until her back was hard against it. She could feel the unit pressing against the base of her spine. Before she realised what was happening he had pulled a cord around her neck, pinning her to the tree. He slipped a metal handcuff around her left wrist, cut the plastic ties with a box cutter, then swiftly grabbed her other wrist, pulled them both together around the tree, and snapped shut the remaining cuff. Vine stood a yard in front of her to admire his handiwork. He smiled insanely.

'And now we wait,' he said.

Caton was in Oakmere, at the junction with Tarporley Road, when he received another call. It was Helen.

'Tom, where are you?' she sounded anxious.

'It's difficult to explain,' he said. 'It's complicated. I'll ring you tomorrow.'

'What do you mean?' She shouted. 'Where the hell is Harry?'

'It's alright, 'he said trying to reassure her. 'I left him next door at Number Seven; with Mr Jones.'

'You did what?'

'I left him next door with Mr Jones.'

'I don't believe that even you could be that stupid!' She yelled.

Caton couldn't believe that she was being this unreasonable. 'You left me with no other option,' he said. 'The door was locked, you weren't answering your phone. I don't see what the problem is.'

'The problem,' she said. 'Is that Mrs Jones moved out last Friday, and there is no Mr Jones. If anything happens to Harry I'll kill you. Do you hear me? I'll kill you!'

When Helen rang back she was so distraught that he had to pull over to the side of the road to deal with it. There was no one in at number seven. She was convinced that Harry had been snatched by a paedophile. Caton doubted it, but he no longer trusted his own judgement when it came to the people he loved. Helen expected him to turn round, and go straight back. Torn between DS Stuart, whom he knew to be in danger, and his son who only might be, his mind failed to function. It was as though his brains had been scrambled. He lowered his head onto the steering wheel, and closed his eyes. In his mind's eye he could see them both. Innocent vulnerable Harry curled up on the sofa, thumb in mouth, Joanne Stuart smiling up at him, confident that she would be safe in his hands. His mind began to project the fate that might even now be befalling each of them. It was a nightmare choice. He opened his eyes, lifted his head, and told Helen precisely why he couldn't go back. Even before he'd started to tell her, he had known that there was no way she was going to understand.

'I'll get onto Wigan, Helen,' he promised. 'And get people out there straight away. Don't worry, I'll make sure they take this seriously, and I'll come back as soon as I've found my officer.'

'That's not good enough,' she yelled. 'I want you here you bastard. You lost him...you can find him!'

'I can't do that Helen, I'm sorry,' he said. I'm going now so that I can ring the duty inspector at Wigan. Harry will be alright. You'll see.'

'I want you here,' she said. 'He's *your* son for God's sake!'

'Helen, I've got to go.' He said, and rang off. Somewhere, somehow I've angered the Gods, Caton told himself, and now they're out to get me. He didn't think there was anything more they could do to him. His world was already falling apart.

35

The rain had ceased. The only sound was the dripping of water through the branches. Joanne Stuart shivered involuntarily. Vine was sitting on the stump of a tree staring at her with a sickly grin. What was taking them so long? She'd switched the unit on. They'd tested it. It was working when she left the apartment, and Vine had certainly not discovered it. They're coming, she told herself; they'll be here soon.

There was a new sound. A car engine approaching, still some way off. Her heart began to beat faster. She strained to hear the sirens; to see the blue lights flashing against the trees. She heard the engine stop. And then there was silence. A minute passed. She saw a figure coming down the narrow path along which Vine had pushed her. Instinctively she strained forward towards him. The handcuffs bit cruelly into her wrists. She didn't care. Caton was coming. As he reached the edge of the clearing he stepped into a pool of moonlight.

'Where are you now Boss?' said Gordon Holmes.

'I'm just approaching Cuddington' Caton replied. 'My sat nav says I'm one point nine miles from my destination.' Just two miles from the Oasis, and two miles from Shemmy Moss. I hope to God it knows something I don't, he thought. It made sense, and it was all they had to go on.

'We're approaching the forest now,' Holmes told him. 'We still don't have a signal of any kind. Are you sure this is right?'

'No I'm not,' Caton replied, but it's the best we've got.' His radio crackled.

'Alpha Bravo, this is Golf Charlie,' said the distinctive voice of Lillian Lucas. 'Now that you're there I want you to take over from Bravo Charlie, do you understand?'

So now he was Bronze Command here on the ground.

'Alpha Bravo…understood.' He replied.

'India 99 is up, Tango Alpha Foxtrot Tango is awaiting instructions, through me. Do you understand?'

'Roger that Golf Charlie.' He told her. Please instruct India 99 to quarter a half mile area centred on…' he switched his sat nav to Destination, and read out the co-ordinates. 'Fifty three, thirteen, North, and twenty three, sixty four, West. Over.'

'Fifty three, thirteen, North, and twenty three, sixty four, West,' came the reply. 'Roger that Alpha Bravo.' There was a pause, and then the radio crackled again. This time Commander Lucas' voice was quieter, less formal. 'Are you sure about this Alpha Bravo?' She said.

'No,' he replied. 'I'm not.'

Barely acknowledging Vine, Stone approached her as calmly as if they were still in his therapy room.

'Hallo Jane,' he said. 'Good of you to make it.'

He reached out, seized her jacket, and tore it open. Then he pulled it roughly over her shoulders, and down her arms, until it met the impediment of the handcuffs, and hung uselessly behind her.

To her right she could see Vine moving closer.

Stone placed a hand on either side of her neck, and let them rest for a moment, taking pleasure in the fear and loathing in her eyes. His hands moved slowly down towards her breastbone. In a single movement he grasped the collars of her blouse, and ripped it apart exposing not only her bra but the slender wire that trailed from it. She saw his expression slide from surprise to anger. He traced the wire, reached behind her back, found, and pulled out the transmitter, slim as a credit card. He stared at it for a moment, then pulled her head forward, undid the buckle, and dragged the horse bit from her mouth, bruising her lips. He held the transmitter up in front of her face.

'What the hell is this?' he snarled.

Joanne stared at the device. The only thing that registered was that the LED display was not lit. Then it hit her. The cattle prod. It must have disabled it. Nobody was coming to save her. She knew that if she started to scream he would end it there and then. And anyway, who was there to hear her. All she had left was the truth.

'I'm a police officer,' she told him. Her voice croaked and it hurt her to speak. 'They know about you. They're coming for you right now.' She nodded towards the device. 'They've been tracking me.'

'Police!' Shouted Vine. 'She's a fucking policewoman. What are we going to do now? What the *fuck* are we going to do?'

Stone turned on him, his face suffused with anger and confusion. 'Calm down Vine,' he said. 'And keep your bloody voice down for a start. We've only got her word for it. She could be a reporter for all we know.'

'Look in my bag,' Joanne urged. 'Check my phone.'

Stone turned back to Vine. 'Where is it?'

'Over there.' He said, pointing to the stump where he had been sitting.

'Well don't just stand there you gormless idiot,' said Stone. 'Get it!'

For a moment Joanne thought that the bigger man was going to turn on the psychotherapist and strike him down. Instead, he turned meekly away, returning with the bag in one hand, and the cattle prod in the other. Stone snatched the bag, pulled the studs apart, and began systematically to examine and discard the contents one by one. He found the rape alarm, the tazer, and pepper spray, and threw them to the ground. In the side pocket he found her mobile phone, and switched it on. If the seemingly innocuous text messages to Caton had not convinced him, a quick scroll through her address book did. The numbers listed included names with prefixes such as DS, DC, and DCI. The confirmation was Chester House; GMP Headquarters.

'You bitch.' He said. He threw the bag on the ground. 'Put those things back in the bag while I deal with her,' he ordered Vine. He advanced towards Joanne holding the transmitter in his right hand. His body was hard against hers, and she could smell his breath, sweet and sickly, in her face. He raised his hand. She flinched instinctively as staring into her eyes he slammed the transmitter repeatedly against the tree beside her head. He stepped back, and flung the remains into the bushes beyond the clearing.

'You're too late,' said Joanne defiantly. 'They'll be here any moment now.'

Vine was backing away towards the path that led out of the clearing. 'That's it,' he said. 'I can't do this anymore. I'm out of here.'

Stone spun around to confront him. 'You managed to do Hatch.' He said.

'That was different,' Vine pleaded. 'She's police for fuck's sake. They know she's here.'

'Listen Vine,' said Stone. 'If they don't catch us, and they don't find her body, we're in the clear. So shut up and help me.'

Vine held the cattle prod out in front of him as he backed away. When he reached the edge of the clearing he flung it deep into the forest, and ran.

Caton screamed to a halt beside the Comm's van; beyond it he could see a squad car with its lights flashing in the murky darkness. Behind that was a Forest Ranger's Landrover.

Holmes leapt out through the rear doors, and ran across to the driver's side. We still haven't got a signal,' he said. 'We have got a Forest Ranger with us who said some kind of four by four went past his cottage not long since.'

'Well it didn't go past me,' said Caton. And I didn't see any side roads where it could have pulled off.'

'There are plenty of tracks the walkers and rangers

use though,' Holmes pointed out. 'But most of them have got barriers across them this time of night.'

'Not all of them,' said Caton, feeling that he was clutching at straws. But then he had been, ever since he sent them all down here. 'It must have pulled off somewhere. You track back the way you came looking for any fresh signs of tyres leaving the road. Take the Ranger with you, and the squad car can come with me.'

Stone turned back to face her. He looked tired she thought; deflated, but not defeated.

'How did you know?' He said.

She shook her head, and grimaced because it hurt to do it. 'I can't tell you that.'

'Why not?'

'Because it would prejudice our case.'

He laughed.

It was the only time she had ever seen him laugh. It made him look as mad as she now knew him to be.

'*You* aren't going to have a case,' he sneered. 'But you *are* going to be the next one'

'It was the landlady wasn't it?' She said, desperate to buy time; doubting that it would make any difference to the outcome. 'Is that when this started?' That stopped him in his tracks. 'That's right,' she said. 'We know all about it. Was she your first?

He looked at the ground, and when he looked up again his expression had changed. It was as though they were back in his consulting room.

'You don't know anything about it,' he said. 'It wasn't like that.'

'So how was it?'

He smiled thinly. 'I can't see any reason why you shouldn't know,' he said. 'It's not as though you're going to be telling anyone, and there certainly isn't anyone listening. If there was, they would have been here by now.'

'Alpha Bravo. We have a location! Over.'

Caton braked so fiercely that the squad car had to swerve to avoid hitting him. 'How? Where?' he said momentarily forgetting protocol.

'The mobile phone belonging to Juliet Sierra has just been switched on.' Replied Lilian Lucas. 'Within a quarter of a mile of your current location. Do you copy that? Over.'

Caton saw pin points of light darting like fireflies through the trees up ahead, and to the left. He slammed his foot down on the accelerator desperate to make the entrance to the track before the vehicle reached the road where it would be that much harder to stop. He knew that he wasn't going to make it. In a blur, the squad car that had been travelling behind him sped past, braked hard as it reached the turning, and skidded broadside to block the vehicle's path. The driver of the Toureg had no time to react, swerved instinctively, and crashed into trees lining the track. The bumper caved in, the bonnet sprung up, and steam billowed from the engine compartment.

Caton leapt from his car, and was first to the driver's door. A voice in his head told him that he was too late. The perpetrator was leaving the scene. It could only mean that Joanne was already dead. Anger, and a flickering vestige of hope, drove him on.

He pulled at the door handle; it was jammed. He could see the driver slumped forward against the wheel, facing away. He braced his foot against the door, and heaved in vain.

'Mind out Sir!'

Caton turned. Behind him stood one of the officers from the squad car. He had an emergency hammer raised ready to strike. Caton let go of the door handle, and stepped back. The officer smashed the tempered steel tip against the window, shattering it, reached in, released the lock, and heaved the door open. Caton pushed him aside, and pulled the driver back from the wheel so that he fell against the back of the seat like a rag doll. It was Max Vine. Blood ran from the place where his forehead met his hairline. His eyes were closed.

Caton shook him. 'Where is she you bastard?' he yelled.

He felt an arm on his shoulder. 'I don't think he's in any state to tell you Sir.'

Caton let go of Vine and stood up. The Toureg was angled across the track, and jammed between two trees. There was no way that they would be able to shift it enough to get their own vehicles past.

Another car pulled up on the road behind his own. DS Aashif Hassan, and DC Jackie Shaw climbed out. Caton looked back down the track in the direction from which Max Vine had come. The uniformed officer was leaning into the car.

'He's alive, but he's still unconscious.' He said.

Caton felt for his personal radio, and realised that he had left it in his car. 'Give me your radio.' He ordered. The policeman unhooked it, and passed it to him. Caton took it.

'With Me!' he shouted to Hassan and Shaw, before sprinting down the track into the forest.

'I couldn't face the rest of them celebrating that day,' said Stone. 'Not when I'd just been thrown on the scrap heap. I went back to the lodgings. She was there on her own. I'd had a bit to drink. I told her I'd been let go. She put her arms around me to commiserate. She had her hand on my arse. I put my hand on hers. She didn't stop me. I slid my other hand down her blouse, felt her breast, her nipple hardening. She looked up at me. I bent to kiss her. She jerked away, tearing her blouse. I grabbed her arms, and went to kiss her. She tried to push me away. She began to scream. I put a hand over her mouth. She was struggling. Her eyes wide with terror. I just wanted her to stop trying to scream. I put my other hand round her neck. Hard up against the wall. Just wanting her to stop. She tried to push away. I felt something give...like a twig snapping. Suddenly she went limp, slid down the wall and crumpled to the floor in a heap. I knew immediately that she was dead. I pulled her away from the wall.'

'You tried to save her didn't you?' She said.

He smiled again, appreciative of the fact that they had worked it out. 'They'd shown us how to do mouth to mouth at the club, but when it came to it I couldn't do it. She just stared up at me. I put her in the recovery position. Then I got out of there, and went back to the club.

'You got drunk, and spilt beer all over your trousers.' She said.

He looked at her oddly, and turned away.

Then it dawned on her. 'You had a premature ejaculation,' she said. 'That's why you spilled your beer…to cover it up.' She couldn't help herself. 'Did you come before, or after, you strangled her?'

He turned and slapped her hard across the face. His expression made her skin creep, her stomach turn over.

'*As* I strangled her,' he said. 'But you don't need to concern yourself. I don't have that problem anymore. As you're about to discover.'

He reached down and hooked one hand inside the belt of her skirt. The other he placed over her right breast, and then slid it slowly up towards her neck.

'Shelley Hassle,' she said desperate to stop him. 'The footballer's girl friend…'

'The footballers' *bike* more like.'

'Is that why you chose her? Because you thought you'd stand a chance with her? Was she the first?' She knew that her voice was becoming ever more desperate.

'He laughed as though she'd told the perfect joke. 'The first? You have no idea…'

'Her strategy had been to distract him, to blow him off course. As his hand encircled her neck she knew that it had backfired.'

'Don't do this,' she pleaded. 'They're coming. Have you any idea what they'll do to you if you do this?'

'I'll be gone long before they get here,' he said.

'They'll find me. They know you were with me. They were following you all the time. They watched you at Piccadilly station. They'll have followed you home. I don't know how you gave them the slip, but they'll know, and they'll have locked onto the tracker. You'll never get away with it.'

He shook his head. 'I will if there isn't a body. They won't find you, not where you're going. Not if they search forever. I'll tell them when you didn't turn up I was worried. I went out looking for you. I should have seen you to your door and waited for you, like I suggested.' He adopted a dramatic grieving tone.

'If only I had. God...I'll never forgive myself.'

'It won't work,' she said. She could think of nothing else to say. She felt his hand tighten on her belt and begin to pull. She tried to thrust her knee into his groin but he was too close, and responded by squeezing her neck ever tighter. Suddenly his grip loosened and his head went back, like a startled animal. She realised that he was listening to something. There were two sounds, one above the other. Someone was running down the path towards them, snapping branches underfoot, and further away but getting louder came the chatter of a helicopter. He let her go, and turned away.

'It's no use running' she said. 'The heat sensors will pick you up. It's best you give yourself up.'

Stone stared at her for a moment, stepped sideways, and within a second she had lost sight of him. She could hear him crashing through the trees behind her.

Caton ran to her. She was shivering, with cold, and crying with relief. He pulled her jacket up and over her shoulders, covering her as best he could. 'God I'm so sorry,' he said. 'I'm so sorry.'

'He's back there,' she told him. 'Behind me. Go and get the bastard.'

'I'm not leaving you,' he said. India 99 hovered above them, catching them in its spotlight. The downdraft snapped some of the smaller branches that began to shower down on them. Caton shouted into his radio over the throb of the whirling blades.'

'He's heading West,' he said.

After a ten second delay, the helicopter lifted and swung away.

Stone weaved between the trees hoping to shake off the searchlight. Fear had overtaken reason; he only knew to run. His heart was thumping in his chest and his breath was laboured. He looked over his shoulder to see if he was being pursued, and failed to notice the partially fallen birch tree ahead of him. Going full pelt, he met it at head height. The blow stunned him, and knocked him to the ground. He managed somehow to get to his feet, and stagger. He lost his footing and suddenly found he was up to his thighs in water. He looked up towards the helicopter now traversing the lake trying to pin him in the beam of its spotlight. His head began to spin. He fell, and sunk like a stone into the inky black, ice cold waters of Shemmy Moss.

As the ambulance carrying Joanne departed, Caton frantically rang Helen back. Her phone was engaged, so he tried the central Wigan police station. It was six nail biting minutes before they put him through to Phil Catterall, the Duty Inspector.

'He's safe,' he said. 'Your son is safe Tom. His

mother is with him. I'm on my way back to the station.'

Caton felt numb, and exhausted. He knew he should have felt something more, but his body was busy leaching the adrenalin from his system.

'Thank God,' he said. 'Where was he?'

'With the guy you left him with. He moved into Number Seven this morning as a tenant on a six month lease while his son builds an annex for him to move into.'

'This morning? But he knew Harry by name.' Said Caton.

'Made it his business to find out who his neighbours are. The old biddy that lives opposite popped in for a nosey, and a cup of tea. She told him.'

'Why didn't he answer the door when Harry's mother rang?'

'Because he wasn't there. He realised he didn't have enough food in to see him through till he could do a proper shop. He nipped down to the supermarket, and took your son with him. He was only gone half an hour.'

Stupid old fool, Caton was about to say before he remembered that he was the one who had left a son he hardly knew with a complete stranger. Some detective I am, he reflected; some father.

'Thanks Phil,' he said. 'I'm sorry I bothered you. I owe you one.'

'Forget it,' said the duty inspector. 'If it was my son I'd have done the same.'

It was fifteen minutes later when Caton received the text. It was short, brutal, and to the point.

You left him with strangers! I warned you. I don't want to see, or hear from you, ever again.

He put the phone back in his pocket. Right now he didn't think he could blame her. Nor did he have the energy to try. Harry was safe. Joanne was safe. That was enough. He sat down on the bonnet of his car, and let the relief wash over him.

36

'Can I come in?'

There was still some tell tale bruising at the sides of her mouth, and she looked tired. Caton made her sit down in one of the easy chairs, and sat facing her.

'I thought I told you not to come back to work until the doctor signed you off?' He said.

'Doctor? You mean shrink.' She grinned. 'I've had enough of those to last a lifetime.'

'I'm sorry I wasn't there when you needed me,' he said. It must have been the umpteenth time he'd said it: in the forest; when they were putting her in the ambulance; in the hospital; over the phone. It didn't matter how many times he said it, it still sounded pathetic.

'That's all right Boss,' she said cheerfully. 'I'm over it. Anyway, from what I gather, we wouldn't have nailed the bastard any other way; leastways, not unless it meant waiting for him to kill again.'

Caton knew that she was right. It didn't make him feel any better. 'I don't suppose I'm Abbie's flavour of the month at the moment.' He said.

She grinned. 'Let's put it this way. I'd stay well clear of her for a while. She's torn between wanting to kill you, and giving you a big hug for saving my life.'

That was at least two people who could cheerfully have killed him. When Kate got home tomorrow it might easily be three. DS Stuart interrupted his ruminations.

'I know it sounds daft, Boss, but I'd like to go back to Bluebell Hollow one last time if that's alright?'

Her face was paler than usual he realised, and that only served to accentuate the dark rings beneath her eyes. Caton understood a thing or two about closure. She might think she was over it, but she was not.

'Are you still seeing the force counsellor Joanne?' he asked.

She nodded. 'Yes Boss.'

He stood up, took his jacket from the back of his chair, and put it on. 'OK.' he said. I'm coming with you.'

She stiffened. 'To the counsellor?'

Caton laughed. 'No you numpty,' he said. 'To Bluebell Hollow.'

'You were probably right,' he told her as they headed out onto the bypass. 'Stone kept handwritten diaries going back ten years or more. He had entries in them covering the dates that each of the girls went missing: theatre bookings, visits to the cinema, meals out; all impossible to check.'

'What about his credit card records?' she asked.

'He paid for the tickets in advance, over the phone. That doesn't mean he actually used them though does it? It was just an elaborate smokescreen. Enough to create doubt in the minds of a jury.'

'What about records of his sessions with the girls?' She said. 'They were all his patients surely?'

'According to his records, none of them were. But then neither were you.

'What has Vine had to say?' She asked.

Caton pulled up at the traffic lights by the entrance to Tesco. He shook his head. 'According to him, Stone had asked him to identify potential clients with a particular physical and psychological profile, and to get Hatch to hand out his business card. Stone paid Vine, and gave him the money to keep Hatch sweet. When Vine became suspicious because these girls were suddenly disappearing, Stone threatened to implicate him. After all, he was clearly the middle man in the enterprise. To make sure that Vine kept his mouth shut, he upped the payments, supplied him with a free cocktail of body building drugs, and started to involve him further. Getting him to abduct the girls; rewarding him by letting him watch while he taunted, abused and killed them.'

Hatch knew nothing about this?'

'Vine says not. But once we turned up he became suspicious. That's when Stone decided to have him silenced.'

'I would never have dreamt that Vine could be a killer, or help Stone to trap and kill those women.' She reflected.

'Nasty things those anabolic steroids,' Caton replied. 'They can cause roid rage, impotence, and schizophrenic symptoms. You'd be surprised how many murders have been attributed to them around the world.'

'Will Vine's testimony, together with mine, be enough to tie Stone to those girls?' She asked, needing to know that the case would be closed as solved.

'Fortunately we have something else to go on as well.' He told her. 'That Range Rover Stone used to get to Delamere Forest belonged to his sister. It turns out she lives and works in London; some financial institution on Canary Wharf. She has a cottage on the edge of the forest that she uses whenever she's up North. That's where she keeps the Range Rover. She bought it with the money she got when their father died. Stone used his share to set up his business. She let him use them both whenever she didn't need to, which was most of the time.'

'He took his victims there before he killed them' She guessed.

Caton shook his head. 'Apparently not. According to Vine they were all killed the night he took them, just as you would have been. But Stone couldn't resist keeping trophies. Clothing mainly. We found their DNA, and his. He also kept tapes of his sessions with them Imagine that. Sitting there listening to them, over and over again. Fondling their underwear, reliving the control he had over them. We found them in a trunk, in the cottage loft space.

Joanne knew that she should be pleased that it was over, or at the very least relieved, but she was only aware of a profound sense of sadness. 'How many?' she asked.

Caton slowed as they reached the mini roundabout by the new police station on the edge of the Hag Fold Estate. It still bothered him that the traditional blue lamp sat atop a minaret style tower here, and at other newly constructed stations in the area. Not that he didn't support the police's role in reflecting an increasingly multi racial society, only that it seemed unnecessarily provocative on the edge of a predominantly white working class estate. As he set off again he glanced across at Joanne.

'There were nine altogether.' He said. He hadn't thought that her face could go any paler, but it did. 'Are you alright, Joanne?' He asked.

She nodded. 'He said I had no idea. I just didn't imagine…' Her voice tailed off.

'Vine has given us the names of eight of them,' he said. 'The other two, we're just hoping we'll get DNA matches for.'

They carried on in silence past Atherton station, and up Newbrook Road. 'So you see, 'Caton said at last. 'Without what you did we might never have caught him.'

'Why did he do it?' She knew that it would make no difference now, but she needed to know.

'According to his sister,' Caton said. 'Shortly after he was let go by the club his father, who had always pushed him like mad, left his mother, and took his sister with him. Stone's mother was already ill. Her husband walking off like that made it ten times worse. She was house bound. Stone became his mother's principal carer. His sister reckons he became co-dependent on his mother. Her need for him fed his own need to compensate for his low self esteem. When their mother died, his controlling behaviour scared off every woman he tried to connect with. When their father died of liver failure – brought on by his alcoholism - she made proper contact with her brother again. They didn't see each other that often, but when they did she said he seemed really pleased to see her. They talked about their mother mainly, and how each of them was doing. She'd sold the house when their father died, and bought a cottage on the edge of the Delamere Forest. Like I said, Stone got to use it. She discovered that her brother had come close to a breakdown, and had gone voluntarily into the Oasis. They recruited him as a mentor. He found he was good at it, and he enjoyed it.'

'He was in control again.' Said Joanne.

'He went to college, qualified as a Counsellor and then became a fully fledged psychotherapist. For a year or so he actually worked at the Oasis; well before any of his victims went there.'

'And he used the contacts he'd made there – Hatch and Vine - to find his victims for him.' Joanne said.

Caton nodded. 'According to Professor Stewart-Baker, Stone would never have lost his need to control. The rejections in his private life sharpened the sexual dimension of his relationship with his victims. And his new profession gave him the means to play out his fantasies. He reckons that first experience with his landlady was hard wired into his brain.'

They were approaching the precinct at Four Lane Ends.

'Can you do me a favour Boss, and just pull in here for a moment.' She said. 'There's something I want to get.'

Caton drove into the car park, and pulled up outside the Co-op Late Shop.

'I won't be a moment,' she said, opening the door.

Caton watched her enter Rosehip, the florists. While he waited, he checked his mobile for texts. He had been doing it obsessively for days. This time he found what he had been hoping for. A text from Helen. He held his breath as he opened it. Just like the last one he had received from her it was short, and to the point. He could tell that it was serious because she'd taken the trouble to ditch the text short cuts.

I read about it. About that serial killer, and the policewoman. Harry has been asking about you. I've decided to give you one more chance. Ring me.

He would have rung her there and then, but Joanne came out of the florists carrying a single spray of flowers, and got back in the car.

They turned right by the Hulton Arms, and drove the remaining mile in silence, past the newly landscaped first phase of the Cutacre workings, where Caton could see that the footpaths had been reopened, and trees had already been planted. He drove into the empty car park beside the Dun Mare.

'Do you want me to stay here?' Caton asked

'She smiled. 'It's a lovely day. Why don't you walk with me?'

The hedgerow on their right was thick and verdant. Litter blown from the council recycling point was still in evidence here, but now there were poignant vestiges of police tape too, fluttering among the branches like so many Tibetan prayer flags. Where the hedge ended, they emerged beside the former race track. Caton could see that more than twenty metres had already been sliced from the top of Cutacre tip. The sides had been cleared right down to the furthest banks of the stream where the bodies of Shirley Hassell and Charlotte Mortimer had been found. Bluebell Hollow was bereft of vegetation, but clumps of deep green and gold marsh marigolds had colonised the bank closest to them. By midsummer the rest of the spoil would have been removed, and the process of returning the entire site to nature would have begun.

Joanne walked on ahead to the tiny cemetery. Caton watched as she made her way between the headstones to the spot beneath the hedge where Verity had been buried. She bent to lay the bunch of flowers on the spot, then stood, head bowed, for several minutes. Then she turned, and walked over to where Caton was looking out across the Cheshire plain towards the ironstone ridge that led to the Delamere Forest, and Shemmy Moss.

'A penny for your thoughts?' she said.

'We recovered his body,' he said. 'But we still haven't found any of his other victims. But we'll keep looking.' He turned, and looked across at the mechanical diggers crawling across the diminishing summit of Cutacre. 'In a few years time all this will have gone. Where that tip is now there are going to be warehouses, and industrial units. Around it, everything else will have been restored to how it was before. There will be nothing to reflect what happened here. There may even be bluebells in the dell again, and wild garlic down by the stream.'

'But this graveyard will still be here,' she said. 'Tended as long as there are people who remember those who are buried here. They may even put a headstone up for Stone's victims. That would be good.'

Side by side they retraced their steps down the lane. Instinctively, Caton placed his arm around her shoulders.

She left it there, soft and warm, in the chill spring air.

The Author

Formerly Principal Inspector of Schools for the City Of Manchester, Head of the Manchester School Improvement Service, and Lead Network Facilitator for the National College of School Leadership, Bill has numerous publications to his name in the field of education. For four years he was also a programme consultant and panellist on the popular live Granada Television programme *Which Way*, presented by the iconic, and much missed, Tony Wilson. He has written six crime thriller novels to date – all of them based in and around the City of Manchester. His first novel *The Cleansing* was short listed for the Long Barn Books Debut Novel Award. His Fourth novel, *A Trace of Blood, reached* the semi-final of the Amazon Breakthrough Novel Award in 2009.

If you've enjoyed
BLUEBELL HOLLOW
You will certainly enjoy the other novels in
the series:

The Cleansing
The Head Case
The Tiger's Cave
A Fatal Intervention
A Trace of Blood
www.billrogers.co.uk www.catonbooks.com

THE CLEANSING

The novel that first introduced DCI Tom Caton.
Christmas approaches. A killer dressed as a
clown haunts the streets of Manchester. For him the
City's miraculous regeneration had unacceptable
consequences. This is the reckoning. DCI Tom
Caton enlists the help of forensic profiler Kate Webb,
placing her in mortal danger. The trail leads from
the site of the old mass cholera graves, through Moss
Side, the Gay Village, the penthouse opulence of
canalside apartment blocks, and the bustling
Christmas Market, to the Victorian Gothic
grandeur of the Town Hall. Time is running out: For
Tom, for Kate...and for the City.

Short listed for the
Long Barn Books Debut Novel Award

Available in Caton Books paperback
ISBN: 978 1 906645 61 8

Also available from Amazon as a Kindle EBook

www.Amazon.com
www.catonbooks.com
www.billrogers.co.uk

THE HEAD CASE

Roger Standing CBE, Head of Harmony High Academy, and the Prime Minister's Special Adviser for Education, is dead. DCI Tom Caton is not short of suspects. But if this is a simple mugging, then why is MI5 ransacking Standing's apartment, and disrupting the investigation? And why are the widow and her son taking the news so calmly?

SOMETHING IS ROTTEN IN THE CORRIDORS OF POWER.

Available in Caton Books paperback
ISBN: 978 1 9564220 0 2

Also available from Amazon as a Kindle EBook

www.Amazon.com
www.catonbooks.com
www.billrogers.co.uk

THE TIGER'S CAVE

A lorry full of Chinese illegal immigrants arrives in Hull. Twenty four hours later their bodies are discovered close to the M62 motorway; but a young man and a girl are missing, and still at risk. Supported by the Serious and Organised Crime Agency, Caton must travel to China to pick up the trail. But he knows the solution is closer to home – in Manchester's Chinatown - and time is running out.

TWELVE BODIES
NO MOTIVE
THE HUNT IS ON
A COLD CASE IS ABOUT TO GET HOT.

Available in Caton Books paperback
ISBN: 978 0 9564220 1 9

Also available from Amazon as a Kindle EBook

www.Amazon.com
www.catonbooks.com
www.billrogers.co.uk

A FATAL INTERVENTION

A SUCCESSFUL BARRISTER
A WRONGFUL ACCUSATION
A MYSTERIOUS DISAPPEARANCE

It's the last thing Rob Thornton expects. When he finds his life turned upside down he sets out on the trail of Anjelita Covas, his accuser. Haunted by her tragic history and sudden disappearance Rob turns detective in London's underworld. A series of rhyming messages arrive, each signalling a murder. Rob must find Anjelita and face a dark truth.

DEEP BENEATH THE CITY OF MANCHESTER
LIES A HEART OF DARKNESS

Available in Caton Books paperback
ISBN: 978-0-9564220-3-3

Also available from Amazon as a Kindle EBook

www.Amazon.com
www.catonbooks.com
www.billrogers.co.uk